THRILLERS
ONE HUNDRED MUST-READS

THRILLERS

100 MUST-READS

DAVID MORRELL

AND

HANK WAGNER

Oceanview Publishing

LONGBOAT KEY, FLORIDA

ISBN: 978-1-60809-040-2

Published in the United States of America by Oceanview Publishing Longboat Key, Florida

Visit our Web site at www.oceanviewpub.com and the International Thriller Writers Web site at www.thrillerwriters.org.

10 9 8 7 6 5 4 3 2 1

PRINTED IN THE UNITED STATES OF AMERICA

ACKNOWLEDGMENTS

The editors are indebted to Stephen Jones and Kim Newman for the example of their influential 1988 volume *Horror: 100 Best Books* and its follow-up, *Horror: Another 100 Best Books*. Mr. Jones provided invaluable advice about how to organize this complex project.

Various thriller reviewers offered helpful suggestions, in particular Larry Gandle, Ali Karim, and David Montgomery. Agent Henry Morrison drew our attention to E. Phillips Oppenheim's *The Great Impersonation*. Nonetheless, the editors of this volume are solely responsible for the final selections.

Hank Wagner thanks his wife, Nancy, along with his daughters, Leigh, Melissa, and Sarah, for making daily life a thrill, and to Theo and Ella for providing comic relief.

David Morrell thanks the many ITW members who contributed to this volume. Without a second thought, they generously donated their time and talent to this educational project. Their commitment to the community of authors and readers is inspiring.

CONTENTS

WELCOME TO THE WORLD OF THRILLERS

David Hewson

Storytellers began thrilling their audiences before human beings learned to write. When a poet-singer called Homer entranced his listeners in the Mediterranean almost three thousand years ago, one of his staples was a tale that could fit on any airport shelf today: Odysseus fighting against extraordinary odds to return home from war to save his threatened wife and son.

Today, thrillers provide a rich literary feast embracing a wide variety of worlds—the law, espionage, action-adventure, medicine, police and crime, romance, history, politics, high-tech, religion, and many more. But old or new—and this vibrant field never remains still—all thrillers share certain characteristics. Like Homer trying to keep his audience captive while telling his tale in ancient Greece, thriller authors are constantly aware that their readers want them to provide the sudden rush of emotions: the excitement, suspense, apprehension, and exhilaration that drive the narrative, sometimes subtly, with peaks and lulls, sometimes at a constant, breakneck pace. By definition, if a thriller does not thrill, it is not doing its job.

But thrillers are also intensely human stories, allegories that find truths in fiction in order to tell us more about the world we inhabit and the kind of people we are. Sometimes, the protagonist will be a classical hero, focused on the challenge ahead, and perhaps a little damaged by his or her destiny in facing it. Other times, the protagonist will simply be an ordinary man or woman on the street, finding a steely thread of heroism inside, one that provides the strength to confront the challenge ahead.

That challenge may be personal, like that of Odysseus. Or, in our modern world, it will often be global, such as averting a pandemic or war or act of terrorism. It may even be both, seeking to crystallize a broader story by focusing on how it impacts the individuals who matter most to the protagonist. Whatever the canvas chosen by a thriller author, it must feel real, often through scrupulous research into science, crime procedures, or history.

Its authenticity will be found, too, through richly rounded characters who rise to challenges in the fictional world that mirror those we face in the real one: how to meet our responsibilities as human beings, even when there is a cost; how to lead a good life in a world where the line between right and wrong can sometimes be hard to discern. Being real means being honest, too. The best thrillers pull no punches. Happy-ever-after endings are, as in life, never guaranteed.

Odysseus, a battle-damaged warrior desperate to save his family. Beowulf, a king determined to protect his people, even at the cost of confronting a creature from hell. Robinson Crusoe, a shipwreck victim alone on a remote island, struggling to find the means of survival, but one day finding something else: footprints. The thriller is the oldest kind of story—rooted in our deepest hopes and fears, for ourselves, those we love, and the world around us.

David Hewson's books have been published in more than a dozen languages. The sixth novel in his Rome-based Nic Costa series, *The Garden of Evil*, was voted best mystery of 2008 by the American Library Association. His first novel, *Semana Santa*, won the WHSmith First Choice Prize for debut book of the year and became a movie starring Mira Sorvino. David is now a regular speaker at writing schools around the world, including International Thriller Writer's annual Craft-Fest and the Book Passage Mystery Writers' Conference in Corte Madera, California. He left school at the age of seventeen to become a cub reporter on one of the smallest evening newspapers in England, in his native Yorkshire. Later he worked as a journalist for the *London Times* and *Sunday Times* before becoming a full-time author.

ONE HUNDRED MUST-READ THRILLERS

David Morrell and Hank Wagner

In October 2004, at the Bouchercon conference in Toronto, Canada, a group of authors celebrated their common interest by creating the International Thriller Writers organization. ITW has grown considerably since then, but its goals continue to include educating readers about thrillers and encouraging ITW members to explore the creative possibilities of the form. Accordingly, ITW sought recommendations from various knowledgeable members and asked advice from several noted thriller reviewers in an effort to compile a list of one hundred thrillers that made a difference. That number was arbitrary. Obviously, more than one hundred important thrillers were published prior to 2000. We could easily have tripled the list, sometimes adding numerous titles by the same author, but practicality forced us to stop at one hundred, and individual contributors often decided which book by a prolific author would be included.

Books were chosen on the basis of the impact each had on the genre. Did the author contribute a new subject, direction, character, and/or technique that had a lasting effect? Did a work make such an impression that it was frequently imitated? After the final list was determined, ITW members were invited to choose a favorite thriller from the list and write an essay that analyzes the work's importance.

Some authors, such as Sandra Brown, had a favorite that they asked to be included. In her case, the book was Evelyn Anthony's *The Rendezvous* (1967), a work that greatly influenced Brown's fiction but that is no longer in the public's mind. Other "lost" novels—E. Phillips Oppenheim's once widely read *The Great Impersonation* (1920), for example—are also on the list, filling gaps in thrilller history. R.L. Stine requested that P. G. Wodehouse's *Summer Lightning* (1929) be included, using the interesting premise that a comedy could also be a thriller.

Brown and Stine are among twelve essayists who also have must-read titles of their own on the list. The others include: David Baldacci, Lee Child, Jeffery Deaver, James Grady, John Lescroart, Gayle Lynds, David Morrell, Katherine Neville, Justin Scott, and F. Paul Wilson. In addition, several essayists have a strong relationship with the topic of the novel they chose to write about. For example, Raymond Benson, author of many James Bond novels, analyzed Ian Fleming's *From Russia with Love*. A. J. Hartley, a Shakespeare professor whose work includes some Shakespeare-based thrillers, wrote about *Macbeth*. Professional pilot Ward Larsen discussed Ernest K. Gann's aviation thriller, *The High and the Mighty*. Emergency physician CJ Lyons wrote about Robin Cook's medical thriller, *Coma*. Attorney M. Diane Vogt analyzed John Grisham's legal thriller, *The Firm*. Sailor Christine Kling provided her thoughts about Erskine Childer's nautical thriller, *The Riddle of the Sands*. Law enforcement officer James O. Born gave his views on Joseph Wambaugh's police thriller, *The Choirboys*. Max Allan Collins, a friend of Mickey Spillane, discussed Spillane's *One Lonely Night*. In many cases, the essayists also composed the biography of the author whose book they discussed. Those brief biographies should be considered part of the essay, providing essential background.

Where to begin the list? When first conceived, this project began with Wilkie Collins, whose contemporaries credited him with inventing "the novel of sensation" when he wrote *The Woman in White* in 1860. But sensational works obviously predate that novel. Next, we thought that Edgar Allan Poe seemed a good place to start. It was intriguing to consider that the creator of the mystery story might also have created the thriller in his only novel, *The Narrative of Arthur Gordon Pym*. Later discussions led us further and further back until, at Douglas Preston's suggestion, we began the list with Homer's *Odyssey*. But then Lee Child made the case that the ancient story of Theseus and the Minotaur (with its labyrinth, monster, and secret weapon of a ball of string) might own that distinction.

Where to end? With an obvious exception like Dan Brown's phenomenally successful and influential *The Da Vinci Code* (2003), it's impossible to assess the long-term impact of any recent thriller, simply because insufficient time has passed and we don't have the perspective to determine what is influential and what isn't. To prevent the list from becoming a mere reflection of current taste, we chose the year 2000 as an arbitrary and symbolic cut-off date, going beyond it only to include Brown's novel.

To elaborate on this point, consider a currently (as of 2010) much-talked-about trilogy by the Swedish author Stieg Larsson, the first book of which is *The Girl with the Dragon Tattoo* (2005, translated into English 2008). Is it impressively written and exciting? Without question. But will it have staying power and be influential? It's too soon to tell. Nonetheless, among recent works, we draw your attention to Kathy Reichs's forensic-anthropology thrillers (*Grave Secrets*, 2002) as well as the eerie FBI Special Agent Pendergast thrillers by Douglas Preston/Lincoln Child, particularly *The Cabinet of Curiosities* (2002). Joseph Finder arguably invented a new genre, the corporate espionage thriller, with *Paranoia* (2004). Similarly, Vince Flynn (*Memorial Day*, 2004) and Brad Thor (*Blowback*, 2005) developed a post-9/11 counterterrorist thriller. Robert Littell's massive fictional history of the CIA, *The Company* (2002) is a primer for any spy novelist. Other contemporary authors of interest are mentioned in the essays.

Henry James once wrote that "the house of fiction has many windows." The same applies to thrillers. As David Hewson notes in his introductory essay, there are many types of thrillers: the spy thriller, the action thriller, the legal thriller, the medical thriller, the political thriller, the romantic thriller, the supernatural thriller, the mystery thriller, and so on. It's an all-inclusive term that can apply to a vast array of genres. The common denominator is that, as John Buchan suggested when he called *The Thirty-Nine Steps* a "shocker," they create excitement and quicken the reader's heartbeat. That doesn't necessarily mean a frantic chase or a devastating gunfight. An unsettling theme, a menacing tone, or an insistent pace—any of these can cause adrenaline to flow. Tastes change, of course, and what was a page-turner two hundred years ago might not seem so today, in which case the essayist puts the book in its historical context so that we can appreciate the effect that the novel had on readers of its era.

In "Tradition and the Individual Talent," T. S. Eliot insisted that every writer had an obligation to learn the history of the literary tradition in which that writer worked. The point is to absorb that tradition and carry it forward, trying to add something new that later writers must take into account. In that way, they can strengthen their technical skills, going in new directions while building on the old. Readers, too, can benefit by understanding the tradition of their favorite kind of fiction and appreciating when a book is truly innovative rather than merely an imitation. Consider each title in this volume as part of a developing tradition, analyzed here in lively essays that we hope will make us better readers and authors.

THRILLERS

ONE HUNDRED MUST-READS

1
THESEUS AND THE MINOTAUR (1500 B.C.)
Lee Child

This ancient Greek myth originated about 3,500 years ago. It has been told and retold many times, by Greek and Roman writers, including Ovid and Plutarch. All versions are slightly different, but all are valuable. The most accessible is found in Plutarch's *Lives*.

The story goes like this: Theseus, the son of the king of Athens, is a privileged but maverick warrior. At the start of the tale, he is away on the coast, attacking and burning enemy ships, in an action that is not fully authorized. He returns home to a crisis. Athens and Crete are in a state of uneasy truce, with Crete holding the upper hand. The price of peace is that Athens must periodically supply young men and women to be sacrificed to the Minotaur, a grotesque creature that lives in a labyrinth on the island of Crete. A demand for fresh victims has just arrived. Theseus insists that he be allowed to go, posing as one of the victims. He arrives on Crete and enlists—by seduction—the help of Ariadne, the daughter of the king of Crete. She supplies him with a ball of string, so that—if he survives the encounter with the Minotaur—he will be able to find his way out of the maze. Theseus descends, unwinding the string as he goes. He kills the Minotaur after an epic struggle. He retraces his steps with the help of the string. He emerges on the surface, ignores Ariadne, and returns home to a mixed welcome.

I first read this tale, in Latin, as a schoolboy. There was something about the story elements that nagged at me. I tried to reduce the specifics to generalities and arrived at a basic shape: Two superpowers in an uneasy standoff; a young man of rank acting alone and shouldering personal responsibility for a crucial outcome; a strategic alliance with a young woman from the other side; a major role for a gadget; an underground facility; an all-powerful opponent with a grotesque sidekick; a fight to the death; an escape; the cynical abandonment of the temporary female ally; the return home to a welcome that was partly grateful and partly scandalized.

I was reading Plutarch's Theseus in the classroom, but on the bus home I was reading Ian Fleming's *Dr. No*, and of course it eventually struck me that I was reading the same story. Theseus was a prince, and James Bond was a commander in the Royal Navy, about as close as Fleming could get to nobility within the confines of "realistic" fiction. For Athens and Crete, read West and East during the Cold War. Ariadne was Honey Rider; the ball of string was an ancient precursor of Q's oddball arsenal; the underground location for the climactic scene and the fight and the escape were all obviously self-explanatory. And so on and so forth.

Even Bond's basic character follows the myth fairly closely. His head-strong willfulness is always apparent—most of Fleming's books (and certainly all the movies) open with a scene of gratuitous violence or action not related to the main storyline. Those are all echoes of Theseus on the coast, burning the enemy ships. Above all, the various bipolar tightropes that Bond walks are prefigured: Is Bond truly valued by M, or merely tolerated? Is he bold, or hot-headed? Is the Secret Service proud of him, or embarrassed by him? And so on and so forth.

Am I accusing Fleming of plagiarism? No, not at all, although I have no doubt that he read Plutarch in school. He came from a much grander family than mine, but our educations would have been very similar. He would have realized—as I did—that the Minoan myth of Theseus from 3,500 years ago is almost certainly a rehash of a constant stream of earlier folktales, but tied to a particular time and place. The story of Robin Hood is similarly instructive: I had always instinctively assumed that the Robin Hood myth was part-fable, part-historical, about that period of English history defined by the regency of Prince John. But serious academic studies show that there were three completely separate Robin Hood myths in England alone, each separated by centuries, and that every culture with a written record of narrative has its own series of "Robin Hood" myths. Equally, a third strand of mythic character exists—the mysterious stranger who shows up in the nick of time to save the day, sequencing through early Scandinavian legends, medieval knight-errant stories, and, as variants on "savior" myths, even religious fables.

What does this tell us? It tells us that certain mythic paradigms—the young, take-charge nobleman, the renegade campaigner for a larger justice, the mysterious loner—are very deeply rooted in our emotional culture. We invented them thousands of years ago because we desperately wanted them to exist. We continue to reinvent them in flimsily disguised forms because we need them to be there, as a matter of catharsis and consolation. Above all, it tells us that the best contemporary thrillers—whenever they are written—will in some way tap into ancient mythic structures. Hollywood variously claims that there are only seven stories, or five, or two, but however many there are, they have all been already written or spoken millennia in the past, in our desperate, insecure infancy as a species. All we can do today is tell them again, and hope to derive the same comfort and excitement we used to, deep in the past.

Lee Child was born in 1954 in Coventry, England, and spent his formative years in nearby Birmingham. He went to law school in Sheffield, England, and after part-time work in the theater, he joined Granada Television in Manchester as a presentation director during British TV's "golden age." During his tenure, his company made *Brideshead Revisited*, *The Jewel in the Crown*, *Prime Suspect*, and *Cracker*. But after being laid off in 1995 at the age of forty, he decided to see an opportunity where others might have seen a crisis and bought six dollars' worth of paper and pencils and sat down to write a book, *Killing Floor* (1997), the first in the Jack Reacher series. *Killing Floor* was an immediate success and launched the series, which has grown in sales and impact with each new installment.

2
Homer's
THE ILIAD and THE ODYSSEY (7th Century B.C.)

William Bernhardt

Both *The Iliad* and *The Odyssey* are attributed to Homer, about whom we have little information, none of it trustworthy. Scholars dispute exactly when Homer wrote these epic poems, but they are approximately 2,700 years old. The ancient historians Herodotus and Aristarchus of Alexandria both wrote about Homer, but their accounts differ on most details. Some ancient sources say he was from Chios, others from Smyrna. Most believed that Homer was blind, that he composed the poems himself, and that he sang them in live performances. Some modern scholars, however, have suggested that the poems may be the work of many poets, while Geoffrey Kirk and others have argued that the consistent brilliance of the writing mandates a single author. Although Homer worked in the centuries-old tradition of oral Greek poetry, some scholars, such as Bernard Knox, now believe that the author wrote the poems out first, probably on papyrus rolls, revising and refining his work, as one might expect from a gifted, professional writer crafting a masterpiece.

Since the dawn of humanity, people have loved thrillers. Long before the written word, men and women told tales that inspired and entertained, that passed information from one generation to the next, that gave their audiences the courage to face the great darkness. The earliest known works of art, among them the cave drawings in Lascaux, France, approximately 17,000 years old, tell stories. The Great Hall of the Bulls contains a painted narrative. Like a Paleolithic comic book, the drawings dramatize the chase and capture of a bison herd. All of the oldest surviving literary works, such as *Gilgamesh*, *The Aeneid*, and *Beowulf*, are ancient heroic thrillers.

Perhaps the greatest examples of these seminal thrillers, and certainly the ones most frequently read today, are *The Iliad* and *The Odyssey*. Both works are written in hexameter verse. *The Iliad* focuses on the character of Achilles, whose wrath—its origin, its execution, and its devastating consequences—have a dramatic impact on the tenth and final year of the Achaean conflict known as the Trojan War. Achilles is enraged when Agamemnon, the commander of the Greek forces at Troy, takes a slave woman given to Achilles as a spoil of war. In protest, Achilles stops fighting. As a result, the Greeks suffer a crippling loss to the Trojans. Achilles refuses the challenge of the Trojan hero, Hector, but his friend Patroclus fights in his place and is killed. In revenge, Achilles slaughters numerous Trojans, kills Hector, and defiles his body. In a moving scene, the repentant Achilles agrees to relinquish Hector's body to his father. The story ends with Hector's funeral.

The Odyssey follows a more traditional story structure: the quest narrative. The hero, Odysseus, a minor player in The Iliad, is the star of the sequel. After the ten-year war is finally over, he spends ten more years journeying home to the island of Ithaca to be reunited with his faithful wife, Penelope, and his son, Telemachus. The god Poseidon is angry with Odysseus and constantly throws storms, squalls, and other obstacles in his path. Odysseus encounters the one-eyed Cyclops, Polyphemus, the lazy lotus-eaters, the enchantress Circe, the nymph Calypso, and passes between Scylla and Charybdis. He eventually makes his way back to Ithaca where his wife is besieged by greedy suitors who are draining the family resources and plotting to kill Telemachus. After employing disguises, deception, and other tricks worthy of a modern-day thriller hero, Odysseus crushes the suitors and is reunited with his family.

Although these two poems are classical literature, I have no problem labeling them as thrillers, not only because they do indeed thrill, but because that was quite evidently the author's intent. The Iliad is filled with what today we call "action scenes," including blow-by-blow descriptions of the combat of Achilles, Hector, and others, some of which are extremely vivid and gruesome. Both poems are replete with ruses, plotting, crosses, double-crosses, and plot twists. There is also plenty of sex. The Trojan War, the setting of The Iliad, begins when Paris abducts another man's wife, Helen, and takes her for his own. In The Odyssey, we learn of Odysseus's sexual encounters with Calypso and Circe. The suitors sleep with housemaids (and are later hanged for it). Interestingly, Penelope only accepts that this stranger who has slain the suitors is her long-lost husband when he accurately describes their marital bed.

The narrative strength of these two epics captivated ancient Greek audiences. They may be challenging for some readers today, but they were the oral bestsellers of the ancient Greek era. Homer's poetry, despite—or perhaps because of—having been written in an artificial, poetic language never spoken by the ancient Greeks or anyone else, was well known in Greece and elsewhere for centuries. Much of the continuing interest in these tales can be attributed to the author's employment of exciting, larger-than-life plots, and heroic yet human characters, devices familiar to fans of the modern thriller.

The influence of these epic poems on all literature, including thrillers, is enormous. The plot of *The Iliad* has been borrowed by such diverse artists as Shakespeare (for *Troilus and Cressida*), John Latouche (for the Broadway musical *The Golden Apple*), the Led Zeppelin song "Achilles's Last Stand," and the recent action-adventure film *Troy*. *The Odyssey* inspired, obviously, James Joyce's *Ulysses* and Margaret Atwood's *The Penelopiad*, just to name a few. But the more obvious descendant of Achilles and Odysseus is the action hero, the protagonist of the modern-day thriller, as represented by Indiana Jones, James Bond, and Rambo.

I first read *The Odyssey* in the sixth grade, as part of a special humanities program offered to youngsters by a local community college. Reading Homer at the age of eleven may seem a daunting assignment, but our teacher, a very young woman named Marcia who dressed in the miniskirts and hip boots iconic of the era, inspired her students (particularly, I suspect, the male ones). We read Homer, Milton, Shakespeare, and anything else she wanted us to read. I devoured *The Odyssey*, this fantastic, comic-book-style story brought to life by characters who were not the perfect superheroes I knew from Saturday morning cartoons. These characters were deeply flawed, but even in Achilles's greatest rage, or Odysseus's most bloodthirsty encounter, I never lost sight of their essential nobility, their honor, their desire to do good. These heroic templates were lodged firmly in my subconscious when I created my series character, lawyer Ben Kincaid. Ben battles in the courtroom and the Senate rather than in the fields of war, but despite his many character flaws and foibles, he is essentially a hero who will not quit and always tries to do the right thing. In this sense, he is squarely in the Homeric tradition and could easily, at least in my mind, sail the seas of ancient Greece with these mythic heroes. After all, once Odysseus slaughtered all those suitors, surely someone had to represent him in court.

Library Journal called William Bernhardt the "master of the courtroom thriller." His twenty-eight books, many of them featuring attorney Ben Kincaid, have sold more than ten million copies worldwide. Bernhardt's novels, which include *Capital Conspiracy* and *Nemesis: The Final Case of Eliot Ness*, are known for their unexpected twists, legal realism, breathless pace, humor, and insightful consideration of issues confronting contemporary American society. He has twice won the Oklahoma Book Award for Best Fiction as well as the Southern Writers Guild's Gold Medal Award. In 2000, he was honored with the H. Louise Cobb Distinguished Author Award, which is given "in recognition of an outstanding body of work that has profoundly influenced the way in which we understand ourselves and American society at large." In addition to his law degree, Bernhardt also holds a master's degree in English literature. He founded HAWK Publishing Group as well as the HAWK Writing Workshops and Seminars, and is a highly sought writing instructor.

3
BEOWULF (between 700 and 1000 A.D.)

Andrew Klavan

Beowulf is the earliest epic poem in English and one of the greatest. Its Anglo-Saxon author is unknown. It may have been composed as early as 700 A.D., but the oldest copy was made by two scribes somewhere around 1000 A.D., the only *Beowulf* manuscript to survive Henry VIII's destruction of monastery libraries. Ironically, though the poem has a hallowed place in the history of English literature, it tells a tale of sixth-century Scandinavia, and is largely drawn from Scandinavian history and mythology. It was, of course, from the language of Anglo-Saxon and Scandinavian invaders that English evolved. These invaders were pagans originally, and *Beowulf* probably began its life as a pagan story. But by the time of its writing, the Anglo-Saxons had become Christians, and the interweaving of Christian morality with a tale of warrior courage is both fascinating and profound. In 1999, the Nobel Prize-winning poet Seamus Heaney translated the epic, winning critical praise as well as the prestigious Whitbread prize. I personally found it a bit too restrained and scholarly and much prefer the more heroic 1963 version by Burton Raffel from which the spellings and quotations below are taken.

Great works of literature often peel away the mask of our piety to expose the raw life underneath. So it is with *Beowulf*, a brooding, blood-soaked celebration of warrior manhood.

We in the modern West have been so powerful, so dominant, so safe in our homes for so long that we slip too easily into the illusion that we live at peace. We are never at peace, not really. When we go to the ballet or walk in the park or stop to smell a rose or read a book, we only do so by the good graces of the fighters who stand ready to kill and die to defend us. Soldiers on our borders, police officers on our streets—only the threat of their physical force keeps those who would murder, rob, or enslave us at bay. Every moment of tranquility and freedom implies the warrior who protects it. The world of *Beowulf* is the real world.

And what a wonderful poem it is, a tale and a tone of such ferocious, melancholy virility that it shocks the sometimes overdelicate modern mind. It's the story of the Scandinavian hero Beowulf and his battles with monsters. It begins when Beowulf travels from Geatland in what is now Sweden to Denmark to come to the aid of King Hrothgar in his towering mead hall Herot. The Danes are being plagued by the swamp monster Grendel, "that shadow of death," who hunts their warriors in darkness, "lying in waiting, hidden in mist, invisibly following them from the edge of the marsh, always there, unseen." Beowulf is such a tough Geat, so bent on winning fame for his courage and prowess, that he disdains to use a sword to kill the beast and wrestles him bare-handed, ripping his arm off by main strength. Grendel slouches home to his swamp to die, thus sparking the rage of his mother, who comes for her revenge.

There's plenty more—including digressive tales of war, betrayal, and tragedy—all set on misty fens and under murky waters and in broken, crumbling towers and halls that seem the earliest inspiration for the setting of many of today's video games. Which is fitting, because really you have to turn to those games to find anything in modern art that so boldly elevates and celebrates the warrior and his drive to "win glory and a hero's fame" in battle.

If you want to see how completely more "sophisticated" modern artists have lost the ability to understand those virtues and their ever-present necessity, take a look at the 2007 CGI film *Beowulf* by director Robert Zemeckis and screenwriters Neil Gaiman and Roger Avary. Note how entirely it subverts and corrupts the vision of the original. In the film, the warriors are drunken thugs and Grendel is King Hrothgar's bastard child. This implies not only a measure of responsibility on the part of the Danes for their own slaughter, but also a tiresome Freudian psychomachy underlying the action. In the poem, conversely, Grendel is the child of "those monsters born of Cain, murderous creatures banished by God." He is roused from his slumber by the music and rejoicing in Herot, especially a poet's song of the world's genesis. The implication in the poem is far more insightful and unflinching than that in the film. The poem's Grendel is a primal force of evil spawned by sinful human nature itself and now perennially at war with the creation. The guilt is not sexual and personal but general in terms of mankind's instinct toward fraternal violence.

That general guilt gives Beowulf's heroism its context. It tells us that evil is woven into human nature, but that individual men may choose to

spearean line, never coming down clearly on one side or the other of key issues—and some scholars think its unusual brevity (by comparison to his other tragedies) shows signs of heavy state censorship. What is clear is that few writers before or since have managed to so shrewdly sketch the mind of someone drawn by ambition and paranoia into acts so terrible that they tear him and his relationships apart long before his head is severed from his body.

Shakespeare had explored assassins before, particularly Brutus in *Julius Caesar* (c. 1599), but never before had he given such weight and attention to a killer who knew the moral enormity of his act before he did it, nor had he given the killer so distinctive and chilling a spouse. Lady Macbeth looms over the first half of the play like the ravens on her battlements, though to blame her for what happens is to deny Macbeth what Shakespeare is so careful to give him: the power of choice. All the same the scenes in which she spurs him to act, using all her powers of persuasion anchored in their intimately personal history, and those after the deed itself in which they grope bloody handed for each other in the darkness, are as riveting today as when they were first written.

Lady Macbeth's subsequent collapse, overwhelmed by the guilt she bears, is marked not just in those memorable and uncanny sleepwalking scenes when she fruitlessly washes and rewashes her bloody hands, but in her steady separation from her husband, who deals with his past by stifling all capacity to feel. At the end of the play, having performed or authorized the slaughter of countless men, women, and children, he cannot even respond to his wife's death, seeing it only as the end of something meaningless: a tale told by an idiot, full of sound and fury, signifying nothing. Whatever its value as a protoexistential statement on the futility of life by a particular character in particular circumstances, the speech has become iconic, an emblem of the play's durability and relevance.

Macbeth is perhaps Shakespeare's most atmospheric drama. From the weird sisters emerging out of the fog on the blasted heath, to the strange sounds carried on the air before Duncan's murder, the play is stiff with dread and the scent of blood. Even when there are no sounds, the killers think they hear them, the terrible knowledge of what they have done turning to panic and apprehension:

> Macbeth: I have done the deed. Did'st thou not hear a noise?
> Lady Macbeth: I heard the owl scream and the crickets cry.
>   Did not you speak?

Macbeth: When?
Lady Macbeth: Now?
Macbeth: As I descended?
Lady Macbeth: Ay.
Macbeth: Hark! Who lies in the second chamber?

Imagined sounds give way to real ones, the pounding at the castle door that the porter imagines to be the gates of hell itself. Part of what Shakespeare does so well, of course, is the marrying of great, even mythic events, with something recognizably human, familiar, even domestic. Ordinary things—as all good thriller writers know—become crucial and telling. Lady Macbeth's sleepwalking and the things she says while doing so ("Yet who would have thought the old man to have had so much blood in him," "The thane of Fife had a wife. Where is she now?") stand out, but just as important is Macbeth's inability to sleep at all. The act that can barely be uttered causes a breach in nature, and the world is turned upside down: hospitality becomes deadly, night that should bring rest bears only horror, and the nation itself is torn apart. Even at the end, with the tyrant dead, it is far from clear that all will be well. The crown of Scotland has passed to Malcom, about whom the play has shown us little, much of it conflicted, and the promised line of kings descended from Banquo is no nearer.

Part of the play's heart is the struggle to balance free will and a sense of destiny or cosmic purpose. For Shakespeare's original audience, this might have been particularly stamped by ideas of rigid social stratification or a Calvinist sense of predestination, but there was also a powerful current in the period—the beginning of what we might call capitalist individualism—to take charge of one's life decisively. So Macbeth's decision to kill for the crown is a seizing of what the witches suggest will come to pass anyway, leaving us with the problem most thriller heroes—and ordinary people—wrestle with: when and how to act decisively, when to let things happen, and when to walk away.

Macbeth is not a novel, of course, but a play, and as such is a must watch as well as a must read. On stage, a production invariably finds the tension, suspense, and horror, which the reader's eye—enmeshed by tricky Jacobean diction and thick metaphor—can sometimes miss. However we experience the play, it's clear that little in literature can match its study of political murder, its consequences, and the impulse to confront a world that seems to be conspiring against our future.

A. J. Hartley is the Distinguished Professor of Shakespeare Studies at the University of North Carolina, Charlotte, the editor of the performance journal, *Shakespeare Bulletin*, and the author of *The Shakespearean Dramaturg* as well as numerous academic articles on Shakespeare and Renaissance drama. He is also the *USA Today* and *New York Times* best-selling author of the archaeologically inflected thrillers, *The Mask of Atreus* and *On the Fifth Day*. His *What Time Devours* centers on the hunt for a copy of Shakespeare's lost play, *Love's Labour's Won*. In addition, he is the author of a fantasy adventure series, the first of which is *Act of Will*.

5.
Daniel Defoe's
ROBINSON CRUSOE (1719–1722)
David Liss

Daniel Defoe (generally thought to have been born in 1659–1661 and to have died in 1731) was a hack writer. In the world of British publishing in the late seventeeth and early eighteenth centuries, there was an explosive growth both in literacy and the popular press. Writing for money was hack writing, and most authors did it proficiently and prolifically. Defoe earned his living by writing political pamphlets (sometimes on both sides of an issue), observations on culture, histories, books on "projects" (useful innovations), and, of course, celebrated works of fiction. These generally took the form of memoirs, for there was no strong market yet for prose fiction, and his works were often believed to be about actual people. In 1719, he published the first of these, *The Life and Surprising Adventures of Robinson Crusoe*, one of the most influential works of fiction ever written. Thereafter, he published numerous other pseudo-autobiographies, many of which are still read today, including *Moll Flanders* (1722), *A Journal of the Plague Year* (1722), and *Roxana* (1724). In addition to writing at an astonishing pace, Defoe also involved himself in numerous, frequently unsuccessful, business projects, including a disastrous effort to extract perfume from civet cats. He spent time in the pillories for authoring a now-famous satire, "The Shortest Way with the Dissenters." A genius who was often his own worst enemy, Defoe died in debt while hiding from creditors.

Anyone who is not a scholar of eighteenth-century British literature would likely be surprised to learn how much ink has been spilled over the question of which book can be called the first English-language novel. The major contenders are Aphra Behn's 1688 romance *Oroonoko*, Samuel Richardson's 1740 epistolary narrative, *Pamela*, and, of course, Daniel Defoe's 1719 fictional memoir, *Robinson Crusoe*. While all three have strong claims, my informal survey (taken over many years) suggests that most eighteenth centuryists give Defoe the prize. I find it remarkable that the first English-language novel also contains so many of the structural elements of the thriller.

To grasp fully why *Robinson Crusoe* is so important, it is necessary to spend at least a moment discussing the history of the novel. Fiction, as we understand it today, developed from the prose romance (not to be confused with the romance novel), which focused on action and on broadly drawn stock characters such as knights who rescue maidens from giants (*Don Quixote* parodies this type of fiction). Think of a fairy tale in which you have a clear sense of character, but there is no depth. By contrast, the novel, as it takes shape over the eighteenth century, injects psychological realism into fiction, producing characters who are broad and deep, well rounded, and emotionally complex. When Defoe set out to write his first work of fiction, he was not attempting to reinvent the romance, but rather he was writing a counterfeit version of another established literary genre, the Protestant spiritual autobiography. *Robinson Crusoe* pretended to be a real memoir, and many people, for a long time, believed it to be so.

Few works of fiction can claim the enduring influence of *Robinson Crusoe*. It spawned two sequels—now read only by the most masochistic of Defoe scholars—and countless imitators. Like Sir Arthur Conan Doyle's Sherlock Holmes or Edgar Rice Burroughs's Tarzan, Robinson Crusoe is a character so firmly embedded in popular culture that most people can tick off elements of the story even if they've never read it or seen an adaptation. Everyone knows that he is cast away on an uninhabited island for a long period of time (twenty-seven years, from 1659–1686), and is befriended by a native whom he names Friday. Readers who have absorbed the story only through cultural osmosis might be surprised that Crusoe has a fair number of adventures both before his shipwreck—when he is made a slave by Barbary pirates—and after—in an extended sequence of fighting wild animals while traveling through Europe. Much of the novel is taken up with Crusoe's spiritual musings as he learns to thank God for what he has rather than curse fate for what he does not.

In other words, by any contemporary novelistic standards, *Robinson Crusoe* is unfocused and disorganized. It is also repetitive and sloppy, and Defoe as often as not will correct things he's already written about in the text rather than going back to rewrite points he wished he'd clarified earlier. He was a phenomenally fast writer. When I first read the book in graduate school, my professor said it would likely take me more time to read it than it took Defoe to write it. He was, of course, joking, but not by much.

And yet for all its many structural faults, Crusoe endures and has cast an indelible mark on fiction in general, and the thriller in particular. There are two principal reasons for this. The first is that *Robinson Crusoe* often operates on the level of what we would call today a novel of "tradecraft," like a spy novel that derives energy from revealing to the reader secrets of a hidden world. The bulk of the action is a surprisingly engaging account of how Crusoe cultivates livestock and crops, how he makes clothes and builds shelters, how he dries his grapes and stores his rice and learns to craft basic comforts with few tools. Only an Englishman would spend as much time as Crusoe does in figuring out how to make a pot so that he might enjoy his meat boiled. The account of Crusoe's self-reliance is what made the book such a staple of boy's literature for so many years. There is something almost addictive about watching this character discover how to function and thrive while so completely isolated.

The second great influence of the book is its pioneering use of the plot twist to create suspense and tension. When Crusoe has been alone on his island for more than two decades, and indeed grown quite used to, if not happy with, his solitude, he travels down to the beach one day and finds a solitary footprint in the sand. In a single stroke, Defoe tells the reader that everything he knows about this universe, every assumption he has made up to this point, is wrong. Other forms of narrative, particularly stage plays, had previously offered readers surprises and turning points, but Defoe stumbled upon the incredible power of the unexpected twist in a fictional narrative. We are inside this character's head, and we are with him while he must understand how to process this new revelation. Religious writers operating the popular press had long known that the intimacy of reading had the power to move and persuade. It was Defoe who discovered how to use this intimacy to surprise and thrill.

Crusoe is a seventeenth-century man, and so he spends perhaps more time than would a modern person in convincing himself that the footprint was probably not left by Satan. This leaves the likelihood that it was cannibals, whom he knows to inhabit a nearby island and occasionally visit a distant portion of his own island to cook and eat their victims. The discovery of the footprint leads to his rescue of one of these would-be cannibal victims, the famous Friday, who becomes his companion for the remainder of his stay on the island and eventually follows Crusoe back to Europe.

There is much that can be said, and has been said, about the problematic relationship between Crusoe and Friday—not to mention the relationship between Crusoe and the boy Xury, with whom our hero escapes from their Moorish captors in the first part of the novel, and whom Crusoe later sells into slavery. Indeed, Crusoe is shipwrecked on his island after he sets out aboard a ship on a slaving expedition, but while he spends a great deal of time reflecting on how wrong it was for him to leave England against his father's wishes, he seems to have no regrets about his abysmal treatment of non-Europeans. He is, in short, a man of his time, and a flawed and complex one at that, but one whose adventures helped to shape thriller fiction.

David Liss's bestselling books include *The Devil's Company, The Coffee Trader, A Spectacle of Corruption, The Ethical Assassin, The Whiskey Rebels,* and *A Conspiracy of Paper* (winner of the 2000 Edgar Award for Best First Novel). His books have been praised for demonstrating the historical roots that led to contemporary flashpoints of injustice, inequity, and corruption. In 2008, at the United Nations Convention against Corruption in Bali, Indonesia, he was named an Artist for Integrity by the United Nations Office on Drugs and Crime. No one is really sure why or what this means, but it very possibly makes him the Bono of historical fiction. Liss's novels have been translated into more than two dozen languages. Both *A Conspiracy of Paper* and *The Coffee Trader* are under development as film projects. He lives in San Antonio, with his wife and children.

6.

Mary Shelley's FRANKENSTEIN, or THE MODERN PROMETHEUS (1818)

Gary Braver

Mary Shelley (1797–1851) was born to the first great feminist philosopher, Mary Wollstonecraft, and novelist and political journalist, William Godwin. Ten days after Mary's birth, her mother died. Too poor to raise his children alone, Godwin married Jane Clairmont, whom Mary never liked nor did she like her stepsiblings. Expected to emulate her dead great mother, Mary educated herself throughout a lonely childhood. Exposed to members of Godwin's intellectual circle, she met Percy Bysshe Shelley. Although still married, the poet eloped with Mary to Switzerland when she was fifteen. In 1816, following the suicide of Shelley's wife, they married, and in a cottage near Geneva the story of Frankenstein was conceived. The 1818 novel was published anonymously, creating curiosity about the author's identity. When subsequent editions listed Mary as the author, critics found fault with the novel because its author was female. Nonetheless, from the start, the book was a popular success, but life soon turned cruel with the death of two children, then Shelley's drowning in 1822. Mary wrote several other books and short stories, but none rose to the greatness of *Frankenstein*.

Frankenstein is one of the most recognized names in English fiction. A name that conjures up iconic images of the flat-headed Boris Karloff monster in ill-fitting clothes and neck electrodes being chased through fields by villagers with pitchforks. A name synonymous with well-intentioned projects going horribly wrong. Clipped to prefix, it is a metaphor of horrific potentials—e.g., *Frankenfood* or *Frankencat*.

Frankenstein is also the title of an English novel that has been in print since 1818. Yet, although most people are familiar with some of the story's elements through the hundred or so movies, *Frankenstein* is a book that few people have read. One reason is that Hollywood has unfortunately made people think that they know the novel's plot, leaving them ignorant about its remarkable insights into human nature, moral responsibility, compassion, justice, and suffering. These insights are especially applicable to the monster, a sentient creature created artificially and forever an outsider to nature and human society, a creature who, in spite of Hollywood, has no name—which is Shelley's point—but who is referred to as monster, as well as demon, vile insect, phantasm, abhorred form, etc. by his own creator, Victor Frankenstein.

There are many reasons why *Frankenstein* is a must-read if for nothing else than appreciation of the brilliant vision of the nineteen-year-old girl who penned the tale. Unlike other gothic narratives of Mary Shelley's day, *Frankenstein* is not a linear narrative but contains, like Chinese boxes, stories within stories told through multiple points of view via diaries, letters, and reported conversations. Together they are organically linked and thematically bound into a coherent artistic whole, which like any thriller, keeps the reader turning the pages as the dread mounts.

The most important storyline is that of Victor Frankenstein, the son of a wealthy Swiss family. From an early age, he hungers for knowledge, but not ordinary classroom knowledge. He yearns to "chase nature to her hiding place." Just before he departs for his studies, untimely death claims his mother. Victor cannot bring her back, but at the University of Ingolstadt, he hopes to conquer death. Rejecting the warnings of his professor, he applies modern scientific methods to the lofty dreams of ancient alchemists. After two years of self-imposed isolation in his lab, disregarding communiqués from his father, his betrothed Elizabeth, and best friend Henry Clerval, Victor discovers the secret of life and animates a lifeless corpse assembled from charnel-house body parts. On a stormy November night the creature comes alive, but Victor is horrified by the enormity of his creation and flees.

For the rest of the book, Frankenstein suffers the consequences of his creation and the dereliction of his responsibility to the monster and those he loves. When the creature begs Victor to befriend him, Victor refuses. When the creature pleas for a female companion, he is denied. Though ugly, the creature is pure in heart and spends two years in the woods, secretly doing chores for a family of cottagers, all the while learning language and admiring their humanity and loving bonds. But when in desperation the monster attempts to befriend the blind patriarch, he is discovered and driven with sticks from the home.

Like Adam banished to the wilderness, the monster is enraged at his existence and decides that he too "can create desolation" and strikes back at his creator, not to murder Frankenstein but to deprive him of all that he has been denied—family, justice, friendship, and love. He kills Victor's young brother, William, frames cousin Justine for the crime, murders Clerval, then strangles Elizabeth on her wedding night. Once his revenge is complete, the creature flees to the North Pole where Frankenstein pursues him, dying in the process, while the monster disappears in the frozen gloom, taking his own life.

Beautifully written, the tragic tale explores such universal themes as the need for friendship and love. On a psychological level, Victor's fate explores the themes of dehumanization and desexualization. Cutting himself off from friends and lover, Victor nearly wastes away in his obsession; and his rejection of Elizabeth in order to create life artificially underscores the desexualization of himself and his fiancée. Likewise, he denies the creature his humanity and a mate. A dark logic plays out when the creature kills Elizabeth moments before she and Victor can consummate their marriage.

Also, the novel explores the difference between knowledge and wisdom. With conscious parallels to Genesis, Victor Frankenstein is both Adam picking the forbidden fruit and God who creates life, then abandons the creature to fend for itself. This hubris, the reckless pursuit of glory and forbidden knowledge, is the cautionary theme of the novel.

Frankenstein has a unique claim in the history of literature as the progenitor of modern science fiction, demonstrating that thrillers can be found in many genres. Written early in the modern scientific age and on the threshold of the Industrial Revolution, the novel is the forerunner of every cautionary tale about science without foresight or ethics, knowledge without wisdom, the abuse of power, the dereliction of responsibility, and the dehumanization and desexualization that results in our slavish dependence upon technology. Likewise, Frankenstein's monster is the prototype of every sci-fi machine, robot, and computer in revolt.

Frankenstein is a manifesto of the dilemmas of living in our scientific age—dilemmas expressed in today's anxieties over genetic engineering, nanotechnology, and other innovations. In essence, the book says that because we can make something, it doesn't mean we should.

Gary Braver is the best-selling author of seven critically acclaimed thrillers including *Elixir*, *Gray Matter*, and *Flashback*, the only thriller to have won the prestigious Massachusetts Book Award. His *Skin Deep* has been called "a gripping, twisty thriller that deserves a wide audience" (*Booklist*). His novels have been translated into five languages, and three have been optioned for movies. He is the only writer to have three books listed on the top-10 highest customer-rated thrillers on Amazon.com at the same time. As Gary Goshgarian, he is an award-winning English professor at Northeastern University where he teaches science fiction, modern bestsellers, horror fiction, and fiction writing. He has taught fiction-writing workshops throughout the U.S. and Europe for over twenty years. He is the author of five college writing textbooks and has written book reviews and travel articles in the *New York Times*, the *Boston Globe*, the *Christian Science Monitor*, and elsewhere.

7

James Fenimore Cooper's
THE LAST OF THE MOHICANS (1826)

Rick Wilber

James Fenimore Cooper was born in 1789 in Burlington, New Jersey, and died in 1851 in Cooperstown, a village founded by his father on the shore of Lake Otsego in upstate New York. One of the earliest American novelists, Cooper is best remembered for his pioneer Leatherstocking Tales and for his sea adventures, though in the course of writing thirty-two novels and several naval histories, he ranged widely in theme. He is said to be the "American Scott," since much of his work followed the example of Sir Walter Scott's successful invention of the historical novel.

James Fenimore Cooper wasn't interested in inventing a new kind of book when he sat down to write his first novel sometime in late 1819; he just wanted to prove that he could write a better book than the one he was reading, a new novel from England (as almost all of them were at the time).

And so he did. By 1820, Cooper's tale, *Precaution*, was published, and the novel did well enough that he decided to write another, *The Spy: A Tale of the Neutral Ground* (1821), which was set in America during the Revolution. This was a daring literary gamble during a time when most American readers still wanted to read English novels by English writers about events happening in England.

More success followed as Cooper continued to write other novels set in America, and then, in 1826, came the book for which he is best remembered, the terrific thriller *The Last of the Mohicans*.

That's right—*Mohicans* is a thriller, the seminal story that began the thriller genre in America. It is also the generally accepted best novel by an author who is important for a number of reasons, including being among the first American novelists, and one of the first to write about American themes using distinctly American characters going through their paces in a distinctly American setting.

The hero in *The Last of the Mohicans* is the taciturn frontier scout and woodsman Natty Bumppo; a man utterly at home in the primeval forest of pioneer America, a man unafraid to do what needs to be done to rescue women—or men—in peril, whether it's being a crack shot, masquerading as a bear, tracking footprints through a streambed, outtalking a venerable and thoughtful tribal chief, or earning the respect and admiration of good-hearted but bumbling British officers. Natty is a man of action, utterly confident and superbly capable, willing and able to use violence when he must, but otherwise soft spoken and serene, a man of quiet strength. He is the first great fictional hero in American literature and sets a pattern for many of today's thriller heroes.

Natty has many names. Cooper calls him variously Deerslayer, Hawk-eye, Long-Rifle (or, in French, *Le Longue Carabine*), Leatherstocking, and Pathfinder. These names serve as useful descriptions of Natty's competence as a hunter, his aim with a rifle, his attire, and his ability as a tracker. Having created this seminal adventurer in his third novel *The Pioneers* (1823), Cooper decided to put him into action in four more novels, *The Deerslayer* (1841), *The Last of the Mohicans* (1826), *The Pathfinder* (1840), and *The Prairie* (1827).

Read in this sequence and not in order of publication, the five novels give us Natty as he grows from an earnest young man to a grizzled veteran of several wars and any number of conflicts with various villains from the 1740s to 1804. But of all the Leatherstocking Tales (as the novels are known collectively), the most enduring has been *The Last of the Mohicans*, a story so engaging that it's been made into several effective films, including the 1993 Michael Mann directed version starring Daniel Day-Lewis as Natty and Madeline Stowe as Cora, the woman-in-peril.

The story follows several main characters during the French and Indian War in 1757, when the French and the British fought for control of North America using various native tribes as allies. (Note that Cooper wasn't only a thriller author but also a historical one inasmuch as the events in his books occurred years earlier than when he wrote about them.) The British lieutenant colonel George Munro, who has his two adult daughters with him, is defending Fort William Henry from a massive French attack. When British reinforcements don't arrive, Munro is forced to surrender. But the honorable surrender turns into a massacre when French-allied Indians attack the unarmed British column as it leaves the fort. Nearly two hundred are killed. (The extensively described massacre is based on historical accounts.)

In Cooper's version of the event, Munro escapes, but his daughters are captured, and the heart of the novel dramatizes the pursuit of the villain-ous Huron chief, Magua, who has the women. The pursuit is led by Natty, along with Munro, the earnest and brave British army major Duncan Heward, a slightly dotty (if ultimately courageous) preacher named David Gamut, and Natty's two Mohican friends, Uncas and his father, Chin-gachgook. Natty and his friends risk their lives repeatedly in order to save the two women. In the action-filled climax, the heroic Uncas dies while rescuing the women, leaving his father, Chingachgook, as the eponymous last of the Mohicans, another stage in the closing of the frontier, one of Cooper's main themes.

The epic scope of this chase novel cements Cooper's and Natty's po-sitions as the first great thriller author and hero in the American literary canon. Cooper's storytelling skills weren't always matched by stylistic ones, however, with the result that critical opinion has waxed and waned about him. In one famous and wonderfully amusing assessment, Mark Twain took Cooper to task for his failings in any number of areas in his essay "Fenimore Cooper's Literary Offences."

But then there's an equally famous essay from Pulitzer Prize winner Carl Van Doren in which he writes that Cooper's imagination "is almost supreme among romancers, and (it) lifts him solidly above all his faults . . . (There is) an intensity (to his writing), by virtue of which he so completely realized imagined, and often imaginary, events."

Today, Cooper is read mostly by students and teachers. His language sounds a little stiff to our ears (as it did to Twain). Also, his descriptive writing sometimes seems a little overwrought. His plotting occasionally relies on the unlikely to fool the bad guys and help the good guys succeed. But the situations and characters found in *The Last of the Mohicans* are completely recognizable to modern-day thriller readers. Replace birch bark canoes with motorcycles and high-performance European automobiles, and the chase scenes are exquisitely familiar. Replace the tomahawk, bow and arrow, and the muskets with sniper rifles, Uzis, and Glocks, and the plot could have been conjured up by any of today's most successful thriller authors.

That's the point: James Fenimore Cooper created an exciting, page-turning, character-driven, audience-pleasing, action-packed kind of writ-ing that found a large audience in the nineteenth century and influenced directly or indirectly countless later thriller writers. Natty and his friends are still a ton of fun to encounter. Go rent the excellent 1993 movie. Better yet, pick up the novel. It's a must-read for anyone who enjoys thrillers.

Rick Wilber first encountered Cooper and Natty Bumppo during study hall in high school and nearly flunked algebra as a result of too much Deerslayer and not enough studying. Rick is the author of the thrillers *Rum Point* and *The Cold Road*; a memoir about his family's life in professional baseball and the challenges of caregiving, *My Father's Game: Life, Death, Baseball*; two short story collections and more than fifty short stories and an equal number of poems published in a wide variety of magazines and anthologies. He has also published several hundred magazine and newspaper travel articles, essays, profiles, and reviews, and is the author of several college textbooks on writing and media studies. He lives in St. Petersburg, Florida, and teaches journalism and mass media at the University of South Florida.

8

Edgar Allan Poe's
THE NARRATIVE OF ARTHUR GORDON PYM
OF NANTUCKET(1838)

Katherine Neville

Edgar Allan Poe (1809–1849) is both the inventor of the detective story and a towering force who raised horror fiction to literary heights. Born in Boston to a pair of theatrical troupers who died by the time he was two, Poe was adopted by the Allans of Virginia—possibly the origin of the "Allan" in the author's name. John Allan was a merchant and took his young ward to England, where Poe was schooled for several years. After their return to Virginia, Poe's life wavered from tragic to maudlin. He had a drinking and gambling problem, and was tossed out of the University of Virginia and West Point, where Mr. Allan had paid the bills. Enraged, Allan stopped supporting his adoptive son. The chaos continued: Poe's succession of jobs, his marriage to his teenage cousin, her death of consumption, his despair, his death at the age of forty, possibly due to alcohol. Throughout, he revolutionized American literature and become a force that the *Encyclopedia Britannica* described, one century after his birth, as "a world author more purely than any other American writer."

My earliest encounters with Edgar Allan Poe were scarcely auspicious. Through years of grammar school, we beleaguered children were force-fed Poe's dark poems and stories almost as a daily diet, until we could regurgitate any of them from our memories at the push of a button. Poe seemed to provide the only tool that teachers found, ready-to-hand, to demonstrate concepts like alliteration and assonance. If I close my eyes, I can still hear the "silken sad uncertain rustling of each purple curtain," and my head still clangs with the "tintinnabulation" of the "bells, bells, bells, bells, bells, bells, bells." Even today, there's scarcely a Poe plot device I can't call upon to furnish some slow, gruesome torture—like bricking someone up into a wall. Indeed, there were times during those endless exams, when I fancied bricking Poe himself up into a wall! So it came as a real surprise when I was twelve or thirteen that the young adventurer Arthur Gordon Pym (himself age sixteen)—hero of Poe's only novel—accidentally sailed into my life and swept me off on a voyage of discovery as no other fictional character had before.

Poe was definitely a man ahead of his time. Today, his writing seems so fresh that it's difficult to imagine just how far ahead of his time he must have seemed during his own life. To place this within historical context: On January 19, 1809 (when Poe was "born in a trunk" in Boston), Thomas Jefferson was still the sitting president of the fledgling United States, Napoleon was trying to conquer Spain, and fewer than twenty years had elapsed since the dawn of the French Revolution. Then, just three days after Poe's birth—on January 22, 1809—something occurred that would impact the world into which Poe was born in a fashion no one could have conceived. On that morning, an obscure young British noble attained his majority: George Gordon, Lord Byron, turned twenty-one and took his seat in the House of Lords. A few short months later, Byron would sail for the Continent, a voyage that—upon the publication of his first adventure/quest, *Childe Harold's Pilgrimage*—would launch a revolution in epic poetry, would electrify Western literature, and would make Byron himself immortal overnight.

Poe's life is often compared to Byron's—their debauchery and massive debts while they were at school, their love of swimming, of shooting, of "manly feats of daring." Interestingly, Poe spent his formative grammar school years in England, just at the time when Byron's reputation raged as "mad, bad, and dangerous to know." At the age of fifteen—in the same spring during which Byron died in Greece—Poe swam Virginia's turbulent James River, comparing this feat to Byron's youthful conquest of the Hellespont. While at West Point, he studied Byron's poetry and became such an admirer that his adoptive father blamed Byron for Poe's excessive behavior. Numerous allusions to Byron appear in Poe's work.

According to Poe, a poem is the perfect vehicle for expressing "Beauty," but as he tells us in his 1842 review of Hawthorne's *Twice Told Tales*, only the short story can convey "terror, or passion, or horror, or a multitude of such other points." He takes great pains to stress the inferiority of the "ordinary novel [which is] objectionable, from its length . . . As it cannot be read at one sitting, it deprives itself, of course, of the immense force derivable from *totality*." Any outside interruption by "worldly interests intervening"—even just setting the book down for a moment—would "be sufficient to destroy the true unity." Poe contrasts this handicap of the novel with the chief advantage of the short story, which can be read in under an hour, during which period "the soul of the reader is at the writer's control."

Given this stance, it is not surprising that, amid Poe's astonishingly prolific body of work—newspaper articles, literary critiques, essays, editorials, puzzles, poetry, mysteries, horror stories—he wrote only one novel: *The Narrative of Arthur Gordon Pym of Nantucket*. (Byron's family name was Gordon.) This complex book—three stories in one really—describes the adventures of a young man who stows away in the hold of a ship, is kidnapped by mutineers and pirates, suffers starvation, encounters cannibalism, explores the little-known Antarctic, and finds a riddle that dates back to ancient Ethiopia, Arabia, and Egypt, providing the key to Western mystical traditions. It is a triumph of swashbuckling-yet-erudite Byronic self-indulgence.

The story at first seems disjointed. It is bracketed by two "testimonials." In the prologue, Pym confesses that he has told his tale to an editor, Mr. Poe, and some "gentlemen from Richmond, Virginia," and that Poe has published some of the tale in the newspapers, under the guise of fiction. Pym is now going to set the record straight with his own true narrative of his adventures. Then, at the apparently dangling end, we suddenly learn that Pym is unable to continue his story: he was killed in an unfortunate "accident." The last vision that Pym recorded in his narrative was of a huge figure, perhaps a divine spirit, rising from a mist of white ashes in the Antarctic Ocean.

Given all these multiple plots, the large cast of characters, the testimonials by others, the diaries, and theatrical asides that we find sprinkled throughout the book, what happened to the rigorous control that Poe demanded over the reader's attention—even his soul? And despite all such baroque qualities, why does this story still live and breathe, some two hundred years later, as surprisingly fresh as the day it was written?

The secret may be revealed in a peephole glance at a fascinating exchange between Poe and Charles Dickens, where Poe states, "There is a radical error, I think, in the usual mode of constructing a story. . . . Nothing is more clear than that every plot, worth the name, must be elaborated to its denouement before anything be attempted with the pen. . . . [It is only then] that we can give a plot its indispensable air of consequence, or causation, by making the incidents, and especially the tone at all points, tend to the development of the intention." The genius of *Pym* is that, not only does the author have foreknowledge of the end, we the readers possess it, too—though when it comes, it is still a complete surprise.

We are informed that the editors discovered something just before going to press with Mr. Pym's memoir. Now this surprise discovery is revealed: three caves in the shape of ancient letters, forming a secret code that chillingly points us toward something sinister involving darkness and light. Readers are left to draw their own conclusions about what it means. This mysterious ending—which is presented almost as an afterthought—is both shocking and thrilling, for we suddenly realize that this cryptic revelation is the very denouement toward which the narrative has been hurtling since before page one.

This literary technique—revealing something critical to the audience that the characters, the "editors," and perhaps even the author do not know—is one of the oldest and perhaps most powerful, dating back to Lord Byron's own mentors, the ancient Greeks. It is irony, a device used with chilling effect in *The Narrative of Arthur Gordon Pym of Nantucket*. As fresh now as the first time I opened its pages, the novel never fails to excite— one of the American progenitors of the modern adventure thriller.

Katherine Neville was born in the Midwest and attended school in Colorado. From the age of eighteen, she worked full time, often taking any job she could get, including computer analyst, commercial photographer, portrait painter, busboy, waiter, and model. These and her postgraduate studies in African literature provided details to enrich her novels. Her twenty years as an international computer executive and consultant in finance and energy took her to six countries on three continents and half of the states in the U.S. After her first novel, *The Eight*, was published in 1988, Neville was described as the female Umberto Eco, the female Alexandre Dumas, and the female Steven Spielberg. Her books, including *A Calculated Risk*, *The Magic Circle*, and *The Fire* (a sequel to *The Eight*), have been bestsellers in nearly forty languages. In a poll by the noted Spanish journal El Pais, *The Eight* was voted one of the top ten books of all time.

9

Alexandre Dumas'
THE COUNT OF MONTE CRISTO (1845)

Francine Mathews

Alexandre Dumas (1802–1870) had a life as outrageous and remarkable as his fictional characters. Born to a Santo Domingo slave girl and a Napoleonic general who was the mulatto son of a marquis, Dumas was a child of fortune from the moment of his father's death, when he was only four. A penniless and ill-educated orphan, Dumas joined the household of the future king of France, Louis-Philippe, where he read extensively and observed the habits of the aristocracy. Following the revolution that placed Louis-Philippe on the throne, Dumas embarked on a career as playwright, then turned in his late thirties to historical novels, producing two of his most famous—*The Three Musketeers* and *The Count of Monte Cristo*—in 1844. In that decade alone, he penned twenty-three plays, forty-one novels, a plethora of travel literature, and tales for children. Possessed of huge appetites for travel, food, and women, Dumas wrote prolifically to pay his constant debts. He claimed to have invented the serial novel (although Charles Dickens might argue the point), and may be the first "franchise" author the marketplace rewarded.

> *When one lives among madmen, one should train as a maniac.*
> —Alexandre Dumas

Let's be frank from the get-go: *The Count of Monte Cristo*, published in 117 installments over the course of two years, from 1844 to 1845, is a *really long book*. The Penguin Classics edition, translated from the French by Robin Buss (1996) with a stormy image of a nineteenth-century beach on the cover, clocks in at 1,243 pages. Most people will heft the volume, observe that it's about as long as Tolstoy's *War and Peace*, and decide to order one of several movie versions from Netflix.

This would be a sad but perfectly comprehensible mistake.

Viewers are forced to choose between a forgettable feature-length 2002 version, the chortle-out-loud pleasures of a Richard Chamberlain television miniseries dating from 1975, and a variety of artier fare that stretches all the way back to 1918. This is a book that, like its brother *The Three Musketeers*, has served as epic rip-off fodder for more than a century. That is, in itself, the ultimate argument for retrieving the tome from its current use as a doorstop and sitting down—preferably by a good fire with a better bottle of wine—for several nights of complete reading bliss.

The Count, as we'll call it for the sake of brevity, is like a caravan through the desert with Scheherazade riding shotgun. It's a collection of tales each more fantastic than the last, with the overarching theme of implacable revenge providing a sense of unity. Like the revolutionary times it was meant to evoke, it's a chaotic mix: infanticide, illegitimate heirs raised in orphanages, a countess who systematically poisons her stepfamily, a girl who runs away with her lesbian lover, smugglers, suicides, and aborted duels, fabulous caves filled with jewels, drug-induced erotic dreams, sex slaves, gruesome public executions, and of course, a wronged man whose innocence is rewarded.

Kind of.

Edmond Dantès, the antihero at the heart of the novel, is nineteen when three jealous rivals frame him as a Napoleonic sympathizer. He's pulled without explanation, charge, or trial from his betrothal feast, and buried alive for fourteen years in the island dungeons of the Chateau d'If, off the coast of Marseille. While he's presumed dead, his rivals make fortunes and win titles. One even marries his fiancée, Mercédès. Meanwhile his beloved father dies of starvation. Dantès, on the other hand, tunnels under his dungeon wall nightly to meet up with an aged priest, Abbé Faria, who spends a decade teaching the young sailor everything he knows—languages, philosophy, mathematics, science. Faria shares his last secret only on his deathbed, however: the key to an immense fortune buried for centuries on the island of Monte Cristo. If Dantès survives, Faria insists, he must claim the treasure and put it to good use. Dantès swears instead to seek his revenge.

The next scene is one I have never forgotten, the one that remains with me through all the books I have ever read or will ever write, the one that registers *The Count* in the annals of great thriller fiction: the old priest dies. And Dantès takes a risk. Dantès takes his place.

He carries the corpse to his own cell and lies down inside Faria's shroud. He sews it shut from the inside. At midnight, his jailers tie a thirty-six pound cannon ball to his feet, and toss him off the Chateau d'If's cliffs into the Mediterranean Sea.

No matter how comfortable your chair or how safe your circumstances, no matter where you read this particular chapter (and remember, it was first read as a newspaper installment, ending with a literal cliff-hanger), Dumas' writing will chill your blood and raise the hair on the back of your neck.

The Dantès who cuts himself free of that watery grave and rises gasping to the surface is a Dantès transformed, a god resurrected: he is the Count of Monte Cristo, an omniscient superhero, from that moment forward.

This all occurs in the first four hundred pages of the book, and in many ways they're the most critical. They provide the reader with an anguished and completely compelling portrait of a good man perverted and destroyed by the randomness of his victimization. It's a profoundly modern concept—Kafka used it a hundred years after Dumas, and the character of Jason Bourne embodies it in our own age. That sense of the modern—of a victim fighting a faceless conspiracy—predisposes us to sympathize and justify everything Dantès does in the years that follow. It's a bloody progress: one enemy shoots himself in the head, another goes bankrupt, a third is driven insane. The collateral damage is immense. Through it all, the count is a model of aristocratic brio. He dresses beautifully. His horses, his houses, his tables are of the finest. He is feared and admired as another Lord Byron, or perhaps—as one woman believes—a vampire. His performance is a perfectly sustained example of heartless cool.

In the end, that's what brings us back to Alexandre Dumas: his accessibility. It doesn't matter that The Count of Monte Cristo was written 165 years ago, about a dangerous political time that has long since faded from memory. Its storytelling is pitch perfect, its revenge plot intricate and swiftly paced. This is rollicking entertainment that keeps us on the edge of our seats. And on that twelve hundred and forty-third page, as Edmond Dantès sails off into the sunrise with his freed sex slave, Haydée, you just might find yourself wishing for a few more installments.

Francine Mathews spent four years as an intelligence analyst at the CIA, which provided some of the material for her spy novels *The Cutout*, *The Secret Agent*, and *Blown*. Her *The Alibi Club* was named one of the fifteen best novels of 2006 by *Publishers Weekly*. As Stephanie Barron, Francine writes the critically acclaimed Jane Austen mystery series. As Barron, she is also the author of *A Flaw in the Blood*, set in Victorian England, and *The White Garden*, about Virginia Woolf.

10
Wilkie Collins's
THE WOMAN IN WHITE (1860)

Douglas Preston

Wilkie Collins (1824–1889) is widely credited with having invented the modern thriller with *The Woman in White*. The son of a well-known Royal Academy artist in London, Collins spent part of his teenage years in Italy, an experience that influenced him greatly; he studied law at Lincoln's Inn, and dabbled in painting before taking up writing. In 1851, Collins met Charles Dickens, thus launching a lifetime collaboration and friendship. The two wrote plays, short stories, and nonfiction works together, and Dickens serialized several of Collins's novels in his weekly publication, *All the Year Round*. Their relationship, dramatized in Dan Simmons's *Drood*, was so close that Collins was later nicknamed the "Dickensian Ampersand," but at the height of his popularity, Collins was the more famous, more beloved, and better-selling writer. Suffering from rheumatic gout for much of his life, Collins grew addicted to laudanum, the notorious Victorian tincture of opium and alcohol. He suffered hallucinations and labored under the delusion that he was being shadowed by a doppelgänger he called "Ghost Wilkie." After the 1868 publication of his celebrated novel, *The Moonstone*, his writing declined as his drug addiction, gout, and corpulence increased. Following Dickens's death in 1870, Collins produced a series of increasingly wretched books until his own death in 1889, at age sixty-five. He left behind a literary legacy of more than two dozen novels, over a hundred nonfiction works, fifty short stories, and at least fifteen plays—and one of the greatest thrillers, *The Woman in White*.

There are literary moments one never forgets. Keats memorialized one in his poem, "On First Looking into Chapman's Homer," when he compared the experience of reading Chapman's translation of Homer to Cortez discovering the Pacific Ocean. One of my memorable literary moments occurred when I cracked a dog-eared paperback of *The Woman in White* I'd bought from a street vendor on Broadway in New York City for twenty-five cents. I was in my early twenties; it was lunchtime, and I sat on a bench next to Central Park Pond, opposite the Museum of Natural History, where I worked as a writer and editor.

After struggling through an unpromising first chapter, I began reading the passage that opens:

> There, in the middle of the broad, bright high-road—there, as if it had that moment sprung out of the earth or dropped from the heaven—stood the figure of a solitary Woman, dressed from head to foot in white garments; her face bent in grave inquiry on mine, her hand pointing to the dark cloud over London, as I faced her.

I was spellbound, and from that moment until I finished, I lived and breathed the novel, walking around in a daze. Dickens called the passage one of the two most dramatic descriptions in all of literature. It is a chapter that every thriller writer should study.

The first installment of *The Woman in White* was published in Charles Dickens's weekly magazine, *All the Year Round*, on November 26, 1859, starting on the same page as the final words of the last installment of Dickens's novel, *A Tale of Two Cities*.

It was an enormous success. Over the course of the serialization, the circulation of *All the Year Round* tripled, and lines formed at newsagents when the next part was due. Thackeray stayed up all night, devouring *The Woman in White*, and William Gladstone cancelled an important engagement to finish it. It was one of the biggest selling novels in English up to that time.

The Woman in White created a new genre of fiction, the "sensation novel," which was the direct precursor to the twentieth-century thriller. The sensation novel dealt with extreme subjects: murder, violence, bigamy, insanity, kidnapping, illegitimate children, nefarious legal machinations, adultery, forgery, fraud, and dark labyrinthine secrets—not in exotic, faraway locales, but seething beneath the placid surface of English domestic life. Because many sensation novels were published in parts, each section had to end with a flourish, a cliff-hanger, a dark note of violence or mystery to keep the reader eagerly awaiting the next installment. The sensation novel was the progenitor not only of the pithy chapter structure of the modern thriller, but also of the episodic nature of most television dramas, thus exerting a vast and subtle influence on modern storytelling.

Collins got the idea for *The Woman in White* from a story recorded by Francois Gayot de Pitaval in his 1735 book, *Famous and Interesting Cases*. Pitaval recounted the ordeal of a woman who was bundled off to an insane asylum by her heirs bent on acquiring her estate. (The story of Martin Guerre was another of Pitaval's cases.) In *The Woman in White*, a brutal baronet and a devious Italian count steal a young woman's inheritance by forcing her marriage to the baronet, who then switches her with a woman in an insane asylum, where her protestations to be a lady of quality become further proof of her insanity.

Structurally, *The Woman in White* is daring and avant garde. The story is mostly told by four narrators, presented through their letters, diary entries, and written statements. Some of the narrators in *The Woman in White* are unreliable, even suspect, which adds to the novel's atmosphere of menace and deception. This shifting of narrative points of view anticipated the literary experimentation of the twentieth century, and in many ways it was more radical than, for example, Faulkner's narrative shifts in *As I Lay Dying* and *The Sound and the Fury*.

The plot of *The Woman in White* is fantastically complex, as ornate and dark as a Victorian wig dresser. After the book was published, one critic analyzed the various timelines and gleefully announced that it was impossible for the events to have taken place. A chagrined Collins ordered the presses stopped and rewrote the book to fix the problem, but modern critics have pointed out further inconsistencies. Despite that, the book moves swiftly and surely, the pacing is perfect, and each terrible scene is like the slow winding of a spring, building up an unbearable tension.

What makes *The Woman in White* a great novel, however, is more than plot and structure: it lies in the extraordinary characters Collins created. Two in particular are unforgettable: Count Fosco and Marian Halcombe, the heroine's best friend.

Collins created deep and powerful portraits of real women in his novels, and Marian Halcombe was his crowning achievement. She is a completely original character, the anti-Victorian woman—independent, sarcastic, highly intelligent, loyal, strong, and courageous; she roundly disparages the idea that women are delicate and weak and in need of protection. Underlying the novel is a subcurrent of outrage at women's lack of rights, particularly property rights, and these are clearly Collins's views, too, a man more than a century ahead of his time. Marian Halcombe is—

do I dare say it?—a more fully realized depiction of a woman than any-thing to be found in English literature before, and that would include the novels of Jane Austen and the Brontë sisters. She is magnificent.

And then there is the exquisite Count Fosco, the corpulent Italian no-bleman of refinement and taste, an aesthete and wit who pets and kisses the tame mice that scamper about his enormous person while remaining mon-strously indifferent to the suffering of his fellow human beings. He com-bines prodigious charisma and charm with a cool, pleasant, and utterly amoral world view; he is one of the most perfectly realized Machiavellian figures in English literature. And yet the reader finds, to his own shock, something deeply attractive about the man. One of the best pieces of ad-vice I ever received as a novelist came from an editor who insisted that a great thriller must have a great villain; Fosco is a villain for the ages, and any writer who aspires to the genre should study him.

When Lincoln Child and I were in the early stages of plotting our novel *Brimstone*, we needed a villain who was an Italian nobleman. Linc brought up Count Fosco, saying we needed a character like him. As we debated who our villain would be, enumerating his traits, arguing about his habits, his looks, and his manners of speech, we kept coming back to Fosco. Finally I said, "Damn it, Linc, why don't we just *steal* him?" And so, with trepidation (and due credit given), we purloined the adipose count—pet mice and all—for our novel. There he appears, exactly as conceived by Collins, updated only slightly into the twenty-first century. It is our little homage to one of our favorite authors, Wilkie Collins, and his greatest novel, *The Woman in White*.

Douglas Preston was born in Cambridge, Massachusetts, and grew up in the deadly boring suburb of Wellesley. He worked as an editor and writer for the American Museum of Natural History in New York. He also taught writing at Princeton University. His numerous books, both fiction and nonfiction, include *Tyrannosaur Canyon* (2005) and *Blasphemy* (2008) as well as *Cities of Gold: A Journey across the American Southwest* (1992). Some of his novels were coauthored with Lincoln Child, featuring FBI Special Agent Aloysius X. L. Pendergast, among them *The Cabinet of Curiosities* (2002). His nonfiction book, *The Monster of Florence* (2008, coauthored with Mario Spezi), chronicles the story of Italy's most notorious serial killer, who ritually murdered lovers in the hills of Tuscany. Preston writes occa-sional pieces for the *New Yorker*, the *Atlantic Monthly*, *Smithsonian*, and other mag-azines. He served on the board of directors of the Authors Guild and International Thriller Writers.

11

Jules Verne's
THE MYSTERIOUS ISLAND (1874)

D. P. Lyle

French author Jules Verne (1828–1905) is the father of the science-fiction genre and, with *The Mysterious Island*, penned one of the great thrillers. Verne's unique gift lies in his ability to meld science fact, fantasy, and speculation with incredible adventure stories. He has taken millions of readers to the center of the Earth, 20,000 leagues beneath the ocean's waves, around the world aboard a balloon in eighty days, the surface of the moon, and all points in between. He imagined navigable aircraft, an electric submarine, and a space rocket long before these existed. He presaged such things as the FAX machine, aerial warfare, astronauts walking on the moon (his were also launched from Florida), and even the now ubiquitous camera phone and text messaging.

> *The desire to perform a work which will endure, which will survive him,*
> *is the origin of man's superiority over all other creatures . . .*
> —Jules Verne, *The Mysterious Island*

It's 1864. The Civil War rages across the rolling hills and fertile farmland of Virginia. Richmond is besieged. Five prisoners commandeer a balloon and escape from a Confederate prison.

> "Are we rising again?"
> "No. On the contrary."
> "Are we descending?"
> "Worse than that, Captain! We are falling!"

With those lines one of the great adventures in all of literature begins. *The Mysterious Island* follows the fate of the five Civil War prison escapees. They are an eclectic group—an engineer, a sailor, a journalist, a young boy, and a black man, who might have been a slave (Verne chooses

39

to refer to him as a loyal butler). The storm carries them from Virginia, across an angry ocean, and deposits them on an uncharted volcanic island in the South Pacific.

Like Daniel Defoe's *Robinson Crusoe* and Johann Rudolf Wyss's *The Swiss Family Robinson*, *The Mysterious Island* echoes the true story of Alexander Selkirk, a sailor stranded on an island off the Chilean coast for five years. As did Selkirk, Crusoe, and the Robinson family, Verne's castaways, who prefer to call themselves colonists, survive by their own ingenuity. They use watch crystals to create fire; manufacture matches from materials found on the island; mold bricks, build a kiln, and fabricate pottery; smelt iron from ore, using a sealskin bellows to stoke the fire, and ultimately make steel; produce various acids to tan hides and make soap; mix up gunpowder and then nitroglycerin, which they use to blow an opening in a rock wall, which releases a waterfall and a steady supply of fresh water; farm; raise animals; build an elevator; and set up a telegraph system.

Each process used by the colonists, and every device they create, are meticulously explained by Verne, revealing the breadth and depth of his scientific knowledge as well as his ability to explain complex subjects to even the most naïve reader. He explores everything from chemistry and physics to zoology and botany, from geology and climatology to celestial navigation, from metallurgy to mathematics and trigonometry, from architecture to hydrodynamics, and even then-current medical knowledge when one of the colonists develops a "pernicious fever."

If *The Mysterious Island* were merely an educational adventure story, it would still rank among the greatest thrillers. But Verne seasons his plot with intrigue, and it is this mysterious element that adds depth and texture to the tale.

The island holds a secret. They are not alone.

Someone or something is out there.

The initial clues are passed off as serendipity or good luck. A large amphibious creature is found slain, a slash across its neck. By what weapon? By whose hand? Maybe the sharp coral sealed its fate. A pig is found dead in one of their traps, yet when it is cooked, a bullet is discovered in the flesh. Where could it have come from? A harpooned whale appears on the beach. A rich source of oil for them, but who launched the harpoon? A chest washes ashore, presumably from a passing or perhaps foundering ship. It contains weapons, tools, scientific instruments, books, maps, and clothing. Exactly what they need. As if someone had packed it specifically for them.

A ship with fifty pirates arrives. They launch a furious attack on the colonists. Death seems imminent, until the vessel suddenly explodes. Surely, it was the powder magazine. But when they inspect the partially sunken ship, the magazine is intact, and it appears as if a mine destroyed the enemy. This fortuitous event convinces them that they are being watched. Six pirates, who were on shore at the time of the explosion, survive, and a cat-and-mouse chase ensues with the colonists being both hunter and hunted. Until the pirates are found dead. Who could have slain them?

Thinking they are now safe, they discover that the island has yet another trick for the colonists. It awakens, spewing smoke and fire, threatening to explode with volcanic fury. On the verge of destruction, the island's true secret is revealed in the person of Captain Nemo, one of the most enigmatic characters in literature. In *The Mysterious Island*, the amazing story of Nemo and his remarkable submarine the *Nautilus*, both initially introduced in *Twenty Thousand Leagues Under the Sea*, comes full circle. To discover the fate of the colonists, the *Nautilus*, Nemo, and *The Mysterious Island*, you'll need to read the book.

Mr. Verne truly achieved his "desire to perform a work which will endure," not only in *The Mysterious Island*, but also in each of the other fantastic novels he wrote. His influence on fiction writers is both long lived and profound.

I first met him on a cool, cloudy October afternoon in 1960 in my hometown of Huntsville. I had just finished football practice—a sport played by most fourteen-year-old Alabama boys—and walked downtown to wait at the library for my dad, who would swing by to pick me up after leaving his job at the post office. The library, built in 1915 by Andrew Carnegie, held row after row of book-stuffed shelves. This day I had no homework, so I wandered through the musty stacks. I had never read a real novel. Just those high-school-sports-hero-wins-the-game-on-a-last-second-miracle-play-and-gets-the-girl books. What we would today call young adult. But never a real novel. A thick, heavy one.

My rummaging ended at a shelf lined with books by Jules Verne. I had seen the Disney production of *20,000 Leagues Under the Sea*, so Verne was not an unfamiliar name. I picked up *Journey to the Center of the Earth*, took it to a table, and began to read. The first page set the hook. When Dad arrived, I got a library card—my first—and took the book home. A week later, I exchanged that one for *The Mysterious Island*. More Verne as well as H. G. Wells, Edgar Rice Burroughs, Hemingway, Steinbeck, and a life-long love of reading followed. Thank you, Mr. Verne.

D. P. Lyle, M.D. is the Macavity Award-winning and Edgar Award-nominated author of the nonfiction books, *Murder and Mayhem*, *Forensics for Dummies*, and *Forensics and Fiction* as well as the thrillers, *Devil's Playground* and *Double Blind*. His other works include *Howdunnit: Forensics: A Guide For Writers*, from Writers Digest Books. He is a practicing cardiologist in Orange County, California, and has worked with many novelists and with the writers of popular television shows such as *Law & Order*, *CSI: Miami*, *Diagnosis Murder*, *Monk*, *Judging Amy*, *Peacemakers*, *Cold Case*, *House*, *Medium*, *Women's Murder Club*, and *1-800-Missing*. Visit his Web site, The Writers' Medical and Forensics Lab, at www.dp lylemd.com

12

H. Rider Haggard's
KING SOLOMON'S MINES (1885)

Norman L. Rubenstein

Sir Henry Rider Haggard (1856–1925) was the eighth of ten children born to a barrister father and a poetess mother. After a lackluster elementary and high school education, Haggard's father arranged a position for Rider with the lieutenant governor of Natal in Africa, where Rider later became the registrar of the High Court of the Transvaal, itself later to become a part of South Africa. Rider married and had four children, the family eventually returning to England, where Rider studied law and became a barrister. However, he soon determined that his heart wasn't in it, and he turned to writing. *King Solomon's Mines* (1885) was Haggard's fourth book and became a hugely popular best seller. The prolific Haggard published over seventy books, including eighteen that featured the hero of *King Solomon's Mines*, Allan Quatermain, along with four novels featuring his other enduring literary creation, Ayesha, "She Who Must Be Obeyed," starting with the also famous novel, *She* (1887).

According to H. Rider Haggard, he came to write *King Solomon's Mines* because of a small wager with one of his older brothers, who bet Rider that he could not write a book "half as good" as the recently published (1883) *Treasure Island* by Robert Louis Stevenson. Rider took the bet and promptly wrote *King Solomon's Mines* in short order (accounts vary from as few as six weeks to at most sixteen weeks). The book originally had trouble finding a publisher, as it was so different and original compared to anything that had come before it, but when after six months of attempts it eventually was published in 1885, it became an immediate best seller and ultimately that year's best-selling book. The novel was one of the first to be the subject of a modern-style advertising and marketing campaign, with billboards and posters inundating London with the announcement that *King Solomon's Mines* was "The Most Amazing Book Ever Written."

The novel is generally and correctly credited with being the first "Lost

World" genre adventure novel and the forerunner and inspiration of such famous novels as Kipling's *The Man Who Would Be King*, Conan Doyle's *The Lost World*, Howard's *Conan* and *Kull* tales, and Lovecraft's *At the Mountains of Madness*, among many others. *King Solomon's Mines* has been filmed at least six times, and the story's hero, Allan Quatermain, is an obvious antecedent and influence upon contemporary heroes such as Indiana Jones. Quatermain himself has appeared as a main character in the graphic novel and subsequent film of *The League of Extraordinary Gentlemen*, where no less an action hero than Sean Connery portrayed him.

King Solomon's Mines is an enduring classic that is still widely read and enjoyed today and owes its continued popularity in part to its engaging, informal first-person narration by Quatermain. It is also notable as the first adventure novel published in English that was based in the African continent. At the time of *King Solomon's Mines*, the African continent was largely unknown to the Western world, and the author's personal knowledge of the geography, flora, fauna, peoples, and fables of South Africa gave the novel a great deal of veracity and flavor that rang true with readers.

The plot involves a small, intrepid band of adventurers who follow an old sixteenth-century treasure map written in blood, that supposedly reveals the location of the lost gold and gemstone mines of the biblical King Solomon. It has epic battles, lost civilizations, and plenty of action, elements that are usually crowd pleasers, yet the novel has been the subject of two major contemporary criticisms.

First, it has been called misogynistic, allegedly reflecting a seeming hatred or at least severe indifference toward women by its author. All four of the main protagonists are male, and the two female characters of any note in the novel are both native Africans from the lost Kakuna tribe. One is Gagool, the ancient, evil witch doctor/sorceress and head advisor to the equally evil usurping Kukuana king, Twala. The other is Foulata, the beautiful tribeswoman who engages in an ill-fated romance with Captain Good, one of the British protagonists. True, none of the protagonists is a female in the contemporary tradition of Lara Croft or even Hermione Granger from the *Harry Potter* series. Admittedly, our Western world has changed in its attitude toward women substantially since this novel was written almost 125 years ago, prior to when women had even been accorded the right to vote. But we need to bear in mind the group that Haggard had in mind for his adventure novel, dedicating it to "all the big and little boys who read it."

The other major criticism leveled against *King Solomon's Mines* is its depiction of the African peoples and their relationships with the British Caucasians. To be sure, there is sufficient content that is directly nineteenth-century British colonialist in attitude and is, by definition, racist. After establishing the interracial romance between Foulata and Captain Good, Haggard has Quatermain attempt to discourage it, based upon the uproar that such a marriage would cause back in England, were Good to bring his African bride back there with him. Quatermain says this, even though he describes Foulata as both beautiful and noble, and has no objection to her otherwise. However, to Haggard's credit, he does endow one of the book's real heroes, a black African prince, with both intelligence and nobility far greater than many of the Caucasians encountered in the novel. Haggard reinforces this when Quatermain declares that he has found numerous Africans more worthy of the title "gentleman," than the British and Europeans who have come to adventure within Africa. Haggard also has Quatermain emphatically declare that he refuses to utter or use the "N" word to refer to black Africans. Remember this is in 1885. In this regard, Haggard was far ahead of his time.

King Solomon's Mines remains a riveting and thrilling adventure yarn that makes for easy, entertaining reading. It has personal resonance in that it remains one of my earliest memories of my father. My paternal grandfather, born around 1880, was a huge fan of adventure stories. I well remember my grandfather almost always carrying a book with him, which invariably was a thriller or a mystery. He passed this love on to my father, who in turn introduced me at an early age to authors such as Haggard, Conan Doyle, Sayers, Christie, Eberhart, Hammett, and Chandler, among others. Even before I was able to enjoy these stories firsthand through reading them, my father would tell my brother and me bedtime stories set in far off lands and involving treasure maps, heroes, battles, and great mysteries. When I was older and reading for myself, I soon recognized many of these tales my father told as being bits and pieces from novels that he cobbled together for our enjoyment. His stories based upon *King Solomon's Mines* were among our favorites. I hope that this novel, the action-packed progenitor of an entire genre of storytelling, will long continue to endure, entertain, and enchant readers of all ages.

Norman L. Rubenstein, like H. Rider Haggard, followed his father into the family business and ran the litigation law firm founded by his father for over twenty years before being appointed a judge. After encountering health problems in his forties that precluded his continued practice of law, Norman, a member of both the Horror Writer's Association and the International Thriller Writers, also like Rider Haggard turned to writing and is currently a columnist for *Shroud Magazine* and for *Fear Zone* as well as a reviewer for *Cemetery Dance Magazine*, *Horror World*, and *Horror-Mall*. He is also associate editor for Bloodletting Press (which received the 2009 Bram Stoker Specialty Press Award from the Horror Writer's Association) and a part-time associate editor for Cargo Cult Press.

13

Robert Louis Stevenson's
THE STRANGE CASE OF DR. JEKYLL AND MR. HYDE
(1886)

Sarah Langan

A prolific, masterful writer, defender of the subjugated, and globe-trotter, Stevenson (1850–1894) led a life that rivaled his fiction. Born in Scotland, he caught the travel bug early, while accompanying his father on sea trips to Shetland. Upon leaving the University of Edinburgh with a degree in law, he spent several years roaming through Europe, where he met the love of his life, Fanny Osbourne. In a storybook-like gesture of wild romanticism, he followed her to San Francisco by boat and then train, living on as little as forty cents per day. By the time he found her in California, the arduous trip had exhausted his health. She nursed and then married him, and together they returned to Europe in 1880, where they spent the next eight years searching for a climate that would heal the respiratory ailments he'd suffered since birth. They never found it, but he continued to write, often from a sickbed, and during this time, he produced the novels that would make him famous: *Treasure Island* (1883), *The Black Arrow* (1883), *Prince Otto* (1885), *Kidnapped* (1886), and *The Strange Case of Dr. Jekyll and Mr. Hyde* (1886). In 1888, the family traveled to the South Pacific and settled in Samoa, where Stevenson became a local hero and defender of indigenous peoples, adopting the native name Tusitala (writer). He died before the completion of his final novel, at the age of forty-four, most likely of a brain hemorrhage, and had already composed his epitaph, which read:

> Under the wide and starry sky,
> Dig the grave and let me lie.
> Glad did I live and gladly die,
> And I laid me down with a will.
> This be the verse you grave for me:

Here he lies where he longed to be;
Home is the sailor, home from the sea,
And the hunter home from the hill.

Within five years of its 1886 publication, *The Strange Case of Dr. Jekyll and Mr. Hyde* became a slow-build commercial success, with two hundred fifty thousand books sold. It remains one of the most translated novels and continues to be read worldwide today. The story inspired the modern trope of the dual personality, from comic book heroes like *The Incredible Hulk* to Stephen King's *The Dark Half*, to perhaps even Thomas Harris's Dr. Lector in *The Silence of the Lambs*. A recent British television miniseries adapted the story to a modern setting. Arguably, the novel inspired modern variations on the werewolf legend, since both stories concern the desire to break free from psychological and social constraints.

Dr. Jekyll and Mr. Hyde concerns a mad scientist who concocts a potion that cleaves the evil part of his nature from his respectable persona and frees it to commit heinous acts. Soon, however, the evil Hyde becomes stronger than respectable Jekyll, and the cleaving occurs without the potion. Hyde subsumes Jekyll, and both men become a single monster.

The short book was written with astonishing intensity in three days, then burned in dismay about its contents, then rewritten in another three days. It was published during the Victorian Era, alongside novels like *Dracula*, *Jude the Obscure*, *The Odd Women*, and *The Picture of Dorian Gray*. At first, these seem unrelated. But in truth, they have much in common: repression. The characters in each of these novels, good or evil, are trapped in worlds whose rules they didn't create, and whose appearance of rectitude is more important than its substance.

Though often dismissed as a populist, Stevenson's fiction has outlasted its critics, and rightly so. What distinguishes *Dr. Jekyll and Mr. Hyde* from its peers, and makes it a stronger novel, is its indictment not just of the cast of characters who witness their good friend's degeneration, but of an entire social order.

Stevenson tended to view the world as an outsider. His health problems engendered in him a sympathy for those less fortunate, and his travels taught him about the world outside stiff, Victorian Britain. He was a furious advocate for reform, and while in Samoa, published a scathing account of the European officials appointed to rule the island, *A Footnote to History*, which resulted in the recall of two government officers. Before that, he visited a leper colony in Hawaii and wrote a letter of complaint to the remote minister overseeing the colony:

> You belong, sir, to a sect—I believe my sect, and that in which my ancestors laboured—which has enjoyed, and partly failed to utilise, an exceptional advantage in the islands of Hawaii. The first missionaries came; they found the land already self-purged of its old and bloody faith; they were embraced, almost on their arrival, with enthusiasm ... This is not the place to enter into the degree or causes of their failure, such as it is. One element alone is pertinent, and must here be plainly dealt with. In the course of their evangelical calling, they — or too many of them — grew rich.

Like the men he condemned, Stevenson considered himself one of the elite. Though his family made their living from engineering lighthouses, they also inherited a substantial sum, and like the rest of the landed aristocracy, not all of it was squarely won. The same can be said for every character in *Dr. Jekyll and Mr. Hyde*, from the kindly scientist to his trusted lawyer Utterson, to Utterson's cousin Enfield, to Dr. Lanyon. All attended school together and are friends of convenience. None has true affection for each other. There is no honesty between them, or even joy—only politeness, and convention. They're trapped. No wonder Jekyll wants to break free and do a little mischief.

When the men learn that Jekyll is involved in bad business, each swears himself to silence. It is this fraternity that Stevenson loathed even more deeply than the evil Mr. Hyde, who consumes his willing victim, proving that once man's darker nature is released, it does not set the good half free, but only corrupts it more deeply, for being a silent participant. It isn't just Jekyll who loses his soul in this story, but every member of Jekyll's class. He condemns the Victorian establishment itself, which, in its silence, commits harm.

In the end, Hyde and Jekyll are not revealed to the world as the same man. Instead, the morally upstanding Utterson reads Jekyll's confessional letters and presumably never looks at them again. Out of loyalty or cowardice, he protects Jekyll's reputation.

Hyde's monstrosity is generic. He threatens to step on a child, canes a man to death, and presumably sleeps with a lot of women, men, or goats—

who knows? Such behavior does not disgust Jekyll, but thrills him, which begs the question: was he ever a good man? Or does the culture in which he lives foster and aid him, simply because he's one of the boys?

What's delightful about this story is its lack of guilt. Jekyll feels pretty bad about getting caught, but not all that bad about the way his alter ego bashed an old guy's head in or maybe knocked a few girls up. In the end, the reader might wonder if committing those small harms is different from being part of a class that ignores all things odious, such as its servants, the families whom the laws it passes condemns to debtor's prison, poorhouses, indentured servitude, winters outdoors, high-priced coal, and rags instead of riches, while all the while these respectable good old boys sniff their brandy at night, and discuss only polite, respectable topics, like the weather.

Sarah Langan's first novel, *The Keeper* (2006), was a *New York Times* editor's pick. Her second novel, *The Missing* (2007), won the Bram Stoker Award for outstanding novel, was a *Publishers Weekly* favorite book of the year, an International Horror Guild outstanding novel nominee, and made several other best-of-the-year lists. She has published several essays and a dozen short stories, one of which, "The Lost," received a Stoker Award. Her young adult series is entitled *Kids*. Her third novel, *Audrey's Door*, received the Horror Writers Association best novel award.

14

Anthony Hope's
THE PRISONER OF ZENDA (1894)

Michael Palmer

Sir Anthony Hope Hawkins (1863–1933) was one of the most beloved and widely read novelists of his era. Writing all his fiction under the name Anthony Hope, Hawkins kept a journal throughout his professional life, which helped readers and literary historians to appreciate his remarkable talent and the breadth of his work, as well as his often painful lack of self-esteem. The man revealed in that journal was a scholar of language and politics, an athlete (rugby), a barrister, a knighted war hero, a devoted father of three, and the first cousin of Kenneth Grahame, author of *The Wind in the Willows*. He was also chronically insecure about money and driven by the need for increasing fame, as well as by a sense of failure for not achieving what he considered true greatness. Although critics considered his thirty-two volumes of novels and short stories to be somewhat uneven, few, if any, failed to acknowledge that his 1894 romantic adventure, *The Prisoner of Zenda*, was a timeless tale, if not a masterpiece. One critic called Hawkins the "new Dumas of the nineteenth century."

Inclusion of this little (50,000 words) gem in a book about the 100 greatest thrillers might be a surprise to some. But having read and reread the story as a suspense writer, many years after my father first brought it home for me from the library, I have no doubt that it belongs. Deathless themes, remorseless villains, intrigue, selfless heroes, a beautiful heroine, relentless pacing, adventure, true love, and an unforgettable, bittersweet ending— what more could any fan of the genre ask for?

Oh yes, memorable use of language.

The more I read, the more impressed I was with the lean, spare prose. I can't remember an adventure story where the author accomplished so much with so little. To write simply, W. Somerset Maugham is quoted as having said, is as difficult as to be good. There are short passages on almost every page of this masterpiece—scalpel-sharp testimonies to the joys and genius of writing simply.

> . . . The fellow's story was rudely told. But our questions supplemented his narrative.
> . . . "The red rose for the Elphbergs, marshal," said I gayly, and he nodded.
> I have written "gayly," and a strange word it must seem. But the truth is I was drunk with excitement. At that moment I believed—I almost believed—that I was in very truth the king. . . .

According to the author, *The Prisoner of Zenda* began taking form in the autumn of 1883 when Hawkins, an attorney returning home from court, passed two men who bore a striking resemblance to one another. Within a short time of encountering the two men near the Westminster County Court, Hawkins, for no specific reason that he could recall, began obsessing on a single word—Ruritania. By the next day, the word had become a country—a monarchy situated roughly between Austria and Germany. Later that day, Hawkins began writing, and a little over a month afterward, the first draft of *The Prisoner of Zenda* was completed (the final version was published eleven years later).

The story features a young Englishman, Rudolph Rassendyll, the cheerful, capable, but totally unmotivated brother of a British lord. Rassendyll, distinguished by striking red hair, has heard that through an ancestral indiscretion, the soon-to-be-crowned King Rudolph the Third of Ruritania, probably a distant cousin of his, features hair the color of his own. Motivated by nothing more than that fact, young Rassendyll decides to attend the coronation. Soon after his arrival in Ruritania, Black Michael, the half-brother to the king, arranges to have Rudolph the Third drugged, kidnapped, and imprisoned in the castle at Zenda. The perpetrator of the crime is the dashing, traitorous, womanizing swashbuckler, Rupert of Hentzau.

While hatching plans for the king's rescue, men loyal to him persuade Rassendyll to impersonate the monarch at the coronation in order to keep Black Michael from seizing the throne. There is, however, a major problem. Rassendyll falls in love with rapturous Princess Flavia who is scheduled to marry the new king and thereby strengthen the fraying bonds between their two countries. The princess, startled by the wit and kindness of the king (Rassendyll) falls in love with him as well. The complications mount as a daring rescue of the prisoner of Zenda is planned and attempted, with Rassendyll leading the way, and Rupert poised to stop him.

The conclusion? Ah, that knowledge awaits your reading—a day or two at the most. To appreciate the impact of this tale, beyond the sudden fame and fortune heaped on Anthony Hawkins, one need only look to the success of the sequel, *Rupert of Hentzau*, and to the multiple adaptations of the novel including a Broadway musical, the operetta *Princess Flavia*, written by Sigmund Romberg, radio and television presentations, and a number of motion pictures starring such screen icons as James Mason, Douglas Fairbanks, Jr., Stewart Granger, Ronald Coleman, and even Peter Sellers in a 1979 comic version.

Nearly all of the political doubles adventures that followed *Zenda* (*Dave*, *Moon over Parador*, and others) are homages to Hawkins's work, along with a whole genre of what came to be known as Ruritanian romances—not bad for a romantic thriller that in length is virtually a novella.

Earlier, I promised not to reveal the conclusion of the book. Well, after reading my favorite passage, I have, at least in part, changed my mind. So stop here if you wish to keep the secret until you reach the end of your own reading. Anthony Hawkins's elegantly simple writing was just too wonderful for me not to share it with you.

> . . . One break comes every year in my quiet life. Then I go to Dresden and there I am met by my dear friend and companion Fritz von Tarlenheim. . . . In the evenings as we walk and smoke together, we talk of Sapt, and of the king, and often of young Rupert; and as the hours grow small, at last we speak of Flavia. For every year Fritz carries with him to Dresden a little box; in it lies a red rose and round the stalk of the rose is a slip of paper with the words written:
> "Rudolph—Flavia—always." And the like I send back by him.

Michael Palmer, M.D., board certified in internal medicine and emergency medicine, is the author of fifteen novels of medical suspense, all *New York Times* best sellers, including *The Society*, *The Fifth Vial*, and *The First Patient*. His fourth book,

Extreme Measures, was made into the motion picture of the same name, starring Hugh Grant, Gene Hackman, and Sarah Jessica Parker. Currently, Palmer is an associate director of Physician Health Services, a Massachusetts agency helping physicians recover from mental illness, physical illness, and chemical dependency, including alcoholism. He is the father of three sons and the pet of two cats. In what spare time he has, Palmer lifts weights, plays bridge, and rides a Harley.

15
Bram Stoker's
DRACULA (1897)
Carole Nelson Douglas

Abraham "Bram" Stoker (1847–1912) was prominent in late Victorian London as the theatrical manager for the noted actor, Sir Henry Irving, a role that consumed his life for twenty-seven years, acquainting him with the day's literary and artistic figures. He bested the closeted Oscar Wilde in winning a celebrated beauty, Florence Balcombe. Stoker wrote eleven novels from 1890–1911, but remained an obscure author during his lifetime. Yet his horror thriller, *Dracula,* became the second-most influential and *the* most critically deconstructed work of that madly fertile period. The blood-sucking boyar from Transylvania is second only to that era's Sherlock Holmes in seizing the global imagination and keeping it captive into the twenty-first century through numerous derivative works. Both Doyle and Stoker were Irishmen working and writing in London, convivial men full of Victorian industry enjoying multiple pursuits. Florence's reputed frigidity led to speculation decades later that Stoker was unfaithful and/or homosexual and died of syphilis. Such speculations would affect later analyses of *Dracula* to the point of undercutting its storytelling genius. Yet the influence of this iconic novel and Stoker's immortal villain is stronger than ever.

The 1890's decadent "Yellow Decade" introduced an astounding number of founding tales for the genre categories that came to dominate twentieth-century fiction: thriller, horror, adventure, mystery, science fiction, and fantasy.

Some consider Anthony Hope's 1894 *The Prisoner of Zenda* the first political thriller. H. G. Wells published science fiction cornerstones, *The Time Machine* (1895) and *The Invisible Man* (1897). The first of Arthur Conan Doyle's Sherlock Holmes stories appeared a few years earlier. Bram Stoker's *Dracula* arrived in 1897. The list seems a roll call of what became iconic 1930–1940 films.

The big best seller of the 1890s was artist George du Maurier's *Trilby* of 1895, which introduced another immortal monster to world literature: Svengali, the evil hypnotic influence who made a young, common, tone-deaf girl, Trilby, a noted concert singer. The novel inspired *The Phantom of the Opera* less than a decade later and has elements in common with Dracula, but compelling storytelling isn't one of them. Yet *Trilby* sold in the hundreds of thousands while *Dracula's* early sales remained wan. Today's readers would drop the episodic memoir-like *Trilby* in no time. *Dracula* can still grab the modern reader by the throat. Why?

First, Dracula's plotline is a ripping yarn of the old school made convincing by being told through a parade of narrators in true crime forms ranging from newspaper clippings to diaries and journals to shorthand accounts to phonograph-recorded notes. The reader becomes the omniscient overseer who assembles the puzzle from the enigmatic pieces the various characters hold. This documentary style—Neil Gaiman has called *Dracula* a "Victorian high-tech thriller"—gives the paranormal and horror elements credence. The plot operates under film director Alfred Hitchcock's famous later example of suspense: moviegoers seeing the bomb planted under the table while the unaware characters gather above it.

The ticking bomb is Dracula and his appetite for fresh victims on the innocent island of England. We meet the monster in the masterfully creepy first five chapters of the novel as mousy English solicitor Jonathan Harker journeys to the rugged Carpathian Mountains of Transylvania and Dracula's castle. There, alone and at the mercy of his undead client, Harker gradually realizes *what*, not *who* he's dealing with.

These opening events have been so memorialized in play, film, and the public consciousness they may seem trite now. Yet, like Ian Fleming's James Bond, "nobody did it better"—and first—than Stoker's setup of Dracula and his minions. Although Stoker took solo walking tours of Europe, he never visited Transylvania. Yet he researched the region with such veracity that Harker's journey becomes a Victorian head trip into an older, more savage, and superstitious place harboring a horrific "other" beyond civilized control. By the time Dracula's three brides drool over the captive Harker's swooning form, the reader shares his horror, helpless sensual thralldom, and burgeoning belief in vampires.

And this is exactly where *Dracula* becomes a very sexy book for its era, and ours. Like early film director Cecil B. DeMille's gratuitously sexy biblical epics, *Dracula* uses its classic battle between good and evil—invocations of God and religious symbols versus a fiendish despoiler of human bodies and souls—to depict scenes barely imagined in Victorian pornography. Stoker makes bloodlust a juicy metaphor for sexual carnality.

Harker, the earnestly engaged solicitor, at first *wants* those bold, red-lipped seductresses to work their lethal charms on him. Later, when Dracula's first English victim, Lucy, has died and will live on as a vampire, her aristocratic husband-to-be lays her to rest by repeatedly impaling her with a three-foot-long stake "two-and-a-half to three inches thick." Her temporary revival and final death provide a paragraph of pure orgasmic description that evades censors because it depicts evil being driven out: exorcism as erotica.

Some scholars say the novel is a misogynistic attempt to deny and control female sexuality, which was escaping Victorian bounds by the 1890s. Another school attributes major homoerotic elements to the novel. Horror as a genre deals with sex and death, and Victorian repression makes both theories worth pursuing. Yet in psychoanalyzing *Dracula* and its author, one has to be careful. Victorian melodrama can be misread by modern eyes, and the novel's enshrining of good women and brave men is purely political correctness for the time.

First, the misogynism charge. Yes, purifying by punishing sexually awakened women is just that and shows up in plots of the era as well as to this day. Still, Mina Murray Harker acts as an industrious partner of the five men—Dr. Van Helsing; Mina's husband, Jonathan; and Lucy's three suitors, who parallel Dracula's three brides. She documents the fiend's methods and pursues him to the bitter end, despite much male lip service about the men protecting her. Significantly, Mina Murray was chosen just a decade ago over Arthur Conan Doyle's Irene Adler as the sole female member of Alan Moore's *The League of Extraordinary Gentlemen* steampunk comic book series.

Then there's that Victorian manly men thing that some see going beyond the "bromance" of Holmes and Watson. Repression was a Victorian addiction, so it's a possibility, but some of these treatises torture the text to make their point. We forget today how strictly the sexes were separated socially then, though there are many reminders in *Dracula*. Much of the genre fiction of the 1890s isn't far above the Victorian "boys' adventure" mode, hence the emotionally united team of men led by an older father figure with arcane knowledge. See a host of later examples from Gandalf in *The Lord of the Rings* to Dr. Kriezler in Caleb Carr's best-selling *The*

Alienist (1994), in which three men and one industrious secretarial woman led by early psychiatrist Dr. Kriezler pursue a "monstrous" serial killer in 1896 New York City. See also many current television crime shows with a similar cast pattern.

It's interesting and often amusing to delve into subtextual decadence in the decades of *Dracula* scholarship, but academic supposition cannot wither nor custom stale the sheer, brisk, chilling fun of rereading the novel (even though we know everything that's coming) and marveling at the visceral legendry Bram Stoker brought to eternal life. Take away Dracula's supernatural powers, and the character would still terrify us, becoming the thriller world's first major serial killer.

Postscript: Rights to *Dracula: the Un-dead*—written by Stoker's great-grandnephew, Dacre Stoker and a Dracula scholar—earned a juicy mid-seven-figure publication deal. The 2009 novel is the first Stoker family authorized project since the 1931 film starring Bela Lugosi and draws on edited-out original text and Stoker's notes. In 1912 London, someone stalks the "band of heroes" who originally defeated Dracula. Two sequels and a film are planned.

So Dracula lives on, giving new blood to the ailing twenty-first century publishing and film industries. How beautifully ironic the old count would find that.

Historical and contemporary mysteries and thrillers number among ex-journalist Carole Nelson Douglas's fifty-five published novels. She's the first author to take a female character from the Canon—Irene Adler, the only woman to outwit Holmes—as the protagonist of a related series, beginning with the New York Times Notable Book of the Year, *Good Night, Mr. Holmes*. Bram Stoker is a continuing character in the eight-novel Adler series. He played a major role in a Jack the Ripper duology within the Adler series, *Chapel Noir* and *Castle Rouge* (the latter suggests what inspired Stoker to pen his signature novel). Douglas also writes the Damon Runyonesque Midnight Louie feline PI mystery series and the noir urban fantasy adventures of Delilah Street, Paranormal Investigator, set in a post-apocalyptical Las Vegas where even Count Dracula can play a cameo role. The first two Delilah Street novels, *Dancing with Werewolves* and *Brimstone Kiss*, received starred *Publishers Weekly* reviews. Her latest titles are *Vampire Sunrise* and *Cat in a Topaz Tango*.

16
H. G. Wells's
THE WAR OF THE WORLDS (1898)

Steven M. Wilson

Herbert George Wells (1866–1946) created fantastic worlds filled with marvelous and frightening inventions in novels such as *When The Sleeper Wakes, The First Men in the Moon,* and *The Shape of Things to Come.* His imagination led him far from the common. "The creations of Mr. Wells," Jules Verne noted, "belong unreservedly to an age and degree of scientific knowledge far removed from the present, though I will not say entirely beyond the limits of the possible." Wells first traveled to the limits of imagination in *The Time Machine* (1895), followed by *The Island of Dr. Moreau* (1896), *The Invisible Man* (1897), and *The War of the Worlds* (1898). He graduated from the University of London in 1890, with a degree in science. Although he never ventured far from that discipline (for a time he was a teacher), it was writing that brought Wells fame. His humanity and hope for mankind gave his work depth. Not until near the end of his life did he acknowledge mankind's failures, and this was only after two world wars.

In *The War of the Worlds,* H. G. Wells wields a sensitive brush on a very large canvas—the story of a people doomed through no fault of their own. Arthur C. Clarke noted that the "novel contains what must be the first detailed description of mechanized warfare," and when one remembers that the work appeared at the end of the nineteenth century, the subject matter is even more astonishing.

To place these fascinating events in historical context, it's important to remember that powered flight, dreadnaughts, submarines (*not* submersibles), and the cataclysmic destruction of world wars were years away. Large scale wars had been replaced temporarily by such regional conflicts as the Boer War and the Spanish-American War. The most devastating weapon to date, the machine gun, had yet to realize its potential. With the arrogance of contemporary superiority coupled with historical myopia, 1898 becomes a quaint period of straw skimmers, bandboxes, and high collars.

In a way, Wells is responsible for perpetuating that cultured innocence with his description of English hamlets, sturdy workmen, and reassurances that all the haste anyone need make was on the train or through a telegram. But that is in subsequent chapters. In the first chapter, Wells makes quite certain that all man is and hopes to achieve has been under scrutiny by "intellects vast and cool and unsympathetic, [regarding] this earth with envious eyes." The invasion begins as distant streaks of light, falling stars, through the night. Urged on by his friends, the narrator (and here the first-person viewpoint works wonderfully, increasing the horrible immediacy of impending death) accompanies them to the pit where one of the Martian machines is half buried.

Wells weaves a sense of confusion, speculation, misinformation, and bravado among the men and boys who make their way to the pit. As with any actual unexpected or shocking event, information is conveyed in bursts of half-truths and rumor. His characters are drawn exactly as a man in a crowd, overawed by circumstances, might see them. Poor Ogilvy is the narrator's friend while many others are loosely identified as boys, unemployed men, or caddies. The author is not dismissing these individuals—he is reinforcing the fact that the Martians will soon make them inconsequential. In a tragic foreshadowing of World War II newsreel footage of refugees fleeing the outrage of war, Wells describes the absurdity of those running from the Martians. People carry children, treasures, ridiculous keepsakes, or pile atop wagons, carts, carriages, all crowding the roads in an insane rush from the horror. Humanity, Wells points out through his narrator, has disappeared in the chaos.

He gives the reader triumphs—enough to heighten the expectation that there is hope. Man is civilized, mechanized, poised on the edge of a new century, and keeper of the planet that he has subdued (at least by nineteenth-century standards). A hidden battery of artillery waiting in ambush for the Martian war machines catches one of the huge invaders in a thunderous volley. It hesitates, its spindly legs collapse, and there is confirmation the machines can be defeated. But the victory is short lived. Where one falls, two more take its place, and the Martian's Heat Ray destroys the battery. Hideous creatures use technology against mankind. Humanity's superiority above animals is challenged and proven false.

The narrator and the world's population have absolutely no bearing on the outcome of the invasion, aside from recording what transpires or the infrequent victory of the English military over the Martians. Conservationists can honestly point out that the honor of defeating the Martians should be awarded to the bacteria that rule the Earth. We humans, Wells notes, have paid the toll for sharing the world with these "germs of disease," in countless deaths over the centuries. Now humans, despite their futile efforts, need only stand aside and let Earth cleanse herself of the unwanted invaders. The lesson may be that mankind is indulged by nature and granted permission to live on Earth.

The thriller aspect of *The War of the Worlds* seemed all too real on Halloween night of 1938 when Orson Welles directed and narrated a one-hour adaptation of the novel. Moving the locale from a small town in England to one in New Jersey, Welles used a news bulletin technique that felt extremely realistic for that decade and convinced millions of listeners that the United States was in fact being invaded by aliens. There is some debate about how much panic actually occurred, but for certain, a large number of people became frightened. In a town in the Pacific Northwest, a power failure occurred during the broadcast, prompting locals to conclude that Martians had caused the blackout. Some townspeople grabbed their guns and ran for the hills.

Germany's growing dominance of Europe prior to World War II no doubt provided some of the emotional atmosphere about fears of being attacked. A 1953 movie adaptation, produced by George Pal and starring Gene Barry, set a new standard for special effects. This time, the fear about being attacked was rooted in Cold War anxieties about the USSR. The climax occurs outside a church and implies that the Earth was saved by God as much as by germs to which humans are immune—presumably the atheistic Communists ought to take note. In 2005, Steven Spielberg directed another film version of the story, with Tom Cruise as the main character. A post 9/11 audience, still reeling from the terrorist attacks, had plenty of reasons to identify with the subject matter, proving again that Wells's novel has an archetypal and psychological resonance that gives it fresh meaning for various generations.

Steven M. Wilson is author of *Voyage of the Gray Wolves, Between the Hunters and the Hunted, Armada,* and *President Lincoln's Spy* as well as *President Lincoln's*

Secret. He writes a column on military history for www.military.com, is managing editor of the *Lincoln Herald,* and an Instructor of History at Lincoln Memorial University. He is also assistant director and curator of the Abraham Lincoln Library and Museum at LMU. Wilson lives in East Tennessee with his wife, Angela, and far too many cats to count.

17
Rudyard Kipling's
KIM (1901)

Tom Grace

Rudyard Kipling (1865–1936) captured the essence of India under the British Raj in a stunning collection of prose and verse that culminated in his groundbreaking adventure novel, *Kim*. His early life alternated between India and England, providing the deep fusion of East and West that would characterize his finest works. During a six-year literary apprenticeship as an assistant newspaper editor in Lahore, Kipling wrote ten to fifteen hours a day, honing his craft in a series of poems and short stories that included "Gunga Din," "Wee Willie Winkie," and "The Man Who Would Be King." Kipling's reputation preceded his return to London, where he joined the city's literary lions and was befriended by fellow adventure novelist H. Rider Haggard. The publication of the short story collection *The Jungle Book* expanded Kipling's oeuvre to include children's literature. From 1890 to his death, Kipling made the world his home, residing in both England and the U.S., and traveling extensively. In addition to his literary works, Kipling's writing credits include speeches for King George V and British PM Stanley Baldwin. He enjoyed wide acclaim during his lifetime and remains the youngest recipient of the Nobel Prize for Literature. Though offered the post of British Poet Laureate and knighthood on numerous occasions, Kipling politely declined.

> He sat, in defiance of municipal orders, astride the gun Zam-Zammah on her brick platform opposite the old AjaibGher— the Wonder House, as the natives call the Lahore Museum. Who hold the Zam-Zammah, the "fire-breathing dragon," hold the Punjab; for the great green-bronze piece is always first of the conqueror's loot.

Rudyard Kipling wastes no time getting to the heart of his 1901 novel, *Kim*, distilling in just two sentences the essence of the hero and his story.

The untamed Kim sits in defiance of the law atop a historic weapon. In the game he is playing, control of the crucial piece on the board is the key to winning.

The story occurs in the 1890s, between the Second and Third Anglo-Afghan Wars. Rugged Afghanistan had the geographic misfortune of standing between tsarist Russia and British-controlled India at a time when both empires were flexing their muscles throughout central Asia. Though there were no direct hostilities between Russian and British forces, a century of intrigue, exploration, and clandestine diplomacy characterized an era known as The Great Game.

The roots of the modern spy novel lay in *Kim* and Joseph Conrad's 1907 novel *The Secret Agent*. These books channeled the energy of an adventure novel into an exploration of the shadowy world of international espionage. The heroic quest became a covert mission, the damsel in distress a captured agent, and the hidden treasure a scrap of timely intelligence that might start or prevent a war. Secrets and hidden agendas, lust and betrayal, aliases and murder—all staged in exotic locales against a larger backdrop of geopolitics. The plot of a well-crafted spy novel plays out like a game of chess, and indeed the spies are often all too aware of their status as pawns.

The Secret Agent defined the typical structure of the genre, that of an established agent dealing with a specific mission in a sprint that races from cover to cover in a matter of days or weeks. In contrast, *Kim* takes the reader on a journey of years in which a boy of raw but unmistakable talent is expertly crafted into a spy. A pair of intelligence missions bookend a tale, introducing the political conflict simmering in Afghanistan, but in between is a series of vignettes in which five men provide the intellectual and philosophical instruction Kim will need to succeed in the game. John le Carré explored similar terrain from the point of view of a spy looking back on his life in *The Secret Pilgrim*.

Kipling's best works explored East-West themes, drawing his readers into the heart of the Indian subcontinent. Kim, the orphaned son of an Irish soldier, is more at home among the Hindus and Muslims of Lahore than the governing British, and his education and adventures in both worlds propel the narrative. *Kim* is something of a rarity in the spy genre in that it is also considered a classic work of literature. In that light, it bears a strong resemblance to another literary classic novel published sixteen years earlier—Mark Twain's *Adventures of Huckleberry Finn*.

Both novels feature a young hero accompanying an adult on a quest for freedom. Where Huck's companion, Jim, seeks to escape physical slavery, Kim's lama desires to free himself from the spiritual Wheel of Things. The heroes travel along a linear feature of geography that dominates the local landscape. Twain's Mississippi River mirrors Kipling's Great Trunk Road as a means for staging movement and adventures over a great distance—a device used a half century later in Jack Kerouac's *On the Road*.

Kipling and Twain employ vernacular language in their storytelling, a rarity at the time but essential to crafting the reality underlying their fiction. Both novels suffered critical historic revisionism decades after their publication, primarily on the grounds of perceived racism and, in Kipling's case, pro-imperialism. Allegations of an anti-Indian bias in *Kim* seem to fly in the face of the book's enduring popularity in India. Acclaimed Indian writer Nirad Chaudhuri declared of *Kim*: "We Indians shall never cease to be grateful to Kipling for having shown the many faces of our country in all their beauty, power, and truth."

In *Kim*, Kipling set a high standard for the spy novel, but things might have turned out differently had his first attempt at a novel seen the light of day. He began writing *Mother Maturin* at the age of nineteen while still working as a newspaperman in Lahore. It was the tale of an Irish woman who ran an opium den in Lahore and traded secrets with a daughter who was married to a government official. He labored on his "masterpiece" for years in India, England, and the United States, but scrapped the book when his father declared the thing not good enough for the printer. Kipling then started fresh on *Kim*.

Two of Kipling's best known works, *Kim* and *The Jungle Book*, feature orphan boys living by their wits in a dangerous and exciting world. Authors of adventure novels often share a Walter Mitty-esque relationship with their protagonists, and in Kipling's case it may have been an attempt to rewrite a desolate stretch of his own childhood in England, which he describes in *Baa Baa Black Sheep*.

In 1899, Kipling published a collection of letters and short stories titled *From Sea to Sea*. The volume included an account of a summer afternoon that he spent on the veranda of a country house in Elmira, New York, smoking cigars with his literary hero, Mark Twain. The encounter occurred in 1889, with Twain at the full height of his fame and Kipling a promising twenty-three-year-old writer. Their conversation meandered through copyright law and book piracy, truth and lies in autobiography, and Tom Sawyer as an adult. On the subject of writing fiction, Twain offered a bit of advice that Kipling bore away in his bosom: "Get your facts first, and then you can distort 'em as much as you please."

Author/Architect Tom Grace is a fortunate soul who enjoys two professions in which he is paid to use his imagination to fill a blank page. He is the author of five Nolan Kilkenny thrillers. He immerses himself in his research and has interviewed the men who deorbited the Mir space station, and traveled to the North Pole just to get the story right. His fourth novel, *Bird of Prey*, was cited in a 2004 National Security Briefing on the deployment of space-based, antisatellite weapons. Grace's recent book, *The Secret Cardinal*, is a jailbreak thriller set amid the incredible church-state conflict between the Vatican and China. This novel won critical praise from the former president of the Vatican and was smuggled into China by members of the persecuted underground church. *El Cardenal*, the Spanish edition of the book, enjoyed an eighty-nine-week run on the best-seller lists in Latin America with over sixty weeks at number one—a stunning achievement considering that Venezuelan pirates illegally manufactured nearly every copy of *El Cardenal* sold in Latin America.

18
Sir Arthur Conan Doyle's
THE HOUND OF THE BASKERVILLES (1901)

Laura Benedict

Sir Arthur Conan Doyle (1859–1930) was born into a prosperous family in Edinburgh, Scotland, and studied to be a physician at the University of Edinburgh. His first short story, "The Mystery of Sasassa Valley," was published in a local magazine in 1879. He eventually established a successful medical practice, and in 1888 published *A Study in Scarlet*, which introduced Sherlock Holmes and Dr. Watson. Throughout his career, Conan Doyle was torn between writing crime novels and what he considered more literary fare. In 1893, he killed off Sherlock Holmes in "The Final Problem" but later brought him back for financial reasons, first in plays, and then in the novel, *The Hound of the Baskervilles*, serialized in 1901. He dabbled unsuccessfully in politics and, after losing his son and brother in World War I, became intensely involved in the Spiritualist movement. Conan Doyle published fifty-six short stories, four novels, and a number of historical works, but is best remembered for the Holmes stories. The last Holmes collection, *The Casebook of Sherlock Holmes*, was published in 1927.

Of my two grandfathers, it was the one I never saw reading anything longer than the evening newspaper who bought me books. He gave me crisp sets of classic stories that were strikingly different from the saccharine drivel peddled by my well-meaning school librarian. At first, I was suspicious and dismissive of them. Then, one dull afternoon, I opened *Treasure Island* and was immediately captivated. *Kidnapped*, *Robinson Crusoe*, and Edgar Allan Poe's stories followed. Though they were all considered boys' books and much scorned by my friends, I was hooked. The crown of my small collection was an oversized, illustrated edition of Sherlock Holmes stories.

Sherlock Holmes intimidated me. He was brilliant and strange, and I sometimes had a hard time following the plots. I could imagine him in the London of *Black Beauty* and *A Little Princess*, yet he was definitely a grown-up, encountering bloody murders, lies, and cruelty. Most strikingly, he was smarter than anybody else.

The Hound of the Baskervilles begins as a mystery. James Mortimer, a country doctor, comes to Holmes with his concerns about the death of his friend, Sir Charles Baskerville. While Sir Charles's death was ostensibly due to natural causes, Mortimer suspects that the death was actually the result of a family curse. He tells Holmes the fantastic legend of Sir Hugo, a Baskerville ancestor who summoned a demonic hellhound to help him subdue a young woman who had scorned him. The hound was subsequently discovered devouring Sir Hugo on the moor, with the young woman dead from fright nearby him.

Many of Sir Hugo's descendents likewise died in gruesome, suspicious ways. Having seen the enormous footprints of a hound near Sir Charles's body, Mortimer fears for the life of Sir Charles's heir, Sir Henry. He asks Holmes to determine if it would be safe for the young man to reside at Baskerville Hall.

Holmes is initially skeptical, but after learning of unusual events that plagued Sir Henry since his arrival in London, he determines that Sir Henry is indeed in danger. Surprisingly, he sends Watson to Devonshire with Sir Henry and Dr. Mortimer, asking Watson to mail reports back to London, where Holmes must remain to work on another case.

Devonshire is stark, surrounded by the moor and the treacherous bog-holes of the Grimpen Mire—a terrible danger to man and beast alike. Watson studies Baskerville's neighbors, dutifully sending reports to Holmes, but before he can solve the case, he discovers that Holmes has been hiding in the nearby hills the whole time, making his own observations. Together, they learn that the hound is a much-abused dog trained to kill by the man who would inherit Baskerville Hall if Sir Henry were to die.

The first clue that *The Hound of the Baskervilles* is more than a standard Holmes mystery is the uncharacteristic amount of action. The legend of the murderous, spectral hound immediately establishes the story's horror credentials, while its Gothic setting and romantic elements echo *Tess of the d'Urbervilles* and *Wuthering Heights*. The escalating danger to Sir Henry produces an atmosphere of suspense throughout. Holmes's obsessive behaviors and ongoing drug addiction combine with the murderer's skillful manipulation of the women he uses in his bid to acquire the Baskerville estate, creating intense psychological drama. The novel has all the makings of a multigenre thriller.

When Holmes reveals himself to Watson in that ancient hut on the moor, he is unkempt from his rough living, but "had contrived, with that catlike love of personal cleanliness which was one of his characteristics, that his chin should be as smooth and his linen as perfect as if he were in Baker Street."

Poor Watson—as well as the reader—has been fooled, and Holmes is shown to be as duplicitous as any common criminal. It's this Jekyll/Hyde duality that tempts me to view Holmes in the context of Sigmund Freud, who had just begun publishing when *The Hound of the Baskervilles* was serialized in 1901.

While Holmes is generally industrious, decorous, and almost always a creature of reason, the dark, disturbing side to his personality makes him a complex, intriguing character. Aside from his bemused affection for Watson, his lack of emotion seems to border on the sociopathic (unless his sudden bursts of energy brought on by developments in a case qualify as emotion). His persistent use of morphine and cocaine suggests that he self-medicates to calm the internal chaos that erupts when he can't keep himself busy. On occasion, he acts like a spoiled child. He is a musician, a mathematical genius, a master of disguise. He toys with the criminals he hunts. He toys with Watson. He is a compulsive manipulator who walks a fine line between breaking the law and upholding it. If he were to become a criminal, he would be a splendid one.

Of course, Holmes is a fictional character, and Conan Doyle had the power to create him in any image that suited his literary purposes. Why shouldn't he have endowed Holmes with extraordinary abilities and interesting faults? Even so, I've always wondered why Watson, a doctor, doesn't speculate on his friend's personality more directly. Although in *The Sign of Four*, he alludes to his friend's "small vanity," Watson primarily acts as an uncritical lens through which we view Holmes. It is as though Conan Doyle is daring us to ask questions in the way that Holmes would.

When Holmes reveals himself to Watson in the hut on the moor, it feels like a dirty trick on us all. Still, the twist is a stunning development that feels as fresh now as it would have a hundred years ago. Conan Doyle's skill at combining compelling story elements with Holmes's fascinating, maddeningly complex character propelled *The Hound of the Baskervilles* far into the future of storytelling so that it serves as a benchmark for the modern thriller.

Laura Benedict is the author of the novels, *Calling Mr. Lonely Hearts* and *Isabella Moon*. Her essays and short stories have appeared in *Ellery Queen's Mystery Magazine* and a number of anthologies, including the *Surreal South* series, which she edits with her husband, Pinckney Benedict. As well, she reviews books for *The Grand Rapids Press* in Michigan. She claims both Cincinnati, Ohio and Louisville, Kentucky, as her hometowns, and currently resides in southern Illinois—a lonely, enchanted place that offers excellent inspiration for writing thrillers.

19

Joseph Conrad's
HEART OF DARKNESS (1902)

H. Terrell Griffin

Joseph Conrad (1857–1924) was born Józef Teodor Konrad Korzeniowski to Polish parents in Ukraine. In 1874, after having lived in Switzerland and Poland, he went to France to join the French Merchant Navy, in which he served until joining the British ship *Mavis* in 1878. In 1886, he became a British subject and acquired his captain's papers. He sailed the world until 1889 when he settled in London to write *Almayer's Folly*. The next year he took employment in the Belgian Congo, and after a year went back to sea for two years as an officer on a British merchantman ship. *Almayer's Folly* was published in 1895, and Conrad left the sea for good. The novella *Heart of Darkness* is based on his year in the Belgian Congo and was first serialized in 1899 in *Blackwood's Magazine*, then published in book form in 1902. However, Conrad did not gain prominence as a writer until 1914 when his novel *Chance* was published. He declined a knighthood in 1924 and died the same year of a heart attack. He is buried at Canterbury.

Heart of Darkness has one of the most intricate beginnings of any thriller. A yacht lies in the port of Gravesend, near London, waiting for the tide. (Given the darkness of the story, the harbor was presumably chosen for the symbolic value of its name.) Aboard are an accountant, a lawyer, a director of companies—personified representatives of civilization—and an unnamed first-person narrator, who describes the gathering night and directs our attention to a fifth person, the only true sailor aboard, Marlow. After the gloom of the scene is established, the narrator tells us what Marlow told the group, thus making us part of the audience to this first-person-within-a-first-person story.

"And this also," Marlow said suddenly, "has been one of the dark places of the earth."

He tells us how he worked for a company that sent him to Africa, where he searched for a man named Kurtz. The search is physical in the sense that Marlow makes an arduous river journey to retrieve the man. It is also metaphysical in the sense that, as Marlow strives to understand what happens to a man when he lives for so long in such an alien place, his quest takes him to the heart of Kurtz's soul—and perhaps ours.

The story mirrors Conrad's frequent despair about the human race, which he once called "the wretched gang." We don't encounter Kurtz until the end of the story. Nonetheless the mysterious character overshadows the plot, his last words providing one of the most famous phrases in literature: "The horror! The horror!" There is indeed plenty of horror. Kurtz is the manager of an ivory station several hundred miles upriver from the sea, a river that is never named, but one presumes to be the Congo. As Marlow pushes onward to find him, he encounters increasing decay, violence, barbarity, and insanity.

Beneath this powerful adventure tale lie the moral ambiguities faced by white men, who fueled by greed, treat the natives with disdain and cruelty, as if they are less than human. Kurtz was once a man of culture and refinement who went to Africa as an idealist and turned into a monster of greed and madness, frightening the mysterious and superstitious natives into following him, subjugating other tribes, and accumulating ivory. One of the most haunting images in the novella is what Marlow describes as a series of poles with balls on top of them. As Marlow gets closer, he notices ants swarming up and down the poles and realizes that the balls are the heads of natives who rebelled against Kurtz. He learns that Kurtz, diseased and demented, was so addicted to the degradation of his life that he even ordered an attack to try to stop Marlow's rescue expedition from reaching him.

Late in the story a native woman appears, "a wild and gorgeous apparition of a woman" who was "savage and superb, wild-eyed and magnificent." She contrasts starkly with Kurtz's frail fiancée whom Marlow visits when he returns to Europe. A lady of wealth, she seems sheltered from the world. She is still in mourning a year after Kurtz's death, and she tearfully implores Marlow to tell her Kurtz's last words. Marlow faces a moral dilemma. Should he tell her the truth, that Kurtz's last words described the horror into which he had sunk? Or should he tell her what she wants to hear, a validation of the man's devotion that she so desperately needs?

Marlow's answer to the distraught woman is, "the last word he pronounced was—your name." In the end, Marlow resolves the dilemma by giving the fiancée something warm with which to remember the man she loved—one of the few kind acts in the story. It is a small gift that costs no one, but it brings a modicum of happiness, or perhaps relief, to a woman who will live the rest of her life with the belief that Kurtz's last thoughts were of her.

Heart of Darkness is a story of good and evil, or at least the evil of white men seeking riches in the jungles of a land they did not understand. It is a morality play and at the same time a disturbing tale of men contesting a continent new to them, full of intrigue and danger, a dark version of exploration thrillers like H. Rider Haggard's *King Solomon's Mines*. Civilization, Conrad seems to say, is what stops us from reverting to our animal instincts and becoming like Kurtz. It keeps the heart of darkness at bay.

Conrad uses understatement to describe violence, a technique that influenced subsequent British thriller writers, notably Geoffrey Household who acknowledged his debt to Conrad in his autobiography, *Against the Wind*. The basic plot of *Heart of Darkness*—a remote outpost, interrupted dispatches from its charismatic leader, an expedition to learn what has happened—was borrowed in numerous later novels and films. Movies based on Conrad's work have been influential also, particularly Alfred Hitchcock's 1936 adaptation of *The Secret Agent*, retitled *Sabotage*. In 1979, John Milius's screenplay of *Heart of Darkness* was famously directed by Francis Ford Coppola as *Apocalypse Now*. There, "The horror! The horror!" became the Vietnam War.

H. Terrell Griffin has spent his adult life soldiering, studying, lawyering, and writing, in that order. Upon graduating from high school, he enlisted in the U.S. Army, and after three years of active duty, he began his history and law studies, eventually becoming a board certified civil trial lawyer in Orlando, Florida, for many years. He is the author of the thrillers *Murder Key*, *Longboat Blues*, *Blood Island*, and *Wyatt's Revenge* featuring trial lawyer turned beach bum, Matt Royal, whom one reviewer described as "Travis McGee with a law degree." Griffin is a lifetime member of the 14th Cavalry Association and holds a U.S. Coast Guard 100 Ton Master's License. He and his wife, Jean, reside in Longboat Key and Maitland, Florida.

20

Erskine Childers's
THE RIDDLE OF THE SANDS (1903)

Christine Kling

Erskine Childers (1870–1922) wrote only one novel, *The Riddle of the Sands*, a sea-going spy thriller that has never gone out of print. Born in England, but raised in Ireland, Childers's own story of his conversion from steadfast supporter of the British Empire to radical Irish Nationalist is as fascinating as his fiction. He studied classics and then law at Trinity College, Cambridge, and began his career as a committee clerk at the House of Commons. An avid yachtsman, he bought his first boat at age twenty-three and frequently sailed the waters of the North Sea and the Baltic, often in the company of his brother, Henry, and later with his wife, Molly. He fought for England in both the Boer War and World War I, but it was his growing support for Irish Home Rule that led him to sail his yacht, the fifty-one-foot Colin Archer design, the *Asgard*, into a full gale to smuggle guns into Ireland in 1914. Childers was sentenced to death by the Irish Free State and executed by firing squad during the Irish Civil War in 1922.

Erskine Childers chafed at calling *The Riddle of the Sands* a novel, claiming instead "it was a story with a purpose." In the preface, Childers wrote that it was a factual tale told to him by his friend Carruthers, and originally the book carried the subtitle "A Record of Secret Service, edited by Erskine Childers." Having stumbled into the world of publishing several years earlier when his sister arranged for the publication of a nonfiction book based on his letters describing the Boer War in Africa, Childers believed the most important aspect of his writing was his call for the modernization of the British military. With his story about two English chaps sailing off the Frisian Islands, he sought to alert England to the potential dangers of a German invasion. While his novel did have a profound impact on politics, and Winston Churchill credited it for Britain's establishing several naval bases on the North Sea, today the book endures as a pioneer of the British spy novel.

The Riddle of the Sands is a great sailing adventure story told from the point of view of Carruthers, a clerk in the Foreign Office martyred to his work when all of his friends have abandoned the city for parties on country estates. When he receives a wire from an acquaintance inviting him to join a yacht in the Baltic, Carruthers packs his jaunty white flannels and boards a steamer for Hamburg. There, he meets up with Davies and discovers that the *Dulcibella* is not the fine yacht he imagined. The hilarious transformation of Carruthers from effete London club man to accomplished sailor is one of the great charms of the book.

Initially, readers are mystified along with Carruthers as to the purpose of Davies's invitation. As the young sailors leave the Baltic and begin their cruise among the Frisian Islands, the taciturn Davies reveals that he was nearly shipwrecked and killed by a duplicitous Englishman. He wants Carruthers to help him solve the riddle of what the traitor and his German navy friends are about. Thus begins their turn as spies listening at windows, donning disguises, and mapping out railway lines, and above all, using Davies's knowledge of the channels and their shifting sands.

Through a combination of Davies's brilliant seamanship and Carruthers's knowledge of human character, these two talented amateurs are able to outwit their enemies and discover Germany's foul plans. In the process, Childers establishes two character types who would later populate the pages of the many spy/adventure novels. First, in Carruthers, one finds the inept and bumbling civil servant who, in the face of danger, is able to rise to heights of ingenuity and self-reliance. This sort of "ordinary man" character was very popular up until the Second World War and the Cold War when the professionals took over. However, in John le Carré's *The Constant Gardener*, one sees that the type has not lost popularity.

The second character, Davies, is a man of stout heart, a patriotic loner and adventurer, a naïve sleuth but brilliant yachtsman who is endearing as he bumbles through the book's romantic sub plot. This archetype of the amateur adventure hero appears in later novels by the likes of John Buchan, Eric Ambler, and Hammond Innes.

It was not only through characters that *A Riddle in the Sands* influenced the next generation of adventure/spy thrillers. Childers's accurate and detailed descriptions of sailing and of Germany's Frisian Islands gave the tale a realism not seen in the romantic tales of the previous century. In the novel, Childers borrowed verbatim from his logbooks of cruises in the North Sea, to the extent that some say the novel can be used as a sailing guidebook.

A few seconds more and we were whizzing through a slit between two wood jetties. Inside a small square harbor showed,
but there was no room to round up properly and no time to
lower sails. Davies just threw the kedge over, and it just got a
grip in time to check our momentum and save our bowsprit from
the quay-side.

Though some critics have complained about the amount of nautical
detail, the book set a standard for the fact-filled techno-thriller that edu-
cates as well as it entertains.

Erskine Childers was the first in a long line of seafaring adventure writers whose lives blur the line between fact and fiction. Hammond Innes,
an experienced yachtsman, sailed his own boat from the Baltic to the Bay
of Biscay, while Sam Llewellyn, author of many wonderful sailing thrillers
including *The Shadow of the Sands*, a sequel to Childers's classic, is a master sailor who has cruised in gold-plated racers and simple open boats. And
then there is Clive Cussler, whose books often feature duos who seem to
be direct descendants from Davies and Carruthers. Cussler created his own
NUMA (National Underwater and Marine Agency) and in over thirty
years at the helm discovered more than sixty undersea wrecks.

On the eve of his execution, Childers wrote in a letter to his wife, "I
die loving England." The enigmatic Anglo-Irishman gave up his life for
his love of Ireland, but he left to us not only a new genre of spy thrillers,
but also a damn good yarn.

Christine Kling has spent over twenty years living in and around boats and
cruising the Caribbean, Atlantic, and Pacific. She recently cruised the Bahamas
singlehanded for six weeks. All her sailing experience led to her first suspense
novel, *Surface Tension* (2002), which introduced Florida female tugboat captain,
Seychelle Sullivan. *Cross Current*, *Bitter End*, and *Wrecker's Key* followed. Christine completed her MFA in creative writing at Florida International University
and is currently working on her first stand-alone sailing thriller. An English professor at Broward College, Christine lives aboard her thirty-three-foot sailboat
Talespinner in Fort Lauderdale.

21

Jack London's
THE SEA WOLF (1904)

Jim Fusilli

Cannery worker, oyster pirate, seal hunter, tramp, and Klondike gold prospector—a well of experience from which he drew during his career as a writer—Jack London (1876–1916) was twenty-three years old in 1899 when he published his first short stories. In 1903, his powerful short novel *The Call of the Wild* (inspired by his prospecting ordeals) became his first best seller. A year later, *The Sea Wolf* was published; it too became a best seller and a critical success, securing his reputation. Ambrose Bierce praised London's skill in creating its title character: "The great thing—and it is among the greatest of things—is that tremendous creation, Wolf Larsen," Bierce wrote. "The setting up of such a figure is enough for a man to do in one lifetime." London went on to write *Martin Eden*, an autobiographical novel, and *John Barleycorn*, a memoir in which he examined his battles with alcohol. The literary heir to James Fenimore Cooper, Herman Melville, and Stephen Crane, he endures as a superb American author, one who influenced Ernest Hemingway, John Steinbeck, and Jack Kerouac, among others. Before his death at age forty in 1916, possibly from uremia, London was quite likely the country's most famous writer. One indication of the lasting merit of *The Sea Wolf*: no American novel has been filmed as often.

The Sea Wolf is a remarkable work—a literary achievement in which London sets opposing philosophies in play in the form of his two main characters. When those philosophies are translated into action, the novel is a thriller so strong that it may very well serve as the model of the form. The writing is crisp, the vivid ocean setting chills the reader's bones, and the exhilarating action is that rare thing—both incredible and believable.

The glittering edge of *The Sea Wolf* rises from the psychological depth London gives to Wolf Larsen, the brutal but enigmatic captain of the *Ghost*, a schooner in search of seals in the waters off the coast of Japan, and Humphrey Van Weyden, a proper gentleman who is rescued by Larsen and pressed into hard labor after Van Weyden falls from a ferry into the Golden Gate Straits.

London uses a device that permits a detailed, multilayered first-person narrative: Van Weyden is a writer of sorts and, as such, a keen observer who reports what he sees and experiences in detail. As the story begins, he filters everything through what he's read; thus we know that he has no firsthand knowledge of a man like Larsen.

In short time, we learn that Larsen is more than a scheming brute, though Van Weyden decides that Larsen possesses a physical "strength savage, ferocious, alive in itself, the essential of life in that it is the potency of motion . . . this strength pervaded every action of his." But Larsen has his intellectual side. As the ship continues its journey, Van Weyden enters the captain's stateroom and finds a rack filled with plays, novels, scientific works, and grammar books. When the two characters debate, calmly at first, Larsen reveals his philosophy:

> I believe life is a mess. It is like yeast, a ferment, a thing that may move for a minute, an hour, a year, or a hundred years, but that in the end will cease to move. The big eat the little that they may continue to move, the strong eat the weak that they may retain their strength. The lucky eat the most and move the longest, that is all.

London permits Van Weyden, the idealistic narrator, to define himself. "I had lived a placid, uneventful, sedentary existence all my days—the life of a scholar and a recluse on an assured and comfortable income," Van Weyden says. "Violent life . . . had never appealed to me."

But Larsen's assessment of Van Weyden is devastating: "You couldn't walk alone between two sunrises and hustle the meat for your belly." Van Weyden knows the captain is right. Whether he will adapt—because we are certain Larsen won't bend—drives the story. Later, Larsen's brother, Death Larsen, appears, as does Maud Brewster, an unexpected passenger who affects the captain and Van Weyden.

The way the principal characters spar and debate is dazzling—to read aloud some of Larsen's soliloquies is to feel the rhythm and power of language. But for all its psychological intrigue and impressive prose, *The Sea Wolf* is an exciting seafaring adventure. On the *Ghost*, Van Weyden struggles as the captain and the crew test him. Each day and night delivers moments of unbearable tension for the narrator and the more vulnerable members of the crew.

Larsen is tested as well, not only by his ship's quest and his steely fanaticism. Crewmembers engineer a mutiny, and the captain is tossed overboard "with his scalp laid open." With Van Weyden in his wake, he makes his way back through darkness onto the ship and descends below deck to confront the mutineers Leach and Johnson. Van Weyden reports, "I heard a great infuriated bellow go up from Wolf Larsen, and from Leach a snarling that was desperate and bloodcurdling . . . By the sounds I knew that Leach and Johnson had been quickly reinforced by some of their mates . . . 'Mash his brains out!' was Johnson's cry." Through sheer force of animal will, Larsen triumphs, and what follows for the traitorous crew as the voyage continues illustrates what Van Weyden calls the captain's mad genius.

Later, when Larsen is weakened by what appears to be a series of strokes, Van Weyden and Maud Brewster manage to escape. They land on what they call Endeavor Island, which is uninhabited by humans, but populated by hundreds of seals. Freed from Larsen's increasing mania, Van Weyden and Brewster, who have a reserved but tender relationship, cobble together a way to survive until rescue arrives. A ship appears and crashes on the island. It is the *Ghost*, and the only crewmember is a weakened Larsen. Van Weyden decides to kill him. But can he?

Larsen says, "You little rag puppet, you little echoing mechanism, you are unable to kill me as you would a snake or a shark . . . Bah! I had hoped better things of you." Clearly, both men cannot survive with each other on an island best fit for animals.

London is renowned for his naturalistic style, a misleading term that doesn't refer to the depth and tactile expression of his natural settings, but to his appreciation for the late nineteenth-century literary movement whose origins are attributed to Èmile Zola. According to Christopher McBride, whose excellent essay prefaces the edition that's part of the Barnes & Noble Library of Essential Reading, Zola "viewed writers as observers of human nature describing the shaping forces from a scientific perspective." Here, the science is provided by Social Darwinism—the survival of the fittest—and London's story may be perceived as an exercise in defining that theory as something other than primal. Van Weyden believes that man is more than brute, more than yeast, and as he tells Maud Brewster, "We have not the strength with which to fight this man; we must dissim-

ulate, and win, if win we can, by craft." Whether Van Weyden can triumph is the crux of the brilliantly told tale.

Jim Fusilli is the author of five novels and one nonfiction book, and is the rock and
pop critic of The Wall Street Journal. He edited and contributed a chapter to ITW's
The Chopin Manuscript, Audible's best-selling "serial thriller," which was named
the 2008 Audiobook of the Year by the Audio Publishers Association, and its
sequel, The Copper Bracelet. His "Chellini's Solution," appeared in the 2007
edition of The Best American Mystery Stories, and his story "The Guardians" was
selected for A Prisoner of Memory, a 2008 anthology of the year's finest mystery
short fiction. His short fiction also appeared in the anthology Boston Noir and
Alfred Hitchcock's Mystery Magazine. In addition to working for the Journal,
Jim has contributed to the New York Times Magazine, the Boston Globe, the Los
Angeles Times, and National Public Radio's All Things Considered.

22

Baroness Emma Orczy's
THE SCARLET PIMPERNEL (1905)

Lisa Black

Emma Orczy (1865–1947) really was a baroness and knew whereof she wrote. Similar to the victims of the French Revolution, she and her family were forced from a privileged life in Hungary by the threat of a peasant revolt. Like her character Marguerite, Emma was spunky, intelligent, and passionately in love with her husband. They returned from their honeymoon to find a crowd around their door—Jack the Ripper had left his latest victim on their sidewalk. Perhaps this prompted Emma's interest in mysteries, and she began to write a series of them after the birth of her first child, creating characters quite different from the premier fictional detective of the day, Sherlock Holmes. Later, a trip to Paris brought up thoughts of the French Revolution, and *The Scarlet Pimpernel* came to her. Publishers considered the story old-fashioned and wouldn't touch it, so Emma turned it into a play. It captured the hearts of audiences everywhere. She went on to write sixteen additional tales about the Scarlet Pimpernel.

In 2002, Donald Maass penned *Writing the Breakout Novel*, which sets out the rules every thriller writer needs to know. His firm lists regarding setting, plot, and character were one of several epiphanies on my road to publication, and so it amazes me that Baroness Emma Orczy managed to satisfy each one of these rules in *The Scarlet Pimpernel* ninety-nine years before Maass's book graced my shelf.

It is the time of the French Revolution, and the lower classes of France—rather understandably—have had enough. They are spouting ideals of *liberté*, *egalité*, and *fraternité* while lopping off heads right and left. The noblemen of England are doing what they can to help their titled friends while avoiding the politics of interfering in a civil war. So far the premise has Maass' trifecta of *plausibility*—we all know this occurred and surely the doomed nobility called on their friends in other countries to help them out; *inherent conflict* of a very basic type, with one group trying to kill and the other trying to save; and the *originality* of looking at a historical event from a unique perspective.

Beautiful French actress Marguerite complained to one of her friends about a nobleman who had mistreated her brother, Armand, and thus accidentally gained the nobleman a date with the guillotine. She confesses this to her new husband, Sir Percy Blakeney, but without any details to explain her action—and the marriage instantly turns into a mannered truce of mutual contempt. Marguerite, lonely and confused, humanizes the us-against-them action by illustrating how good people can do bad things when the pressure ramps up, as when the French agent Chauvelin approaches her for help in identifying the widely admired Pimpernel. If she does not cooperate, Chauvelin will denounce her brother as a spy and ensure his death. Marguerite is up against it, with no one to talk to, not even her husband. What the reader knows or quickly figures out, of course, is that her husband *is* the Scarlet Pimpernel.

Here we have Maass's idea of "Conflicting ideals or values create tension" taken to extreme. Percy is not a snob, but the victims are his friends. Marguerite agrees in theory with the revolutionaries, but not in practice. She is closer to her brother than anyone in the world, especially given the temporary emotional distance of her husband, but does not want more blood on her hands and feels the dashing Pimpernel embodies all that is good in humanity. The political has become extremely personal to her.

Thus does Orczy "combine high public stakes with high personal stakes." Then, although Orczy wrote her book a hundred years after these events, she "conveys a sense of the times" by taking current locations and explaining their use then, and tossing in details such as the average person's fear of the plague. She "portrays historical forces and social trends through characters" who all, major or minor, have firm opinions regarding their world and its facets.

As for Percy Blakeney, the Pimpernel: Percy remains one of the most unique characters ever created. He is a superhero, a master of disguise and keen student of human foibles with a preternatural competence for moving around unseen in a foreign country, despite being tall, blond and English. He is capable of outwitting his enemies with an embarrassing insouciance, going so far as to pen a silly poem to his alter ego and then recite it to his enemies:

They seek him here, they seek him there,
Those Frenchies seek him everywhere.
Is he in heaven, or is he in hell,
That damned elusive, Pimpernel?

Orczy builds up her hero for us at every turn until we are thoroughly schooled in his wonders. Yet he is also an antihero, rich, bland, considered by all who know him—at least on the surface—to have the keenest of fashion sense only to make up for having no other sense at all. Dilettante by day, hero by night, he seems the obvious ancestor to Zorro, the Shadow, and Batman. He is barely mentioned until the third chapter, does not appear until the sixth, and we are given no insight into his thoughts until the sixteenth, and then only as they concern his wife. We never read a scene from his point of view and never learn what he thinks of anyone else, or how he became so adept at his work or why he chose to enter the fray. Is he passionately committed to the care of human life or is he simply a bored rich boy looking for a little adventure? We suspect it's the former, but Percy gives no hint. The bored rich boy act works well for him, and he sticks to it. "The highest character qualities are self-sacrifice and forgiveness," Maass says. Percy risks not only his safety but his self-image, letting the rest of his society mock him, the privileged son of nobility, as an idiot.

On a side note, Percy's catchphrase "Sink me!" used so liberally on stage and screen, is never uttered. Instead, characters of all genders and ages say "Faith!" to express surprise, irritation, confusion, or any other emotion—constantly. Also, Marguerite and the pursuing Chauvelin are old friends, not ex-lovers, as in the stage musical; Orczy does not allude that they were ever more than acquaintances, to the disappointment of the prurient.

All the characters—even the villain—have Maass's suggested self-sacrificing motives. The Pimpernel and his team take every step while acutely aware that they are the last and only hope of entire families. If they fail, not only aristocrats but their children will be slain. Chauvelin pursues both these groups for the greater good of making France a more egalitarian state (though we suspect that pride, challenge, and a touch of sadism are also present). Marguerite is desperate to save both her brother and her husband and is constantly reminded that she cannot do both, and what is worse, is forced more than once to choose. Orczy even mastered the art of ending chapters with a cliffhanger to keep things moving.

She did all this without the benefit of Maass's book, or even Zucker-man's *Writing the Blockbuster Novel*, which wouldn't come along for an-other ninety-one years. In fact, except for the telling and not showing of the characters' lengthy internal musings, which can be excused as charac-teristic of novels written at the time, it seems Baroness Orczy wrote as near perfect a thriller as is possible. She provides every required factor: a sym-pathetic and unique hero, a coldhearted but intelligent adversary, a stun-ningly distinctive setting, the highest personal and public stakes possible, and a pace that will keep readers of every century turning the pages.

Lisa Black spent the happiest five years of her life in a morgue. After ten years as a secretary, she went back to school for a degree in biology. In her job as a foren-sic scientist at the Cleveland area coroner's office, she analyzed gunshot residue on hands and clothing, hairs, fibers, paint, glass, DNA, blood, and many other forms of trace evidence, as well as crime scenes. Now she works as a latent print exam-iner for a police department in Florida, dealing with fingerprints and crime scenes. She has testified as an expert witness in over fifty trials. She has also written two books under the name Elizabeth Becka, *Trace Evidence* and *Unknown Means*. Her novel, *Takeover*, appeared in 2008 and its sequel, *Evidence of Murder*, in 2009.

23

Edgar Rice Burroughs's
TARZAN OF THE APES (1912)

W. Craig Reed

Edgar Rice Burroughs (1875–1950) was a mythmaker of the highest order. In 1912, he began his writing career with "Under the Moons of Mars" for *The All-Story Magazine*. That same year, he wrote two novels for the same magazine. One of those novels was *Tarzan of the Apes*. From then until his death in 1950, Burroughs penned almost seventy science fiction, western, historical, and jungle adventure novels. He purchased a ranch near Los Angeles in 1919, which he named Tarzana, and the citizens of the community incorporated under that name in 1928. He served during World War II as the oldest war correspondent. The Burroughs crater on Mars is named in his honor.

Edgar Rice Burroughs did not enter this world destined to be a writer. He did not spend his childhood immersed in fictional worlds where heroes swing from trees, rescue damsels in distress, and call upon nature to assist. Danton Burroughs, in the foreword to *Tarzan, My Father*, the book I coauthored with Johnny Weissmuller, Jr., described his grandfather as "restless in other professions he'd tried, be it railroad policeman in Idaho, or member of the Seventh Cavalry chasing Apaches in the last years of the Wild West in the 1800s. Finally, he tried writing, and his third novel was *Tarzan of the Apes*. That was in 1912."

    The son of a businessman, Edgar Rice Burroughs was born in Chicago, Illinois. After graduating from the Michigan Military Academy in 1895 and failing the entrance exam for West Point, he enlisted with the cavalry at Fort Grant, in the Arizona Territory. Following his army stint, Burroughs worked for his father and married Emma Hulbert in 1900. By 1911, after years of meager earnings, he became disillusioned with the writing in pulp fiction magazines. This fueled a desire to write his own stories, the third of which was "Tarzan of the Apes."

That novel brought to life a cultural icon. A muscled protagonist in dozens of movies, most of them starring Johnny Weissmuller during the days of black-and-white film, Tarzan still looms large as the hero whom boys emulate and girls admire. As one of those boys, I recall the first time I heard the epic story of Tarzan.

While turning the page, my grandfather's voice rumbled like a volcano on the verge of a cataclysmic event: "...and Tarzan, the young Lord Greystoke, rolled unconscious upon the dead and decaying vegetation..."

Unconscious? Did that mean . . . ?

My heart raced. How could it be that Tarzan of the Apes had just met his fate at the hand of a giant gorilla?

My grandfather set the book on the nightstand and rubbed his tired eyes. Dozens of lines covered his face, etched by time and toil and the tolerance of things my young mind had yet to comprehend. His voice now soft, he said, "That's all for tonight. We'll read some more tomorrow."

Flinging the blankets from my chest, I sat up straight. "No! You can't stop now, Grandpa! I have to know what happens next!"

Grandpa smiled and placed a sympathetic hand on my shoulder. "Don't we all."

With that, he turned off the light and left the room.

My blanket now clutched tightly about my neck, I shivered as every darkened shadow threatened to devour me like an angry lion, and every strange noise announced the stealthy approach of a maneater—eyes glaring and fangs dripping with saliva.

I glanced at the book on the nightstand, illuminated now only by the dim moonlight filtered through half-open window shades. The white and swirling block letters appeared as native dancers set against a purple sky. TARZAN OF THE APES ran across the top, and the name EDGAR RICE BURROUGHS across the bottom. In the center, a fierce lion struggled in vain against the strong grip and lethal blade wielded by the King of the Apes.

I smiled. Though surrounded by evils lurking in the jungle of my world, with Tarzan but an arm's length away, fear no longer owned me. I closed my eyes and dreamed of eating delicious fruits and swinging through the trees, high above the angry carnivores below.

Many years later, when given the assignment to once again explore the pages of the first title in the *Tarzan* series, I initially had misgivings. Although the book became a best seller in the 1900s, before the Internet made us all "Google stupid," I questioned whether this thriller could stand the test of time. Would not this manuscript now receive only rejections from the publishing community? After all, writing that employs an omniscient point of view and velvety English-accented prose, and lacks a flawed protagonist, would never get past a discerning literary agent today, let alone find its way onto a bookshelf.

But as I turned the first page, I rediscovered something I had found decades earlier. Something that filled my chest with pounding anticipation, my eyes with joyful mist, and my soul with a wonder and excitement I hadn't known since childhood. Once again, I felt compelled to keep turning pages. Then I smiled as I recalled the protest voiced to my grandfather, so long ago, when he dared to stop reading for the night.

I have to know what happens next!

"Don't we all," Grandpa replied.

One could say that this is the essence of a thriller—that special something that sweeps us along like a rushing river that threatens to shatter us against the rocks. But most of all, that special something that keeps us wanting to know what happens next. Few writers can lay claim to a mastery of all these ingredients in the way that Edgar Rice Burroughs blended them into one of the best thrillers ever written. Burroughs brilliantly splashes each chapter with cliffhangers, suspense, and foreshadowing, as evidenced by a short but powerful sentence near the beginning:

> It was on the morning of the second day that the first link was forged in what was destined to form a chain of circumstances ending in a life for one then unborn such as has never been paralleled in the history of man.

Only somebody devoid of curiosity could dare put this book down after reading such a proclamation.

I have to know what happens next!

When Burroughs wrote his Tarzan books, the world was in desperate need of a hero. Rumblings of the First World War threatened world peace. Soon, a deadly influenza epidemic, starvation, and economic upheavals claimed the lives of millions. Enter Tarzan, King of the Jungle and Master of the Beasts. One fierce man who engaged the wild and the foreign, the bestial and the brutal, and defended us against the enemies and ideologies that threatened our way of life. A man who possessed the strength to strangle a lion and the cunning to manipulate a tribe of savage aborigines. Yet a man whose gentle heart could win the love of a beautiful Baltimore girl.

Critics claim that Burroughs's works "failed to gather critical acclaim, yet influenced a generation." But Burroughs never courted critical acclaim. He had as his only goal to entertain, to sweep us away, if only for a day, from our worries and our fears. To bring a smile, a gasp, and perhaps a tear of joy. To bring us a hero: courageous, pure, merciful, and even romantic.

And for this young boy, and then again for this half-life writer who hopes to someday wield a pen half as well, Edgar Rice Burroughs has done just that.

W. Craig Reed is the author of the thriller *DNA* (2008) and the nonfiction book *Crazy Ivan: A True Story of Submarine Espionage* (2003). Craig is also the coauthor of *Tarzan, My Father* (2002) with the late Johnny Weissmuller, Jr.—a Borders Best book that chronicles the life of the most well-known Hollywood star of the early Tarzan films. Craig is currently writing *Six Minutes*, the thriller sequel to *DNA*, and *Red November: Inside the Secret U.S.–Soviet Submarine War*, a nonfiction book about Cold War espionage programs. Craig is also a general partner with Aventi Group, a marketing consulting firm in Northern California, which services leading technology firms. Craig has won numerous awards for client campaigns and professional writings, and is a former board member and vice president of the Silicon Valley American Marketing Association. A decorated veteran, Craig served during the Cold War as a submariner, navy diver, and special operations photographer, and completed several recon missions with Navy SEAL teams.

24.
Marie Belloc Lowndes's
THE LODGER (1913)

James A. Moore

There's something to be said for a book's longevity when it's been made into five films (one of them by Alfred Hitchcock, another—the latest—in 2009) as well as a television drama. That's the case with *The Lodger* by Marie Belloc Lowndes. Lowndes (1868–1947) was born in France, to parents Louis Belloc and Elizabeth Rayner Parkes. Four years later, the family moved to London, but she spent a good deal of her childhood in both locations. Her first novel, *The Heart of Penelope*, was published in 1904, although by that time she was already an accomplished writer, much like her brother (Hilaire Belloc) and mother. Her last published work appeared in 1949, two years after her death. All told, she produced close to sixty novels, plays, and collections, many dealing with the criminal mind. 1913 saw the publication of *The Lodger*, her best known work, an intriguing study in how horrific events shape one family and the people connected to them. It sold over a million copies.

The situation in *The Lodger* starts off desperate and gets worse from there. Ellen and Robert Bunting are in serious financial straits, and despite all of their best efforts, the aging and unemployed couple is having no luck getting in a better place. Then comes an ominous knock on the door. Set in London in Victorian times, the story is told in a straightforward fashion that emphasizes the increasing terror.

Lowndes was one of the progenitors of the psychological thriller. The careful revelation of clues, the deliberate examination of the main characters and their gradually increasing awareness of the dangerous man dwelling with them provide a virtual road map of how to create tension without giving away too much.

As the story evolves, a new lodger comes into the Bunting household, Mr. Sleuth, a man of obvious good upbringing and culture, who takes more than one room and pays for a full month in advance, enough money to keep the Buntings from the poorhouse.

Now if only there weren't all those unsettling murders taking place in the area.

The Avenger is the name given to the killer, who bears a striking similarity in his levels of violence to Jack the Ripper. Other stories have taken a villain from history, but few have stood the test of time as well as *The Lodger*. I exclude only Bram Stoker's *Dracula* from that assessment, but let's remember the difference in timelines. The real Dracula had been dead for centuries, while the 1888 crimes of Jack the Ripper were still relatively fresh in people's minds when Mrs. Lowndes penned her 1913 tale. For all anyone knew, the man was still alive.

As the story progresses, it focuses on Ellen Bunting and her growing convictions that the man who saved her family from financial ruin might very well be the killer who is haunting London's late night streets.

The evolution of the tale is well handled. At the beginning, Ellen makes it clear that she has no desire to hear the sordid details of the murders, even though one of the family friends, Joe Chandler, is a detective working the case. But as time goes on and her suspicions grow, Mrs. Bunting's desire to be kept in the dark is tested and finally replaced by a growing dread, even as she excuses all that she suspects in an effort to give her family the financial stability offered by the odd gentleman now living in their home.

Ellen spends more and more time trying to disprove her suspicions and instead runs across more and more reasons to accuse the man she's unconsciously trying to protect. Meanwhile, her husband, a visiting daughter, and the family friend who's investigating the case discuss the sort of person capable of committing the atrocities and escaping without being seen. The author provides a careful look at the lives of one family and the slow disintegration of that unit as tensions mount and the murder spree continues.

The plot has a simple, natural flow. There are no forced revelations, and the pacing, which might seem slow at first, is a fine complement to the mounting threat. There are no sudden revelations, no red herrings to confuse the issues. There is simply the examination of a husband and wife who begin to come to unsettling conclusions about their lodger at the same time that they struggle with financial worries and their extremely strict code of Victorian ethics. At one point, the mention of a reward being offered to anyone who learns the identity of the Avenger is enough to offend Ellen, who finds the notion of turning in a murderer for profit not only distasteful, but absolutely improper.

Given the novel's taut psychological edge, it's easy to understand why *The Lodger* remains fresh almost one hundred years after its publication. Its influence has been considerable, especially because of the strong way it investigates the psychology of suspicion. Arguably, Alfred Hitchcock's career and its emphasis on suspicion wouldn't have been the same if not for his silent screen adaptation of this novel. His 1954 film *Rear Window* can be seen as a variation on *The Lodger*, with the suspected killer living in a neighboring apartment rather than in the same household. Interestingly, Cornell Woolrich, the author of the *Rear Window* source material, was once compared to Marie Belloc Lowndes. This is merely one example of her influence. Although Lowndes is no longer a familiar name, she left a permanent mark on the psychological thriller.

James A. Moore was born in Atlanta, Georgia, and moved all over the country in his earlier years. He is the author of more than twenty novels, including the critically acclaimed *Fireworks*, *Under the Overtree*, *Blood Red*, the *Serenity Falls* trilogy (featuring his recurring antihero, Jonathan Crowley) and his most recent novels, *Cherry Hill* and *Deeper*. He has twice been nominated for the Bram Stoker Award and spent three years as an officer in the Horror Writers Association, first as secretary and later as vice president.

25
John Buchan's
THE THIRTY-NINE STEPS (1915)

Janet Berliner

John Buchan was a prolific author who began life as the first of four sons and a daughter to a Free Church of Scotland minister in Perth, Scotland, in August 1875. After a brief stint in law, he entered politics as the private secretary to Alfred Milner, high commissioner for South Africa and Governor of Cape Province. In 1907, he married Susan Charlotte Grosvenor, and they had four children. During the First World War, he spent time in the British Army Intelligence Corps and later became director of information under Lord Beaverbrook. In 1935, King George V named John Buchan governor general of Canada. Preferring to have a peer in that position, the king created and bestowed on him the title of Baron of Tweedsmuir. Early in 1940, while shaving, he suffered a stroke and hit his head upon falling. Despite the best medical care available, he succumbed to his injuries on February 11, 1940.

John Buchan left behind an impressive legacy in print, publishing around one hundred books, including biographies and histories, as well as thirty novels and seven collections of stories and poetry. In 1910, he wrote his first adventure, *Prester John*, set in South Africa, as many of his works would be. Then, in 1915, he wrote what would become his most famous work, *The Thirty-Nine Steps*, which almost by itself launched the chase thriller genre. His final work, *Sick Heart River*, published posthumously in 1941, found a dying adventurer trapped in the Canadian wilderness and contemplating the meaning of life. While we now remember Buchan for his adventure stories, in his day he was as well known for his horror stories such as "Witch Wood" and "The Green Wildebeest." He was also, for a time, a partner in a publishing company and later founded the Governor General's Awards, recognizing Canadian literature.

His works strongly influenced such subsequent political intrigue thriller writers as Eric Ambler, Geoffrey Household, Ian Fleming, and just about any novelist or screenwriter whose innocent main character is blamed for a serious crime and forced to run from the police or the CIA or whatever while desperately trying to figure out who the real criminal is.

I first encountered John Buchan's work through *The Thirty-Nine Steps* when I was a precocious young girl in South Africa around 1950. Having worked my way through all of the Nancy Drews available in the library in Cape Town, I wandered into the adult section to look for something more to read. My hand fell upon John Buchan's book largely because it was shelved around my eye level, and it was undauntingly slender. It was my first lesson in less being more.

The book also had an enormous effect on my future life and my future books. Richard Hannay's adventures reinforced my natural wanderlust, but also the novel instilled in me a subconscious quest for thirty-nine steps. So much so that when I moved to Grenada for a year, I rented a house because it had thirty-nine steps from the porch down to the beach. More importantly, Buchan's direct prose and talent for mixing dry humor with suspense would become for me almost a template for how to write a thriller.

The book itself is significantly different from the 1935 Alfred Hitchcock film that so many people in our modern era of short attention spans and DVDs remember. For example, it doesn't include a female companion for the protagonist. The book, probably not even forty thousand words long, would be considered a novella to current publishers. In that short space, John Buchan takes the reader on a breathless ride.

Richard Hannay is a man bored by life in London while the rest of Europe seethes its way into what would be the First World War. He becomes an accidental secret agent when his peculiar upstairs neighbor, Franklin Scudder, beguiles him with a tale of intrigue and begs Hannay's assistance in hiding from unknown enemies. When Hannay comes home to find Scudder stabbed to death, he is forced to go on the run, first in London, and later in the Scottish countryside, trying to avoid the police and Scudder's mysterious foes while he tries to unravel whatever machinations the dead man has gotten him mixed up into. He takes with him Scudder's journal.

Reading the journal, Hannay learns that the United Kingdom appears to be in danger of an invasion by Germany and its allies. He reads about an enemy group called The Black Stone and of something called The Thirty-Nine Steps. After much deliberation, he realizes that the phrase "the thirty-nine steps" could refer to a landing point in Kent, where thirty-nine steps lead down a cliff to the sea. Hannay goes to Kent and finds the spies about to board a yacht. The scheme is thwarted, and the United Kingdom enters World War I, having kept its military secrets from the enemy.

The inspiration for the title was wonderfully mundane, as Buchan's son later explained. His father was convalescing from a serious illness at a private nursing home. "There was a wooden staircase leading down to the beach. My sister, who was about six, and who had just learnt to count properly, went down them and gleefully announced: there are thirty-nine steps." Some time later the house in Kent was demolished and the original steps were replaced by concrete. A section of the old stairs, complete with a brass plaque, was sent to Buchan.

In addition to Hitchcock's famous work, Buchan's story has been adapted into four more films, most recently one premiering in 2008 on BBC television. While the subsequent films are all more faithful to the source work, it will of course be Hitchcock's version that is most remembered for the meeting of two masters of thrills in works that, while not their first, certainly helped to forge their legacies in the minds of fans.

For those who know only the film, I cannot advise strongly enough taking the short time needed to read the original book, which has almost never been out of print since its initial publication nearly a century ago.

Some of the passages may seem offensive to a modern reader. For instance, the murder victim, Scudder, is a vocal anti-Semite, but Buchan did not share those views and arranged for the Jews in the novel to proclaim how crazy Scudder is for obsessing about an imagined Jewish conspiracy. Indeed, later in life Buchan found himself on Hitler's "hit list" as a supporter of the Zionist "Palestine Parliamentary Group" in the 1930s.

Readers with more interest in Buchan and his times would do well to read his autobiography, *Memory, Hold-the-Door* (published in the U.S. as *Pilgrim's Way*). The book was one of President John F. Kennedy's favorite works, which he often quoted to friends and acquaintances. Buchan's Richard Hannay appeared in several other thrillers, what Buchan called "shockers," including *Greenmantle*, *Mr. Standfast*, and *The Three Hostages*.

Janet Berliner is the Bram Stoker Award-winning author of six novels, including the *Madagascar Manifesto* trilogy with George Guthridge, and *Artifact*, her four-way collaboration with friends Kevin J. Anderson, Matthew J. Costello, and F. Paul Wilson. She has sold over one hundred short stories to magazines and anthologies.

She is also the editor of six anthologies, including two with illusionist David Copperfield, and one with Joyce Carol Oates. She is a member of the Council of the National Writers Association, a past president of the Horror Writers Association, and a member of the Authors Guild, the International Thriller Writers, and the Science Fiction and Fantasy Writers of America. Born in South Africa, Janet now lives in Las Vegas, while she plans her escape to the Caribbean.

26

E. Phillips Oppenheim's

THE GREAT IMPERSONATION (1920)

Justin Scott

Edward Phillips Oppenheim (1866–1946) was one of the most popular authors of his day. Born in London and raised in Leicester, he began writing fiction in his teens, an ambition that so distressed his domineering, leather merchant father that Oppenheim was removed from school and forced to work in the family business. Thereafter he devoted nine hours each day to commerce, eight to sleeping, and the remainder to writing fiction. By the time his father died and Oppenheim sold the leather business, his publishing career was so successful that he could afford to leave England and set up housekeeping on the French Rivera. Many of his books, including *The Great Impersonation*, were dictated, a technique that presents an interesting contrast between the effect of the words on the page as opposed to the way they sound when read aloud.

Midway in a career that spans sixty years, two world wars, and one hundred and fifty novels, a guy sits down and writes a masterpiece. His sales, already huge, increase dramatically. He continues to write excellent novels. None quite equals the masterpiece, but he enjoys by all accounts a deeply satisfying writing life. The wealth of bestsellerdom permits him to live on the French Riviera among the rich and titled people he loves to write about.

His name was E. Phillips Oppenheim.

The masterpiece is *The Great Impersonation*. It's a spy story set in 1914 in the fleeting, desperate months before England and Germany fought the Great War that decimated two generations of husbands and sons. He published it in 1920, just two years after the slaughter.

While beloved by legions of readers, *The Great Impersonation* is really a writer's book. Halfway through it dawns on you that not only has he written a gripping thriller; he's also written an intriguing mystery, a strange and emotional love story, and a Gothic novel complete with a haunted wood and a howling demon. And he's integrated them so smoothly that you're straining a wrist to turn the pages. He's also writing about good and evil, duty to God and country, and redemption. But first and foremost he is writing about that greatest of all human fantasies—the second chance.

It's a battle cruiser of a novel, both fast and stately. To propel it, Oppenheim invents a plot device so clever that words like twist or gimmick can't begin to do it honor.

It starts when a dissolute English baronet stumbles out of the African jungle into the remote camp of a German nobleman on a mission. A writer is allowed one coincidence early in a plot, and Oppenheim takes full advantage: Not only were Sir Everard Dominey and Major General Baron Leopold von Ragastein at school together at Eton, but when Dominey and Von Ragastein were boys they looked exactly alike. Doubles. The former schoolmates catch up over dinner. Von Ragastein is military commandant of the colony of German East Africa, and Dominey is a drunk living off the last of his wasted inheritance.

Oppenheim makes it brutally clear that we have not entered the doppelgänger territory of *The Prince and the Pauper* or *The Prisoner of Zenda*. *The Great Impersonation* is not about doubles trading places. It is about war, and there is room for only one winner.

After von Ragastein and Dominey fight to the death, we meet the victorious von Ragastein in England, where Dominey's solicitor is astonished. Ten years in Africa have so toughened and matured his wastrel client that he hardly recognizes him. The solicitor is even more astonished that the ever impecunious Sir Everard is not looking for a handout, or to borrow on his already mortgaged-to-the-hilt estate, but intends to pay off his debts and restore his Norfolk house and lands to a glory not seen by generations of struggling Domineys.

Equally astonished is Von Ragastein's former mistress, the Hungarian Princess Stéphanie Eiderstrom who refuses to believe that he is Dominey and threatens to expose him if he won't resume their affair.

Similarly, Dominey's wife, who has vowed to kill him if he ever sets foot in their house again—having been insane since Dominey evidently killed a man before he fled to Africa—is sufficiently confused by the changes in her husband that she decides not to stab him in his sleep and instead throws her dagger down a well.

You can be forgiven for wondering if this entire situation could be fodder for a comic stage farce, particularly when wrapped gaily in the trappings of wealth and privilege: elegant restaurants, splendid palaces, town houses, pheasant shoots, cellars of old brandy and ancient port. In fact, one character actually raises the point. But the stakes are so high. The hor-

rific war looms. And the German spymaster running von Ragastein reminds him, and us, how the love and hope of Dominey's wife is something
too fragile to be abused.

The writing, too, rises above farce. Oppenheim is subtle, yet clear.
Dominey and his beautiful older cousin, the Duchess Caroline who is married to Duke Henry, were obviously very fond of each other before
Dominey went to Africa. We feel a wonderful heat between them, or is it
merely flirtation?

Oppenheim is as subtle with his action scenes. There are a grand total
of two instances of violence on stage. First, when Dominey/von Ragastein
awakes to the aforementioned dagger at his throat in a terrifying moment.
The second occurs at the end, a sudden attack that would seem tame if it
weren't so rare in the novel.

The main reason that *The Great Impersonation* never descends to farce
is that Oppenheim exploits the doppelgänger device to a new degree by
placing the reader in the same position as the characters who are stunned
and fascinated by Dominey's miraculous improvement. How could a man
have changed so much? How does a wastrel become an upright citizen? At
the same time, the reader asks when will some Englishman realize that this
newly constituted Everard Dominey is too good to be true. How long can
a spy hide in plain sight?

Which leads the reader to the big and constant question that weaves
relentlessly through the novel. Will he get caught? The German plan is
for their impersonator to influence British war decisions at the highest
level. He can't be a secretive spy. He can't skulk. To be effective, he must
be charismatic, even larger than life, a man who makes people curious. He
has to march boldly through British society.

The Germans are glad to put up the money to pay off the mortgages
on Dominey Hall because that transforms him into a nobleman of substance—a public figure to influence public figures. A high point in his effort is a weekend party at Dominey Hall attended not only by the Lord
Lieutenant of Norfolk, but a powerful cabinet minister. Of course—Oppenheim being Oppenheim—also showing up for the weekend are the
Hungarian princess and Dominey's wife newly sprung from the asylum.

Will he get caught? I won't tell you. You'd hate me for it. Just as you'd
hate me if I revealed Oppenheim's miraculous plot device, one of the most
stunning revelations in thriller history. I will say that part of the pleasure
comes from wondering just how Oppenheim plotted his thriller. What did

he know at what point while writing? Was it all laid out, or was he making decisions on horseback? I repeat—this is a writer's novel, filled with great writing lessons, especially about pacing and twists. You don't have to be a writer to be thrilled by it, though you may want to become one after you read it.

Justin Scott has written twenty-four thrillers, historicals, and mystery novels, including *The Shipkiller* and *Normandie Triangle*. With many books set at sea, he has been called "the Dick Francis of yachting." He writes the Ben Abbott detective series (*HardScape, StoneDust, FrostLine, McMansion,* and *Mausoleum*), and has been twice nominated for the Edgar Allan Poe Award by the Mystery Writers of America. His main pen name is Paul Garrison under which he has written five modern sea thrillers including *Red Sky At Morning, Sea Hunter,* and *The Ripple Effect*. He has collaborated with Clive Cussler on the Isaac Bell novels, *The Wrecker* and *The Spy*.

27
Richard Connell's
"THE MOST DANGEROUS GAME" (1924)

Katherine Ramsland

By the time he was ten, Richard Edward Connell, Jr., (1893–1949) had a role model for his future as a writer: his father, who edited the *Poughkeepsie News-Press* in Poughkeepsie, New York. In high school, Connell, Jr., wrote features for the paper and covered baseball games, absorbing material for short stories he would later compose. He was only eighteen when he became city editor. Although he began college at Georgetown, he quit to be a secretary for his father, now in Congress. Connell, Sr., died less than two years later, so Connell, Jr., entered Harvard. There he edited the *Harvard Lampoon* and the *Harvard Crimson*. Enlisting during World War I, Connell penned items for the camp newspaper, *Gas Attack*. Later, his work in advertising inspired other short stories, and he sold his first one in 1919, the same year he got married. Five years later, he published the biting tale that would gain him lasting renown: "The Most Dangerous Game." Even as he became one of the best-known short story writers of his time, he moved to California, where he tried his hand at novels and screenwriting. In 1941, he received an Oscar nomination for best original story for *Meet John Doe*. However, his career ended prematurely in 1949 when a heart attack took him at age fifty-six.

Average men rising to a challenge is a theme that populated most of the short stories that Richard Connell, Jr., penned during the 1920s. He usually wrote for the masses. Yet it was only when he took up a truly sinister subject for "The Most Dangerous Game" that he ensured his philosophical legacy. A contest Connell described between the hunter and the hunted that had seemed nearly unthinkable in 1924 has inspired numerous imitations, both fictional and actual.

The tale was first published in *Collier's Weekly* and received the prestigious O. Henry Memorial Award—Connell's second such win in two years. While engaging as fiction, "The Most Dangerous Game" (aka "The

Hounds of Zaroff") was also a cynical commentary on big-game hunts that were fashionable during the 1920s among the wealthy. In fact, both the protagonist and antagonist participate in this sport with a disturbingly callous zest.

Sanger Rainsford shows up first. He's an arrogant New Yorker, renowned for his publications on big-game hunting. While traveling by ship to Brazil, he gets stranded on an isolated Caribbean island and soon meets its lone inhabitants: the Russian aristocrat, General Zaroff, and his deaf mute Cossack slave, Ivan. Zaroff is himself a big-game hunter, familiar with Rainsford's publications. In fact, he's delighted to have the company of a kindred soul. While they wine and dine, Zaroff freely admits what he's doing, believing that only someone like Rainsford could fully appreciate it.

Zaroff describes his boredom with even the most ferocious animal and how this pushed him toward hunting much more interesting prey—an animal that can *think*. Toward this end, he lures ships to his island, making them crash and forcing surviving crew members to play a "game"—*as* game. To earn their freedom, they must survive on his island for three days while he hunts them. Of course, Zaroff has all the advantage, including a pack of vicious hunting dogs.

Rainsford realizes that Zaroff will now seek to hone his skill against a master hunter—*him*. He knows that any moral objections will fail, since he himself has openly affirmed Zaroff's attitude about the hunter's superiority over the hunted. Thus, Rainsford has no choice but to "play," and win or lose, he will have to ponder this savage reflection of his own arrogance.

Connell's story, a typical mirror-image tale meant to turn a protagonist on his head, has been widely anthologized and adapted for film, although the notion of a mad human-savage on an island was not new. For example, H. G. Wells had portrayed this in 1896 in *The Island of Dr. Moreau*. But Connell was also illustrating the moral quicksand of arrogance.

Hollywood made its most famous rendition in 1932, utilizing sets from the Skull Island scenes in *King Kong*. (Fay Wray acted in both films, although no female character appears in Connell's story.) While there were other films over the years, the basic plot also emerged in countless television series, from *Star Trek* to *Criminal Minds*. More disturbing, its central tenet—hunting humans—inspired real-life psychopaths who fancy themselves "above the herd."

The infamous "Zodiac" seems to have read the story or seen a film of it. With at least seven victims in the San Francisco area during the late 1960s, he sought public notoriety. As he claimed responsibility for a double homicide and threatened more, he divided a code among three local newspapers and demanded that the entire cryptogram be published. The papers complied, and a reader deciphered it. Part of the message echoed Zaroff: "I LIKE KILLING PEOPLE BECAUSE IT IS SO MUCH FUN IT IS MORE FUN THAT KILLING WILD GAME IN THE FORREST BECAUSE MAN IS THE MOST DANGEROUS ANAMAL OF ALL TO KILL [original spelling retained]." In addition, in one film version, Zaroff dresses in black, wears a knife in a sheath on his left side, and keeps a rifle in his right hand. A surviving witness of a Zodiac assault described the hooded figure that approached him in similar terms.

Investigators searched for men who viewed themselves as hunters, and a strong suspect was Arthur Leigh Allen, who admitted familiarity with Connell's story. Acquaintances of his said he often spoke of the "most dangerous game" and "man as true game." However, after Allen died, a DNA analysis exonerated him.

Serial killer Robert Hansen also seemed to replicate Zaroff's agenda. In 1980, he flew prostitutes into wilderness areas in Alaska to turn them loose without resources and hunt them with a high-powered rifle. The FBI finally brought him to ground, persuading him to confess to the torture murder of seventeen young women. (This resembles the 1972 film, *Woman Hunt*, considered a "remake" of *The Most Dangerous Game*.)

It's disturbing that humans can become so callous and cruel as to treat their own kind as prey, yet such dehumanization clearly works as entertainment. This theme is likely to show up again and again—in fiction and otherwise—as an archetypal truth about human nature.

Dr. Katherine Ramsland holds graduate degrees in philosophy and psychology. She has published sixteen short stories, more than eight hundred articles, and thirty-four books, including *The Devil's Dozen: How Cutting Edge Forensics Took Down Twelve Notorious Serial Killers*, *True Stories of CSI*, *Inside the Minds of Serial Killers*, *The Human Predator*, and *The Criminal Mind: A Writers' Guide to Forensic Psychology*. With former FBI profiler Gregg McCrary, she coauthored *The Unknown Darkness*, and with forensic science professor James E. Starrs, *A Voice for the Dead*. She has been translated into ten languages, and has written biographies of both Anne Rice and Dean Koontz. In addition, she pens a regular feature on historical forensics for *The Forensic Examiner* and teaches forensic psychology and criminal justice at DeSales University in Pennsylvania. Appearing on numerous news programs and documentaries, she is considered an international expert on serial murder.

28

W. Somerset Maugham's
ASHENDEN or THE BRITISH AGENT (1928)

Melodie Johnson Howe

W. Somerset Maugham (1874–1965) was a prolific and successful English novelist, playwright, and short story writer. He was also one of the most significant travel writers between the two world wars. His first major novel, *Of Human Bondage* (1915), was decried by the critics, but saved from obscurity by Theodore Dreiser who thought it a work of genius and compared it to a Beethoven symphony. The book has never been out of print. *The Moon and Sixpence* (1919) and *The Razor's Edge* (1944) are among his best known books. His short story, "The Letter," was turned into a brilliant noir film starring Bette Davis. Numerous other stories, novels, and plays were adapted into movies, such as *Rain* staring Joan Crawford. Many of his works, including *Liza of Lambeth* and *Cakes and Ale*, featured female characters who were ruthless in serving their sexual needs while not thinking of the cost to others. Critics often condemned Maugham for letting his villains off too easily. "It must be a fault of mine that I am not gravely shocked at the sins of others unless they personally affect me," he responded. During the latter part of his career, he fell from favor, thinking of himself as the "very first row of the second raters." He died while reading a mystery.

W. Somerset Maugham was a great short story writer. He was also a spy in World War I. Blending his talent and personal experience, he wrote *Ashenden or the British Agent* (1928). The book is a group of sixteen short stories connected by the character Ashenden, a writer/spy, and R., a British colonel, Ashenden's recruiter and handler.

Maugham writes in the preface to a later edition, "The work of an agent in the Intelligence Department is on the whole monotonous. A lot of it is uncommonly useless. The material it offers for stories is scrappy and pointless; the author has himself to make it coherent, dramatic, and probable. That is what I have tried to do in this particular series."

Each story contains an order from R. that Ashenden must fulfill. Sometimes he succeeds, and sometimes his goal is lost in a maze of emotion created by the unpredictability of human beings. Maugham's sharply observed characters, wit, and stiff English compassion bring these stories to life. Here, Maugham gives us a sense of Ashenden and R., the old soldier:

> . . . so long as the fine weather lasted he was prepared to enjoy himself. He did not see why he should not at least try to combine pleasure to himself with profit to his country. He was traveling with a brand-new passport in his pocket, under a borrowed name, and this gave him an agreeable sense of owning a new personality. He was often slightly tired of himself and it diverted him for awhile to be merely a creature of R.'s facile invention . . . R. it is true had not seen the fun of it: what humor R. possessed was of a sardonic turn and he had no facility for taking in good part a joke at his own expense. To do that you must be able to look at yourself from the outside and be at the same time spectator and actor in the pleasant comedy of life. R. was a soldier and regarded introspection as unhealthy, unEnglish, and unpatriotic.

The reader never sees the effects of the war in these stories, except in eerily empty European cities where spies maneuver, scheme, and contrive against each other in the name of their country. This is Lucerne as seen through Ashenden's eyes:

> Most of the hotels were closed. The streets were empty, the rowing boats for hire rocked idly at the water's edge and there was none to take them, and in the avenues by the lake the only persons to be seen were the serious Swiss taking their neutrality, like a dachshund, for a walk with them.

Maugham is brilliant at going from the languid overview, then moving swiftly in for the kill with a sharp devastating observation.

One of my favorite stories is "Giulia Lazzari." It is a love story turned into ugly betrayal by the war. A dancer has captured the heart of an East Indian terrorist who spies for the Germans. Ashenden must get this uneducated creature to write letters to her lover, enticing him to come from neutral Switzerland to France, so he can be captured. The main part of the story takes place in a hotel room where Ashenden cajoles this volatile, angry, sobbing woman into betraying her lover. When writing the letter, she asks him:

"How do I spell *absolutely?*"

"As you like."

How succinct. How perfectly put for a spy who wants to give nothing away to the love-obsessed terrorist. When the Indian learns that he has been deceived, he swallows poison in a train station in front of his captors. In the hotel room, Ashenden tells the lady what has happened and that she is free to go. She cries and wails and then suddenly clearheaded asks:

"What are they going to do with his things?"

"I don't know. Why?"

"He had a wristwatch I gave him for Christmas. It cost twelve pounds. Could I have it back?"

And that is the end of love. Maugham captures not only the everydayness of being a spy, but the deadening loss for all those involved.

As with many of his stories, this one is based on an actual event. There was a British agent sent to assassinate the real Indian terrorist and German spy, Chattopadhaya. How deeply was Maugham involved? We don't know. But Winston Churchill reportedly told Maugham to burn fourteen of his short stories because they gave too much information away.

Another story, "The Hairless Mexican," is about a hit man so overly confident in his murderous skills and sexual prowess that he fails miserably at his mission. Maugham uses irony in place of a gun every time

In creating the Eton-educated Ashenden, Maugham paved the way for Eric Ambler, Ian Fleming, John le Carré, and many more. I even see Ashenden in P. D. James's Inspector Dalgliesh. Also, R. is in all likelihood the prototype for M. in the James Bond novels. Alfred Hitchcock used elements from Ashenden in his 1936 film, *Secret Agent.*

This group of stories was written in a long-ago era. The element of the ticking time bomb so popular in thriller writing today does not exist in them. But the human element does. And its accuracy—on a special tour of the CIA in Langley, I learned that they have a best spy novel list. It's very short. *Ashenden or the British Agent* is on it.

After a career in acting, Melodie Johnson Howe turned to writing. Her first novel,

The Mother Shadow, was nominated for Edgar, Anthony, and Agatha Awards. Howe's second novel, *Beauty Dies*, soon followed. Her numerous Diana Poole short stories about a middle-aged actress in Hollywood have been published in *Ellery Queen's Mystery Magazine*, *The Best Short Fiction of the Year*, and other anthologies. Her short story, "Facing Up," was nominated for the Barry Award. She is also the author of *The Diana Poole Stories*. Janet Hutchings, editor of EQMM, says "the critical acceptance her work has received is well deserved . . . Howe is one of the genre's best short story writers and novelists." As Howe says, "I write about what I know. Hollywood, women, men, love, betrayal, and then I throw in a murder or two." She taught at the UCLA Writers Program and the Santa Barbara Writers Conference. She blogs on www.criminalbrief.com.

29.
P. G. Wodehouse's
SUMMER LIGHTNING (1929)

R.L. Stine

P. G. (Pelham Grenville) Wodehouse (1881–1975) had a literary career that spanned more than seventy years. He lived to be ninety-three and published ninety-three books of humor and brilliant farce. He was also a playwright and lyricist for more than thirty Broadway musicals. He wrote with such composers as Cole Porter, George Gershwin, and Jerome Kern. His most popular novels and stories feature the foppish, upper-class twit, Bertie Wooster, and his indomitable and wise butler, Jeeves. He also wrote many *Blandings Castle* novels and stories, featuring the eccentric, almost dim-witted Lord Emsworth and the Empress, his treasured fat pig. Wodehouse was a golf enthusiast and wrote many of the funniest stories about golf ever written. British born, he spent much of his later life on Long Island and became a U.S. citizen in 1955. In 1975, he was knighted by the queen of England and died a few months later with an unfinished *Blandings Castle* novel in his typewriter.

What ugly secrets does the old mansion hold?

Why is more than one visitor willing to pay *big money* to have the teller of these secrets silenced?

Can it be that several guests are not who they claim to be? Why do they sneak off in the dark of night to meet in secret?

Which guest is responsible for the shocking theft of the owner's most priceless possession?

Yes, I'm describing a novel with lots of mystery, intrigue, twists, and surprises. This book is a great classic—but not a classic thriller. I'm talking about *Summer Lightning*, a comic masterpiece by P. G. Wodehouse, an author few would ever confuse with Ken Follett, Frederick Forsyth, or even Dorothy L. Sayers.

When I was asked to nominate a book for this volume, I decided to give myself a challenge. Having written both humor and thrillers, I've chewed many an ear off with my theories about how the two are closely connected.

P. G. Wodehouse is my favorite author. He wrote ninety-three novels, and I've read most of them with great pleasure. I admire them for their impossibly convoluted plots, and for the ease and splendor of Wodehouse's language. His mastery of language has been compared to Shakespeare, and his brilliantly tangled story lines have been compared to Dickens.

However, as big a fan as I am, even I know that Wodehouse's novels cannot be considered thrillers. So, that's the challenge I gave myself: to use *Summer Lightning*, one of his superb *Blandings Castle* novels, to prove my theory about the close relationship between comedy and thrillers.

To begin, the story is driven by a heinous crime.

Lord Emsworth, the dotty and absent-minded master of Blandings Castle, has one interest in life—his most prized possession, the Empress, an enormous pig, which he enters annually in the local Fat Pig Competition. Early in the book, the pig is stolen, throwing Emsworth and the castle into an uproar.

Alfred Hitchcock described the object that sets the plot of a thriller in motion as the *MacGuffin*. It can be a suitcase holding a million dollars, an incriminating love letter—or, in this case, a fat pig. The stolen object begins a chase that can lead to thrills—or laughs.

I hope this doesn't spoil it for you—but the pig was stolen by Lord Emsworth's nephew, Ronnie Fish. Ronnie doesn't plan to keep it or sell it for bacon. His idea is to return it to his uncle in a few days in order to win Emsworth's undying gratitude.

This leads us to our second connection to thrillers—the cover-up.

When Hugo Carmody, Emsworth's secretary, comes to tell Ronnie the upsetting news, Ronnie realizes he must put on a good face to hide his connection to the crime. This funny dialogue ensues:

Hugo: "You know that pig of your uncle's?"
Ronnie: "What about it?"
"It's gone."
"Gone?"
"Gone!" said Hugo, rolling the word round his tongue. "I met the old boy half a minute ago, and he told me. It seems he went down to the pig-bin for a before-breakfast look at the animal, and it wasn't there."
"Wasn't there?"

"Wasn't there."

"How do you mean, wasn't there?"

"Well, it wasn't. Wasn't there at all. It had gone."

"Gone?"

"Gone! Its room was empty and its bed had not been slept in."

"Well, I'm dashed," said Ronnie.

He was feeling pleased with himself. He felt he had played his part well. Just the right incredulous amazement, changing just soon enough into stunned disbelief.

"You don't seem very surprised," said Hugo.

Ronnie was stung. The charge was monstrous.

"Yes, I do," he cried. "I seem frightfully surprised."

Other thriller techniques that can also be used for comic effect? How about misdirection. Most thriller writers misdirect their protagonists to create surprises and plot twists in their novels. And they misdirect the readers to keep them from guessing where the book is going.

Wodehouse keeps everyone misdirected as often as possible! In fact, very few guests at Blandings are who they claim to be.

The young woman who claims to be Myra Schoonmaker, an American heiress, is actually Sue Brown, a chorus girl. The detective Percy Pilbeam, who appears to be on the trail of the stolen pig, is actually after different game. He's there to steal Galahad (Gally) Threepwood's manuscript of his memoirs.

Which brings us to the *second* MacGuffin. Wodehouse isn't satisfied with only one. And as with many thrillers, this subplot bumps against the main story.

It seems that Lord Emsworth's brother, Gally Threepwood, is staying at Blandings to write his memoirs. This has caused great horror among many guests. They knew Gally in their younger years and don't want to be embarrassed. Some will do anything to keep his salacious memoir from the public—even *steal* it.

In this funny scene, Threepwood is asking Emsworth and his imperious sister, Lady Constance, about a scandalous incident he's including in his memoir:

> "What year was it there was that terrible row between young
> Gregory Parsloe and Lord Burper, when Parsloe stole the old

chap's false teeth and pawned them in a shop in the Edgeware Road?" . . .

Lady Constance uttered a sharp cry. The sunlight had now gone quite definitely out of her life. She felt, as she so often felt in her brother Gallahad's society, as if foxes were gnawing her vitals. . . ."Gallahad! You are not proposing to print libelous stories like that about our nearest neighbor?"

"Certainly I am," the Hon. Gallahad snorted militantly. . . . And leaping lightly over the spaniel, he flitted away across the lawn.

Stories like that must be suppressed, Lady Constance believes. Soon, more than one thief is plotting to take possession of Gally's hot reminiscences.

With stolen pigs and purloined memoirs and chorus girls pretending to be heiresses, there are enough misdirections and complications here for any thriller.

And what about suspense? Every thriller thrives on suspense. Will the hero overcome all the life-threatening odds to achieve his mission, defeat the tightening net of foes who are out to destroy him—and live to star in a sequel?

There is suspense in Wodehouse, but it's a little different. I think the true suspense is: how will the author untangle the impossible, tangled mess he has created and get everyone straightened around by the last, happy chapter? This kind of suspense keeps you reading as avidly as the first kind, I believe.

I guess my main thought is that thrillers and comic stories both set out to produce a visceral reaction in readers. A good thriller will keep you in suspense, make you gasp, startle you, and even frighten you.

Comic novels have a similar goal, and their writers want to elicit a visceral reaction as well. They want to keep you in suspense, startle you—and make you laugh.

Have I proven the connection between the two kinds of writing?

I'm not so sure.

But I see that my space is up. It's time for me to leap lightly over the spaniel and flit away across the lawn.

R.L. Stine is one of the best-selling children's authors in history. His scary novels—

including the *Fear Street* and *Goosebumps* series—have sold over 350 million copies worldwide. Stine began writing joke books and humor for kids. But his career took off when he became scary, writing his first YA horror novel, *Blind Date*, in 1986. He is currently at work on a new *Goosebumps* series called *Goosebumps HorrorLand*. In addition, he recently published two thrillers for adults—*The Sitter* and *Eye Candy*. Bob lives in New York City with his wife, Jane, and King Charles spaniel, Minnie.

30
Edgar Wallace's
KING KONG (1932)

Kathleen Sharp

Conceived by a widowed actress and a romantic lead, Edgar Wallace (1875–1932) was born in 1875 with drama in his blood. A stint in the British army, a job reporting on Boer Wars, and a brush with some Russian spies inspired his first book *The Four Just Men* (1905). Wallace went on to create twenty-four plays and one hundred seventy-four more novels, an amazing output that included *The Green Archer* and *The Mind of Mr. J.G. Reeder*. His cinematic vision was also unparalleled: over one hundred sixty films have been made of his novels, far more than any other author. In 1931, he traveled to Hollywood and started the screenplay for *King Kong*. Two months into that project, however, he died suddenly on Feb. 7, 1932. His coffin was shipped home and carried through the streets of London, where flags flew at half-mast, church bells tolled, and mourners paid respect. Even in death, the novelist produced great theater.

Before Frank Buck and Indiana Jones, there was Carl Denham. Perhaps you remember the adventurous agent. He brings a shipload of humans to Skull Island, finds a gigantic monster, and transports him to New York City to exploit him for money. Denham's scheme is foiled when the wild beast breaks free of his chains and nearly destroys Manhattan.

Every nine-year-old boy and his thirteen-year-old sister know the story of *King Kong*. The 1933 movie was billed as "The Most Awesome Thriller of All Time" and has continued to deliver in each remake over the past eighty plus years. The seminal story was said to be the brainchild of the movie's swashbuckling co-director, Merian C. Cooper, who once boasted: "Edgar Wallace didn't write any of *Kong, not* one bloody word. I'd promised him credit and so I gave it to him." But as usual Cooper was exaggerating. Wallace toyed with *Kong* as early as 1925 when he published *The Hairy Arm*, also known as *The Avenger*. In this novel, a stalker threatens to kill a starlet and uses an apelike man to kidnap her. Still, Kongaphiles unfamiliar with Wallace's books insisted for years that the movie script was Cooper's. But when Wallace's original script turned up for auction in the 1980s, they had to concede that *King Kong* was more the Englishman's creation than Hollywood would have us believe.

Certainly, the film was a collaboration of talent. But Wallace wrote the story in five days in January 1932, producing the original 110-page script. Entitled *Kong*, it opens on Vapor Island (not Skull) with a P. T. Barnum-like showman named Danby (not Carl) Denham who wants to find "something colossal." Denham baits his prey with a heroine named Zena (not Ann), her rescuer John (not Jack), and the crewmen of Captain Englehorn, all of whom are chased by a string of terrifying creatures. The entire pursuit climaxes atop the Empire State Building. In his treatment, Wallace established the major characters, their relationship to one another, and the overall plot, imbuing it with a menace that can still turn your knuckles white.

Most of Wallace's suspense tales had a simple cast. There was a hero, usually a working man; a pretty woman who is deeply, albeit innocently, involved in the problem; a few villains whose motives are somewhat unclear; and a monster of superhuman strength. But great thrillers are often driven by plot, and Wallace excelled at constructing a story's bones. He created a problem, some characters, a solution, and, most important, a dramatic end. Because the ex-reporter published his stories first in serial form in newspapers, he didn't always know *how* his tale would develop. All he knew was that each installment had to stand on its own. That's why his novels have imaginative twists that seemingly doom the hero until we read the following chapter (or weekly episode), when he manages to extricate himself to face another harrowing adventure.

In time, Wallace built his plots on two frames. Inside the main story arc are smaller sagas driven by calamities that have quick short runs and often overlap. The author solves the small setbacks as they appear so he doesn't burden readers with tedious explanations. Many of his tales feel formulaic, but they click inexorably toward their big denouement, hastened by a pursuit so gripping we almost forget how implausible it is.

Wallace devised a prototype for the modern thriller. How fitting then that three months before his movie premiered, *King Kong* the book was published in December 1932, marking one of the first movie novelizations. RKO studio pulled out all the stops to promote Wallace's movie, producing lobby cards, posters, magazine features, and advertising. The effort paid off, too. When the film opened nationally on April 10, 1933, it smashed all attendance records and made box-office history with a then-astounding $1.8 million. It was enough money to save RKO from bankruptcy. Over the subsequent twenty years, the studio reissued and reran *Kong* so many times, it practically lived off the big gorilla.

To this day, *Kong* remains the most thrilling jungle quest ever, partly because it's archetypal—like all great thrillers. It borrows a little from Hieronymus Bosch, Jonathan Swift, Teutonic folktales, and Greek myths, reminding us that there are some realms where we dare not tread. As extreme capitalist Denham warns: "(T)here's something . . . that no . . . man has ever seen." Despite our science, technology, and super-secret surveillance tools, humans can still be thrown over by the sudden appearance of a primordial creature smashing through the brush.

It must be acknowledged that part of *Kong*'s power lies in its primitive sex appeal. For the thirteen-year-old girl, it's the realization that the love Kong feels for Ann can never be consummated and is therefore more "pure." For the nine-year-old boy, it's the extreme gigantism. To talk of such primal desires, however, is to violate both the sacred *and* profane. It's so much better to keep our fantasies locked in the subconscious or at least inside the darkened movie theater, where they can paw at us mutely like some hairy arm.

But there are other stirrings too. It's no coincidence that Wallace developed his story during the nadir of the Great Depression, in 1932, when the U.S. financial system was flailing to the horror of our allies. With the market's lupine stock traders, buffaloed officials, and sheep-like investors, Wall Street resembled a pin-striped jungle run amuck with ambition, greed, and ruthlessness. Denham represented the dark side of that sort of businessman, a dodgy fellow who could be charming when he wasn't scheming. He's a uniquely American creature, a real Yankee Doodle Dandy who, along with skyscrapers, tommy guns, and shrieking starlets, fascinates the rest of the world. Who else but a well-bred English playwright could reveal our hucksterlike traits and still make them awe inspiring?

Wallace's *King Kong* not only presaged the corporate thriller; it became a reliable economic indicator of sorts. Whenever the S&P 500 index drops significantly, *Kong* resurfaces like an old debt. Consider that in 1976, when ordinary people were getting squeezed by a U.S. recession, inflation, and oil-rich sheiks, voila! Along came Dino De Laurentiis to remake the movie, turning Denham into a rapacious executive at Petrox Corp. who in his lust for oil colludes with the U.S. government. Some thirty years later, Peter Jackson made his own film version by expanding on Wallace's 110-page script. Once again, *Kong's* timing was remarkable. Main Street was getting bludgeoned by rising oil prices, deceptive financial instruments, and crooked little chiefs even as Wall Street bonuses swelled. But by the time this *Kong* remake was playing on cable TV, Wall Street was crashing yet again. How odd that the British, Italians, and New Zealanders can predict U.S. economic disasters better than our own Federal Reserve bankers, but never mind all that. Let's thank Mr. Wallace for exalting the stereotype of the evil capitalist system—a theme that continues to animate global headlines and today's thriller genre.

With *King Kong*, Wallace updated the ancient struggle between man and nature, beauty and the beast, money and heart. He left enough space in his story for these basic elements to switch roles, overlap, and catch us by surprise. But make no mistake: *Kong* reflects the darkest corner of our own secret selves—the smooth, hairless arm of clever Carl Denham.

Kathleen Sharp writes true suspense stories for national magazines and film. An award-winning journalist, she's written for *Vanity Fair, Playboy, Parade,* the *New York Times Magazine,* and *McCall's* among others. The author of the acclaimed *Mr. and Mrs. Hollywood: Edie and Lew Wasserman and Their Entertainment Empire,* she helped turn that book into a film documentary, *The Last Mogul,* which was distributed by ThinkFilm and aired on Bravo. Her other books include *In Good Faith* and *Stalking the Beast.* She has consulted for A&E's *Biography,* produced stories for NPR, and has been honored with several writing awards, including a journalism fellowship from the University of Southern California. Sharp is also a former editor of the ITW Newsletter *The Big Thrill.*

31

Lester Dent's
DOC SAVAGE: THE MAN OF BRONZE (1933)

Mark T. Sullivan

Lester Dent (1904–1959) was born in La Plata, Missouri. After moving to New York City, he became arguably the most successful author of the Pulp Era. He was a polymath, mastering a topic or talent fully, then dropping it after it exhausted his interest. He loved technology. As his biographer Philip José Farmer noted, Dent rivaled Jules Verne. The list of gadgets that first appeared in the Doc Savage stories and then came into existence years later is impressive.

When I was twelve, I first encountered Doc Savage as a powerhouse of a man with a cowl hairdo and a torn shirt on the cover of Bantam's 1964 reprint of *The Man of Bronze* by Lester Dent writing as Kenneth Robeson. I found the paperback in a cottage my family was renting on a lake in Vermont. On a chilly, rainy day, I huddled under blankets near the woodstove and read the book in two hours, so captivated by the startling action that I never moved.

As pulp historian Will Murray points out, before Doc Savage, heroes were largely limited by what seemed physically or mentally possible. Doc changed that. He was the original superhero, and an amazing number of superheroes that followed him owe one trait or another to the star of 181 novels that Lester Dent and others wrote between 1933 and 1949.

Doc Savage was called The Man of Bronze seven years before Superman became The Man of Steel. After Doc's father was murdered, Doc inherited a huge fortune and vowed to right wrong seven years before Bruce Wayne found himself in similar circumstances on his way to becoming Batman. Nineteen years before James Bond appeared, Doc exhibited uncanny investigative instincts, loved high-tech gadgets, fast cars, and faster planes; and he attracted beautiful women wherever he went.

Doc had a habit of climbing buildings on slender silk ropes twenty-eight years before Spider-Man swung onto the scene. Thirty-four years before *Mission Impossible* appeared on television, Doc worked with a team of specialists. He inhabited a massive chiseled body and was a weapons expert and deadly hand-to-hand fighter thirty-nine years before Rambo. Doc reveled in anthropology, archaeology, and hidden treasures forty-eight years prior to Indiana Jones. He was also deeply versed in symbols, codes, art, and history seventy years before Robert Langdon.

The character was conceived in 1932, gestated for a year, and finally; was born in March 1933, the fictional stepson of three minds: Lester Dent; Dent's editor, John L. Nanovic; and his publisher, Henry William Ralston. At the height of the Depression, Ralston was the business manager of Street & Smith Publications, a successful New York purveyor of dime novels and pulp magazines that had published Jack London, Theodore Dreiser, and Upton Sinclair.

In 1930, Street & Smith released the first issue of *The Shadow* magazine, and despite the nation's economic woes, it became a hit. Ralston believed the single hero magazine format could be repeated and set about trying to invent a new character. He soon devised a leading man loosely based on Colonel Richard Henry Savage, a hero of the Spanish-American war, a soldier, a diplomat, a lawyer, and an author who had, in fact, written for Street and Smith in the previous century.

Ralston thought of Doc Savage as a man raised from birth to right wrong. Over lunch one day, Ralston gave a sketch description of Doc and his assistants to John L. Nanovic, one of Street & Smith's top editors. Nanovic, in turn, talked to Lester Dent about further developing the characters. Over the course of a year, Dent, Nanovic, and Ralston mapped out the vast terrain of Doc's character and skills. Doc was built like Adonis, with dark bronze hair and skin that was tanned and weathered to a lighter bronze, burnished that way by years spent under the tropic sun and in the harsh elements of the Arctic. He was a scientist, surgeon, research chemist, inventor, anthropologist, and linguist. He could drive like a racecar driver, pilot like a dogfighter, run and swim like an Olympian, and brawl like no man on Earth.

Dent wrote *The Man of Bronze* in seven days. But no one in March 1933 cared about the rushed feeling of the story. It was the height of the Depression. People were looking for cost-conscious entertainment, and *The Man of Bronze* more than fit the bill. The first Doc Savage story was a huge success. Once a month, twelve months a year, for the next fourteen years, Dent produced a *Doc Savage Magazine* story of approximately sixty thousand words. That's seven hundred and twenty thousand words a year. I, who take eighteen months to come up with a hundred-and-twenty-thousand-word book, feel in slow motion. Sure, Dent worked in the world of pulp, where money was the primary motive. But I'm convinced that the true source of Dent's superhuman productivity was Doc Savage. No hero without Doc's seemingly limitless abilities and knowledge could have spawned such a library of work from a single person. By the time Dent put his pen down in 1948, he had written 165 of the Doc Savage novels and outlined most of the others.

Dent himself was a big man with an outsized personality, a broad intellect, and a monstrous appetite for adventure and travel, which are also aspects of Doc's personality. But Dent added so much more to his hero, once describing the spectrum of Doc Savage as a melding of the strength of Tarzan, the deductive mind of Sherlock Holmes, the morals of Jesus Christ, and the scientific acumen of Craig Kennedy, the original scientific gizmo sleuth in mystery and suspense literature.

Armed with that formidable character, Dent followed a winning formula. In every story, he put Doc and his men in a new, exotic location, where they battled a cunning new villain in pursuit of a new and amazing treasure. Along the way, Dent created dozens of twists and turns in his plots, which were intricate masterpieces of suspense. In later adventures, Dent gave Doc a secret hideout in the Arctic called the Fortress of Solitude where he conducts experiments. He also gave Doc an oath that he lives by:

> Let me strive every moment of my life to make myself better and better, to the best of my ability, that all may profit by it. Let me think of the right and lend all my assistance to those who need it, with no regard for anything but justice. Let me take what comes with a smile, without loss of courage. Let me be considerate of my country, of my fellow citizens and my associates in everything I say and do. Let me do right to all, and wrong no man.

Okay, it's not as succinct as "Truth, Justice & The American Way," but the oath, the secret hideaway, and a dozen other Doc Savage quirks accompany superhero after superhero that followed him. Within a few years after the character's debut, there was a successful Doc Savage radio show, and comic books as well. Eventually, Dent's stories became a numbered paperback series geared toward men. In 1964, Bantam rereleased *The Man of Bronze* as the first in that series. It featured James Bama's stunning rendition of Doc as the hyperrealistic powerhouse with the torn shirt that I remember from the book cover I admired on that rainy day when I was twelve. All these years later, after finishing the first installment of what I hope will be a series about master thief and government agent Robin Monarch (who saw his own parents murdered, who has a moral code, and attracts beautiful woman), I can't help but feel indebted to Lester Dent, Doc Savage, and *The Man of Bronze*. Together they created a whole new class of character—the superhero—and changed the world of thrillers forever.

Mark T. Sullivan grew up outside Boston. He attended Hamilton College, graduating in 1980 with a B.A. in English. He later attended the Medill School of Journalism at Northwestern University. Before embarking on his writing career, he worked as a journalist at Reuters, States News Service, and the *San Diego Tribune*. His first novel, *The Fall Line*, was published in 1994, followed by *Hard News* one year later. But it was not until 1996, with *The Purification Ceremony*, that his career took off. A finalist for the Edgar Award for best novel, it also won the W.H. Smith Award for best "new talent." His other works include *Ghost Dance*, *Labyrinth*, *The Serpent's Kiss*, and *Triple Cross*. Sullivan lives in southwest Montana with his wife, Betsy, and two teenage sons, Connor and Bridger.

32

James M. Cain's
THE POSTMAN ALWAYS RINGS TWICE (1934)

Joe R. Lansdale

Born in Annapolis, James M. Cain (1892–1977) studied at Washington College, in Chesterton, Maryland, earning his B.A. and master's there. He worked as a journalist, screenwriter, and novelist. His novels are often mentioned in the same breath with those of Dashiell Hammett and Raymond Chandler as a key contributor to the so called hard-boiled school of crime fiction. Cain resisted that label, however, stating that he belonged "to no school, hard-boiled or otherwise." Several of Cain's novels were adapted into films. Three—*The Postman Always Rings Twice* (1934), *Double Indemnity* (1936), and *Mildred Pierce* (1941)—are considered classics of the American screen. Cain's post World War II works include *The Butterfly* (1947), a story of incest and murder set in Kentucky, as well as his personal favorite, a Depression hobo novel, *The Moth* (1948). In 1970, he was named a Grand Master by the Mystery Writers of America.

James M. Cain was the master of hard-boiled prose, lean clean dialogue shiny as a new dime. He wrote like a demon on holiday, sexed up and hung over, and he changed the landscape of literature as surely as Ernest Hemingway or William Faulkner or Raymond Chandler. But as Tom Wolfe wrote: "Nobody has quite pulled if off the way Cain does, not Hemingway, not even Raymond Chandler."

In fact, Chandler thought very little of Cain and then adapted one of his best books into Billy Wilder's noir film *Double Indemnity*. The dialogue is snappier than Cain's, and some of the scenes have a kind of high poetry about them. But Cain's fiction stands quite well on its own and has about it a kind of working man's muscular poetry, soaked in sweat and hormones so ripe you can almost smell it.

The characters themselves are not poetic at all. At first glance, they appear to be everyday people. They want what most people want. A good life. But the cold difference is they're unwilling to work for it. At their core they feel entitled, above and beyond the working person's code. With *The Postman Always Rings Twice*, Cain established this theme at the start of his career, and in most of his novels it's hammered at with the hardworking mentality of a blacksmith shaping a horseshoe. Later, he perhaps shaped too many similar horseshoes, but he pounded out two masterpieces that changed the landscape of crime writing and other forms of writing dramatically. His work inspired so many novels, films, and even comic books, that if they were piled on top of one another they'd reach to the moon and beyond.

Those two masterpieces were *The Postman Always Rings Twice* and *Double Indemnity*. The former is possibly the most famous, if for no other reason than the title is a mystery unexplained by the book. Nowhere inside the story does the line appear, or anything that resembles the title, but the title works. It brings to mind a kind of dead certainty like the arrival of the postman, who, if you don't answer the call on the first ring, you will on the second. And that's exactly what happens in the novel; there's a chance to miss that first ring, to not reach out and take hold of the bad choice, but it's a chance you know will be denied and that these characters will most certainly open the door on the second ring. What's behind the door is not mail delivery, but a fate carved deep into the walls of hell.

"They threw me off the hay truck about noon" is one of the best opening sentences ever written. Simple though it is, it carries a lot of information. The main character, Frank Chambers, telling his story in first person, with that one line has revealed all we need to know about him. He's a loser, constantly cast aside by mainstream society. He's someone on the edge, trying to get a free ride through life. And there's something about him that makes certain people, those in the know, not want to have anything to do with him. They realize he's, well, "wrong." They can sense the shark under the water.

The plot is simple as well. In fact, it's boy meets girl. But the problem is the girl is married to a Greek named Nick Papadakis, an unattractive guy with an accent and a tourist court, a filling station, and a sandwich joint. The woman, Cora, though not classically attractive, has a hot body and a look about her that makes a man want to mash her lips. For Frank Chambers, she's a walking, talking, sex-charged dream; she's everything he's ever wanted, and if the dice roll right, she comes with a sandwich shop.

Cora is the fine, shiny, tasty-looking apple on the outside with the big fat worm in the middle. She's everything a mother fears for her son. She's the hot patootie with her soul on ice. She's just what Frank Chambers has been looking for when he's thrown off that hay truck at noon and comes walking into Cora's and Nick Papadakis's life. As for Cora, Frank is what she's been looking for, a big, handsome lug with all the willpower of a marionette; the only thing she needs to do is fasten the strings.

Written so tightly that it squeaks like new shoes, the story shows Frank and Cora embracing their doom in their sleazy quest for easy money and minor position. Cain dramatizes their destruction step by relentless step, and it's like watching someone walking down a railroad track with a train coming, lacking the will to step off. For Frank, it's suicide by sex drive. For Cora, it's suicide by greed. There's real attraction between the two, but there's no trust. The clock is set, and all we need to do is wait and watch until the alarm goes off.

I've always loved Chandler and Hammett and Hemingway, but over the years, I've come to think that Cain, with this novel and *Double Indemnity*, was the master of the lean mean writing machine, and that although his reputation is high, it might have been higher yet had he written fewer books that were weak specters of this perfect little gem.

Where does mojo storytelling come from? How does one learn to spin yarns in any genre, whether it be horror, suspense, science fiction, or western? First you need to see the world, like Joe R. Lansdale, who has lived most everywhere, if you count a small area of east Texas as everywhere. Second, you need to learn how to take a punch. Or a kick. Then, learn how to avoid them. (Lansdale has long been an ardent student of the martial arts.) The author of dozens of novels (including seven featuring the delightful Hap Collins and Leonard Pine) and several short story collections, Lansdale has been called "an immense talent" by *Booklist*. The *New York Times Book Review* declares that he has "a folklorist's eye for telling detail and a front-porch raconteur's sense of pace." He received numerous awards, among them the Edgar, seven Bram Stoker horror awards, a British Fantasy Award, the American Mystery Award, and two *New York Times* Notable Book citations. His novella "Bubba Hotep" was made into a film by the same name and is considered a cult classic. Lansdale lives in Nacogdoches, Texas, with his wife, Karen.

33

Daphne du Maurier's
REBECCA (1938)

Allison Brennan

Dame Daphne du Maurier (1907–1989) penned one of the most famous first lines in any novel: "Last night I dreamt I went to Manderley again." *Rebecca* remains one of the best-known novels of the twentieth century and the first major Gothic romance, paving the way for modern-day romantic thrillers. Du Maurier wrote fifteen novels and numerous short stories ("Don't Look Now"), many of which were made into film and stage productions, including Alfred Hitchcock's Academy Award winning adaption of *Rebecca* in 1940, starring Laurence Olivier and Joan Fontaine. Hitchcock also directed film adaptations of du Maurier's *Jamaica Inn* and her short story, "The Birds."

I have a confession. I first read *Rebecca* in 2005, shortly after I sold my first novel. For years, friends talked about the book, and I nodded and contributed where I could, and over time I came to know the story so well it was as if I'd read it.

When I sat down one Sunday afternoon to finally read cover to cover a copy I'd purchased years before, I couldn't put it down. I was transfixed not only in another time and place—Cornwall, England, in 1938 and the grand estate of Manderley—but thrilled with the realization that Daphne du Maurier had created the genre I love and write: romantic suspense.

Romantic suspense novels are unique to thrillers in two primary ways: first, there are usually two protagonists, a hero and a heroine, who are equally important to the story. Second, there is a happily ever after as in a traditional romance. In all other ways, they follow the traditional thriller format: high stakes, something personal at risk, and strong pacing.

In *Rebecca*, Daphne du Maurier created a world that is as relevant today as it was more than seventy years ago. The timeless quality of the story causes us to reflect on the nature of love, betrayal, and loyalty, and could happen today just as easily as 1938. A young, innocent, naïve hero-

ine—who is known only as "the second Mrs. de Winter"—falls in love
with an older, experienced widower. The heroine, a first-person narrator
who is given no name by the author, is now part of a world she's never
known. She's taken to the estate of Manderley. She has wealth and position through her marriage to Maxim de Winter, but she's still timid and insecure. How can this kind, older, wealthy man truly love her? In many
ways, *Rebecca* is a Gothic version of *Cinderella*.

Had the story been merely about the second Mrs. de Winter over-
coming her insecurity—which she does—the reading public wouldn't have
been enthralled for more than seven decades. What *Rebecca* did was take
a rather common romance premise—young poor woman falls in love with
older rich man—and turn it completely around. Immediately, you're drawn
into the story because it starts at the end: *Last night I dreamt I went to Manderley again.* Chapter one ends: *For Manderley was ours no longer. Manderley was no more.*

Who doesn't want to know what happened to Manderley?

When the young second Mrs. de Winter moves into her new home
with her new husband, she sees Rebecca—the first Mrs. de Winter—everywhere. In the décor, the paintings, and of course, the antagonist: the cold,
evil Mrs. Danvers. Mrs. Danvers loves Rebecca—is in fact rather obsessed
with her—and in every way possible manipulates, degrades, and tries to
destroy our young heroine.

The second Mrs. de Winter is much stronger than she thinks. Although she walks into Manderley the first time timid and insecure in her
relationship with Maxim—believing he still loves his dead wife—she grows
into a woman all of us can be proud of. She learns to stand up for herself,
to accept that she has value, and that she is worthy of being loved. The
heroine becomes the strength of the relationship, as Maxim's guilt and
pain make him turn to her for solace and support.

Yet it's precisely as the heroine begins to grow and mature that the
story kicks into high gear. In the beginning, the atmosphere and the psychological suspense provide the page-turning thrills—the sense of foreboding is on every page. When Rebecca's body is found, all bets are off as
secrets become threats, and not only is the future happiness of the hero
and heroine at stake, but their lives as well.

Over and above the story itself, the novel's structure and style play a
huge part in its success. Starting at the end to hook the reader, showing the
future strength of the heroine so the reader is already engaged and curious

about how she became such a woman, and, of course, what happened to Manderley; never naming the heroine, to further show her sense of worthlessness both to herself and to others; and using a deceptively simple storyline that, only as it goes on, allows the reader to appreciate the complexities of both character and plot.

Many analysts have suggested that du Maurier created the relationship between Rebecca, Maxim, and the heroine to parallel her own marriage with Sir Frederick Browning, who had been engaged to a beautiful and vibrant woman before breaking it off and marrying Daphne. Others have suggested that the relationship between Maxim, Mrs. Danvers, and the heroine was Daphne's view of her relationship with her parents. But all good authors draw upon their own pain and happiness, twist it around, and shake it up to tell a unique story. This authenticity creates characters that seem so real they could walk off the page.

Daphne du Maurier herself was surprised at her novel's popularity, saying it was "simply a study of jealousy." It's often the case that an author doesn't see the depth in their stories. Even critics don't understand a novel's enduring qualities, such as V.S. Prichett who wrote in the *Christian Science Monitor* in 1938: "I have no doubt that anyone who starts this book will not be able to put it down until he has finished it; after that, I hope that he will wake up and laugh at himself . . . It would be absurd to make a fuss about *Rebecca*, which will be here today and gone tomorrow like the rest of publicity's 'masterpieces.'"

The point of a good thriller is precisely that readers can't put down the book until they are finished. In that, Daphne du Maurier was a truly brilliant storyteller, and there is nothing "simple" about her work.

I leave you with these words that Daphne du Maurier wrote near the end of her life:

> I walked this land [Cornwall] with a dreamer's freedom and
> with a waking man's perception—places, houses whispered to
> me their secrets and shared with me their sorrows and their joys.
> And in return I gave them something of myself, a few of my
> novels passing into the folk-lore of this ancient place.

New York Times and *USA Today* best-selling and award-winning author Allison Brennan writes romantic suspense and supernatural thrillers. A four-time RITA nominee for best romantic suspense, her novel *Fear No Evil* won the Daphne du

Maurier award in 2007 for Best Mainstream Mystery/Suspense. Allison's recent romantic thrillers include her FBI trilogy—*Sudden Death*, *Fatal Secrets*, and *Cutting Edge*. In 2010, she launched her "Seven Deadly Sins" supernatural thriller series. A former legislative consultant, Allison lives in Northern California with her husband and their five children.

34
Agatha Christie's
AND THEN THERE WERE NONE (1939)
David Morrell

Agatha Christie (1890–1976) was born Agatha Miller in Torquay, England. In 1912, she met Archie Christie; they married in 1914. When Archie left her in 1926, Christie disappeared for eleven days. Exactly what happened during that time remains a mystery. Christie later met and married archaeologist Max Mallowan in 1930. They remained together for forty-six years. According to her official Web site, Christie "is the best-selling author of all time. She has sold over two billion books worldwide and has been translated into over forty-five languages." She also wrote over a dozen plays, including *The Mousetrap*, the longest running play in theatrical history. Christie published her first novel, *The Mysterious Affair at Styles*, in 1920. That book featured the debut of her famous character, eccentric Belgian detective Hercule Poirot. Another notable creation was Miss Jane Marple, who bowed in a short story in 1927 and appeared three years later in *The Murder at the Vicarage*. Her most controversial novel is *The Murder of Roger Ackroyd* (1926) in which the murderer turned out to be the first-person narrator.

Agatha Christie's *And Then There Were None* is a brilliant example of how a mystery can also be a thriller. Ten strangers are invited to an estate on a remote island. Trapped there, each is murdered in a way that mirrors a line from a children's ditty about ten little indians. "One went to sleep, and then there were seven. . . . One broke his neck, and then there were six." As the bodies accumulate, the survivors become convinced that one of them is the killer. Eventually, though, all ten people are found dead, and searchers fail to discover anyone hiding on the island. A police inspector reviews the evidence and can't figure out who the killer is. Finally, the murderer (one of the ten) solves the mystery by leaving a note in which he explains that a terminal disease motivated him to select nine people whom he felt had committed an unforgiveable crime and who had escaped punishment. In his final days, he resolved to see that justice was served. An apparent early victim, he pretended to be dead and then was at liberty to kill the others, one by one, while they focused their suspicions on their companions. When his goal was achieved, he committed suicide, appearing to be one of the victims.

Summarized this bluntly, the plot feels strained, but in actuality it's a tour de force of invention, executed so efficiently that the reader doesn't have a chance to question details. The pace and the tension, not to mention the atmosphere of fear and violence, are the elements that make this mystery a thriller—as opposed to mysteries that emphasize the reader's intellectual satisfaction in assessing clues and trying to solve a puzzle before the fictional detective does. If a mystery focuses solely on the cerebral aspects of a criminal investigation, it lacks the sensational aspects of a thriller.

To make the point, it's worth taking a brief look at the way mysteries evolved. As Max Allan Collins notes in *The History of the Mystery*, the first detective book was published in 1828—the nonfictional *Mémoires* of François Eugène Vidocq, a former criminal who was chief of the first police detective bureau, France's *Le Sûreté Nationale*. Edgar Allan Poe read Vidocq's memoirs and was inspired to invent the first detective story, "The Murders in the Rue Morgue" (1841). He even mentioned Vidocq in the story and gave his main character, the first fictional detective, a French name: C. Auguste Dupin. Although the story emphasizes clues and detection, it also has a Gothic tone, not to mention two gruesome murders (a woman is stuffed up a chimney, another is beheaded) and a sensational revelation—the murderer is an orangutan. Thus it's both a mystery and a thriller.

In 1842, one year after Poe's story was published, the first English detective bureau was established in London, in an area called Scotland Yard near Trafalgar Square. Charles Dickens was fascinated by these detectives, especially their almost uncanny powers of observation and their knowledge of the secret parts of London. He spent a great deal of time with them and created the first fictional English detective, Inspector Bucket, in *Bleak House* (1853), which isn't a thriller but has an amazing extended thriller sequence, a long climactic pursuit through London.

It's generally acknowledged that the next memorable English police detective is Sergeant Cuff in Wilkie Collins's *The Moonstone* (1868), even though other detective stories were published in the meantime. But what hasn't been emphasized until recently is how a gruesome 1860 murder in an English country house influenced Collins's novel and the mystery genre in an incalculable way. That murder and its long-lasting significance are analyzed in Kate Summerscale's *The Suspicions of Mr. Whicher: A Shocking Murder and the Undoing of a Great Victorian Detective* (2008).

Twelve people lived in remote Road Hill House: Mr. and Mrs. Kent, their seven children, a nursemaid, a housemaid, and a cook. In addition, six servants came to work there each day. When the household wakened on Friday, June 29, 1860, they discovered that one of the children, a three-year-old boy, was missing. After a long, frantic search, the boy was discovered dead, crammed down a privy into excrement, his head nearly cut off. When the local police couldn't identify the killer, renowned Detective-Inspector Jonathan Whicher was dispatched from Scotland Yard to investigate the seventeen suspects and solve the crime.

The lurid nature of the murder and the public's fascination with police detectives attracted the attention of newspapers throughout England. Every step of the investigation was chronicled. After painstaking analysis, Whicher accused one of the remaining children, a conclusion that was so distasteful to the public that Whicher was discredited, his career destroyed. Years later, the child confessed (the motive was jealousy), too late to benefit Whicher.

Summerscale points out one other factor that made Whicher's investigation disturbing. The Victorians had an obsession about the privacy of the home. The idea of a stranger poking around in the laundry room and the kitchen—and the privy—made most people shudder. Moreover, the detective was a member of the working class whereas the husband and wife who lived in Road Hill House held a station above him, another reason to be horrified by his intrusion.

A remote house, a ghastly murder, numerous suspects, the arrival of a master detective. This combination became a template for countless fictional mysteries since 1860. *And Then There Were None* represents a variation of it, but Agatha Christie was hardly alone in using it. At the start, these elements were so fresh and disturbing that many early mysteries were indeed thrillers. In time, however, the memory of what happened at Road Hill House faded. During the 1860s and '70s, the very idea of a police inspector poking into someone's life was shocking, but as the years passed, fictional detectives became more like the intellectual puzzle solver that Poe had created years earlier in "The Murders in the Rue Morgue."

This figure was, of course, fully realized in Sir Arthur Conan Doyle's Sherlock Holmes, who first appeared in 1887's A *Study in Scarlet*. Doyle generously acknowledged his debt to Poe and gave Holmes even more Gothic qualities than Dupin has (in one paragraph, Dupin sounds like a vampire). As Laura Benedict notes in her essay about Doyle's *The Hound of the Baskervilles*, Holmes with his moodiness, violin, and heroin addiction sometimes seems close to being deranged.

In the United States, another real-life detective, Allan Pinkerton, provided the inspiration for the hard-boiled private detective, whose zenith appears in the works of Dashiell Hammett, Raymond Chandler, Mickey Spillane, and Ross Macdonald (although Macdonald's Lew Archer is more medium-boiled than hard). Spillane dramatized plenty of action, but novels by the other authors (Hammett's *The Maltese Falcon*, for example) tend to follow the traditional structure of a crime that requires the detective to conduct a series of interviews, collect clues, and solve the puzzle. There are occasional moments of sensation, but not enough to call them thrillers as well as mysteries. The exception is Hammett's *Red Harvest* (1929) which has a jaw-dropping body count.

When comparing mysteries and thrillers, it's useful to bear in mind that Wilkie Collins, whose *The Moonstone* was the first significant detective novel, also is credited with inventing "the novel of sensation." That element—brilliantly demonstrated in Agatha Christie's *And Then There Were None*—is what makes this mystery an utterly engaging thriller.

David Morrell created the character of Rambo in his award-winning 1972 novel, *First Blood*. A former professor of American literature, he is the author of numerous *New York Times* best sellers, including the classic *Brotherhood of the Rose* spy trilogy. In 2009, International Thriller Writers honored him with its Thriller-Master award.

35
Eric Ambler's
A COFFIN FOR DIMITRIOS
(UK TITLE: THE MASK OF DIMITRIOS) (1939)

Ali Karim

Eric Ambler (1909–1998) was born and raised in London but traveled extensively in his later years, residing in mainland Europe and America. He is regarded as one of the greatest thriller writers, with many of his novels adapted for film, including *The Mask of Dimitrios*, *Journey into Fear*, and *The Light of Day*, the title of which was changed to *Topkapi*. Ambler worked in the film industry, living in Los Angeles for a period. Most of his fiction was set in the boundary where politics and espionage meet. His protagonists were rarely professional spies. Instead they were usually amateurs out of their depth who overcame the professionals who had trapped them. Ambler's education and early employment involved engineering; however his family were music hall entertainers, so it was natural that in later life he became a professional storyteller. During World War II, he was an army photographer and filmmaker with the rank of Lieutenant Colonel. He won several literary awards including the Mystery Writers of America's Edgar and the Crime Writers Association's Gold and Diamond Dagger. Married twice, he died in 1998 in Switzerland.

It was over twenty-five years ago when I first read Eric Ambler's *A Coffin for Dimitrios*, so it was a delight to rediscover this epic, unusual, and highly influential work. How fresh and relevant it is today. Focusing on the dark side of human nature, it makes us realize that the problems faced in the Balkans have always been around, rooted in politics and money. Although the novel has little action until the end, it uses dark imagery to increase tension that makes the reader shiver. Ambler's 1930's Europe is a volatile and dangerous place. The storm clouds of war loom on the horizon.

The plot at first appears simple. We have Charles Latimer, a former academic turned detective novelist on holiday in pre-World War II Turkey. Latimer meets Colonel Haki, a Turkish police official (and fan of detective fiction) who wants the Englishman to base his next book on a plot that Haki has invented. Latimer tries to decline gracefully, but when Haki tells him about the discovery of the body of underworld enforcer, master criminal, and spy, the Greek Dimitrios Makropolous, Latimer's curiosity is piqued.

Perhaps the inspiration for the mythical Keyzer Soze in the 1995 film *The Usual Suspects*, Dimitirios was an international gangster, murderer, pimp/woman trafficker, spy, and assassin who hid behind different names and identities, operating for a shadowy banking group, Eurasian Credit Trust, and carrying out dark deeds when required by his paymasters. Latimer is drawn to learn about the drowned man who lies on Colonel Haki's morgue slab, and decides to trace Dimitrios's life. The journey will change Latimer as the trail snakes from the East to Paris and also through the criminal deeds that defined Dimitrios. But can Latimer trust the recollections of Dimitrios's enemies? And how will Latimer's liberal value system be challenged when he unearths the truth and extent of the evil lurking in Dimitrios's soul?

Latimer begins his search by reading a copy of Dimitrios's criminal record, which opens with the murder of a moneylender named Sholem. Together with an accomplice, Dimitrios slit Sholem's throat and stole his money. While the slippery Dimitrios fled, the less quick-witted accomplice was caught and hung by the authorities. Colonel Haki describes Dimitrios as "A dirty type, common, cowardly scum." Latimer, however, sees that as Dimitrios's criminal career progressed, he became far more sophisticated, and perhaps a man representative of his amoral times. Latimer comes to believe that greed has created a "new theology. Dimitrios was not evil. He was logical and consistent; as logical and consistent in the European jungle as the poison gas called Lewsite and the shattered bodies of children killed in the bombardment of an open town."

So Latimer—like Marlow searching for Kutrz in Joseph Conrad's *Heart of Darkness*—sets out to learn who and what Dimitrios was. This is a classic quest motif, in which Ambler makes the figure of Dimitrios even more sinister by keeping the ultimate truth about him concealed until the very end, using letters, rap sheets, and the recollections of others to build up his notoriety. Latimer's journey twists and turns from Turkey to Athens, Sofia, Geneva, and ends in Paris, providing a dark profile of much of prewar Europe. In a chilling interlude, Latimer meets the former spymaster Grodek, who has retired to Switzerland. Via a series of letters, we learn how Dimitrios and Grodek entrapped a greedy low-level government clerk named Bulic. In a casino sting operation, Dimitrios and Grodek obtained secret government maps for their paymasters, the Fascist Italian Government. Then Latimer discovers that Dimitrios was behind a Balkan political assassination, that in Paris he ran a heroin smuggling operation and a prostitution ring involving kidnapped Asian women, that his crimes stretched far and wide across the continent—and beyond—until the authorities got too close to him and he faked his own death.

At the end of Latimer's search, he helps to flush Dimitrios from behind his mask/coffin. In a tense climax, Latimer comes face to face with his quarry and concludes that Dimitrios is really the personification of the crisis that the world was facing (and still is) because he acted as an instrument for the dark side of big business by carrying out the dirty deeds that his paymasters at the shadowy bank, the Eurasian Credit Trust, could not. Alfred Hitchcock wrote in an introduction to a 1943 omnibus edition of Ambler's novels, "[Ambler's villains] are not only real people, they are actually the kind of people who have generated violence and evil in the Europe of our time." And Dimitrios is just that, a psychopath whose need to accumulate wealth convinces him that morality and conscience mean nothing.

A pivotal novel in the thriller genre, A Coffin for Dimitrios influenced scores of writers and filmmakers. A version of Dimitrios shows up as Harry Lime in Graham Greene's screenplay for The Third Man (1949). Robert Ludlum's Carlos the Jackal in The Bourne Identity (1980) has overtones of Dimitrios. Many later writers, such as Robert Harris, John le Carré, Len Deighton, Alistair MacLean, and Alan Furst explored and extended Ambler's themes. The novel blends politics, espionage, banking, and the underworld to show how all of these factors influence society and the dark side of the human condition.

Ali Karim is Assistant Editor at Shots eZine, a contributing editor at January Magazine & The Rap Sheet, and writes for Crimespree magazine, Deadly Pleasures, and Mystery Readers International. He is an associate member of both the Crime Writers Association and the International Thriller Writers organization. Karim contributed to Dissecting Hannibal Lecter (edited by Benjamin Szumskyj), a critical examination of the works of Thomas Harris, as well as The Greenwood Encyclopedia of British Crime Fiction (edited by Barry Forshaw). Karim blogs about existential thrillers at www.existentialistman.blogspot.com

36
Geoffrey Household's
ROGUE MALE (1939)
David Morrell

An Oxford graduate with a degree in English literature, Geoffrey House-hold (1900–1988) rebelled from what seemed an inevitable career as an international banker and instead led an adventurous life that took him from England to Romania, Spain, Latin America, the United States, and the Middle East, where he worked for British military intelligence during World War II. As he remarked in his autobiography *Against the Wind*, he couldn't recall an occasion when, if asked to go somewhere, he did not accept. A prolific author of thrillers that draw on his global experiences, Household is at his best in *Rogue Male* (filmed by Fritz Lang as *Man Hunt*), *Watcher in the Shadows*, *The Courtesy of Death*, and *Dance of the Dwarfs*, as well as the frequently anthologized short story, "Taboo." In his obituary, the *New York Times* praised him for developing suspense into an art form.

Few authors influenced me more than Geoffrey Household. In the summer of 1968, while studying American literature at Penn State, I wrote a hunter-hunted short story that would soon morph into *First Blood*, and when I showed it to my writing instructor, he said the outdoor scenes reminded him somewhat of Geoffrey Household's work. Not knowing anything about Household (graduate school sheltered me from popular fiction), I borrowed *Rogue Male* from the library, finished it in one night, and eagerly set out to read everything else Household had written. Until then, my attempts at thrillers had felt scholarly and academic, but the visceral elements of *Rogue Male* woke me up to the power that could be achieved in the high-action genre.

The pace of *Rogue Male* is stunning, as is its premise, which made Household famous among thriller writers. With war looming in the late 1930s, a British big-game hunter makes his way across Europe, stalking an unnamed dictator, who is almost certainly Hitler. The hunter (who is also not named) establishes a sniper's position on a ridge above the dictator's country estate. He focuses his telescopic sight on his quarry, pauses to correct his aim, and at that moment is discovered by the dictator's security team. They torture him in an effort to learn if he works for the British government. When they finally decide that he acted on his own, they throw him off a cliff, hoping to make his death look like an accident while at the same time accounting for the serious damage that their torture inflicted on his body. But he survives, landing in mud that cushions his fall and prevents him from bleeding to death.

All of these incidents occur in the first four pages. *Four pages*. Astonishing. I can't think of another novel that establishes so much story so quickly. The rest of the book moves with equal relentlessness as the main character musters all his wits to hide, regain his strength, and get out of the country. His interrogators hunt him to prevent him from making another assassination attempt. The chase narrows from Europe to England to a couple of miles of farmland and finally to within a dozen feet of where the main character lives like an animal, digging a burrow between two hedgerows, remaining underground for days at a time.

Few novels have a more claustrophobic atmosphere. The mud at the start and the burrow at the end are paralleled by an empty water tank in which the main character is compelled to spend a night. He survives a lethal fight in a dark subway tunnel. Chased, he squirms into clay amid soaked cabbages on a field drenched by rain. He hides in night-shrouded ditches. While these constricted settings add to *Rogue Male*'s tension, they also reinforce one of the elements that make the book distinctive—the vividness with which the protagonist merges with his surroundings, particularly fields, woods, and streams, as if Household felt a kinship with the transcendentalism of Wordsworth's nature poetry.

But this is a version of Wordsworth channeled disturbingly through Robert Louis Stevenson's *Robinson Crusoe*, Joseph Conrad's *Heart of Darkness*, and John Buchan's *The Thirty-Nine Steps*, antecedents that Household acknowledged. In the end, the big-game hunter is so absorbed into nature that he descends to the level of one of the animals he used to hunt, a theme suggested by the book's title and by an epigraph that discusses the fear and cunning of a rogue animal who relies on ferocity after pain or loss separates it from its fellows.

In *Rogue Male*'s most harrowing moment, the protagonist's hunters try to force him to sign a propaganda document that falsely links the British government to his assassination attempt. They close the narrow hole through which air comes into his burrow. He nearly suffocates amid the stench of his excrement until he manages the strength to pull toward him the object with which they stuffed the air hole. The object turns out to be the rotting corpse of a polecat that he befriended, one rogue recognizing another. This drives the hero to such a frenzy that he uses a knife to cut the polecat apart. He attaches strips of the animal's gut to a primitive catapult, with which he fires a metal stake through the hole at one of his captors. "I noticed the surprise in his eyes, but by that time I think he was dead. The spit took him square above the nose. He looked, when he vanished, as if someone had screwed a ring into his forehead."

The detachment of those sentences illustrates something else that makes *Rogue Male* distinctive. The main character writes the bulk of his narrative during the fearful days he spends hiding underground. He tells his story partly to set the record straight in case he is killed and his diary survives, but the main purpose is to objectify his ordeal and preserve his sanity. The horror of what happened to him is presented in an unemotional, understated way, to the point that the contrast between his words and what they cloak can be shocking. The tension behind each subdued sentence dramatizes the narrator's fiercely repressed pain and mental anguish. "By that time I had, of course, been knocked about very considerably. My nails are growing back but my left eye is still pretty useless."

I eventually learned how much Household believed in his nongraphic approach to depicting violence. After I finished writing *First Blood*, my admiration for his work prompted me to send him a copy of the manuscript in the hope that my outdoor action scenes would motivate him to recognize a kinship and supply a publicity quote. It didn't take long for him to reply. The author of a novel in which a rotting polecat is skinned, its guts used to build a catapult to drive a stake through someone's forehead told me that he couldn't possibly give me a quote. "Your novel is far too bloody."

David Morrell is the author of *First Blood*, the award-winning novel in which Rambo was created. He holds a Ph.D. in American literature from the Pennsylvania State University and taught in the English department at the University of Iowa until he gave up his tenure to write full time. "The mild-mannered professor with the bloody-minded visions," as one reviewer described him, Morrell is the cofounder (with Gayle Lynds) of the International Thriller Writers organization. His numerous best-sellers include *The Brotherhood of the Rose* (the basis for a top-rated NBC miniseries), *The Fraternity of the Stone*, *The League of Night and Fog*, *Creepers*, and *Extreme Denial* (set in Santa Fe, New Mexico, where he lives). He is also the author of *The Successful Novelist: A Lifetime of Lessons about Writing and Publishing*.

37

Helen MacInnes's
ABOVE SUSPICION (1941)

Gayle Lynds

Helen MacInnes (1907–1985) was known around the globe as the Queen of International Suspense, writing twenty-one spy novels over a remarkable forty-five-year career. A new MacInnes book was an event, eagerly awaited and loudly heralded. Of course, it would be a *New York Times* number one bestseller. Of course, it would be on the list for months. In her day, no other female author in the field achieved her popularity. She stood alone at the top of the literary espionage mountain, gazing down on the likes of le Carré, Fleming, and Ludlum—until their sales and reputations finally caught up with hers. MacInnes was born in Glasgow, Scotland, and in 1932 married the love of her life, Oxford classicist Gilbert Highet. They moved to New York in 1937 and became U.S. citizens in 1951. Four of her books were made into movies: *Above Suspicion* (published 1939, Britain; 1941, USA), *Assignment in Brittany* (1942), *The Venetian Affair* (1963), and *The Salzburg Connection* (1968). She was awarded the Columba Prize for Literature in 1966.

Seldom does a novelist have a career as long and distinguished as Helen MacInnes's. All of her books—from her first, *Above Suspicion* (1939, 1941), to her last, *Ride a Pale Horse* (1984)—hold up well to critical scrutiny and to the modern reader's demand for a compelling tale. In the course of those forty-five years, MacInnes consistently excelled in several ways. She was a writer of great imagination yet firmly rooted in factual research. She reveled in politics and could explain the intricacies of global events in crisp dialogue. She had an acute sense of place, bringing foreign settings vibrantly to life. She knew how to string out suspense until not only her protagonists but also the reader broke into a sweat. She could make a sentence sing, a description ooze texture and scent, and a reader cry or laugh.

Her first novel, *Above Suspicion*, was not only extraordinarily good, it changed the future of the spy genre. Here is the background: MacInnes earned an M.A. in French and German from the University of Glasgow in 1928, then a Diploma in Librarianship in 1931 from University College in London. She was a linguist and a librarian, working on translations with her husband, Oxford don Gilbert Highet. They traveled often to the Continent, where their ability with languages and their many return trips gave them intimate knowledge that he, and later she, used in their books.

All of this came into play in 1937 when Highet joined the faculty at Columbia University and they moved to New York. There he read his wife's journal in which she reflected on Nazi Germany's violent activities and expansion. Because of her clear analyses, interesting ideas, common sense, and accurate forecasts, he encouraged her to write a novel. At the same time, it is also possible that by then he had been approached by British intelligence. We know only that he worked for them during and after World War II. "A peaceful country needs a good intelligence service," MacInnes said in an interview years later. "Freedom will not survive unless we know the nature of the attack on it. That is what my books are all about."

Above Suspicion was a surprising sales and critical success. Set in 1939 white-knuckle Europe, it chronicles a young English couple—Oxford professor Richard Myles and his wife, Frances—who are asked to turn their summer vacation into a secret undercover mission to find out whether a British spy working covertly in Germany is still alive. They have been chosen because they are "above suspicion." Of course, they also sound very much like the real-life professor and Mrs. Highet.

Such a simple story idea, but in such simplicity lies genius — and risk. Frances and Richard leave for Paris, Nürnberg, Munich, Innsbruck, Pertisau, Innsbruck again, and finally Verona. In another's hands, this could be a trite travelogue. Instead we have brainy and resourceful protagonists (no perils of the hapless Pauline here) who deal with secret codes, dead drops, safe houses, disguises, searched suitcases and hotel rooms, narrow escapes, and betrayal. Complexity is added by several subsidiary characters who enter and leave naturally, each bringing suspense and information to the plot.

MacInnes tells the story almost entirely from the viewpoints of the two protagonists, slipping smoothly between them, sometimes paragraph to paragraph. The skill of this technique for a first novelist is impressive. In the opening third of the book, we see quick vignettes of unnamed, dangerous professionals who are uncannily smart and adept at surveilling our hero and heroine. It gives us chills, waiting—waiting—waiting for the Nazis to close in.

Occasionally over her career, MacInnes was criticized for writing "types," not characters. Sometimes that was true, but often she was already using a more daring and today more contemporary means of characterizing—allowing the characters to show who they are through their thoughts, words, and deeds, rather than writing long paragraphs of personal history.

While the private detective novel is an American invention, originally a novel of the proletariat, the spy novel arises primarily from Britain's literary soil, and MacInnes, who was British by birth and American by choice, took the understatement, occasional stuffiness, and velvet-cloth-over-cold-steel conventions of the long-beloved British conception, giving it an American robustness and a global viewpoint.

An example is Henry van Cortlandt, an outspoken American newspaperman, who bluntly questions Frances about whether the Brits, who had been appeasing Hitler, would ever stand up to the Nazi juggernaut: "And you're telling me Britain is going to take off its nice clean coat and get its nose all bloodied up defending Poland?"

"A country fights for two main things, either for loot or for survival," Frances explains. "If Poland, or any other country, is attacked, then it is the signal for any other nation who doesn't want to become part of Germany to rouse itself. It may be the last chance."

A citizen of the world, Helen MacInnes wrote like one, displaying a keen and nuanced understanding of history, politics, culture, and geography, all in service to her taut and exciting adventure tales. The result is that *Above Suspicion* enlarged and refined the international espionage novel, forever changing it and becoming a template for those to come.

New York Times best seller Gayle Lynds is the award-winning author of eight international espionage novels, including *The Last Spymaster*, *The Coil*, *Masquerade*, *Mesmerized*, and *Mosaic*. Her books have won such awards as Novel of the Year (*The Last Spymaster*) given by the Military Writers Society of America, and the 2006 American Author Medal given by the American Authors Association. They have also been hailed by *People* magazine as "Page-Turner of the Week" and "Beach Read of the Week." *Publishers Weekly* lists *Masquerade* along with books by John le Carré, Frederick Forsyth, Robert Ludlum, and Helen MacInnes as one of the top ten spy novels of all time. With Ludlum, she created the Covert-One series and wrote three of the novels, including *The Hades Factor*, which became a CBS miniseries. A member of the Association for Intelligence Officers, she is co-founder (with David Morrell) of the International Thriller Writers organization, and is listed in *Who's Who in the World*. Born in Nebraska, raised in Iowa, she lives in Southern California.

38

Cornell Woolrich's
"REAR WINDOW" (1942)

Thomas F. Monteleone

Cornell Woolrich (1903–1968) was as odd and tortured as many of his characters. The product of a broken marriage, he was raised by his mother in New York City. He attended Columbia University, but never graduated. His first novel, *Cover Charge* (1926), was a contemporary homage to F. Scott Fitzgerald, as were several to follow, but they didn't reveal his true talent—the ability to capture the angry desperation of the doomed. He is well known for his famous line: "First you dream, and then you die." In the 1930s, he began writing darker tales of crime and suspense, which found an appreciative market in pulp magazines. As he continued to write short stories and novels under his own name, he also created two successful pseudonyms: George Hopley and William Irish. Woolrich is a founding father of noir fiction, although he also wrote many stories in the *Weird Tales* mode that were beautifully strange and hinted at the supernatural. He published several collections of his short stories and twenty-five novels, one of the most viscerally compelling of which is *Rendezvous in Black*. Thirty-six films were based on his work, including *Phantom Lady*, *Night Has a Thousand Eyes*, and François Truffaut's *Mississippi Mermaid* (adapted from *Waltz into Darkness*). Despite such apparent success, he spent most of his life staying in cheap hotels with his mother and drinking himself into oblivion. It's fitting that so many of his titles have "black," "night," or "darkness" in them. By the time he died just before the age of sixty-five, he was a shattered ghost of his prior self.

Because of the famous 1954 film by Alfred Hitchcock, "Rear Window" is the most well-known and widely recognized work by Cornell Woolrich. Given the memorable performance by James Stewart, this shouldn't be surprising, but the short story has also been honored in its original form with its inclusion in *The Mystery Hall of Fame*, edited by Bill Pronzini, Martin H. Greenberg, and Charles G. Waugh, based on a poll of the Mystery Writers of America selecting the greatest mystery, crime, and suspense tales of all time. The story first appeared in the February 1942 *Dime Detective* magazine under the title "It Had to Be Murder," but when Woolrich included the tale in his 1944 collection, *After Dinner Story*, he changed the name to "Rear Window."

The plot is deceptively simple. The protagonist, Hal Jeffries, is confined to his apartment because of a broken leg and passes the time by observing the lives of his neighbors across the courtyard of his New York building. He watches them through their open windows and begins to suspect one neighbor, a man with the ominous sounding name of Thorwald, of murdering his wife. Woolrich cleverly ratchets up the suspense and tension by building his case against Thorwald through a series of voyeuristic scenes described in great detail. Each account of the target's actions, taken separately, appears mundane and unremarkable but, when examined sequentially and layered with the nuances of close observation, coalesces into a damning portrait of guilt.

This technique demonstrates one of Woolrich's enduring talents as a writer. He was able to describe overly familiar scenes and clichéd dramatic situations with fresh, often poetic feeling.

> There was a woman living there with her child, a young widow I suppose. I'd see her put the child to bed, and then bend over and kiss her in a wistful sort of way. She'd . . . sit there painting her eyes and mouth. Then she'd go out. She'd never come back till the night was nearly spent. Once I was still up, and I looked and she was sitting there motionless with her head buried in her arms.

Woolrich's attention to details—often oddly dark and inappropriate additions to a scene or a setting—became a powerful narrative tool in his hands. A gradual compilation of elements and objects and actions that somehow did not "add up" allowed Woolrich to create a sense of something terribly awry, or worse, with abject dread as the consequence.

The story also exemplifies a recurring plot device in Woolrich's fiction—the difficult determination of innocence or guilt in many of his characters. Some of the more successful ones include "You'll Never See Me Again," and "If the Shoe Fits." Woolrich creates doubt almost effortlessly because even the nominative heroes of his tales have their own flaws and personal demons laid bare to the reader.

What makes "Rear Window" compelling, and ultimately thrilling, is not only the growing sense of culpability in the suspect, but the equally disturbing obsession that surges in Jeffries. He becomes utterly convinced that his neighbor is a murderer and uses his belief to justify acts (such as persuading his assistant to break into the suspect's apartment) that are not only illegal, but possibly dangerous. As the story ramps up to its powerful climax, the reader becomes as fearful and suspicious of Jeffries as Thorwald, the obvious villain in the piece.

With this in mind, it is not surprising that Hal Jeffries comes across as less than likeable, less than honorable, and certainly not an acceptably satisfying hero that was typical of the age in which the story appeared. Woolrich delighted in dealing with characters like Jeffries because of the added ambiguity and doubt they injected into his fiction.

In the typical noir tale, the protagonist is plagued by powerful, most likely sinister, forces. Often he feels overwhelmed, not only by the palpable sense of danger, but also by the realization that he may lack the ability to *understand* the forces which threaten, much less control them.

"Rear Window" is a brilliant inversion of that basic noir paradigm. Hal Jeffries, the protagonist, through his latent voyeurism and ever-increasing obsession, creates his *own* world of menace, then enters blindly into a labyrinth of deception and suspicion that could ultimately destroy him. Although he ends up solving a crime, the reader is left in the annoying position of having to cheer for a protagonist who may not be all that admirable. Perhaps, suggests Woolrich, Jeffries is a little too real, a little too much like ourselves.

Thomas F. Monteleone has been as equally prolific as Woolrich, but a lot happier. He sold his first short story to a science fiction magazine in 1972, and since then has published more than a hundred others, as well as twenty-eight novels and four collections. He has also edited seven anthologies and is a four-time winner of the Bram Stoker Award in four different categories—novel, collection, anthology, and nonfiction. He is the author of the *New York Times* best seller and Notable Book of the Year, *The Blood of the Lamb*, and the immensely popular *The Complete Idiot's Guide to Writing a Novel*. His work has been translated into fourteen languages. He lives in Baltimore with his wife, Elizabeth, and daughter, Olivia, and likes it a lot.

39
Vera Caspary's
LAURA (1943)

M. J. Rose

Vera Louise Caspary (1899–1987) became one of the most prominent female authors and playwrights of her generation, writing more than twenty-one novels. Several of her books were turned into movies, including *Bedelia*. Caspary also wrote plays and movies. Fritz Lang's *The Blue Gardenia* and Joseph L. Mankiewicz's *A Letter to Three Wives* were both based on her screen stories. The *Washington Post* called Caspary's life "a Baedeker of the twentieth century. An independent woman in an unliberated era, she collided with or was touched by many of its major historical and cultural events: wars, the Depression, the Spanish Civil War, Hollywood in its romantic heyday, Hollywood in the grip of McCarthyism, the footloose life of the artistic rich, publishing, Broadway." *Laura*, her best-known work, was adapted into a popular film in 1944, directed by Otto Preminger with Gene Tierney in the title role and Dana Andrews playing the detective.

Vera Caspary wrote thrillers—but not like any other author of her time, male or female. Her specialty was a specific type that she pioneered—the psycho thriller. Typically, thrillers emphasize plot development as opposed to character development. They focus on an action arc as opposed to a psychological arc. But a successful psychological thriller does both, more or less equally. The suspense comes from the human interaction between characters who prey on each other, trying either to confuse, destroy, or deceive.

Laura is a superb example of a perfect melding of all those elements. This haunting novel written in 1941 (its working title was *Ring Twice for Laura*) and published in 1943 is about a dead woman—or so we think when we start to read. Laura Hunt started as a daring and ambitious secretary at an advertising agency and worked her way up to become a top executive (Caspary had a similar background). Laura's inability to balance her professional and private lives results in her murder.

If a mystery is a *who*-dunit, this thriller is a *how*-dunit. And Laura sat-
isfies both definitions. Who killed her (a jealous suitor) is certainly a mystery that needs to be solved. But there's also the mystery of who in fact was
killed. As soon as the supposed murdered woman shows up unharmed and
very much alive, we're not only startled—we're reading nonstop suspense.
(Hitchcock's 1958 *Vertigo*, based on the Boileau/Narcejac novel *D'Entre
Les Morts*, seems strongly influenced by Caspary's device, as does the Brian
De Palma 1976 film *Obsession*.)

At its heart, the novel is about a woman and the men in love with her.
Each is a narrator in the novel: there's the fifty-year-old man of letters, her
fiancé who is a Kentucky gallant, and the detective investigating her violent death. And when Laura reappears and it turns out that another woman,
Diane, was murdered (a shotgun blast obliterated her face, preventing her
from being identified), Laura herself becomes a narrator and a suspect.

This groundbreaking suspense novel thrills in the way it playfully toys
with the reader's expectations and emotions. It's about obsession, and as
such it mesmerizes the reader, just as Detective McPherson is mesmerized
by Laura's portrait hanging over her fireplace and the mental image he
constructs of her while he spends days in her apartment, studying her journals and fantasizing about her thoughts. (Again, *Vertigo* comes to mind.)

Reading this novel today, we forget how many advances Caspary
brought to the genre. First, her feminist themes were far ahead of her time.
Second, she delivered a stylistic tour de force. Like Wilkie Collins's *The
Moonstone*, Caspary's novel utilizes multiple narrators who each move the
story forward. Part one is told by journalist and critic Waldo Lydecker,
Laura's benefactor and companion. In part two, we hear from Detective
Mark McPherson, who investigaties Laura's murder. Part three is narrated
by Laura herself, the presumed murder victim. The fourth part is a police
transcript, and the fifth and final part returns us to Detective McPherson.

Laura is an astonishing blend of a murder investigation and a woman's
quest for love and success. Caspary once said, "I'm not nearly as interested
in writing about crime as I am in the actions of normal people under high
tension." As the *New York Times* noted in her obituary, her principal theme
is "the working woman and her right to lead her own life, to be independent." That emphasis on character is, for me, what makes *Laura* one of the
must-read thrillers.

You can feel the tension on every page, starting with the book's evocative opening.

The city that Sunday morning was quiet. Those millions of New Yorkers who, by need or preference, remain in town over a summer weekend had been crushed spiritless by humidity. Over the island hung a fog that smelled and felt like water in which too many sodawater glasses have been washed. Sitting at my desk, pen in hand, I treasured the sense that among those millions, only I, Waldo Lydecker, was up and doing. The day just past, devoted to shock and misery, had stripped me of sorrow. Now I had gathered strength for the writing of Laura's epitaph.

You feel the suspense in every scene.

The doorbell is ringing. Perhaps he has come back to arrest me. He will find me like a slut in a pink slip with a pink strap falling over my shoulder, my hair unfastened. Like a doll, like a dame, a woman to be used by a man and thrown aside.

The bell is still ringing. It's very late. The street has grown quiet. It must have been like this the night Diane opened the door for the murderer.

M. J. Rose, is the international best-selling author of ten novels of psychological suspense (*The Reincarnationist* and *The Memorist*) and coauthor of *Buzz your Book*. She's the founder of the first marketing company for authors, AuthorBuzz.com, and a founding member of ITW. Getting published was an adventure for Rose who self-published *Lip Service* in 1998 after traditional publishers turned it down because it didn't fit into any one genre—today it would be called a psycho thriller. After selling over 2,500 copies, *Lip Service* became the first e-book and the first self-published novel chosen by the Literary Guild/Doubleday Book Club as well as the first e-book to be published by a mainstream New York publishing house. Rose has been profiled in *Time*, *Forbes*, the *New York Times*, and appeared on *The Today Show*, CNN, and other television programs. FOX's TV series *Past Life* is based on *The Reincarnationist*. Rose lives in Connecticut, with Doug Scofield, a composer, and their very spoiled dog, Winka.

40
Kenneth Fearing's
THE BIG CLOCK (1946)

Lincoln Child

Although Kenneth Fearing (1925–1961) is chiefly remembered as the author of *The Big Clock*, he was better known by his contemporaries as a poet, his work appearing in many of the leading literary journals and magazines of his time. Born in Oak Park, Illinois, he attended the University of Wisconsin, editing its literary journal. He also developed a drinking problem, which, coupled with his iconoclastic personality, led to a tumultuous personal life. After moving to New York in 1925, he began writing poetry in his spare time, eventually publishing several volumes. Fourteen years later, he wrote his first novel, *The Hospital*, and only in 1946, after many intervening works, did he publish his classic novel, *The Big Clock*.

People familiar with *The Big Clock* today—if they're familiar with it at all—most likely know it as a sleek, stylish 1948 film noir starring Ray Milland as the put-upon hero, George Stroud; Elsa Lanchester as a dingbat painter; and a smug Charles Laughton as the murderous Earl Janoth, head of a sprawling media conglomerate. Or possibly they know the 1987 remake, *No Way Out*, which starred Kevin Costner and was set in the Pentagon.

But they are not likely to know the story in its original incarnation—a 1946 novel—and that's a shame. Because it's a remarkably poisonous little puff adder of a thriller—eccentric and louche—with language sharp and bright as a rhinestoned buzz saw.

Here's an example: "She was tall, ice-blonde, and splendid. The eye saw nothing but innocence, to the instincts she was undiluted sex, the brain said here was a perfect hell."

Here's one other: "Hagen was a hard, dark little man whose soul had been hit by lightning, which he'd liked. His mother was a bank vault, and his father an International Business Machine."

See what I mean? It's a self-confident, in-your-face style of writing, so great when done right but so very, very easy to get wrong.

Fearing's self-confidence spills over into every facet of the story. He's not afraid to paint his hero—so different from the Ray Milland character of the movie—as a rather unlikable fellow, a heavy-drinking serial philanderer, drifting through his career with prematurely shrunken ambition. Nor is Fearing afraid to break the unspoken rules of fictioneering, often bizarrely, in ways both big and little. For example, the hero of *The Big Clock* is named George; his wife, Georgette; and his daughter, Georgia. This perverse bit of surrealist three-card monte might sit easily in the works of Beckett or Cocteau, but one is surprised to find it in a straight-ahead noir thriller.

George Stroud is the executive editor of *Crimeways*, a part of the sprawling magazine syndicate of Janoth Enterprises (think Time Inc. and Henry Luce). True to character, Stroud has struck up an adulterous relationship with Earl Janoth's glamorous girlfriend (and rumored lesbian), Pauline Delos. All too soon Pauline is killed by Janoth, who, learning there's a rival for her affections, flies into a murderous rage. When he calms down, Janoth is naturally more than eager to learn the identity of this rival and, if possible, pin the murder on him. He assembles the vast resources of Janoth Enterprises to find the man. Most particularly—in the book's central irony—he relies on George Stroud and the staff of *Crimeways* to learn the man's identity and bring him to justice.

And so we have a familiar thriller conceit, used frequently by Hitchcock in films such as *The 39 Steps* and *North By Northwest*: a hero who, in order to clear himself, must solve the crime on his own while at the same time eluding the law. But in *The Big Clock*, Fearing gives this familiar setup a clever spin. At first, Stroud is unaware that Janoth is the real murderer—yet he is all too aware that the man Janoth is searching for so fiercely is none other than himself. Thus he must not only solve the crime, but he must do so while hiding in plain sight. He is forced to play a double game: On the one hand, he has to find the real killer. But on the other he has to subtly manipulate the *Crimeways* staff to ensure they don't track him down first—while not getting caught at it.

The Big Clock unfolds primarily in the towering Janoth Building, a fantastic set piece where the various magazines, *Crimeways* and *Futureways* and *Homeways* and the rest, are like interconnected segments of some vast hive, humming with ceaseless activity. And at the very heart of the hive lies the Big Clock itself. This device is employed very differently in the book than it is in the subsequent movie. In the film version, the clock is very real: a larger than life automaton that runs all aspects of the Janoth empire, and in whose mechanical innards some very intense action scenes play out.

In the book, the clock is more subtle and metaphorical, an emblem for George Stroud's own outlook on things: the futility of life and the point-lessness of ambition.

> Sometimes the hands of the clock actually raced, and at other times they hardly moved at all. But that made no differ-ence to the big clock. The hands could move backward, and the time it told would be right just the same. It would still be run-ning as usual, because all other watches have to be set by the big one, which is even more powerful than the calendar, and to which one automatically adjusts his entire life.

It is interesting to compare *The Big Clock* to Fearing's first novel, *The Hospital*. Both books use a chain of first-person narrators, bouncing from character to character as new chapters are introduced. But the earlier book is much more linear in style, a minute-by-minute recitative of events in a large city hospital that, in certain ways, presages the novels of writers like Arthur Hailey: it's a kind of urtext for *Airport* and television shows such as *ER*. And yet it shows very little of the remarkable character delineations and cynical playing with tropes that characterize *The Big Clock*. Nor does the plot have the kind of Chinese-puzzle complexity of the later book: a nightmarish construction that perfectly suits the nihilistic worldviews of both the author and protagonist.

The most telling difference between the two books is most likely George Stroud. He is selfish, amoral, deeply cynical, and—perhaps most shocking of all—seems to learn nothing from his grueling ordeal. In the last pages of the story, Stroud, having been saved from the gallows and divorce, is already trying to hustle the free-spirited *artiste* played in the film by Elsa Lanchester, one of whose paintings helped save his sorry ass.

One cannot help but wonder if this jaundiced outlook of the later-period Fearing isn't in part a reflection of what was increasingly going on in his personal life. Originally known best as a poet—he won multiple Guggenheim Fellowships, and his poetry appeared in many of the leading literary journals and magazines of his time (is this why the lines I quoted earlier sing so true?)—he scored big commercially when *The Big Clock* was published. However, such later novels as *Loneliest Girl in the World* (1951) and *The Generous Heart* (1954) were comparative failures. Improvident business decisions, combined with a long-standing and accelerating drinking problem, combined to dissipate the small fortune he'd made on *The Big Clock*. In his final decade, as both his financial problems and his alcoholism worsened, he became known for questionable personal hygiene and a decidedly unkempt appearance. He died of cancer in 1961, just short of his sixtieth birthday. Reading between the lines of *The Big Clock*—and observing the kind of dreadful roller-coaster ride Stroud allows himself to experience as a result of his lustful appetites and chronic apathy—you cannot help but sense that Fearing's spectacular self-destruction lies just over the horizon.

But while it lasts, it's a hell of a ride.

Born in Westport, Connecticut, in 1957, Lincoln Child demonstrated an interest in writing as early as second grade, and by the time he finished high school he had written two dozen short stories, a complete novel, and a half-finished fantasy saga. Child graduated from Carleton College in Northfield, Minnesota, majoring in English. In 1979, he secured a position as editorial assistant at St. Martin's Press, rising ultimately to full editor. While there, Child assembled several collections of ghost and horror stories, including *Dark Company* (1984), *Dark Banquet* (1985), and *Tales of the Dark 1–3* (1987,1988). In 1995, he and coauthor Douglas Preston published *Relic*, the first of many novels to feature the quirky FBI Special Agent Aloysius X. L. Pendergast. The team has published numerous stand-alone thrillers, including *Mount Dragon* (1996) and *The Ice Limit* (2000). Child has also penned several solo thrillers, including *Terminal Freeze* (2009).

41

Graham Greene's
THE THIRD MAN (1950)

Rob Palmer

Graham Greene (1904–1991) was born in Hertfordshire, England. He took
a degree in history at Oxford and, a few years later, published his first novel,
The Man Within (1929). He traveled widely and was recruited into MI6,
the British spy agency, continuing to file reports until his death. Some literary critics later wondered if writing was only a cover for Greene's spying
activities. If so, it was a brilliant ruse. In total, he wrote over twenty novels, dozens of short stories, and ten screenplays as well as eight stage plays.
He suffered from bipolar disorder, a condition that made a wreck of his
personal life, but that he claimed was the wellspring of his writing. Greene
had a talent for portraying moral ambiguity, an ability to write in shades of
gray, that made his characters and stories unique and memorable. He was
one of the most celebrated novelists of his era and was considered a strong
candidate for the Nobel Prize in Literature. When he did not win, he joked
to his publisher that only one Nobel judge stood in his way, someone "determined to outlive him."

Graham Greene's choice of approaches varied widely. His books are sometimes outrageously funny (*Travels with My Aunt*, 1969), sometimes political (*The Quiet American*, 1955), sometimes religious (*The Power and the
Glory*, 1940), and sometimes pure suspenseful entertainment (*The Min-
istry of Fear*, 1943). *The Third Man* (1950) is clearly in the latter category,
a thriller in its heart and soul.

The idea for *The Third Man* came from Alexander Korda, head of the
movie studio, London Film Productions. Korda wanted to make a movie
about post-World War II Vienna, with Carol Reed as director. He raised
the concept with Greene, who was interested but initially had little to offer
except a character he had envisioned years before: the roguish underworld
figure, Harry Lime.

Postwar Vienna was the perfect place to set a story of intrigue. Divided into four Sectors—Russian, French, British, and American—and governed by an absurdly complex system of checks and balances, the city was a haven for smugglers, thieves, and scoundrels of every stripe. In some ways, Vienna itself seems to be the star of the story, a shadowy game board where the weak are constantly terrified and the strong are always looking for a quick and easy score.

Greene agreed to write the screenplay, but he first wrote the story as a novella to give it substance and background. He had no intention of letting the public read this work. Only after the movie became a huge success did he consent to publication. In prose form, *The Third Man* is brief, only slightly over one hundred pages. Still, every one of those pages contains something of a masterstroke.

The novella opens with the arrival in Vienna of Rollo Martins (changed to Holly Martins in the movie). Martins, a hack writer of pulp westerns, has come to visit his old friend, Harry Lime. Martins is greeted by shocking news: Lime is dead, struck by a car only a few days earlier.

Like most of Greene's protagonists, Rollo Martins is no paragon. He drinks too much, speaks out of turn, and comes up a poor second in every fight. He's also thin-skinned. When a British army colonel named Calloway claims that Harry Lime was a racketeer, Martins is deeply offended. He vows to prove Calloway wrong and resurrect the good name of Harry Lime. Here the wheels of the plot begin to turn, as Martins tracks through the snowy, war-blasted streets of Vienna looking for the remaining threads of his friend's life. What he finds isn't pretty, as Lime was a dealer of stolen penicillin. He diluted the medicine, which led to the deaths of hundreds of patients. Many others lie ruined in the hospital.

Along the trail, Martins turns up Lime's girlfriend, Anna Schmidt. Martins has a troubled history with women. He has "incidents"; he "mixes his drinks." He, like his creator, Greene, has had too many shabby liaisons in too many cities. Anna—distraught, vulnerable, one of Vienna's weak ones—is like a drug to him. After a single evening, Martins falls in love with her.

At its core, *The Third Man* is about loyalty. Anna is loyal to the memory of her love for Harry Lime; Calloway is loyal to his duties with the army; even Lime is loyal—like any sociopath, loyal to his own self-interest. For Martins, the choices are much more difficult. He must decide whether to help his old friend, or help Calloway rid the city of a villain, or help himself—to Anna.

Though *The Third Man* covers serious themes, Greene intended it primarily as one of what he called his "entertainments," a category that includes *Orient Express* (1933) and *The Confidential Agent* (1939). As a thriller, *The Third Man* delivers, from the first line—"One never knows when the blow may fall."—to the final, searing chase scene through the Vienna sewers.

The movie version of *The Third Man* stars Joseph Cotton, Orson Welles, and Alida Valli. It was released to instant critical acclaim. In 1999, the British Film Institute named it the best British film of the twentieth century. If the film is so good, why read the novella? The same question could be asked of most of Greene's books, nearly all of which have been made into movies. With *The Third Man*, both versions are well worth a look. The novella shows, page by page, the creative decisions made by Greene. These can be compared with the decisions made by Carol Reed in directing the movie. Both are brilliant in their own way.

Perhaps the greatest achievement in *The Third Man* is the character, Harry Lime. This was a true collaborative effort between Greene, Reed, and Orson Welles, who played Lime in the movie. An evolution of the title character in Eric Ambler's *A Coffin for Dimitrios* (1939), Lime was a new form of criminal mastermind: selfish, manipulative, deadly, yet possessing an overpowering charm. Though well dead at the end of the story, Lime lived on for years in the public light, in a radio drama, *The Lives of Harry Lime* (voiced by Welles), and in a television series (*The Third Man*, starring Michael Rennie).

Reed, as director, received most of the accolades for *The Third Man*. Greene's contribution was quickly relegated to second tier. This must not have bothered Greene, as he dedicated the novella to "Carol Reed in admiration and affection."

Graham Greene had a profound effect on the way thrillers are written and received by the reading public. For example, the influential noir film *This Gun for Hire* was based on his novel *A Gun for Sale* (1936). His style is terse but sophisticated, leaving the reader waiting for the next beautifully turned phrase, the next tick of plot development, the next layer of character revealed. He perfected the shady, furtive hero, with whom readers secretly and uncomfortably identify. Greene influenced a whole generation of younger writers. His guiding hand can be seen in the powerful descriptive prose of John le Carré, the strong political themes of Charles McCarry, the dark world view of Len Deighton, and dozens of other greats.

At age twelve, Rob Palmer read his first Graham Greene novel. He has been hooked ever since on the great British suspense writers, especially Conrad, Greene, and le Carré. Rob is the author of two thrillers. *No Time to Hide*, his first, won the Eric Hoffer Award in suspense fiction. *Eyes of the World*, Rob's second book, opened to great reviews and was short-listed for three prizes in the mystery and suspense field. In addition to writing, Rob is a lawyer and law professor in Washington D.C. His practice focuses on international finance and investment. He has written dozens of articles and book chapters on the law, current events, and politics. He's currently working a thriller involving the assassination of John F. Kennedy.

42
Patricia Highsmith's
STRANGERS ON A TRAIN (1950)

David Baldacci

Born in Fort Worth, Texas, in 1921, Patricia Highsmith spent the latter part of her life in Europe; she died of leukemia in 1995, while residing in Locarno, Switzerland. Highsmith attended Barnard College, studying English composition. For several years after graduation, she earned a living writing for comic-book publishers. Her first novel, *Strangers on a Train* (1950), written with the encouragement of Truman Capote, sold well; in 1951, Alfred Hitchcock turned the book into a classic film of suspense. Highsmith's most popular literary creation was Tom Ripley, the antihero of her 1955 novel, *The Talented Mr. Ripley*. Ripley appeared in four subsequent novels. A 1999 film version of the first Ripley book, featuring Matt Damon as the sociopathic con artist, generated new interest in Highsmith's work in America, where she had been largely ignored in recent years. The author of twenty-two novels and eight short story collections, Highsmith won the O. Henry Memorial Award, Le Grand Prix de Littérature Policière, and the Silver Dagger Award of the Crime Writers Association of Great Britain.

Oh, how courageous Patricia Highsmith was. Or perhaps the lady was supremely confident in her storytelling prowess. Then again, it might have been both. Her great gift was to let the tale develop slowly, over a bubbling of ingenious plot points, with a few hard jabs thrown in from time to time to keep the reader honest and alert.

Some suspense writers today go for the quick bang over the sophistication of a more developed yarn. Perhaps thinking the entire world has gone ADD, they pop you in the first chapter, which may only be a page long. Next, they steamroll you with one gory event after another told in as few (and simplistic) words as possible. Well, if "Yee-ha" doesn't constitute a foreign policy, as I once read in a newspaper while overseas, then "quick and slick" doesn't constitute a well-told tale.

With Highsmith, the dread builds slowly but inexorably as the characters develop like film before our hungry eyes. Finally, the denouement eases into view before it explodes, eviscerating every soul within range. The effect is not unlike an underwater earthquake transforming later into a towering tsunami that devastates all before it.

Strangers on a Train could be a textbook on the art of constructing suspense noun by adjective, small interaction by informative interior monologue. The satisfying result is that the characters are developed to such a degree that on closing the book you realize you know the protagonists better than you do some *real* people of your acquaintance. The critical details are seemingly insignificant yet told movingly, confidently, without a trace of unnecessary baggage. We can tell from the words she uses that Highsmith knows that it all matters. She is giving you the oxygen to breathe that the story requires. You suck it down and wait for more, fully realizing that this writer knows exactly what she's doing.

The story's touchstone is that of the everyman, Guy Haines, dropped into a nightmare that may well vanquish him. The tone is dark, the mood darker still. The characters bleed red right through the pages, right onto our fingers. It is *Rear Window* on steroids, but with a bigger heart. It is *In Cold Blood* in the symmetry of an ill-fated pair of young men who share a terrible secret. Yet the creep of sheer foreboding in *Strangers*, the palpable anxiety, is arguably even fiercer than in Capote's masterpiece. Is there any wonder Hitchcock leapt at the chance to turn the novel into film? It seemed created just for the iconic director. All he had to do was transfer it from book page to cinematic frame.

So here we are with Guy and Charles Anthony Bruno, surely one of the most original fictional characters ever. They meet on a train. They eat, they drink, they talk, page after page; emotions run hard and swing fast. Yet nothing much seems to happen for a long time. The doomed Miriam isn't dispatched until page eighty-one; the dreaded Bruno senior not until much later. And while Miriam's death scene is brief, it hangs with you far longer than the cumulative effect of a thousand spiritless murders in lesser books. Yet despite the leisurely pace, Highsmith cements your hands to the pages by the sheer force of her wordplay, by the mounting tension, by the absolute assurance in the heart of the reader that when it all comes together the effect will be catastrophic.

My first reaction to Bruno was, naturally enough, revulsion. Poor Guy I pitied. They were good and evil personified. Yet life is not that simple, and

Highsmith knows it. As she meticulously turned on and off the information tap, as the character arcs burned and churned across the pages, my opinion of the two leads changed. In sum, I liked Bruno better and Guy less. Pity turned to disgust at Guy's weakness, his display of all the right emotions at all the wrong time. My initial disgust at Bruno's homicidal streak, of his casual entitlement to live off the largesse of others—even the incestuous undertones between mother and son—started to drift to something else, understanding perhaps, occasionally even sympathy.

As the walls closed in on Guy, my emotional barometer swung again. I was now rooting for the doomed architect. In some ways, Highsmith had, in the end, transformed me into Guy Haines. I wanted to survive. I wanted the tenacious detective Gerard to lose and me to win. No, of course, I meant I wanted *Guy* to survive, I wanted *Guy* to win. Didn't I? That really is Highsmith's point after all. Not only that any one of us could be Guy Haines, but, also, perhaps more significantly, that any one of us could be Charles Bruno.

Yet, even as Guy should have hated Bruno more than any man alive, he attempted to save his life when a drunken Bruno went over the side of the sailboat. How can two men with such a horrific secret between them bond in such a way? Bruno blackmailed Guy into murdering someone. He even blueprinted the crime for his hapless foil. It seems too incredible, too implausible that Guy would attempt to wrench his nemesis from death. However, in the hands of a master writer it all works. Indeed, it works as well now as it did when Highsmith first wrote it. Isn't that the definition of a classic?

David Baldacci is the author of numerous consecutive *New York Times* and worldwide best sellers, including *Absolute Power, Total Control, The Camel Club*, and *Divine Justice*. With books published in over forty-five languages in more than eighty countries, and with over sixty-five million copies in print worldwide, he is one of the world's favorite storytellers. He's also the cofounder, along with his wife, of the Wish You Well Foundation, a nonprofit organization dedicated to supporting literacy efforts across America. Still a resident of his native Virginia, he invites you to visit his foundation at www.wishyouwellfoundation.org.

43
Mickey Spillane's
ONE LONELY NIGHT (1951)

Max Allan Collins

Mickey Spillane (1918–2006), the most translated American writer of the twentieth century, sold hundreds of millions of books. A bartender's son born in Brooklyn, Spillane was a flight instructor in World War II and was among the first wave of comic book writers, penning scripts for the likes of *Submariner* and *Captain America*. His rugged private eye, Mike Hammer, was a sensation in the 1950s, sparking a comic strip, radio series, four TV series, and numerous films, notably the highly regarded *Kiss Me, Deadly* as well as *The Girl Hunters* in which Spillane played Hammer. His paperback reprints were so successful that Gold Medal Books—the first paperback original publisher—was created to fill the market Spillane had uncovered. Mike Hammer is widely regarded as the father of the modern vigilante action hero. In 1995, Spillane was named a Grand Master by the Mystery Writers of America.

The enormous success of Mickey Spillane's first three Mike Hammer mysteries—*I, the Jury* (1947), *My Gun Is Quick* (1950), and *Vengeance Is Mine!* (1950)—is hard to fathom today. Even Stephen King did not enjoy blockbuster status so early in his career, and the most apt comparison that comes to mind is Elvis Presley's sexual impact on popular music.

Like Presley, Spillane was attacked by self-appointed arbiters of public taste and morality, getting hit on all sides—liberals outraged by Hammer's vigilante tactics, conservatives appalled by Spillane's then-explicit sexual content. In literary circles, Spillane was derided as a vulgarian, his work condemned as worthy only of men's room walls.

The public didn't care about such opinions and bought the books in the millions, worldwide, and along the way Spillane changed the notion of how a tough hero behaves, opening doors on sex and violence in popular fiction that could never again be closed. The writer (not "author," a term Spillane despised) made a big public show throughout his lifetime of thumbing his nose at critics, even once getting his publisher to take out a huge ad in *Publishers Weekly* consisting of negative excerpts from reviews. "Let's hope they *really* hate the next one!" Spillane gleefully bragged.

Spillane, however, was in secret badly stung by this criticism. It may have led to his joining the conservative religious sect, the Jehovah's Witnesses, and certainly was a factor in his almost decade-long absence from writing novels (1952-1961). *One Lonely Night* (1951) was written by Spillane at the peak of all this negative criticism and is clearly designed to be his response.

The novel begins with Hammer, in Manhattan of course, on the George Washington Bridge on a rainy night, possibly contemplating suicide, certainly awash in self-doubt. The scene is set in an evocative manner typical for Spillane but one for which his critics never gave him credit:

> Nobody ever walked across the bridge, not on a night like this. The rain was misty enough to be almost fog-like, a cold gray curtain that separated me from the pale ovals of white that were faces locked behind the steamed-up windows of the cars that hissed by.

The private eye is enraged and guilt ridden, having been humiliated in court by a liberal judge ("He was little and he was old with eyes like two berries on a bush") who has branded Hammer an unrepentant murderer, reluctantly releasing the PI on a self-defense plea. From out of the snow that the rain has become emerges a damsel in distress, and Hammer rises to the occasion.

But he so viciously dispatches the villain pursuing her ("I only gave him a second to realize what it was like to die then I blew the expression clean off his face") that she assumes Hammer is a "monster," too, and throws herself off the bridge. "She twisted and slithered over the top of the rail and I felt part of her coat come away in my hand as she tumbled headlong into the white void."

In Spillane's novels, Hammer rarely has a client—he has a friend or an innocent to avenge, and here he sets out to settle the score for the girl he inadvertently scared into suicide. He works with the police, his friend Captain Pat Chambers of Homicide, who represents the legal alternative Hammer rejects, and gets embroiled in national politics. He even becomes the protector of a Joe McCarthy-esque senator who is attempting to purge Washington of subversives but has a terrible secret—a twin brother who is a homicidal maniac and is stalking him.

Such over-the-top melodrama is typical in Spillane. He is not a realist—Hammer's world is an expressionistic, even surrealistic nightmare landscape, a metaphor for the disappointment of the postwar world to which veterans like Hammer (and Spillane) returned. The "Commies" who are the chief villains in *One Lonely Night* should not be viewed in political terms—they are the boogie men in Hammer's nightmare, and dismissing the vivid first-person prose and breakneck narrative on political correctness grounds is a madness that surpasses even Mike Hammer's.

While Hammer is a detective, *One Lonely Night* is more thriller than mystery, as is clear in the famous climactic action scene in an abandoned paint factory, where the crazed PI goes up against scores of "Commies" who are torturing Velda, his beloved secretary and partner (she is also a PI and handy with a "rod"). She hangs naked from the rafters as Hammer takes on an army of evil.

And he is ready. Contemplating this probably suicidal assault, he has—after sixty thousand or so words of soul-searching—decided that he has been put on earth by God to fight evil with evil's means.

> I lived to kill so that others could live. I lived to kill because
> my soul was a hardened thing that reveled in the thought of tak-
> ing the blood of the bastards who made murder their business
> . . . . I was the evil that opposed other evil, leaving the good
> and the meek in the middle to live and inherit the earth!

While the mystery will be solved in the final chapter, in a manner that turns the apparent pro-Joe McCarthy bias of the book on its head, Hammer is in full action-hero mode in the second to the last chapter. For a book now sixty years old, *One Lonely Night* can still shock:

> I aimed the tommy gun for the first time and took his arm
> off at the shoulder. It dropped on the floor next to him and I let
> him have a good look at it. . . .The music in my head was going
> wild this time, but I was laughing too hard to enjoy it.

Mickey has answered his critics. And he has sent his psychotic PI Mike Hammer to deliver the message.

Max Allan Collins is the author of the *New York Times* best-selling graphic novel *The Road to Perdition*, the basis for a film starring Tom Hanks that was nominated for six Academy Awards (it won for cinematography). His other credits include such comics as *Batman*, *Dick Tracy*, and his own *Ms. Tree*; film scripts for HBO and Lifetime; and the innovative, Shamus Award-winning Nathan Heller historical detective novels. His movie and TV tie-in books include *Air Force One*, *Saving Private Ryan*, *American Gangster*, and ten *CSI* entries. He was chosen by Mickey Spillane to complete half a dozen unfinished Mike Hammer novels in the writer's files. The first, *The Goliath Bone*, appeared in 2008 to much acclaim, followed by *The Big Bang* in 2010. Collins is an independent filmmaker, and his *Eliot Ness: An Untouchable Life* aired on PBS. He lives in Iowa with his wife, Barbara Collins; they write the Trash 'n' Treasures "cozy" mystery series, including *Antiques Bizarre* (2010).

44

Jim Thompson's
THE KILLER INSIDE ME (1952)

Scott Nicholson

James Myers Thompson, (1906–1977) was a journalist, screenwriter, and novelist known primarily for his pulp fiction and questionable morality. The son of a sheriff who left office under a cloud of suspicion, Thompson's teenage education consisted of running drugs, women, and bootleg booze for hotel clients, providing fodder for the grifters, double-crossers, floozies, and misanthropes that would populate his fiction. He embraced that early opportunity to launch his career as an alcoholic, which no doubt contributed to his uneven output and sometimes bizarre surrealism. After a couple of attempts at more realistic fiction, he veered into crime novels in 1949 with *Nothing More Than Murder*. He followed that up with *The Killer Inside Me*, then released a barrage of bleak crime novels in the following decade, most notably *Savage Night* and *Pop. 1280*. He also had a brief flirtation with Hollywood, working with director Stanley Kubrick, who provided the cover blurb for posthumous releases of *The Killer Inside Me*: "Probably the most chilling and believable first-person story of a criminally warped mind I have ever encountered." Thompson fell out of favor in the latter part of his career, and most of his work was out of print when his lifelong addictions to drinking and smoking sent him to his deathbed. However, he wheezed out a prediction that his works would make a lasting impact, fulfilling the prophecy in the title of one of his short stories, "This World, Then the Fireworks."

Jim Thompson's classic noir thriller, *The Killer Inside Me*, published as a paperback original in 1952, could be single-handedly credited with spawning the serial killer subgenre, a lineage that includes Robert Bloch's *Psycho*, Bret Easton Ellis's *American Psycho*, Thomas Harris's Hannibal Lecter, and Jeff Lindsay's Dexter series. But Thompson's first-person narrative did more than open the gates for aberrant behavior in literature—it blew off the barn roof and pushed winds into heaven and hell.

Thompson's brand of grit came along at the perfect time. After World War II, an explosion of genre paperbacks replaced the pulp magazines that had given them birth. Tough-guy crime fiction began showing up alongside more traditional whodunits in the magazines, and their subject matter lent itself to lurid covers, often with veiled promises of lascivious excess, unseemly women, and shadowy morality. At the same time, paranoia and a fear of the "Other," typified publicly by the McCarthy-driven Red Scare and personally by Thompson's own problems stemming from a brief Communist Party affiliation, were creating an undercurrent of distrust and uneasiness.

Following the success of Mickey Spillane, original paperbacks from writers like Thompson, John D. MacDonald, and David Goodis opened vast territory for exploration, but Thompson dove more deeply into the dark waters of human sociopathy than any of his peers. Incestuous, duplicitous characters acted out of impulses that he only casually attempted to explain. His writing style, like his first-person protagonists, offered no apologies and presented a culture in which depravity lurked beneath the placid surface of routine behavior.

Protagonist policeman Lou Ford is the personification of this viewpoint and seems to be an exaggerated extension of Thompson's core beliefs. In calming one of his victims just before dispensing a bizarre brand of justice, Lou offers a bit of philosophy: "It's a screwed up, bitched up world, and I'm afraid it's going to stay that way. And I'll tell you why. Because no one, almost no one, sees anything wrong with it. They can't see that things are screwed up, so they're not worried about it."

In Thompson's milieu, it's not Lou Ford who is insane—it is society. Its rules make no sense, and civilization is only a pretense, a playing field in which the score shifts to those who know how to rig the game. Ford approaches his grisly tasks with a world-weary sense of duty, built on a belief that he's only undertaking the necessary evils because other people are too weak or afraid to face them.

"It was funny the way these people kept looking for it," Lou muses. "Why did they all have to come to me to be killed? Why wouldn't they kill themselves?"

Lou is not a textbook sociopath inasmuch as he possesses a rudimentary sense of right and wrong, at least as society holds those qualities. Then again, Lou is not consistent either, facilely shifting from an intellectual who solves calculus problems for fun to a drawling, easygoing dumb cop whom no one would suspect of murder.

"I guess I kind of got a foot on both fences," Lou claims. "I planted them there early and now they've taken root, and I can't move either way and I can't jump. All I can do is wait until I split."

Among Ford's supporting cast, those who are kind and trusting are most likely to come to a bad end, validation that life is unfair and those that can't grasp the simple guiding principles won't last, while those who set their own laws, like mogul Chester Conway, consolidate their power over the weak and the timid. As the net tightens around Lou, he outflanks the first criminal psychologist sent to shrink him in a scene that could have inspired the famed Clarisse Starling-Hannibal Lecter face-offs in the classic *The Silence of the Lambs*. Not only is Lou more well read in the field of aberrant behavior than his questioner, quoting texts and theories; he also manipulates the conversation to ensure no one can form a solid opinion. He fully believes himself above judgment, whether mortal or divine.

"They could only find proof in me—in what I was—and I'd never show it to 'em," good ol' Lou muses after reviewing all the evidence stacked against him.

To Thompson's credit, he offers little Freudian groundwork for Lou Ford's motivation. Reminisces of a childhood incident, heavily veiled, slowly emerge as Lou's spree accelerates. However, the core foundation of his pathology is that Lou simply *is* a creature of nature doing what nature does best. If a few people feel a little pain, that's just the way the game is played, and Thompson's peculiar brand of justice and balance are always restored: "I wiped my gloves on her body. It was her blood and it belonged there."

When Lou is finally snared, it's a love letter and not a tactical slip that does him in. With a cunning and amused nod to society's expected norms, he responds to his incarceration with a studied indifference: "I put on a pretty good act, it seemed to me. Just good enough to let 'em think I was bothered, but not enough to mean anything at a sanity hearing."

Lou is often referred to as an unreliable narrator, primarily due to the novel's abrupt conclusion that some feel breaks established rules of narrative fiction. But with Thompson's brave blend of surrealism, genre convention, autobiography, psychological treatise, and social satire, he emerges as simultaneously both more realistic and experimental than his crime-writing peers. In truth, Lou is the most reliable narrator possible, a metafictional hero who just doesn't cotton to arbitrarily imposed rules.

Ultimately, it's not just Lou who "wanted so much and got so little, that meant so good and did so bad." Lou's not to blame, and neither is anyone else. It's just the way the game shook out, the way the cookie crumbled, the way the dice fell, the whole clichéd march of time that gets us in the end.

Much like Jim Thompson, Scott Nicholson is a journalist, screenwriter, and novelist known primarily for his pulp fiction and questionable morality. He's the author of seven supernatural thrillers, including *They Hunger* and *The Red Church*, which was an alternate selection of the Mystery Guild and a finalist for the Bram Stoker Award. He is an original bass playing member of the International Thriller Writers' Killer Thriller Band. He's currently developing several comic book series, including *Dirt*, in which he plays a creepy, over-the-top version of himself as the Digger, an undertaker narrating adaptations of his numerous short stories. Nicholson's other comics titles include *The Gorge*, *The Red Church*, and *Murdermouth*. As if this exposure to words weren't lethal enough, he's also a freelance editor and has written numerous articles about writing in addition to hosting an annual paranormal conference.

45

Ernest K. Gann's

THE HIGH AND THE MIGHTY (1953)

Ward Larsen

Ernest K. Gann (1910–1991) was the creator of the "aviation thriller." As is so often the case, Gann's success was earned through both hard work and good fortune. Not only blessed with a knack for the writing craft, Gann was an accomplished pilot. He was uniquely positioned to witness the birth of aviation, experiencing first-hand the trials of a profession that was tailor-made for storytelling. His body of work is a thoughtful analysis of the interaction between man and machine. His first novel, *Island in the Sky* (1944), was a commercial success. But it was *The High and the Mighty* that carried Gann to a new level of recognition. Both novels became movies, as did *Soldier of Fortune*, *Twilight of the Gods*, and *Fate Is the Hunter*. His historical novel, *The Antagonists*, was adapted into a well-known television miniseries, *Masada*. Throughout his career, be it as a writer of novels, short stories, or screenplays, Gann brought to his audience an authenticity borne from the trials of experience, and it was this realism that consistently brought his stories to life.

There is a long-held maxim that those who exhibit vitality in their writing do the same in their lives. Perhaps no author better illustrates this maxim than Ernest K. Gann. Gann grew up in Lincoln, Nebraska, and began developing his storytelling gift at an early age. In 1926, when he was sixteen, he made his first film, a modest but entertaining feature that started a lifelong association with the big screen. It also set a standard for success—the picture cost two hundred dollars to make and grossed four hundred in its first week. This relationship with motion pictures would blossom later in Gann's life, but not until he had made his mark as a writer.

Gann was an adventurer first and foremost. He took up flying at an early age, beginning as a barnstormer, and advancing through the ranks of aviation until he was hired by American Airlines. During World War II, he signed on with the Army Air Corps and flew DC-4 Stratocruisers for Transport Command, a duty that took him quite literally across the world.

It was during Gann's period of flying for the commercial airlines that he decided to pursue writing. He put long layovers to good use, creating fiction that was drawn from his firsthand experiences in the cockpit. The early days of aviation were far removed from today's aerial mass transit system. Aircraft of the early decades were prone to malfunction, and maintenance was a mixed bag with the quality varying widely. The aviators themselves were a rich lot: colorful characters who spent long days in a cockpit where the command structure was absolute. The captain was the master of the vessel, an authority of undeniable nautical heritage. Indeed, many parallels can be drawn between Gann's leading men and other infamous literary skippers—the Blighs and Ahabs of legend.

Gann's first three books were nonfiction, brought out in the early days of World War II. *Island in the Sky*, however, published in 1944, was the work that launched his career. The story was based on a harrowing Arctic rescue mission and became an instant bestseller. Gann continued producing a book roughly every two years until 1953, when *The High and the Mighty* was published.

Its plot is an adaptation of an actual commercial flight Gann had worked from Honolulu to Portland, Oregon, while flying for Matson Airlines. Gann later revealed that the flight in question was laced far more with comedy than the taut suspense delivered in *The High and the Mighty*. In any case, the essence of the plot follows standard Gann form—take an exotic setting, populate it with colorful characters, then furnish an extraordinary situation (a passenger plane running out of fuel over the Pacific Ocean), and let the drama come.

As with many of Gann's books, the exotic location in *The High and the Mighty* did not involve palm trees or foreign tongues, but rather isolation and machines. Passengers and crew prepare for a Pacific crossing, and soon all are gliding miles above an unforgiving ocean. The cabin of the ship is a world to itself, functioning as a containment chamber to test the wits and nerves of everyone aboard. Throughout the story, there's some contact with the outside world, but Gann is effective in using this distant chatter of radios and signals to reinforce the aircraft's seclusion.

The skipper is a troubled man, an experienced aviator who has lost his confidence. In Gann's words, it was Captain Sullivan's "secret which he intended to keep to himself. He was a man in charge, but a man losing his nerve. A man who will lock up when the chips are down—as they most certainly will be." Countering the skipper is copilot Dan Roman. Roman is vastly experienced, but carries demons of his own, guilt centered on a long-ago decision made when he was the pilot in command. The book relies heavily on flashbacks to develop characters, a technique made necessary by the physical and chronological constraints of the story. *The High and the Mighty* flies to a satisfying conclusion, but not before testing everyone involved.

The book was later adapted into a film classic under the same name, John Wayne delivering perhaps the most famous slap in cinematic history. The later twisting of the story line into the Hollywood spoof *Airplane* (1980) gave aspects of Gann's original work a near iconic status.

Ernest K. Gann's work had a significant impact on the thriller genre. *The High and the Mighty* set the groundwork for a slew of disaster novels, beginning with Arthur Hailey's *Airport* (1968). The technical detail that gave his stories such authority was eventually brought to another level, with a military bent, by Tom Clancy in *The Hunt for Red October* (1984).

In 1979, when Ernest Gann was sixty-nine years old, he was given the opportunity to fly in a U. S. Air Force U-2 spy plane. He never hesitated. Writer, rancher, sailor, and adventurer—through his books, Gann gave his readers an enticing sample of a rich life. His gift continues long after his passing, and *The High and the Mighty* remains his indelible signature on the world of thrillers.

Ward Larsen's first novel, *The Perfect Assassin*, was honored with numerous awards, including the Florida Book Award Silver Medal for popular fiction, and the Military Writer's Society of America Gold Medal. He was a fighter pilot in the United States Air Force for seven years, including twenty-two missions in Operation Desert Storm, and also served as a federal law enforcement officer. His recent novel, *Stealing Trinity*, a World War II thriller revolved around the Manhattan Project, garnered rave reviews. Ward is both a commercial airline pilot and a trained aircraft-accident investigator, skills that are the subject of his international thriller, *Fly by Wire*.

46

Jack Finney's
INVASION OF THE BODY SNATCHERS (1955)

James Rollins

Writing about him in *Danse Macabre*, Stephen King said that one of Jack Finney's great abilities as a writer was "his talent for allowing his stories to slip unobtrusively, almost casually, into another world." What makes this talent so unique, however, was that it was on display in all of Finney's work, whether it was mainstream, comedy, fantasy, science fiction, or thriller. Born in Milwaukee, Wisconsin, Finney (1911–1995) worked in a New York advertising agency (a background he later used in his novel, *Good Neighbor Sam*) before becoming a full-time writer. His first novel, *Five Against the House* (about college students who try to rob a casino), was published in 1954. Aside from *The Body Snatchers* (1955), Finney's greatest success came with his science fiction thriller, *Time and Again* (1970), which is about a secret government project involving time travel to New York City in 1882. The author of nearly two dozen novels and three short story collections, Finney was given the World Fantasy Award for Life Achievement in 1987, proving that the ingredients of a thriller, especially as demonstrated in *The Body Snatchers*, are not limited to any genre.

"The book is much better than the movie."

Who hasn't heard that statement from time to time? That hope prompted me to pick up a copy of Jack Finney's *Invasion of the Body Snatchers*. I was a high school student, and I had just seen the 1978 remake of the 1956 black-and-white film. I vaguely remembered Don Siegel's original masterpiece—with the haunting last scene of a raving Dr. Miles Bennell running through the streets yelling, "You're next!" But as an avid reader of all things pulp, I wanted to look at the source material upon which these two movies were based.

It wasn't easy to find. The novel was first published in 1955 under the shorter title, *The Body Snatchers*, but I finally managed to locate a battered reprint in a second-hand store that specialized in science fiction. I read the dog-eared copy in one long session, baking under a window as the sun moved across the sky. It was a simple story. Aliens invade a small town, replacing its inhabitants with perfect copies. The novel opens with the narrator, a small town doctor in Mill Valley, California, being faced with a peculiar patient, a woman who believes her uncle is not her uncle. While the man looks exactly like her uncle and talks like him, even has all his memories, she insists "his responses aren't *emotionally* right . . . there's something *missing*."

This opens the way for a taut tale of mounting paranoia and suspicion. The effect is heightened by the first-person perspective, a narrator of unflagging commonness, along with a setting as familiar as Mayberry. Dr. Miles Bennell is no swashbuckling hero or brawny champion, nor is he particularly bright or inventive. He is freshly divorced, rather bumbling, too quick to trust, and easy to sway. He lives in a town where "from down the block you could hear the far-off clatter of a lawnmower" and where one could sit "on the wide old porch in the comfortably battered wicker furniture, or the porch swing, eating bacon and tomato sandwiches on toast, sipping coffee, talking about nothing much."

This simple setting, with events narrated by an ordinary man, slowly and inexorably persuades the reader to believe in alien seed pods that burst during the thick of night and grow human copies. Richard Matheson and Stephen King (the latter acknowledges the influence of both Finney and Matheson) employ a similar technique in their novels, populating unremarkable towns with ordinary folk and challenging them with extraordinary horrors. The device brings the terror directly into the reader's everyday world.

But the dread becomes even more powerful when considered in relation to the decade when it was written. Jack Finney, a native of Marin County, where the story takes place, was also reflecting the paranoia of his time. Much has been written about the story's parallel to the growing "red menace" of Communism. Between 1950 and 1954, the political witchhunts of Joe McCarthy created fierce suspicion throughout the United States. Many 1950s critics linked the cold and emotionless pod-people with Communist infiltrators, while later critics maintained that the pod-people were a metaphor for a political culture determined to make everyone identical, tolerating no dissent.

Finney drew on other real-world tensions to add resonance and topicality to this multilayered novel, to stoke the fear and uneasiness lurking in the hearts of his readers. For example, the narrator, Dr. Bennell, relates a past encounter with a shoeshine man named Billy, a middle-aged black man.

> Billy professed a genuine love for shoes. He'd nod with approv-
> ing criticalness when you showed up with a new pair. "Good
> leather," he'd murmur, nodding . . . He obviously took content-
> ment in one of the simpler occupations of the world, and the
> money involved seemed actually unimportant.

But one night, Dr. Bennell overhears Billy speaking to a friend when there aren't any patrons around. The black shoeshine man reveals the truth about himself, parodying his own antics: "Please le'me kiss your feet! Le'me kiss 'em!" As he continues mocking his customers, Dr. Bennell is forced into a terrible realization.

> Never before had I heard such ugly, bitter, and vicious contempt
> . . . contempt for the people taken in by his daily antics, but
> even more for himself, the man who supplied the servility they
> bought from him.

This same mimicry and deception is what Bennell witnesses in the pod-people when they drop their masks, revealing their true nature. So, it isn't just the extremes of McCarthyism that give this novel power, but also the racism prevalent at the time. How can anyone read the above section and not squirm? It forced both sides of the racial divide to wonder who were wearing masks of hypocrisy and what lurked beneath them.

The novel's topicality also touched upon another social turn during the mid 1950s: the slow deterioration and wasting of small towns across America following the end of World War II. Mill Valley seems a bucolic, idyllic community, but the fear and heightened attentiveness of our nar-rator finally completely open his eyes to the true dilapidated condition of his town.

> Everything I was seeing now had been here to see then, except
> that—you don't really see the familiar until it's thrust upon you,
> you don't actually notice, until there's a reason to do so.

In this ultra-aware state, Dr. Bennell notes the empty stores, the fly-specked windows, the sun-faded signs, the closed up inns, the shuttered Sequoia theater. His girlfriend notes it, too. "When did all this *happen?*"

"A little at a time . . . We're just realizing it now; the town's dying."

And most disturbing—it is not the aliens that caused this deterioration. It's another sign of the times, continuing all the way to today's battle between small town businesses and the cold calculation of major corporations, those vast conglomerates that destroy the mom-and-pop outfits across America, wearing their own masks, imitating and intimidating. Finney uses all these root fears—of outsiders trying to control us, of racial conflict, of changing times—to draw his readers into a screaming edge of terror that has a significance the movies based on *The Body Snatchers* (there are four) don't attempt. Such is the work of a true master of his craft.

But it's worth noting one last difference between the book and the movies, one last proof of the power of Finney's words over the cinematic flicker. And that lies at the end of the book. All the movies conclude with a cynical and pessimistic hopelessness. In the original black-and-white film, our hero is reduced to a wailing Cassandra, with no one to heed his call.

But what about the book? In the final section, Dr. Bennell and his girlfriend have a chance to escape, but instead the two remain behind to burn a field of growing alien seed pods, sacrificing their own freedom. Contrary to our expectations, Bennell becomes a hero whose last act of defiance has an unexpected result. The pods abandon their invasion, forsaking the planet and its implacable inhabitants, searching for easier targets. Finney offers hope, suggesting that it takes only one person to stand up against the tide, whether it's ruthless conformity, racism, or the trampling spread of corporations, and for this reader, that makes the book indeed much better than the movie.

James Rollins is the *New York Times* best-selling author of adventure thrillers, sold to over thirty countries. You'll often find him underground or underwater as a caver and scuba diver. These hobbies have helped in the creation of his earlier books, including *Subterranean*, *Deep Fathom*, *Amazonia*, and *Sandstorm*. His thrillers *Map of Bones*, *Black Order*, and *The Judas Strain* earned national accolades, such as one of 2005's "top crowd pleasers" (*New York Times*) and as one of 2006's "hottest summer reads" (*People* magazine). He was also handpicked to novelize *Indiana Jones and the Kingdom of the Crystal Skull*. His works include *The Last Oracle* as well as his first middle-school book, *Jake Ransom and the Skull King's Shadow*, and his Sigma thriller, *The Doomsday Key*. His most recent thriller is *Altar of Eden* (2010).

47

Hammond Innes's
THE WRECK OF THE MARY DEARE (1956)

Matt Lynn

Hammond Innes (1913–1998) is the missing link in British thrillers, a writer who took the adventure stories of writers such as H. Rider Haggard and John Buchan and updated them for the audiences of the 1950s and 1960s even as the Cold War spy stories of Ian Fleming, John le Carré, and Len Deighton were starting to emerge. Innes was a prolific author and journalist, who, over a career that spanned four decades, produced more than thirty novels, as well as several nonfiction books. Born in Horsham in Sussex, and educated at Cranbrook School in Kent, he started working for the *Financial News* (now the *Financial Times*) in 1934, and published his first thriller *The Doppelganger* in 1937. But it was only after World War II, in which he served in the Royal Artillery and rose to the rank of major, that he hit his stride as a writer. A succession of masterfully plotted action stories such as *The Blue Ice* and *The Angry Mountain* were published after the war. But it was *The Wreck of the Mary Deare*, later made into a film starring Gary Cooper, which transformed Innes into a global best seller. He carried on writing well into the 1990s.

For the English, the Channel—that narrow strip of water that separates their country from Continental Europe—is no more noticeable, or remarkable, than a few light clouds in winter. The ferries that plough the short section of sea from Dover to Calais, taking only an hour and a half, are the closest most of us ever get to it. Viewed from those massive ships, over such a short distance, it is a toy town sea, about as threatening as a suburban garden, and about as interesting.

But there is, of course, much more to the Channel than that, as there is to any sea-lane. The genius of *The Wreck of the Mary Deare* is that it brings the Channel snarling to life. The novel, the finest of more than thirty that Hammond Innes turned out in a long career, has many fine characters, but none finer than the teasing, vengeful sea in which it is set.

Innes belonged to the tradition of action adventure writers that started with storytellers such as H. Rider Haggard, Anthony Hope, John Buchan, and Edgar Wallace. The rules of the genre are relatively straightforward, and Innes doesn't deviate from them. Typically, an ordinary man is pitched into a conspiracy and has to fight his way out, relying on only his resources and wits.

In Innes's work, as in Buchan's, there are no supermen, special agents, or sleuths: just men, probably much like the readers themselves, who happen to find themselves facing terrible and overwhelming odds. But, while he drew on that tradition, Innes also refined the form, pushing it toward a new level of literary achievement by virtue of his painstaking research and the drama and detail he brought to his extraordinary settings.

Nowhere is that more true than in his breakthrough work. With an ordinary man in an ordinary place, *The Wreck of the Mary Deare* displays Innes's mighty talent at full sail. John Sands is steering his boat, the *Sea Witch*, out across the Channel in a bad gale. A salvage operator, Sands is no hero: he isn't especially brave or clever, but he does have a sense of honor and, like most sailors, is willing to help a fellow seaman in trouble. A shipwreck looms out of the distance, pitching wildly into the stormy seas, apparently abandoned by its crew. After climbing aboard, Sands discovers its captain, Gideon Patch, alone on the damaged ship. After a long battle against a terrible storm, the ship is ultimately broken on the Minkies, a treacherous series of rocks often hidden under the waters between Jersey and Saint-Malo in France.

The plot is straightforward enough. Sands and Patch, a man with a past, are caught up in a conspiracy by the ship's owners to switch cargos and claim the insurance. There is an inquiry, and eventually the return to the wrecked ship. What starts as a mystery turns quickly into a chase. There is nothing particularly original about it—insurance scams have been a frequent plot device in thrillers. But the setting and the skill with which Innes handles his tale set the story apart.

The sea is so well described you can taste the salt on every sentence. The lights from the wrecked boat that Sands first notices across the water have "a ghastly brilliance like a bloated glow worm." The waves and spray are "cold and clammy," the water sticking to the skin. The rough sailing conditions where the Atlantic meets the Channel, and the rocks and reefs that lurk off the coast of Brittany, are a constant menace, waiting to ensnare the unwary.

Then there is the captain, Gideon Patch, a man driven to the point of insanity by the conspiracy around him. "Sweat had seamed his face, making grime streaked runnels as though he had wept big tears," notes Sands when he first spots him on board. The captain is as wild and unpredictable as the seas he sails in, and every bit as dangerous. It is a measure of Innes's skill that he can make Patch both threatening and sympathetic at the same time: he can switch from one to the other in the space of a paragraph. The captain is a man searching for redemption—after an earlier ship was lost, his career was also lost in the doldrums for many years—and when he is offered the bridge of the Mary Deare, it is only so he can be set up to sink the vessel.

But it is the Channel that is the true major character of the story, and which inevitably controls its outcome. At times punishing, at others forgiving, the Channel lives and breathes on every page. Innes was a keen yachtsman, and all his experience of sailing off the English coast is distilled into the narrative, but there is nothing flat or technical about the descriptions of the gales, the wrecks, and the rocks.

As a writer, I've always identified with Innes. That's partly because I live close to where he was born and grew up. Indeed, my daughters go to Cranbrook School, a couple of miles down the road from my house, where Innes himself was educated. It is also partly because Innes was a financial journalist before becoming a thriller writer, the same path I have followed. But it is mostly, because, along with near contemporaries such as Alistair MacLean, he is part of a tradition of British adventure writing: a tradition that my own work, successfully or otherwise, attempts to tap into. There is something instinctively appealing about taking an ordinary man, with no special skills or exceptional courage, and then pitching him loose in a grand, dramatic narrative. He grabs readers with a raw energy, identifying them with the action, in a way that more accomplished heroes can't, and achieves the ultimate aim of popular fiction, which is to take readers on an enthralling journey both to a different place and to a different self. Innes was a master of that, and nowhere more so than in *The Wreck of the Mary Deare*.

Matt Lynn was born in Exeter and grew up in London. He started his career as a financial journalist and worked for *The Sunday Times in London* from 1992 to 2000. Today, he writes a weekly column on European economics for Bloomberg and is a regular contributor to *The Spectator*. His career as a thriller writer began with

Insecurity in 1997. *The Watchmen* was published the following year. In 2000, *The Month of the Leopard* appeared under the pen name James Harland. Over the next five years, he embarked on seven ghostwritten action adventure thrillers, for a series of well-known writers, three of which were number one bestsellers. In 2008, he returned to writing under his own name with *Death Force*, the first in a new series of thrillers featuring a group of mercenaries thrown into action around the world.

48

Ian Fleming's
FROM RUSSIA, WITH LOVE (1957)

Raymond Benson

Ian Fleming (1908–1964) created one of the most famous characters in thriller history—James Bond, 007—arguably inventing a new genre, the "fantasy" spy novel. After a career as a journalist, he began writing novels in his forties. During World War II, he served as the personal assistant to Britain's director of Naval Intelligence, an experience that shaped the fictional background of his suave but ruthless secret agent. Fleming's first novel, *Casino Royale*, was published in 1953. A new Bond thriller was published each subsequent year until 1966—a total of twelve novels and two collections of short stories. A hugely successful James Bond film series began in 1962 and is now the longest-running movie franchise in cinema history, although few of the movies present Bond as Fleming envisioned him: humorless, cold, ruthless, and brooding.

During his lifetime, Ian Fleming never received the critical appreciation he deserved. In his native England, the James Bond novels were politely acknowledged as entertaining reads but generally disregarded among the literati. Fleming began to see the huge international sales of his thrillers only after President John F. Kennedy expressed admiration for the books in a 1961 *Life* magazine article, and especially a year later when the successful film series got underway. By 1964, however, the author was dead of a heart attack and was unable to benefit from the huge acclaim his character subsequently enjoyed. Now his character is known around the world, not a bad legacy for an author who borrowed James Bond's name from that of someone who wrote a guide about birds of the West Indies.

Picking a quintessential Bond novel is a difficult task. One might say that *Dr. No* (1958) encompasses all the necessary ingredients—a larger-than-life villain, an exotic locale, a beautiful but flawed heroine, elements of the fantastic, and plenty of "sex, sadism, and snobbery," as one critic put it. Typical of the series, it emphasizes Bond's taste for the material aspects of life—food, alcohol, cars, gambling, and women—because he knows that the next morning he might not be alive. Other favorites are *Goldfinger* (1959) and *On Her Majesty's Secret Service* (1963). However, most hardcore Bond fans agree that *From Russia, with Love*, Fleming's fifth novel (1957), remains the most striking and innovative of the 007 thrillers.

The book's narrative structure is a departure from most of the series—the protagonist doesn't appear until nearly a third of the way into the novel. (Fleming tried a similar experiment in *The Spy Who Loved Me*, 1962, which is written in the first person by the female main character—Bond appears only in the last third of the book.) The first ten chapters of *From Russia, with Love* deal exclusively with the villains and their attempts to fashion a foolproof plot to assassinate 007 in an embarrassing fashion. In addition, the book ends with a surprise shocker, a completely offbeat change from Fleming's previous books—the reader is led to believe that James Bond is dead.

While *From Russia, with Love* contains everything one expects from a Bond novel—a sweeping, fast pace; colorful, descriptive prose; exotic locations (Russia, Turkey, the Orient Express); and a wonderfully clever plot—it also demonstrates Fleming's attempt to "elevate the Bond books to a higher literary level" by providing a greater degree of characterization.

The story concerns the Russian spy outfit SMERSH's elaborate plot for revenge against the British Secret Service and, in particular, James Bond. (In the movie version, the villains are the criminal organization SPECTRE instead of SMERSH, evidently an attempt by the filmmakers to practice a bit of detente.) Rosa Klebb, head of operations and executions, handpicks an assassin, Red Grant, as well as a beautiful, innocent Russian girl, Tatiana Romanova, to act as pawns in SMERSH's ploy. The Secret Service learns from Kerim, their man in Istanbul, that Romanova is willing to defect to the West and hand over a much coveted Russian Spektor Coding Machine only if James Bond will come to Istanbul and rescue her (she claims that she fell in love with the agent after seeing his photograph in the KGB file). Tatiana insists on escaping via the Orient Express, so the couple joins Kerim aboard the famous train. But Red Grant is also present. After drugging the girl and murdering Kerim, Grant reveals his true identity and explains the entire scheme to Bond. After a furious battle, Bond kills Grant and manages to escape from the train with the girl and the Spektor. Later in Paris, Bond locates Rosa Klebb in a hotel room. The woman attempts to stab Bond with poison-tipped knitting needles, but the

Deuxième Bureau arrives in time to take the woman away. Before she is arrested, however, she kicks Bond in the shin with a poison-tipped blade contained in her shoe. Bond falls to the floor, presumably dead, and the novel ends.

The startling finish validates Fleming's courageous structural experiment of focusing entirely on the villains in the first third. By elaborately detailing SMERSH's plot to kill Bond in the beginning, the feeling of imminent danger is present throughout the book and the suspense builds to a shattering climax aboard the Orient Express. Once Bond escapes this danger, the tension is momentarily relieved until he meets Rosa Klebb in Paris. With that unexpected kick in the shin, all the looming disaster that hung over Bond throughout the novel finally hits home.

In fact, when Fleming wrote the book, he was discouraged by Bond's lack of success and really did want to kill him off, but his publisher and a few friends persuaded the author to resurrect the character the following year (in *Dr. No*). In that book, we learn that 007 was rushed to the hospital in the nick of time and that his life was saved.

From Russia, with Love is arguably the only real Cold War espionage tale in Fleming's series. It's spy vs. spy, and that isn't always the case with Fleming, even though all his thrillers take place during the shady political arena of the fifties and early sixties. Notable as well is that Fleming provides Bond with the first of the spy "gadgets" that appear from time to time in the novels (and are used to an absurd extreme in the films). Here, the Armorer equips 007 with an attaché case that has secret compartments for money, ammunition, and a silencer for his Beretta. The case also contains two throwing knives hidden in the lining, one of which saves Bond's life in his fight with Grant.

From Russia, with Love might not be representative of the Bond series because of its unusual structure and surprise ending in which Bond doesn't "win"—but it is the book with the most successful blend of full characterizations in addition to a highly original, fascinating, and suspenseful plot.

Between 1996 and 2002, Raymond Benson was commissioned by the James Bond literary copyright holders to take over writing the 007 novels. In total, he authored six original 007 novels, three film novelizations, and three short stories. Some of his Bond work appeared in the anthologies *The Union Trilogy* and *Choice of Weapons*. His *The James Bond Bedside Companion*, an encyclopedia of the 007 phenomenon, was nominated for an Edgar Award by the Mystery Writers of America for Best Biographical/Critical Work. As David Michaels, Raymond also penned the *New York Times* best-selling books, *Tom Clancy's Splinter Cell* and *Tom Clancy's Splinter Cell—Operation Barracuda*. Along with his novelization of the popular videogame, *Metal Gear Solid*, Raymond's original suspense novels include *Evil Hours*, *Face Blind*, *Sweetie's Diamonds*, and *A Hard Day's Death*, the first in a series of rock 'n' roll thrillers that includes *Dark Side of the Morgue*.

49

Alistair MacLean's
THE GUNS OF NAVARONE (1957)

Larry Gandle

Alistair MacLean (1922–1987) was born in Glasgow, Scotland. He was the son of a Scottish minister and learned English as a second language after Scottish Gaelic. He spent most of his childhood near Inverness. In 1941, he joined the Royal Navy and spent two and a half years aboard a cruiser as a torpedo man. His experience in the East Coast Convoy Escorts gave him intimate knowledge of the navy and the northern Atlantic during wartime. After the war, he studied English at the University of Glasgow and graduated in 1953. He then worked as a teacher. In his spare time, he wrote short stories and won a competition in 1954 for his maritime tale, "The Dileas." The story was published in the *Glasgow Herald*, where the wife of an editor at Collins read it and showed it to her husband. The editor tracked down MacLean and convinced him to write a full-length novel. The result was MacLean's first novel, *H.M.S. Ulysses* (1955), a huge commercial success that was partially based on MacLean's wartime experiences and was favorably compared to Herman Wouk's *The Caine Mutiny*. This was followed by *The Guns of Navarone* in 1957, another best seller. In 1961, it became an Academy Award-nominated film starring Gregory Peck, David Niven, and Anthony Quinn. A 1968 film based on another of his novels, *Where Eagles Dare*, starred Richard Burton and Clint Eastwood. Over the next thirty years, MacLean published a total of twenty-eight novels. After his death in 1987, his popularity went into a decline with few books now in print in the U.S., although most are still available in the UK.

The Guns of Navarone is a riveting tale about a team of mission specialists in World War II who are given the assignment of destroying huge guns on the island of Navarone, off the coast of Turkey. The guns disrupt a shipping lane that British ships need to use in order to rescue twelve hundred men from the nearby island of Kheros. Keith Mallory, a world famous mountain climber, is chosen to lead the group. Mallory is also a skilled saboteur and speaks Greek and German fluently. The others in the group are Lieutenant Andy Stevens, who will navigate the boat and is also a skilled Alpine climber, Corporal Dusty Miller, an explosives expert, Casey Brown, engineer of the boat and guerilla fighter, and finally the hulking presence of Andrea Stavrov, skilled in hand-to-hand combat and a "complete fighting machine." Andrea is Greek and knows the intricacies of the language and customs. Together, they must accomplish what the British Navy and Air Force could not. They must infiltrate the island of Navarone and blow up the enormous guns. The mission appears to be suicidal.

There are, of course, multiple obstacles to achieving success. First, they sail to the island in a dark storm in a boat with a very unreliable engine. They encounter a Nazi ship on the way. The storm batters them against the rocks. Once on the island, they must overcome guards, then climb the sheer cliffs. They are confronted by more guards at the top, are captured, shot at by Stuka dive-bombers and troops on the ground. They must also discover the identity of a traitor in their midst, who keeps the Germans on their tail continuously. One escapade follows another until the great climactic scene when they finally reach the guns.

MacLean uses the techniques he is famous for, bringing together a group of greater-than-life heroes who must beat insurmountable odds to achieve the seemingly impossible. Their resilience and determination are qualities that he favored throughout his career, although in many books one of the group is a traitor, with the consequence that loyalty is emphasized as another virtue. Sex and romance aren't present because the author thought these elements slowed the action. The plot has an episodic structure as the heroes struggle from one crisis to another. In a sense, the book is a serial novel with each scene ascending to a climax and a very brief denouement before the next scene begins. While the characters are not complex, the descriptive prose creates a strong sense of realism. At heart, the entertainment value and the imaginative storytelling are what make MacLean's books effective. Nobody had a better grasp of how to plunge readers straight into the meat of a story and to keep them gripped through the twists and turns of the next three hundred pages.

Of course, there are elements of MacLean's work that appear old-fashioned these days. He brought a very British sense of fair play to his work. His heroes fight by the rules. They don't ever actually complain about "something not being cricket," but there is little question that they think it.

Nonetheless, MacLean had several great achievements. He is one of the writers who defined the fictional version of World War II. A "good war," fought by honest, hardworking men, pressed into a civilian army that was fighting for a noble cause. It was a war that turned ordinary guys into heroes. And it was a war where stealth, courage, and determination allowed the ordinary soldier to make a difference. Watch any World War II drama since the late 1950s, and the image of the war they portray is essentially MacLean's.

Next, he had a major influence on the adventure story. His heroes were men pitched into conspiracies, wars, conflicts, who struggled against impossible odds, both to overcome their opponent and to maintain a sense of decency. The work of later authors such as Frederick Forsyth and Tom Clancy owes a huge debt to MacLean. Through the qualities of his heroes, his lean, punchy prose style, and the furious pacing of his stories, he helped to create the contemporary adventure thriller. Indeed, it is hard to watch any modern Hollywood action movie without seeing MacLean's fingerprints all over the script.

In addition, MacLean's work had a significant impact on the maritime thriller, influencing authors like Clive Cussler, who acknowledged that he studied MacLean's fiction and used it as an example when he began his career. But MacLean had an even broader influence, providing a modern template for the Mission Impossible or Dirty Dozen type of story in which a band of various and sometimes mismatched heroes takes on a seemingly unachievable task against overwhelming odds.

Given all this, it's puzzling why his books are no longer in print in the United States. One reason might be that these days there is little interest in stories about World War II or the Cold War. Nuclear weapons in the hands of Arab terrorists are perhaps more relevant to contemporary readers. A pity. With one of the greatest thriller plots ever invented, *The Guns of Navarone* is a novel that deserves to be in print and enjoyed for many more decades to come.

Larry Gandle is the assistant editor of *Deadly Pleasures Mystery Magazine*. He is also a creator of the Barry Award for best thriller, one of the first awards to have that objective. Now there are others such as the Ian Fleming Steel Dagger Award of Great Britain's Crime Writers Association and the Thriller Award of the International Thriller Writers organization. Larry works as a radiation oncologist in Florida and resides in Tampa.

50

Richard Condon's
THE MANCHURIAN CANDIDATE (1959)

Robert S. Levinson

Richard Condon (1915–1996) published his first novel, *The Oldest Profession*, in 1958, and a year later scored his first major success with *The Manchurian Candidate*, a bravura thriller that brought him fame, fortune, and a writing career that included two dozen other books that bristle with wit, satire, and irreverent, often wicked, wisdom. His themes were frequently political in nature, among them *Winter Kills*, a critical success dealing with a family not unlike the Kennedys, *The Final Addiction*, and *Emperor of America*, while he more memorably invaded Mafia lore with *Prizzi's Honor* and three sequels. Condon turned to fiction after twenty-two years working as a movie publicist, including a long term with Walt Disney Productions promoting *Snow White and the Seven Dwarfs*, *Fantasia*, *Pinocchio*, and *Dumbo*. A native New Yorker, he settled for a time in Paris, before moving with his wife and two daughters to homes in Spain, Ireland, and Switzerland, ultimately settling in Dallas prior to his death. Condon called himself a compulsive writer, who spent seven hours a day, seven days a week at the typewriter, and often quoted "Condon's Law" about writing fiction: "When you don't know the whole truth, the worst you can imagine is bound to be close."

> If you write one book that, for whatever reason,
> becomes iconic it's an extraordinary blessing.
> —John le Carré

That's precisely what Richard Condon did, bless him.

He wrote a book fifty years ago that has come to be considered a cultural icon of another time in America's history, containing elements that have continued to ring true through the decades, seem relevant today, and suggest a relevancy that will continue into the future.

The Manchurian Candidate was an instant best seller, pitched into controversial orbit by unorthodox storytelling as chilling as it was thrilling, a volatile mix of Cold War politics, sex, cynicism, satire, suspense, humor, intrigue, incest, murder, suicide, and blackmail. The overload of information frequently threatened to crash a story praised for its brilliance and originality by some, condemned by others for a pulp prose style that elevated kitsch to another dimension.

As Condon laid it out, an American army patrol is captured during the Korean War and taken to a Chinese research facility where the members are brainwashed into believing they're attending a ladies' garden club meeting. In fact, they're witnessing the murder of two members of their unit by Sergeant Raymond Shaw, who has been programmed to obey commands triggered by the suggestion that he pass the time by playing a game of solitaire. No one who has read the book or seen the movie can forget the significance of the queen of diamonds.

The patrol members are set free, convinced that Raymond rescued them from death at the hands of an overwhelming enemy force. Raymond returns home a walking time bomb, chosen by the Communists to commit an unspecified assassination sometime in the future because of his ties to the corridors of power. His stepfather is U.S. Senator Johnny Iselin, a clownish lush being steered to higher office by his wife, Raymond's domineering mother, through the use of repeated and wholly invented claims about Communist agents occupying sensitive positions in various agencies of government.

At the same time, once back home, the patrol's leader, Captain Ben Marco, suffers a recurring nightmare. Visions of the garden club meeting conflict with images of Raymond killing the two soldiers and feed a growing belief that the enemy encounter never happened. He brings his suspicions to the military authorities, who judge Marco to be a mental invalid of the Korean War until another platoon member reveals he's tortured by the same nightmare.

Marco, leading the government's pursuit after the truth, locks onto Raymond who, although suffering his own anxieties, remains completely controlled by his Soviet handlers and will commit five murders on command—his beloved wife among the victims—before he turns the queen of diamonds face up in a game of solitaire and is directed to his ultimate assassination target.

The clock is ticking as Marco finally pieces together the puzzle. He charges after Raymond in a desperate pursuit that leads to Madison Square

Garden and the political convention where Senator Iselin is about to be introduced as his party's nominee for vice president and to a series of climactic twists that play out like a Greek tragedy.

Upon publication, *The Manchurian Candidate* was awarded immediate cachet as a mirror of the times. It dealt with the first armed conflict of a Cold War so failed and open-ended (to this day, unresolved between North Korea and the U.S.) that it was labeled a "police action" in official records; an ultimately disgraced U.S. Senator Joe McCarthy, who kept changing the number of Communists he'd allegedly uncovered in our government; and, especially, the concept of mind control through a technique that proved to be valid and ultimately came to be known as brainwashing.

I couldn't afford the hardcover when it was published to all the hoopla and huzzahs, so I had to wait for the paperback edition, which I began reading on a business flight to New York. I was less than thrilled. For one thing, the plot was frequently nonlinear. For another, Condon's writing offered more details than a Bond Street tailor lavishes on a suit, far too many for this off-the-rack guy. If Condon mentioned the Medal of Honor, he felt the need to interrupt the story to provide a page about its history. The same for political conventions. The same for—

I set aside the book after twenty-five or thirty pages, quietly cursing the reviewers who had convinced me to invest two bits and my time ("A breathlessly up-to-date thriller," *New York Times*; "Brilliant," *The New Yorker*), but I've never been one to quit a book (or a movie), no matter how bad, without seeing it through to the bitter end. I went back to *The Manchurian Candidate* after returning from an evening at the theater. Settling in bed, I expected Condon's expansive, occasionally mind-numbing prose to shuttle me to dreamland after a few pages.

Au contraire.

The story took off, kept me awake all night, riveted to an innovative thriller that a half century later handily holds its own against changes in storytelling techniques, whose influence is often revealed in the themes and conceits of more than a few authors working today.

The movie versions, the first in 1962 with Frank Sinatra as Marco and Laurence Harvey as Raymond, and the second in 2004 with Denzel Washington and Liev Schreiber, practiced a less diabolical form of brainwashing, tricking people into believing they know the book. Not so, if only because they're denied the greater truths Condon packed into his final paragraphs.

For any doubters among you, why don't you pass the time by playing a little solitaire?

Robert S. Levinson, best-selling author of *The Traitor in Us All, In the Key of Death, Where the Lies Begin, Ask a Dead Man*, and the Neil Gulliver-Stevie Marriner mystery-thrillers *The Elvis and Marilyn Affair, The James Dean Affair, The John Lennon Affair*, and *Hot Paint*, was an award-winning newspaperman, public relations executive, and television writer-producer before he turned to writing fiction. Among other credits: short stories in *Ellery Queen* and *Alfred Hitchcock* mystery magazines, Ellery Queen Readers Award recognition three times, stories in four "year's best" anthologies, stage plays premiered at RiverPark Center's International Mystery Writers Festival, 2007 and 2008. He wrote and produced two Mystery Writers of America Edgar Award galas, as well as two International Thriller Writers Thriller Award shows. He also served on the Writers Guild of America-West board of directors, four years on the Mystery Writers of America national board, and six terms as president of the Hollywood Press Club.

51

Len Deighton's
THE IPCRESS FILE (1962)

Jeffery Deaver

Len Deighton (1929–) is the only cook-artist-historian-spy writer that I know of. The proclivity toward cooking, and later food journalism, came from his chef mother, the art from innate talent later nurtured by training at the Royal College of Art. The historian-spy part? Certainly a stint with Royal Air Force's Special Investigations Branch could be cited as an influence. But equally important was the boy's experience in wartime Britain—where one couldn't escape either the blunt or subtle aspects of global conflict and the intrigue they engendered. Born in England, Leonard Cyril Deighton worked a number of jobs in countries all over the world: photographer, chef, waiter, illustrator, advertising executive, airline steward, and food columnist. He wrote his first novel, *The IPCRESS File*, in the early 1960s. It became a successful movie, released in 1965, starring Michael Caine. (The film was titled *The Ipcress File*—note the difference in capitalization—the word an acronym, whose meaning I won't reveal, in the interest of, well, keeping covert what should remain covert.) Deighton has been writing successful spy and thriller novels, short stories, and nonfiction history books ever since.

Set in the fog of the Cold War, *The IPCRESS File* features an unnamed protagonist (he was Harry Palmer only in the movie version). The agent (I'll call him our "Spy") was a former military intelligence officer now working as an operative for one of the smallest of the British security organizations. When brilliant British scientists begin disappearing, a very 1960's conceit, our Spy is recruited to handle the case, and he soon tumbles into a web of brainwashing and mind control plots, Eastern Bloc shenanigans, and home-front intrigue and infighting. The exotic locations of Lebanon and the South Pacific figure prominently.

The novel was a huge bestseller when it was first published in 1962. Three years later, the book was successfully adapted to the screen (minus the Mideast and Asian settings), and Michael Caine's subtle and wry Cockney-inflected characterization of the protagonist set the standard for portraying an unsuperhero spy (I'm thinking especially of European New Wave and noir cinema of the '60s and some of the grittier TV shows like Patrick McGoohan's *Secret Agent*, which originated as *Danger Man* in the UK, and *The Prisoner*).

The plot of *The IPCRESS File* is more than serviceable—and offers up a good whammy twist at the end—but the storytelling is elliptical, even meandering; one doesn't read *The IPCRESS File* for Matt Damon *Bourne Identity* roller-coaster speed. Its significance lies elsewhere.

First, of course, with our Spy.

Though Deighton refined his plotting in later books, *The IPCRESS File* is at heart a character-driven look at a man in conflict and those whom he crashes up against or glances off of. And what a character he is—a classic antihero from the 1960s: a forty-something civil servant obliquely making his way as best he can through life, contemptuous of classist British society, paranoid (he's weirdly fastidious about keeping an escape package with a new identity up to date), and flippant and fast with his wry asides (words as a shield, it always struck me). When we think of Len Deighton and *The IPCRESS File*, we are immediately reminded of Alan Sillitoe (*The Loneliness of the Long Distance Runner*) and John Osborne, creators of working-class antiheroic protagonists smoldering in gritty postwar England.

Yet our Spy's skepticism about the Establishment doesn't derail his strong moral center and his courage to act upon it. "I have a clear mind and pure heart," he says. "I am a loyal and diligent employee and will attempt every day to be worthy of the trust my paternal employer puts in me." He's cynical yet not bitter—a very hard act for an author to pull off.

We are with this unnamed fellow 100 percent, even when he plods along without much direction—largely, I think, because that is how most of us live our lives: stumbling in the general direction of our rather vague missions.

He comes alive within us.

And so, I should point out, does the world he inhabits. For this, we have to marvel at Deighton's narrative ability to create a character with a keen eye and observant nature and the intelligence to articulate those observations for our benefit.

Deighton, through the Spy, nails the personalities of those he meets, in the same way that a perceptive observant journalist/psychotherapist might. We immediately feel the avarice, cowardice, foolishness, courage, nobility, and sleaze of those who populate the book. In compensation for breathless plotting, the author offers a breathtaking journey into the murky world of gray versus gray—and that shading refers, if I may indulge, both to geopolitics and the human mind.

As a rebellious teenager in that turbulent era, I picked our Spy as my preferred espionage protagonist. He taught me cool, he taught me healthy skepticism . . . and he taught me a thing or two about living on one's own and self-reliance. Why, he even provided cooking lessons! (Some trivia: A gourmet cook, Len Deighton taught Michael Caine how to crack an egg like an expert during the filming of the movie.)

Another reason that *The IPCRESS File* appeals to me is the author's prose. It's weighty and complex, far from the staccato, pop vernacular of most crime fiction of that era. You sift through it slowly, enjoying. Deighton showed that spy writing could be both stylish and yet not a pastiche of Graham Greene. I like to think that his style derived from his love of drawing and of cooking, two skills whose success depends more on inspirational improvisation than hewing mindlessly to preliminary sketches and printed recipes.

The *Sunday Times* of London called him "the poet of the spy story."

I also appreciate *The IPCRESS File* for its role in the history of espionage literature. The triumvirate of that era, of course, was composed of Ian Fleming, John le Carré, and Len Deighton. Of their creations, James Bond was the flashy superhero, George Smiley the tireless, yet world-weary bureaucrat. Deighton's unnamed Spy was a combination of the two: a physically brave field agent informed by cynicism and a complex worldview and with a disdain, if not contempt, for glitz and gimmickry. Deighton's writing was more accessible than le Carré's dense narrative, but transcended Fleming's journalistic prose.

While Fleming was well established when Deighton first published (and indeed would survive the publication of *The IPCRESS File* by only a few years), I can't help but speculate that le Carré—just getting his own writing career underway—was a careful reader of Deighton's fiction.

Finally, the novel stands as a vivid historic tableau of life in the Cold War era. We've largely forgotten about those days of East vs. West, of simple enemies in simple conflict, thanks to the emergence of nonstate threats like Al-Qaida. But read *The IPCRESS File*, and, if you're of a certain age, you'll get vivid flashbacks to a time when you'd lie awake nights, worried about warmongering Bolsheviks poised over nuclear missile launch buttons.

There were several other novels featuring our unnamed Spy, including *Funeral in Berlin*, which was, in my opinion, the best in the series.

So why did I pick *The IPCRESS File* as my must-read selection?

Because it was the first Len Deighton book, it was *my* first Len Deighton book, it was the first to elevate an antihero to such heights in popular culture. And is anything ever better than the *first*? I don't think so—whether it's your first beer, your first car, your first lover.

Or your first covert assignment snatching a roll of stolen microfilm from a dead-drop site on a foggy night in East Berlin, right under the noses of those nasty Stasi agents.

We've all been there, right?

A former journalist, folk singer, and attorney, Jeffery Deaver is an international number-one best-selling author. His numerous books include *The Bodies Left Behind*, *The Broken Window*, and *The Sleeping Doll* as well as *A Maiden's Grave*, which became an HBO film starring James Garner and Marlee Matlin, and *The Bone Collector*, which was adapted into a major feature film starring Denzel Washington and Angelina Jolie. He's been awarded the Steel Dagger and Short Story Dagger from the British Crime Writers Association. In addition, he is a three-time recipient of the Ellery Queen Reader's Award for Best Short Story and has been nominated for six Edgar Awards, an Anthony Award, and a Gumshoe Award. In 2009, ITW gave him its Best Novel Award for *The Bodies Left Behind*.

52
Fletcher Knebel and Charles W. Bailey's
SEVEN DAYS IN MAY (1962)

James Grady

The superb Cold War political thriller, *Seven Days In May*, came from two Washington journalists, fact hunters who added street savvy to classical educations and created fiction. Fletcher Knebel came to big-time D.C. journalism via the Sorbonne and rural Pennsylvania reporting. For this book, their fiction debut, he partnered with Harvard scion Charles Bailey II, who came out of the *Minneapolis Tribune* and who, even as his book career flourished, went on to be Washington editor for National Public Radio. They used newspaper skills to sharpen inspiration into a blockbuster that couldn't be ignored as implausible. Their other novels include *Convention* and *No High Ground*. On his own, Knebel wrote *Night of Camp David*, *Vanished*, and *Dark Horse*, among others. Knebel (who died of cancer) famously said: "Smoking is one of the leading causes of statistics." Together they created a masterpiece, one that inspired legions of their fellow D.C. reporters to spend long nights tapping keyboards and failing to produce a political thriller better than *Seven Days in May*.

Fall back in time and space to the mushroom cloud fears of 1961 and Washington, D.C., a post World War II "sleepy Southern town" rebranding itself after the witch-hunting McCarthy era as a modern Camelot for young President John F. Kennedy. Come back to a world dominated by the Cold War with sideshows in places like Vietnam that few Americans could find on a map, though we all knew where Cuba was after a failed invasion at its Bay of Pigs, which was not so secretly backed by our Central Intelligence Agency. World news in that era skimmed stories of military coups dotting the globe—coups that we now know often bore the fingerprints of our spies. Autumn in the next year meant "the missiles of October," a nuclear-tipped showdown again triggered by Cuba, when the U.S. and the U.S.S.R. went eyeball to eyeball and blinked our way back from atomic Armageddon.

In 1961, Fletcher Knebel was a newspaper journalist and the driving force for a thriller he cowrote with Charles W. Bailey II, a book ignited by the paranoia of the times and little-known twists of American history, a novel that created a template for the American political thriller for the next half century: *Seven Days in May*.

The plot is simple: a charismatic Air Force general sets up a coup to overthrow America's democracy and an unpopular, diplomacy-driven president "for the good of the nation." A Marine colonel named Jiggs discovers the plot by accident, then works with the president and a handful of Washington insiders to thwart the plot against a ticking countdown clock of seven days—all without alarming the trusting nation or the trigger-nervous world.

Seven Days in May is a literary triumph of the big "what if."

There'd been "American loses its democracy" books before—notably Nobel Prize winner Sinclair Lewis's anti-Fascist 1935 novel *It Can't Happen Here*. Living memory in 1961 included challenges to America's rule of law and civilian control of the military such as the 1933 "Businessmen's Plot" when big money tycoons tried to convince retired Marine Corps hero General Smedley Butler to lead a coup against President Franklin D. Roosevelt (Smedley blew the whistle). President Harry Truman had fired the pompous but vastly more popular General Douglas MacArthur over Korean war policy disagreements, and Washington during Camelot buzzed with rumors about how Air Force General Curtis LeMay (later vice presidential candidate for George Wallace) considered his commander in chief JFK a weak-willed appeaser of America's enemies.

But it took Knebel and Bailey to "what if" all that into a page-turning, feels-real novel that scared the hell out of Americans and showed them the fragility of democracy. The Academy Award-nominated movie adaptation that starred Burt Lancaster as the egomaniacal coup leader general and Kirk Douglas as the square-jawed Marine hero turned *Seven Days in May* into an American cultural icon.

What's amazing nearly a half century of "big idea" and "what-if" novels later is how the book still grips a reader—even though it's a thriller with almost no action.

Conversations and conjectures drive the novel. The most dynamic scene fills a few lines when an Army sentry gets knocked unconscious by his honorable commanding officer and a secretly imprisoned United States senator. A Secret Service agent tails villains without getting caught.

People meet and move the plot forward . . . by talking. "Off camera" an admiral confesses, a plane accidentally crashes, and Jiggs—after crude sweet talk—makes love to his own wife. The greatest personal peril our Marine hero faces comes from his irresistibility to a New York career woman whom he asks . . . for gossip. The showdown comes in a long mano a mano debate between the evil general and the virtuous president, with a "double tap" bullet of speechifying fired into the general on the White House lawn by the president's buddies who promise to expose the general's extramarital affair if he fails to disappear from public life. The epilogue wrapping up loose ends is a transcript of a Monday morning presidential press conference in which nothing nefarious is revealed.

More action explodes in chapter one of many post-JFK assassination thrillers than in the whole of *Seven Days in May*. And yet, most of them are forgotten while Knebel and Bailey's work lives on—in our cultural consciousness, though not on our bookshelves. It's out of print.

Seven Days in May triumphs because it never loses sight of its big idea and because it personifies a few good men confronting a massive evil. The authors set the fiction in *their* distant future of 1974—ironically, the spring of the Watergate hearings that brought about the downfall of a rogue president, not a renegade chairman of the Joint Chiefs of Staff—and while many of Knebel and Bailey's assumptions about that era's everyday life never came true, their big "what if" endures because the challenges to government, politics, freedom, law, justice, and loyalty are ever present.

If we'd never been blessed with *Seven Days in May*, which I read as a teenager, I'm not sure I'd have written *Six Days of the Condor*. Knebel and Bailey—along with Frederick Forsyth's *The Day of the Jackal*—showed a new generation of authors like me how to use a ticking clock as the central and endemic organizing principle for a big "what if." *Seven Days in May* perhaps more than any other novel showed how to create powerful fiction by spinning an ultrarealistic plot "behind" the reality that's believable to readers when they start page one *and* after they lift their eyes from the end, so that "what if" becomes not only "what could happen" but "maybe it already did."

That's a classic thriller.

James Grady published his first novel, *Six Days of the Condor*, in 1974 when he was twenty-five. A former U.S. Senate aide and national investigative reporter, he is the author of a dozen more novels, including *Runner in the Street* and *River of*

Darkness, plus numerous short stories as well as scripts for television and films. Grady received an Edgar nomination for his short story, "Kiss the Sky," won France's 2001 Grand Prix du Roman Noir, Italy's 2004 Raymond Chandler medal, and Japan's 2008 World Baka-Misu Award for fiction. In 2008, London's *Daily Telegraph* named Grady as "one of fifty crime writers to read before you die." He lives inside Washington, D.C.'s Beltway with his writer wife, Bonnie Goldstein. Their son, Nathan, is a college student; their daughter, Rachel, is a documentary director/producer nominated for a 2007 Academy Award.

53

Lionel Davidson's
THE ROSE OF TIBET (1962)

Milton C. Toby

Lionel Davidson (1922–2009) may be an unfamiliar author to many readers on the American side of the Atlantic. In England, though, Davidson was touted as a rising superstar when his first novel, *The Night of Wenceslas*, was published in 1960. He drew immediate comparisons to Eric Ambler, John le Carré , and other masters of spy fiction, and that debut novel won the Crime Writers' Association Gold Dagger. Davidson won a second CWA Gold Dagger with *A Long Way to Shiloh*, published in 1966, and his third with *The Chelsea Murders*, published in 1978. In 2001, Davidson received the CWA Cartier Diamond Dagger for his sustained excellence and for a significant contribution to crime fiction. Davidson later called his four CWA awards "extraordinary," telling an interviewer that only *The Chelsea Murders* was "even *about* crime." There is no pretense of crime in the author's second novel, *The Rose of Tibet*, and his most recent work, *Kolymsky Heights*, written thirty-two years apart. Both are great adventure stories. Despite Davidson's numerous honors, his novels are difficult to find these days, but the search is well worth the effort.

H. Rider Haggard established a lofty standard for adventure novels with his Victorian classics *King's Solomon's Mines* and *She*. It was another seventy-five years before Lionel Davidson raised the bar even higher with *The Rose of Tibet*. Although sharing some thematic and stylistic elements with *King Solomon's Mines* and *She*, *The Rose of Tibet* is far more than a simple retelling of the Haggard tales. And, thankfully, it has little in common with an early film version of *King Solomon's Mines* that had actor and singer Paul Robeson as Umbopa breaking into song at odd times during a hazardous trek across the African desert.

   An account by protagonist Charles Houston of his eighteen-month journey to Tibet to search for his brother, *The Rose of Tibet* is presented a first-person narrative told by a third-person narrator. This unusual literary device allows Davidson, the author, to appear in the book as Davidson, the character, a dubious book editor who takes it upon himself to verify, and then to prepare a record of, Houston's amazing story for publication.

Readers are introduced to Charles Houston when Davidson learns that Houston dictated the details of his travels to an elderly friend, who offers the notebooks for publication. Unfortunately, Houston is not in a position to confirm any of the details surrounding his time in Tibet; having returned to England with £500,000 and an injury requiring the amputation of his right arm, he has vanished somewhere in the Caribbean.

In the introduction, sprinkled through the narrative, and finally in a lengthy epilogue, Davidson tries to pin down elements of Houston's story, communicating with Tibet scholars and government officials while trying to locate eyewitnesses to the astonishing events described by Houston. H. Rider Haggard employed a similar technique in *She*, where the author-as-editor publishes a manuscript ostensibly written by L. Horace Holly, who was mysteriously absent in "Thibet" without a forwarding address.

Both Haggard and Davidson had real-world experience reworking and publishing the manuscripts of others. Employed as fiction editor at the magazine *John Bull* during the early 1950s, following time in the submarine service during World War II, Davidson serialized the likes of authors Agatha Christie and Graham Greene. His attention to detail in recounting the investigation into Houston's story, and throughout the book itself, lends an air of credibility to the whole affair. It leaves the reader wondering if there might be some factual basis to the novel.

The Rose of Tibet starts slowly, building momentum for the first fifty or so pages while Houston debates whether to travel to India, and then to Tibet to search for his brother, a filmmaker who vanished during an assignment. By the time Houston commits himself to the quest, there is no doubt that he is singularly ill suited to the task and that things won't proceed as planned.

Arriving in India, he is stonewalled by the Tibetans, who are reluctant to give outsiders any information about the missing film crew. He hires a young Sherpa named Ringling who leads him over the Himalayas to the monastery at Yamdring, where rumors hint that a group of foreigners are being held. Mistaken for the god Hu-Tzung because Ringling mispronounces his name as Hoo-tsung, Houston locates his brother and makes frequent visits to the bed of Mei-Hua—the high priestess of the monastery, the eighteenth incarnation of the Rose of Tibet.

In spite of its remoteness and inaccessibility, or perhaps because of it, Tibet has been coveted by outsiders for centuries. A delegation of Russian Cossacks was turned back near Lhasa in 1879. Then in 1904 the British staged a brutal military invasion led by Sir Francis Younghusband in which thousands of Tibetans were killed. The most recent invaders, the Chinese, are still there. They stormed into Tibet in 1951 and created a "hell on earth" according to the Dalai Lama, who fled to India a step ahead of the invaders.

With the Chinese invasion as a backdrop, Houston, Mei-Hua, Ringling, and the British film crew attempt a tortuous escape from Tibet. The final third of the book holds its own with any thriller as the party tries to dodge the Chinese army and struggles to survive in a harsh and unyielding environment. Nearly everyone dies, leaving Houston and Mei-Hua to spend months wintering in a tiny cave near a village occupied by the Chinese.

The Rose of Tibet works on several levels, as a tale of high adventure and as a richly textured glimpse into an exotic place that few people ever will experience firsthand. When the book was published in 1962, most outsiders knew little about Tibet, and Lhasa was considered the Holy Grail of exotic destinations. Not a lot had changed when I visited Tibet in 1985, shortly after the area was opened to foreigners by the Chinese, although my arrival by airplane was far less arduous and eventful than Houston's overland treks by bicycle, mule, horseback, and on foot.

Obvious tensions between Tibetans and the Chinese notwithstanding, Tibet was, and is, a special and magical place. Lionel Davidson has done it justice, and The Rose of Tibet is clear evidence that a rousing adventure is timeless.

Milton C. Toby is an attorney and author who lives in Georgetown, Kentucky. His practice includes the representation of death row inmates and equine law, an unlikely combination of interests that has been the basis for several award-winning short stories. Before becoming a lawyer, Toby worked as a journalist and freelance photographer in the United States, China (from where he traveled in Tibet), Costa Rica, and Colombia. He is the author of five nonfiction books, including Ruffian, a biography of the ill-fated filly that might be the best Thoroughbred racehorse of all time, and The Complete Handbook of Equine Law and Business, as well as numerous magazine articles on legal topics. He serves as chair of the Contracts Committee for the American Society of Journalists and Authors and speaks on copyright issues affecting writers and photographers.

54
Richard Stark's (Donald E. Westlake's)
THE HUNTER, aka POINT BLANK (1962)

Duane Swierczynski

Donald E. Westlake (1933–2008) was born in Brooklyn and raised in Yonkers and Albany. He attended colleges in New York state without graduating. Considered a writer's writer by his peers, Westlake received an Academy Award nomination for his screenplay, *The Grifters*, three Edgar Awards, and the Grand Master Award from the Mystery Writers of America. His first novel, *The Mercenaries*, was published in 1960. Thereafter Westlake wrote under his own name as well as several pseudonyms, in part to combat skepticism over his rapid rate of production. His pen names included Tucker Coe, Samuel Holt, Edwin West, and Richard Stark. Under his own name, he invented the comic caper genre (*The Fugitive Pigeon*, 1965) and wrote a number of humorous novels about a luckless criminal named John Dortmunder. Meanwhile, as Richard Stark, he chronicled the brutal existence of career criminal Parker. Combining the two, Westlake's comic caper novel, *Jimmy the Kid* (1974), features Dortmunder's gang of bumbling kidnappers using a Richard Stark/Parker novel as a blueprint for a crime. Westlake wrote over one hundred novels, many of which were made into movies, *The Hot Rock* and *Bank Shot*, for example. *The Hunter* was filmed twice as *Point Blank* (with Lee Marvin) and *Payback* (with Mel Gibson).

I discovered Richard Stark in Stephen King's *The Dark Half*. In an afterword, King talked about how fictional tough guy writer George Stark was modeled on Donald E. Westlake's "Richard Stark" alter ego. I was seventeen years old, and I remember thinking I really needed to track down some stuff by this Stark guy. He sounded like my kind of writer. But this was an Internet-less 1989, and I couldn't find a single book by Stark, in print or used.

Life moved on. In 1997, I read and loved a novel called *The Ax* by Westlake, and later remembered that, oh yeah, this was that Stark guy, under his real name. The first Stark novel I finally laid hands on was *The Damsel*, in a beat-to-hell Signet edition I found on the bargain shelves at Otto Penzler's Mysterious Bookshop (shelves, I later learned, that Westlake helped build.) I read it in a gulp and instantly craved more. By that time, after a hiatus that lasted from 1974 to 1997, Stark had resumed writing the Parker novels (the first of the new ones had the appropriate title, *Comeback*), and slowly . . . very, very slowly . . . older Starks returned to print. In the years that followed, I finally managed to track down all of the 1962–1974 Parker novels, from *The Hunter* through *Butcher's Moon*. If there's a better series of American crime novels, I have yet to discover it.

I also devoured all of the Westlakes I could find. While he is famous for his comic caper novels, I enjoyed his hard-edged stuff better: *The Ax*, *Killing Time*, *361*, *The Hook*, *Don't Lie to Me*, *Murder Among Children*, *Killy*, *The Smashers* (aka *The Mercenaries*). But it was Stark's novels about Parker, a tough amoral heister with no first name, that really grabbed me. So much so that when I decided to write a straight crime novel, I wrote one about a mute getaway driver named Lennon. Needless to say, *The Wheelman* owes a serious debt to Richard Stark—the pace, the clipped emotions. So do a lot of other tough guy novels in the Stark mode, including Max Allan Collins's Nolan series, Garry Disher's Wyatt, and more recently Dan Simmons's Joe Kurtz and Tom Piccirilli's Chase. The influence goes beyond novels. Whenever I see a character like Terence Stamp's Wilson in Steven Soderbergh's *The Limey*, or even Clint Eastwood's *Dirty Harry*, I think of Parker. Whenever I read a Punisher comic, I think of Parker. Richard Stark infused the crime genre with fresh, cold blood. He made it okay to root for the bad guy.

Funny thing is, I don't believe Westlake set out to revolutionize anything. At the time, he was being published in hardback and wanted to write paperback originals under a pen name. So Westlake came up with a story about a remorseless, cold operator who, by novel's end, would be caught and punished. Because that's what you did to bad guys in crime novels back in the 1960s. You caught them. And then you punished them.

But something weird happened along the way. Gold Medal, which had been Westlake's intended target, passed on *The Hunter*. Pocket Books accepted it, but editor Bucklin Moon asked for one change. He wanted Westlake to let Parker get away at the end, so that the novel could serve as the first in a series. Westlake once told an interviewer: "So I wound up with a truly cold leading series character, which was an interesting thing to do and to try not to soften him. We came in here with this son of a bitch and we're going out with this son of a bitch."

And that's the nasty appeal of the Parker series: *it's fun to read about sons of bitches.* It's fun to watch how they respond when you start to apply the screws to them. The key to the Parker novels is that they aren't about good guys vs. bad guys, or even flawed hero vs. bad guys. No—they're about one bad guy versus *even worse guys.* You may not want to invite Parker over to the house to roll around with your kids in the backyard, but you can't help admiring the way he operates. Parker doesn't do office politics. He's not passive-aggressive. He's not going to lead a life of quiet desperation, like the rest of us mooks. Instead, Parker cuts out all of the bullshit we deal with on a daily basis, and figures out the straightest line between himself and his goal (which in *The Hunter* is $45,000 he's owed). Then he walks that line. And God help those who try to stop him. Who wouldn't want to be Parker?

The series has a remarkable unity, not only because of its impressive tough tone, but also because each book has four sections. The first, second, and fourth are presented from Parker's viewpoint, while the third is presented from the viewpoint of Parker's antagonist, usually a fellow criminal who has double-crossed him. In addition, the books usually begin with a sentence that has the following structure: "When a fresh-faced guy in a Chevy offered him a lift, Parker told him to go to hell." "When he didn't get any answer the second time he knocked, Parker kicked the door in." "When the car stopped rolling, Parker kicked out the rest of the windshield and crawled through onto the wrinkled hood."

Despite Parker being a "son of a bitch," my wife and I named our first-born son Parker, in honor of the Richard Stark character (as well as Peter Parker, the Amazing Spider-Man). A couple of years ago, I was lucky enough to meet Donald Westlake at the MWA Edgar Awards. Sarah Weinman introduced us, and I believe I just stood there, trying like hell not to say something stupid/stammer/collapse. What do you say to the writer who showed you the way? Thankfully, Westlake was gracious, funny, and totally laid-back—not at all like his cold-blooded creation. I shook his hand and thanked him for his "body of work," or something geeky like that. Incidentally, this was the Edgars where Stephen King received the MWA Grandmaster Award. I wish I could have gathered both of them in the same place to tell them: You two! You're the ones who did this to me!

Duane Swierczynski is the author of several thrillers, including the Stark-inspired heist-gone-wrong story, *The Wheelman*, as well as *The Blonde* and *Severance Package*—which he's currently adapting as a movie for Lionsgate. He also writes the monthly X-Men series, *Cable*, for Marvel Comics, and has penned adventures for such various heroes (or antiheroes) as Punisher, Wolverine, and the Immortal Iron Fist. Swierczynski recently collaborated with *CSI* creator Anthony E. Zuiker on *Level 26: Dark Origins*, the first in a series of "digi-novels" that combine traditional book publishing with digital video. He lives in Philadelphia with his wife, son, and daughter.

55

John le Carré's
THE SPY WHO CAME IN FROM THE COLD (1963)

Denise Hamilton

John le Carré is the pseudonym of David Cornwell, a former British intelligence officer who revolutionized the Cold War espionage thriller in the early 1960s with his character-driven, elegantly plotted, and morally ambiguous books. Born in 1931, le Carré worked for MI5 and later MI6 under diplomatic cover and as a political consul in Germany. He knew British double agent Kim Philby and ran spies, conducted interrogations, and debriefed defectors from behind the Iron Curtain. Le Carré is famous for his icy, intelligent writing and his insider details about the tradecraft of espionage. Many of his best-known novels feature British spymaster George Smiley. But Smiley plays only a fleeting role in *The Spy Who Came in from the Cold*, le Carré's third book and his widely acknowledged Cold War masterpiece. *Spy's* international success allowed le Carré to quit government work and devote his life to fiction. In 1965, *Spy* was turned into a movie starring Richard Burton. Other le Carré novels adapted into films include *The Little Drummer Girl*, *The Russia House*, *The Constant Gardener*, and *Tinker, Tailor, Soldier, Spy*, a television miniseries with Alec Guinness as Smiley. After the collapse of Communism, le Carré settled into writing novels about the ambiguities, abuses, and secret operations of the war on terror. In a recent BBC interview, he ranked *Spy* as his favorite and best book.

In 1963, a British intelligence officer stationed in Hamburg published a 256-page novel called *The Spy Who Came in from the Cold*. Set inside the murky world of British and East German intelligence, *Spy* was a departure from popular espionage novels of the time. There were no Bondian pyrotechnics, little glamour or gadgetry, and negligible violence. What there was—in spades—was cool, elegant writing, moral ambiguity, and almost unbearable psychological suspense.

Alec Leamas, the book's middle-aged antihero, embarks on a dangerous mission behind the Iron Curtain to frame the head of East German intelligence as a British spy. Trapped in a world of shifting realities, allegiances, and betrayals, Leamas begins to wonder if he's also a sacrificial pawn. This is a masterful chess game of a novel, spinning out feints within feints in prose all the more haunting for its simplicity. Its plot reversals and twists are concealed one inside the next like a series of Russian nesting dolls, and the true purpose of Leamas's mission and MI6's perfidy is revealed only in the book's final pages.

The book lays out themes that le Carré returned to time and again—the morally corrupt world of the spy; the fussy, donnish spymasters spinning webs from the safety of Whitehall; innocents ensnared in sinister plots and agents on both sides of the Curtain whose similarities might just outweigh their differences. But if it was a "game," it was deadly serious and played with real lives.

When Leamas's lover asks whether he cares that innocent people may die because of his lies, Leamas admits that the possibility makes him sick with shame and anger. But he can't see things in black-and-white. His only concern is whether an operation, however foul, will be successful. Indeed few of le Carré's spies see the world in black-and-white, which makes them infinitely interesting characters. The book's bleak ending, where Leamas finally takes a doomed stand, suggests his disillusionment at realizing that all governments, regardless of ideology, regard their citizens as expendable cogs in the wheel of politics.

Spy's enduring appeal is that it illuminates a dark corner of mankind while also hinting at the redemptive power of love. Almost fifty years after publication, it remains as haunting and devastating as the day it was written. But le Carré has also captured a historic epoch, deftly sketching postwar Berlin's "half-world of ruin, drawn in two dimensions, crags of war"; the virulence of anti-Semitic East German officials even *after* the Holocaust, and the rigidity of the British class system.

Protagonist Leamas is far from a privileged Oxbridge scion. He's eminently unclubbable, lacks a degree, and is considered stubborn and willful by his Whitehall superiors, who suspect he may be part Irish. But Leamas gets results, which is all that counts. For years he ran the important Berlin station, where he cultivated a successful network of East German spies. But slowly they began to be picked off by his nemesis in East Berlin, an icy, unrepentant Nazi spymaster named Mundt.

Spy opens with one of the most riveting scenes in thriller fiction, as

Leamas's last double agent tries to make it across the East German border into the Western sector on a bicycle and is shot down by guards within twenty feet of freedom as Leamas looks on, helpless. With his network blown, Leamas returns to London, where the Service has hatched their clever plan to bring down Mundt. Whitehall also hints about a mysterious "asset" left in East Germany, whom it is eager to protect from Mundt's clutches.

And so le Carré sets the first deception in motion. Leamas pretends he's been sacked, starts to drink and brawl, and is approached by Communist operatives in London who hope to bribe the dissolute "ex" spy into revealing a rumored mole in the East German service. Spirited away to East Berlin, Leamas plants the seed of Mundt's treason with his Jewish Communist interrogator, Fiedler, who itches to replace his Nazi boss. Mundt is put on trial, but then the plot twists jaggedly. When Whitehall's schemes are exposed and Mundt is vindicated, suspicion falls on Fiedler. Was he Whitehall's secret asset, Leamas wonders? Will Mundt now kill them both?

Then le Carré lowers the boom. "Suddenly, with the terrible clarity of a man too long deceived, Leamas understood the whole ghastly trick." The slight of hand that le Carré pulls off is diabolically clever. Check. Check. Checkmate.

The book ends as it begins, with a nail-biting East German border scene as two people dash madly across the no-man's-land to scale the towering, sinister wall to freedom. Le Carré keeps readers in suspense until the final two paragraphs, then sends them reeling in disbelief. Many will want to start rereading immediately to figure out how exactly the author did it, to pinpoint every hinge on which the plot turned, and catch the hints they missed the first time around.

The Cold War is history now, and the covert battles waged by Soviet and Western spy agencies seem almost quaint after the visceral terrors of 9/11 and the ensuing "hot" wars in Iraq and Afghanistan. Back then, captured spies were often exchanged rather than killed, and both sides waged mainly psychological warfare, played according to strict rules. There were no suicide bombers, videotaped beheadings, and other bestialities. At its core, the Cold War was fought between Western peoples with similar cultural backgrounds and reference points. No wonder we see it through a scrim of nostalgia.

John le Carré was the bard of Cold War literature. He pierced the veil of secrecy and ideology and taught us about spycraft and skepticism while writing about universal human themes like honor, betrayal, and love. *The Spy Who Came in From the Cold* was a thriller of its time, but through the alchemy of le Carré's words, it has grown into a novel that is timeless.

Denise Hamilton's latest novel, *The Last Embrace*, is set in 1949 Hollywood and features a missing starlet, gangsters, cops, and a special effects studio wiz. Denise also writes the contemporary Eve Diamond series and is editor of *Los Angeles Noir*, a best-selling anthology that won a Southern California Independent Booksellers' award for best mystery of the year. Denise's books have been shortlisted for the Edgar, Macavity, Anthony, and Willa Cather awards. Her debut, *The Jasmine Trade*, was a finalist for the prestigious Creasey Dagger Award given by the UK Crime Writers Association. Prior to writing novels, Hamilton was a *Los Angeles Times* staff writer. Her award-winning journalism has also appeared in *Wired, Cosmopolitan, Der Spiegel*, and *New Times*. During the Bosnian War, Hamilton lived and taught in Yugoslavia as a Fulbright Scholar, where she met many spies. She now lives in a Los Angeles suburb with her husband and two boys.

56

Wilbur Smith's
WHEN THE LION FEEDS (1964)

W. D. Gagliani

Wilbur Smith (1933–) was born in Northern Rhodesia (Zambia) and nearly died of cerebral malaria. After a miraculous recovery, he spent his early life on his father's huge cattle ranch. A reader from early on, his hated years at boarding school and university led him to an unwanted—and blessedly brief—career in accountancy, and an ardent desire to write fiction. The second novel he wrote became his first to be published and attracted a lot of attention, including the sale of film rights, foreign and book club sales, and critical acclaim. *When the Lion Feeds* was based on Smith's formative years in Africa, focusing on Sean and Garrick Courtney, competitive brothers who stand poised to participate in some of South Africa's greatest historical moments, especially the Zulu War of 1879 and the subsequent gold rush. Following this auspicious debut with more chapters in the Courtney saga (*The Sound of Thunder*, *A Sparrow Falls*, *The Burning Shore*, etc.), then adding stand-alone contemporary and war thrillers, and eventually returning to the distant past, Smith made the best of the old writer's advice to write what you know: his books are all set in the Africa he loves, albeit in different historical contexts. Many of them have been filmed with star power such as Lee Marvin, Roger Moore, and Rod Taylor (*Shout at the Devil*, *Gold Mine*, *Dark of the Sun*), and all have made him perhaps the most popular African-born author of all time.

Already a voracious reader long before reaching high school, the boy has worked his way through Jules Verne and found an affinity for African adventures, fueled by Verne's *Five Weeks in a Balloon* and lesser-known *Dick Sands: The Boy Captain*. Moving on to H. Rider Haggard's *King Solomon's Mines* and *She*, and later Robert Ruark's *Uhuru*, the boy then stumbles onto a Reader's Digest Condensed Books version of Wilbur Smith's *The Sunbird*. Awed by the author's ability to tell parallel stories set in present-day and ancient Africa, the boy hungrily seeks more by this author. He finds

When the Lion Feeds, Smith's first published novel, and the African landscape opens up anew.

I was that boy, and I'd already consumed as much African adventure as one could stand, and more. I was enthralled by the movie *Zulu*, which recounted the unvarnished story of the British defense of Rorke's Drift in the Zulu War of 1879, and I was pleasantly surprised to find that the battle figured prominently in Wilbur Smith's book. Despite the artistic license of placing a Gatling gun at Rorke's Drift when no other historical text agrees (Gatlings were used by the British elsewhere in the war, but not at the mission station), Smith's portrait of the battle, and the war itself, brought that conflict to life for a young military history buff. The rest of his works would prove as compelling to the writer-in-training I happened to be in the 1970s, but it was the hook of the Courtney saga that would keep me reading.

In *When the Lion Feeds*, the brothers Sean and Garrick Courtney share a competitive bond ruined early in the book when a shooting accident costs Garrick his leg and opens up a bitterness between them that consumes the rest of their lives. Garrick is the weaker, more studious brother, and the accident further sentences him to succeed in far lesser fashion than his guilt-ridden (but often thoughtless) brother Sean. Later they are caught up in the Zulu War—their father killed in the disastrous battle of Isandlhwana, Garrick managing almost accidental heroism in the defense of the hospital at Rorke's Drift, and the gallant Sean believed killed but instead saved by Mbejane, his future footman and loyal Zulu servant/companion.

The Courtney brothers emerge from the war as competitors in many ways: for the affections of a young woman, for the love of their mother, and eventually for ownership of the family holdings. Sean departs rather than fight his brother and heads into the bush with Mbejane. A brawler by nature, Sean meets Duff Charleywood during a fight and forms a fast friendship with the Englishman. Using skill, ingenuity, their fists, and occasionally guns, Sean and Duff manage to carve themselves huge fortunes on the Transvaal during the gold rush, becoming respected mine owners and feared speculators as the boomtown slowly evolves into Johannesburg. Betrayed in a stock swindle scheme gone awry, they're driven into the wilderness nearly penniless, forced to turn to elephant hunting in a bid to rebuild. Duff's sudden death nearly kills Sean, too, until he meets and falls for a young Boer woman. And the story's not over—tragedy, love, hate, revenge, war, betrayal, all are played out on the vast African landscape.

Wilbur Smith uses the imperfect Sean Courtney (and, in later books, both his descendants and ancestors) to tell many of the stories of his native Africa, not all of them tame, pretty, or what we would call politically correct. None of them is devoid of racial hatred, pride, and political machinations. Occasionally criticized for the racism displayed by many of his characters, Smith never flinches from portraying class distinctions, separations, and resentments among both white and black Africans toward each other and among themselves, presenting Africa as a troubled continent mired in its colonial past and its constant struggle to reach a better future. Smith usually balances his portrayals of black and white Africans by including admirable and despicable examples of both and often lecturing on the dignity of fellow humans who have more in common than they like to admit.

Male characters in Smith's novels usually display chauvinistic qualities, but are also undone by women who are often stronger—and smarter—than they appear. Sex and brutal violence always play a part, though mostly kept offstage or somewhat muted. An always concise use of strong visual detail displays the beauty and drama—and occasionally horror—of life in Africa. Even in the less sweeping books, Smith's prose leads to a unique sense of place that elevates each novel. His wartime thrillers, such as *Shout at the Devil* (1968) and *Cry Wolf* (1976), recall the early work of Jack Higgins (Harry Patterson) crossed with the thrillers of fellow South African Desmond Bagley. Perhaps *The Diamond Hunters* (1971) and *The Eye of the Tiger* (1975) are, among Smith's work, more representative of the contemporary thriller as we know it. Another, 1979's *Wild Justice* (aka *The Delta Decision*) also deals with terrorism in more modern contexts.

The resulting Wilbur Smith canon, as perfectly exemplified by the high-octane, machismo-fueled *When the Lion Feeds*, is a potent blend of thriller, historical fiction, and family saga. Whether dealing with the present or the past or, occasionally, both in the same work, Wilbur Smith has perfected the modern African adventure and kept it alive in the twenty-first century.

W. D. Gagliani is the author of *The Wolf's Trap*, a Bram Stoker Award nominee, and its sequel, *Wolf's Gambit*, as well as numerous short stories in anthologies such as Robert Bloch's *Psychos*, *More Monsters from Memphis*, *Wicked Karnival Halloween Horror*, *Extremes 3: Terror on the High Seas*, *Extremes 4: Darkest Africa*, *The Black Spiral*, *The Asylum 2*, *The Midnighters Club*, and others. With collaborator

David Benton, he has also published fiction in *Malpractice: An Anthology of Bedside Horror*, *Dark Passions: Hot Blood 13*, and *Masters of Unreality*. His essays and book reviews have appeared in *On Writing Horror*, *Cemetery Dance*, *Chizine*, *HorrorWorld*, *Hellnotes*, *Crimespree*, *BookPage*, *The Scream Factory*, the *Milwaukee Journal Sentinel*, and many others.

57

Evelyn Anthony's
THE RENDEZVOUS (1967)

Sandra Brown

Evelyn Anthony (1928–) is the pseudonym of Evelyn Ward Thomas. She first gained fame and commercial success with her exhaustively researched historical novels. In the 1960s, she switched to writing contemporary thrillers and spy novels featuring strong female leads, such as her famous series character, Davina Graham, the head of British spy services. Her books became known for their memorable protagonists and twist endings. Her 1971 novel, *The Tamarind Seed*, was adapted into a 1974 film starring Julie Andrews and Omar Sharif as lovers involved in Cold War intrigue. However, Anthony effortlessly adjusted to the end of the Cold War and wrote nearly a dozen thrillers set in the post-1990 world, including her most recent work, 2004's *No Resistance*.

"Count yourself lucky to read this new treat from Evelyn Anthony." So said the *Buffalo Courier-Express* in 1973. I agree. If you haven't read this British author, you've missed some excellent storytelling, suspense, and sexual tension.

She began her career in 1949 by writing novels about historical figures, *Elizabeth*, *Anne Boleyn*, *Victoria*, *Charles the King*. But like her contemporaries Mary Stuart and Helen MacInnes, she gravitated to novels of suspense, espionage, and intrigue. These are what made me a devotee, an admirer, and, ultimately, a student.

Because every work by Evelyn Anthony is noteworthy, it's difficult to isolate a favorite. So I settled on three, which, in my opinion, are among the best of romantic suspense by this or any author: *The Rendezvous*, *The Assassin*, and *Sleeping with the Enemy*.

The Rendezvous was published in 1967, roughly twenty years after the end of World War II. It opens at a cocktail party in a swank Park Avenue apartment in Manhattan. Chic, glittery, and glib people are making droll conversation. The only newcomer to this gathering is an architect of recent renown. Everyone is impressed by Karl Amstat's urbanity, wit, and natural charm.

But when his hostess pulls him aside and introduces him to her sister-in-law, Karl (aka Colonel Alfred Brunnerman) finds himself face to face with Terese Masson, a member of the French Resistance whom he had put through a grueling interrogation twenty years earlier when he was a Nazi SS officer.

Oops.

Lucky for him, Terese's memory was wiped clean by the traumatic experience. Lucky for readers, they're drawn into a tantalizing agony of suspense, waiting for the moment when Terese's memory will return and she'll recognize her new lover as the former SS officer. Even as their passion for each another escalates, so does the threat of Israeli operatives, whose mission is to find and kill war criminals.

Bet you're wondering how it's going to end. Anthony holds you in suspense right up to the final paragraph.

She was an adolescent during World War II, and that conflict influences much of her fiction. Nazis and their capacity for evil are frequent themes. In *Sleeping with the Enemy*, Louise, an American, is married to a Frenchman, Comte de Bernard. They live in his chateau in the village of St. Blaize, where the Germans have assembled a top-secret laboratory for the production of a lethal nerve gas that will ensure victory.

The comte is a decent, peaceable man who wishes to protect his village from the worst ravages of the war. To that end, he maintains a civil relationship with the Germans and extends them his hospitality. Louise regards her husband's cordiality as collaboration, causing disharmony in the household.

Enter the American secret agent. Savage—don't you just love it?—has been commissioned to find the nerve gas laboratory and destroy it, or die trying. He infiltrates the village, and therefore the Germans, by passing himself off as Louise's Swiss cousin. So now, under the lichen-crusted, red tile roof of the chateau, you've got the wishy-washy French aristocrat, the odious German officer, the brash American, and the brave and beautiful Louise, whose loyalties are divided.

Summarized like this, this situation sounds melodramatic. It isn't. Especially the cruelty of the Nazis. To encourage the villagers to produce the Allied saboteur among them, the Germans inflict atrocities on the children of the village.

Before the denouement, in order to achieve his mission, Savage must live up to his name. The comte realizes that passivism is no way to win a war. And Louise is forced to make difficult choices that will haunt her for the rest of her life.

What one is willing to sacrifice for love is also a recurring theme in Evelyn Anthony's writing. *The Assassin* is the story of an American heiress, Elizabeth Cameron, who is unwittingly drawn into a Communist plot to murder a politically outspoken Catholic cardinal. It begins with her granting what seems a small favor, and results with her having to aid and abet Keller, the professional hit man hired to commit the murder. As if that isn't enough, her former lover is the CIA agent hot on the trail of the assassin.

I hate when that happens.

Now why would this cultured, well-educated heiress be willing to put her life on the line for Keller, who is uncouth and predatory? Because for all his brutality, Keller has honor. Elizabeth comes to trust him more than she does the so-called good guys.

Which brings me to a trait found in all Evelyn Anthony's books, the distinction that elevates them above others of the genre: *the lines between good and evil are blurred.* She creates delicious ambiguities. I ask myself, "Why am I rooting for SS Colonel Brunnerman as he's trying to outrun the justice he deserves—death—for his heinous war crime?"

Savage, in *Sleeping with the Enemy*, is a hero, but in order to carry out his mission he allows children to be torn from the arms of their parents and sent to Nazi death camps, sacrificing a few to save millions. Meanwhile, Louise, definitely the heroine, must seduce the German officer for the sake of Savage, the comte, and the Allied cause. And, while the German officer is a pig, his love for her is sincere.

How can I, as a reader, feel anything but loathing for Keller, the assassin, when he accepts fifty thousand dollars for a hit, before even knowing or caring that his target is a beloved Cardinal? He seems so unprincipled. But once his background is revealed, isn't his law-of-the-jungle mentality understandable?

Reading Evelyn Anthony, I find myself in the same moral tug-of-war as her protagonists. Are evil and good totally distinct, or do they intersect? Her characters are forced to make a choice that violates the ideals and loyalties of their past and present. That decision will determine their future and possibly even the fate of the world. And, as in all nail-biting thrillers, their success depends on beating a ticking clock. In Anthony's books, each tick reverberates.

Evelyn Anthony made an enormous contribution to the genre of romantic suspense. Indeed, she helped create it. *The Rendezvous*, *The Assassin*, and *Sleeping with the Enemy* define it. These books resonate with the humanity of the characters. They teem with nuance. They are taut with sexual tension. Each tells an exciting story, but leaves the reader with more to think about than simply the plot. They're realistic in that they don't always end happily, but always satisfactorily.

I've reread them for pleasure and for study. As a reader, I'm always entertained. As a writer, I'm continually inspired.

Sandra Brown is the author of fifty-eight *New York Times* best sellers, twelve of which jumped onto the list in the number one to five spot. These include *Smash Cut, Smoke Screen, Play Dirty, Ricochet, Chill Factor, White Hot,* and *Hello, Darkness*. A lifelong Texan, she was born in Waco, grew up in Fort Worth, and attended Texas Christian University, majoring in English. Before embarking on her writing career in 1981, she worked as a model, a television weathercaster, and a feature reporter on the nationally syndicated program *PM Magazine*. Court TV also sought Brown to host the 2007 premier of its popular series, *Murder by the Book*. In 1992 her novel, *French Silk*, was made into an ABC-TV movie. She has seventy million copies of her books in print worldwide and has been translated into thirty-three languages. In 2008 she was named ThrillerMaster, the top award given by the International Thriller Writer's organization.

58
Michael Crichton's
THE ANDROMEDA STRAIN (1969)

Josh Conviser

Michael Crichton (1942–2008) has become an institution. His name is shorthand for science, technology, fiction, and filmmaking. Many credit him with creating the "techno-thriller." At the very least, he popularized the genre. While attending Harvard Medical School, he wrote thrillers to pay for his studies. One of them, *A Case of Need*, written under the pseudonym Jeffery Hudson, received a Mystery Writers of America best novel Edgar Award in 1969. That same year, Crichton published *The Andromeda Strain* under his own name and became a publishing phenomenon. His subsequent international bestsellers include *Congo*, *Rising Sun*, *Jurassic Park*, *The Lost World*, and *State of Fear*. He worked in multiple genres, including travel writing, historical fiction, and science fiction. He also made his mark in film and television, notably writing and directing *Westworld*, an influential movie about a theme-park robot that becomes homicidal, as well as creating *ER*, one of the most popular TV series of all time. Crichton's work tackles complex technology and controversial political issues with a dramatic inventiveness that few can match.

My name is Josh Conviser, and I'm an insomniac. For that I blame Michael Crichton—and I'm not alone. There's a whole generation of readers who grew up on Crichton's work. Through our formative years, we spent night after night lost in his books. As spokesman for that generation, I take it on myself to demand recompense for all those sleepless nights!

Sure, Crichton opened our eyes to the wild possibilities of science, technology, world politics, history, and travel. I'll give him that. Yes, *The Andromeda Strain* was the first real book I read for my own enjoyment. And, yes, I went on to read everything Crichton wrote, and then became a writer of techno-thrillers myself. But those all-nighters were brutal. I was young— I needed my rest!

In preparation for writing this essay, I was "forced" to reread my wall of Crichton. The marathon only confirmed his mastery of the "what if." What if dinosaurs could be reborn? What if we discovered a spaceship on the bottom of the ocean? What if historians could travel back in time? What if our analysis of global warming is wrong? Crichton's dexterity with emerging technology opened these speculations to a broader audience. Indeed, he took speculative fiction out of the future and slammed it into our backyard. This shift is both at the root of his popularity and emblematic of the world in which we live.

With the exponential rate of our scientific and technical progress, nearly any "what if" could happen right now and around the corner. Crichton's work delves into that new reality. He opened our eyes to the beauty, majesty, and possibility of progress. He also revealed the pitfalls (psychological, sociological, political, and apocalyptical) that may impede our path forward. In Crichton's books, we see that what once lay in the realm of magic may now be occurring down the street. This reality offers tremendous possibility, forces hard decisions, and opens us to ever greater calamity.

The Andromeda Strain was one of the first books to tackle this reality in popular fiction. In it, fact drives fiction, and science informs drama. The book uncovers worlds within worlds, peeling back layers of science, even as it drives the reader through the story. Its plot deals with a military satellite that inexplicably falls back to earth. In a matter of hours, nearly everyone in the vicinity of its crash point is dead. Only an infant and an old man survive. A team of scientists is called to a supersecret facility in the Nevada desert to study the satellite and survivors. They uncover the Andromeda Strain—a never before seen, and possibly extraterrestrial, biological agent that is causing the deaths. With humanity's fate, and their own, on the line, we accompany the scientists through their discoveries, mistakes, achievements, and disasters as they deal with the threat. It's science. It's speculation. It's a killer ride.

The book appears to be a factual recounting of actual events. It melds false documents with a journalistic style to create fiction that sits flush with fact. Even the opening acknowledgments work to this end. In them, Crichton thanks the characters in his own story for their help in filling out its details (an example of metafiction worthy of Borges). He includes bogus but real-seeming graphs, diagrams, and interview transcriptions along with a three-page invented, but persuasive, bibliography.

With the line between reality and possibility blurred, Crichton weaves a story that is both gripping and terrifying. Rereading the novel, I found it interesting to see how much of that possibility has become reality. Many threads of our modern tech-heavy life make their way into the book: voice-activated computer systems capable of complex analysis, satellite surveillance, and the hazmat outfits made popular in *ET*, among others. Today, the technology in *The Andromeda Strain* feels very comfortable. That it was written in the 1960s (before we landed on the moon) is amazing.

After *The Andromeda Stain*, Crichton went on to many other successes—each book positing a wild "what if" that grows ever more plausible with each turn of the page. He had a two-pronged genius. First, he saw magical (and often frightening) possibilities in our world. He was then able to take these possibilities and fashion them into stories of gripping intensity, ripe with emotion. Many of his books are cautionary, warning us that as we drive forward, we need to be aware of the course we take. At the same time, he revealed to us the possibilities that lie on the cutting edge and beyond.

Crichton's inventiveness changed the thriller landscape. His wild musings continue to keep me up nights and inspire me to find the magic in our world. Insomnia is a small price to pay for that gift. Thanks, Michael.

Josh Conviser grew up in Aspen, Colorado, went to high school in Santa Barbara, California, and graduated from Princeton University in 1996. He has lived in Europe, Asia, and Australia. An avid mountaineer, he climbed in ranges around the world, including the Himalayas, before giving up the mountains for the jungles of Hollywood to pursue a career in screenwriting. He was the executive consultant on HBO's series, *Rome*, and has several films in development. His first novel, *Echelon*, a techno-thriller, was published in 2006. His second book, *Empyre*, came out a year later.

59

James Dickey's
DELIVERANCE (1970)

Terry Watkins

Atlanta-based poet James Dickey (1923–1997) burst onto the national scene in 1970 with the publication of *Deliverance*, his most famous and enduring work. The multifaceted Dickey wore many hats: writer, teacher, hunter, athlete, copywriter, and air force officer. In 1965, his book of poetry *Buckdancer's Choice* won the National Book Award. But it was *Deliverance*, the terrifying and visceral story of four Atlanta businessmen seeking escape from their mundane lives by canoeing down the doomed, soon-to-be-dammed Cahulawassee River that thrust Dickey onto best-seller lists. A combative, Hemingwayesque personality, the burly, hard-drinking Dickey waded through the literary scene with both fists clenched. He excoriated other poets, lectured with passion, and struggled the rest of his life to live up to the hype that *Deliverance* bestowed upon him. He was never able to recapture that glory or garner the further critical acclaim he sought. Battling with critics, alienated from his wife and family, Dickey continued writing what he considered his best work even as his health deteriorated. He died three days after giving his last college lecture.

Deliverance illuminates the unique American male zeitgeist and its connection to Old West frontier values. Few works by American writers express the conflicts ingrained in our mythologies and frontier legacy as does this simple canoe trip that propels four urban dwellers into decisions that are irrevocable and morally uncertain. In 1972, two years after the novel was published, the John Boorman movie adaptation—a powerful kinesthetic thrill ride with Jon Voight cast in the role of Ed and Burt Reynolds as Lewis—was a masterful cinematic rendering of the story that earned three Academy Awards and six Golden Globes, further enhancing Dickey's reputation and fame.

The four adventurers are unprepared for this journey into the darker regions of the American experience. They begin in the mountain town of

Oree, and immediately display a disrespect for the primitive hillbilly "out-siders," one of whom informs the sarcastic Bobby, who's made a comment about his hat, "You don't know nothing." This portends the first violent ac-tion that fractures the chaste, male bonding, wilderness experience with a violent homosexual rape of Bobby by two hillbillies and transforms the journey into a terrifying nightmare. This rape takes place on the banks of a virginal river that is itself about to be raped and destroyed by civiliza-tion.

The trip's organizer and enthusiast is Lewis, a self-styled macho sur-vivalist who fantasizes he's preparing for the collapse of civilization and the return to wilderness existence. Lewis kills one of the hillbillies involved in the rape. The other man escapes. Ed, the viewpoint character who leads us through the story, is a graphic designer who admires the macho, mus-cular Lewis and sees himself as soft and weak in comparison. Ed will ulti-mately be forced to replace Lewis, who is rendered impotent by a broken leg at the moment of the final crisis. The unmarried, wisecracking Bobby, now the victim of the most feared of male defeats, is useless. The fourth member, Drew—the most adjusted to his life, a man who loves his family and his job with a major soft drink company, and who embraces the laws and believes they are applicable under all circumstances—finds himself having to choose between those very laws and the potential threat the death of the hillbilly might pose to himself and his family. He decides to join a cover-up of the killing. Soon after, Drew dies in the river rapids. But was it by a rifle shot from the cliffs by the hillbilly who escaped, or did Drew hit his head on the rocks and drown? That question sets up the final crisis.

With Lewis injured, Drew dead, and Bobby useless, it falls to Ed to save the day and carry the survivalist banner by ascending a dangerous cliff in order to kill the man they believe is trying to kill them. Ed's climb and his actions must transcend his own self-image. He needs to become his macho hero, Lewis. The weakness that made Ed's arm shake so that he missed his opportunity to kill a deer earlier in the story must now become steady so he can kill a man. When Ed finds his quarry on the top of the cliff, his decision to execute him to protect the group comes with doubt. Is this the man who is after them? Maybe he's just wandering through. But the predicament cannot be escaped. A decision has to be made, and made quickly. To guess wrong could be a death sentence for Ed and the others. Or it could mean a cold-blooded execution of an innocent. Ed sees no third option. No way out of the dilemma. Is it of greater moral value to kill and be wrong, or not kill and be wrong? This is an inescapable quandary, when the truth cannot be known in the moment of crisis and a decision has to be made.

The aftermath for the survivors hints at the impact on their lives. Lewis is a gimp. Bobby slinks off into the shadows. As for Ed, the ordeal pushed him into the role of the mythological warrior, the savior, but he has a big price to pay. His triumph leaves him unable to ever integrate fully back into the protective skin of normal life. He has killed. He has lied and participated in the big cover-up, and with these dark secrets comes the fear that "Somebody may be after me," suggesting this is something he will never escape. He has seen the dark side of life and has suffered the same post-traumatic syndrome as soldiers, accident victims, and others who have encountered an event that rips away the thin veil of civilization to reveal the primitive, violent realities underneath.

Deliverance challenges the reader to confront the same difficult questions that Ed faces. What are we willing to do under the pressure of extreme circumstances? What value triumphs in a survival crisis? What will this mean later? The decisions to take violent and deadly actions under great duress, and the consequences to those who survive, are what elevates the book well beyond sheer entertainment and places it firmly on the shelf of great thrillers.

Terry Watkins, author of screenplays and the thrillers *The Big Burn* and *Stacked Deck*, is an outdoorsman and Vietnam veteran who grew up in the mountains of north central Pennsylvania on a steady diet of Western myths. He spent so much time roaming the hills that he acquired the nickname "Little Daniel Boone." When he went off to Vietnam, he carried with him the blinding baggage of the mythologies of the Old West from the Indian Wars to the Alamo and the OK Corral. When he returned from that conflict, many of these long-held views underwent challenge. He found in *Deliverance* a powerful expression of the conflicts and contradictions inherent in those iconic macho ideals.

60

Frederick Forsyth's
THE DAY OF THE JACKAL (1971)

F. Paul Wilson

Born in Ashford, Kent, England, Frederick Forsyth (1938–) was educated at Tonbridge school, and later Granada University, Spain. After serving in the RAF from 1956 to 1958, he worked as a reporter for the Eastern Daily Press in Norfolk, before joining Reuters in 1961. In 1965, he began working for the BBC. There, he covered the Biafran side of the Biafra-Nigeria war. In 1968, he left the BBC to return to Biafra, where he reported on the war, first as a freelancer and later for the *Daily Express* and *Time* magazine. In 1970, he decided to write a book using the research skills and methods he had developed as a reporter. That book, *The Day of the Jackal*, became an international bestseller and spawned two feature films. Subsequent novels include *The Odessa File*, *The Fourth Protocol*, *The Dogs of War*, and *The Afghan*.

Frederick Forsyth's first novel (that last bit bears repeating: *first* novel) put a new twist on a number of spy-thriller conventions. Although not a true spy novel, it's structured as one: Its titular character, a professional assassin, functions very much like a spy—forging new identities, moving secretly from country to country, dealing with traitors. It's also very much a procedural, leading the reader in great detail through the intricate measures the Jackal takes to avoid detection and all the methods his pursuers employ to track him down.

Set in 1963, the novel also takes the unprecedented step of making Charles de Gaulle the assassin's target.

Excuse me? Charles de Gaulle was not assassinated; he died of natural causes the year before the novel was published. So unless this takes place in an alternate universe, the Jackal is doomed to failure. How can you possibly build suspense—let alone maintain it for the length of an entire novel—when the reader knows from the get go that the plot is going to fail?

In the hands of Frederick Forsyth, it doesn't matter. He makes it work.

The Day of the Jackal was inspired by the real-life assassination attempt on de Gaulle in 1962 after he endorsed independence for Algeria. A group of French militants calling itself the OAS waged a campaign of terror against it. A fellow named Jean Bastien-Thiry was executed for masterminding the plot.

The novel opens with Bastien-Thiry's execution and a recap of the failed attempt on de Gaulle. Shortly thereafter, a remnant of the OAS hires a professional assassin known only as the Jackal to finish the job. Wisely, the Jackal tells his employers nothing about his plans, and just as wisely, Forsyth tells the reader nothing as well. Instead, he does what all good storytellers do: He *shows*. We follow the Jackal, whose true identity we never know, through England, France, and Belgium as he researches de Gaulle, sets up false identities, and purchases the weapon he'll use for the assassination. Slowly, piece by piece, we see the plan begin to take shape.

On the other side, the French police realize that the former OAS reprobates are up to something. They capture a bodyguard named Kowalski and brutally interrogate him (believe me, he'd pray for waterboarding instead of the electric wires attached to sensitive parts of his anatomy) to extract what he knows, which isn't much beyond the name "chacal" (French for jackal). Eventually, a doggedly persistent French cop, Inspector Claude Lebel, is set on the trail of this nameless, faceless killer. He traces the Jackal to an apartment in England occupied by a man named Charles Calthrop (note what the first three letters of those two names spell) but misses him.

Now the cat-and-mouse game begins in earnest, with the Jackal receiving tips from an OAS contact in the French government that help him stay one step—sometimes less than that—ahead of Lebel.

In contrast to Robert Ludlum, who published his own first novel, *The Scarlatti Inheritance*, that same year, there's little passion in Forsyth's prose. The affect is generally flat, with the Jackal showing scant or no emotion. He isn't a radical firebrand; there's no pleasure for him here (other than, perhaps, the satisfaction in bringing off this nearly impossible feat), no emotional or ideological stake. It's simply a job—a challenging one, yes, but still a job.

Forsyth writes in what I call movie mode. We witness the action from outside; rarely are we allowed into the hearts and minds of the characters. This should make for an uninvolving read, but in Forsyth's hands it's curiously compelling. The torture scene is a perfect example. Its matter-of-fact presentation is utterly chilling.

Unlike the characters in James Bond-style novels, the Jackal is no bon vivant. He doesn't high roll in casinos or dally in five-star hotels. He's more at home in the underworld, the demimonde of gunrunners and forgers. He even has an interlude in a gay bar.

Whether we're following the Jackal or the police, Forsyth renders the locations in exquisite detail. Never do we question that the author has spent time in these places. And it is perhaps this attention to detail that empowers the Herculean suspension of disbelief necessary to overlook the historical contradiction so central to the plot. Everything is so real, the Jackal is so skilled, so expert at his profession that, yes, never mind what history says, this man just might be able to assassinate de Gaulle.

And as we read on (perhaps to our dismay, perhaps not), we find ourselves rooting for the Jackal. He may be a cold-blooded killer, but his foes are equally ruthless. And he's the underdog, a man on a high wire with no safety net, single-handedly facing down the combined police forces and intelligence networks of Western Europe. Every time the authorities start closing in, we can't help hoping he outwits them . . . again.

In the end the story comes down to a battle of wits between the Jackal and Lebel, and along the way the two men develop a grudging mutual respect. The final scene between the pair is delivered in Forsyth's typical affectless style:

> Lebel stared into the eyes of the other man...
> "Chacal," he said. The other man said simply, "Lebel."

After that it's a matter of who can shoot first.

Born and raised in New Jersey, F. Paul Wilson misspent his youth playing with matches, poring over Uncle Scrooge and E.C. comics, reading Lovecraft, Matheson, Bradbury, and Heinlein, listening to Chuck Berry and Alan Freed on the radio, and watching Soupy Sales and Shock Theatre. He is the author of more than forty books: science fiction (including the novels Healer, Wheels within Wheels, and An Enemy of the State), horror thrillers (among them The Keep, The Touch, and Reborn), contemporary thrillers (The Select, Implant, Deep as the Marrow), novels that defy categorization (The Fifth Harmonic and Virgin) and several collaborations. In 1998 he resurrected his popular antihero, Repairman Jack (who first appeared in the 1984's The Tomb). The thirteenth installment in the series, Ground Zero, was published in 2009. Much of his short fiction is collected in Soft and Others, The Barrens and Others, and Aftershock and Others. He edited two anthologies (Freak Show and Diagnosis: Terminal) and has also written for stage, screen, and interactive media.

61
Brian Garfield's
DEATH WISH (1972)

John Lescroart

Brian Garfield (1939–), a major creative force in American popular culture over a good part of the past half century, has forged a career that is nothing less than staggering in breadth, depth, and longevity. The author of over seventy books of Westerns, mysteries, action thrillers, spy novels, history, and biography, with total sales of over twenty million copies, Garfield has screen credits that are hardly less impressive. To date, eighteen films and/or television programs—including *Hopscotch, Recoil, Relentless, The Last Hard Men*, and the many iterations of *Death Wish*—have been based on his work (and two more are currently in production). As a young man, Garfield performed the hit song "I Can't Quit" on American Bandstand with the band, The Palisades. His musical comedy, "Legs," based on the Rockettes, played at Radio City Music Hall. Garfield has proven himself a master in all of the original American popular arts. In *Death Wish*, he created an archetypical hero who continues to be a mainstay of popular fiction and film—the average man driven by circumstances outside of his control to become an avenging vigilante.

There isn't a novelist in the world who wants to hear this, but Brian Garfield wrote *Death Wish* in about two weeks. This was in 1972. After visiting a friend in New York City on a snowy night, he came back to his car for the two-and-a-half-hour drive back to his home in New Jersey, and found that someone had slashed the canvas roof of his ten-year-old convertible. The rage he felt—and that grew over the long drive—led him to the question, "What would happen to somebody who got that furious—and stayed that way?"

The protagonist in *Death Wish* is a middle-aged, slightly paunchy accountant named Paul Benjamin. (In the many movies based upon the novel, Charles Bronson's character is named Paul Kersey—"for no more sinister reason," Garfield says, "than the fact that there's a good character actor in movies named Paul Benjamin, and anyhow 'Kersey' was easier for both Charles Bronson and Vincent Gardenia to pronounce.") In almost all important ways, Benjamin is an extremely unlikely hero. Not only is he physically unprepossessing; he is by his own admission an unexciting specimen. In his job, he works with numbers and spreadsheets. His two friends are stereotypical, dull accountants. He and his wife, Esther, never quite let their marriage bloom into something romantic—rather, they are what he calls Aquarian acquaintances.

In short, no one would normally think to cast Paul Benjamin as the hero of a thriller. He is pretty much the opposite—an Everyman with a reactive, rather than proactive, temperament. The character arc tracing his development from nebbish accountant to avenging urban vigilante has changed the landscape of the thriller world ever since.

The novel begins with a superb first sentence: "Later he worked out where he had been at the time of the attack on Esther and Carol." Strong as this opening is, its true power comes from Garfield's strategy in writing the next few pages, where we follow Paul as he takes a cab with one of his friends back from a bibulous lunch to his job—they're bellyaching about crime and the generally benighted state of New York City. Next, at the office, Paul enters into a lengthy, essentially meaningless discussion with one of his colleagues. Finally, he has a phone call with a client.

Each of these encounters, unremarkable and even boring in themselves, might in a lesser author's hands have been little more than scenes with talking heads. But because of the pulled-pin character of the book's opening sentence, these scenes become excruciatingly, almost unbearably, suspenseful. More importantly, they establish our identification with Paul Benjamin's character since the point of view is consistently and always his. We've *got to find out* exactly what happened to Esther and Carol, and no matter what it was—whatever it is, it's *bad*—we're with Paul, the second-hand victim, every step of the way.

When we learn how bad it is—Esther is dead and Carol is well on her way to life in a near-vegetative state—we keep our faith with Paul as he tries to come to grips with the tragedy that has altered his life so completely. At first, and fittingly for his character, his reactions are muted and restrained. He doesn't really know how to react, what to feel, how to respond to the inner turmoil that is inexorably changing his worldview. By degrees, his emotions find outlets—he weeps, he slams his fists on the bed, he walks naked around his apartment, he checks with the progress of the police, he throws up, he starts to drink. All pretty normal stuff.

Until he fashions a roll of quarters in a sock into a makeshift weapon.

This is where things start to change for Paul, for us as readers, and for the modern urban thriller.

Suddenly, Paul Benjamin has broken out of his reactive mode and has started to think about the problem of crime in New York City. Mostly, he's still very much in a defensive mode. If something happens to him, he's going to want to protect himself. This is a reasonable desire, and we readers continue to identify with him and completely approve. This is a smart guy taking appropriate steps to insure his own safety in a dangerous environment.

When Paul ventures out again into the city, Garfield provides an extended metaphor of urban detritus to show just how dangerous the environment is. (This is one of the great things about *Death Wish*: the tiny telling details that carry enormous emotional weight.) So we've got groups of young toughs laughing, garbage on the sidewalks, bums and drunks, "discarded newspapers, crumpled lunch bags, rusty bottlecaps, rustless empty cans, broken bottles." All these details, though mundane, serve as a shorthand for the breakdown of civilization in the city as a whole, and lead Paul to the perilous thought: "*All right, they've been told, they've had their chance.*

"He didn't follow the implications of the thought through: he was afraid to."

But the implications are clear enough. Paul is moving toward an active confrontation with the world he lives in. These nonthreatening details of everyday life come to represent for him, and for us, a very real, clear and present danger. Somebody is indeed out to get him—in fact, the entire city is out to get him, and everyone like him.

The extremity of the paranoia might start to lose us here, except for another inspired bit of plotting. Paul walks home through this terrifying urban jungle, and suddenly a young man comes up behind him, ordering him in the most vulgar terms to stop and turn around. Suddenly—aha!—Paul's concerns are not paranoia; they are real, and here is the proof.

His reaction is still reasonable and sane. He has been carrying his roll of quarters all this time, and now has the presence of mind to swing it at his would-be attacker. He misses, and (to Paul's amazement) the mugger

runs off, but the incident marks another step along Paul's path from victim
to avenger. He can actually, by his own actions, assert his dominance over
the threatening world he inhabits.

That same night, Paul happens to turn on the TV, and here Garfield
fills in anything that might be missing in our understanding of Paul's evolution:

> Cowboys picking on sodbusters and a drifting hero standing
> up for the farmers against the gunslingers . . . It was easy to see
> why Westerns were always popular and he [Paul] was amazed he
> hadn't understood it before. It was human history. As far back
> as you wanted to go, there were always men who tilled the soil
> and there were always men on horseback who wanted to exploit
> them and take everything away from them, and the hero of
> every myth was the hero who defended the farmers against the
> raiders on horseback, and the constant contradiction was that
> the hero himself was always a man on horseback.

Now Garfield gives it to us straight—the fundamental paradigm shift
that turns out to have shaped so many variations of the modern thriller.
Paul Benjamin is about to do the job of the man on horseback. He is going
to defend the sodbusters against the gunslingers. But, unlike all the mythic
heroes before in human history, Paul Benjamin is not one of the men on
horseback. He, himself, is one of the sodbusters.

As the novel progresses, so does Paul's paranoia, but amid a now-calm
coolness that is both agonizing in its suspense and deliberate in its apparent rationality. We readers are carried along as Paul goes off to Arizona on
business. He is back to living his humdrum existence. He handles a complicated audit, he meets and beds a woman from a bar, he has many normal interactions with regular people.

And then he buys a gun.

By the time he returns to New York, Paul Benjamin has become the
prototypical urban avenger, intent on going out into the neighborhoods
and eliminating the evil that lurks there. He starts shooting criminals. He
is clean, efficient, self-righteous, and deadly. In the last scene of the book,
Paul kills three vandals after they attack a train, and as he is walking away
he notices that a uniformed policeman has seen the whole thing. The cop
turns around and does nothing.

Clearly, the cop, who represents civilization, is grateful to Paul Benjamin and to all the people who would be like him.

Paul Benjamin was the first in a whole generation of fictional urban vigilantes, avenging real or imagined wrongs without feeling the need to resort to the hierarchy and rules of formal law enforcement. The novel, *Death Wish*, became the template for how this apparent acceptance of unfettered violence turned into an acceptable, even moral, characteristic for a hero to possess. Garfield gave us the rationale—step-by-step, emotionally convincing, powerful, with a relentless logic that made its argument seem universally true.

Ironically, Brian Garfield himself never wanted the book to be a clarion call for revenge, or for Paul Benjamin to be an admired hero: "I meant it," he says, "(if you believe in the influence of subtext) as a cautionary lesson, not a recommendation. Revenge is a universal fantasy but, in practice, it isn't a solution; it's a problem."

John Lescroart is the author of nineteen novels, fourteen of them in the San Francisco–based Dismas Hardy/Abe Glitsky series. Libraries Unlimited has included him in its publication *The 100 Most Popular Thriller and Suspense Authors*. His books have been translated into twenty languages, and his short stories appear in many anthologies. His first novel, *Sunburn*, won the San Francisco Foundation's Joseph Henry Jackson Award for best novel by a California author, and *Dead Irish* and *The 13th Juror* were nominees for the Shamus and Anthony Best Mystery Novel, respectively. *The 13th Juror* was also selected for inclusion in this volume. *Guilt* was a Readers Digest Select Edition choice. *The Mercy Rule*, *Nothing But The Truth*, and *The Suspect* were major market book club selections. *The Suspect* was also the 2007 One Book Sacramento choice of the Sacramento Library Foundation, and was chosen by the American Author's Association as its 2007 Book of the Year.

62

David Morrell's
FIRST BLOOD (1972)

Steve Berry

David Morrell (1943–) was born in Kitchener, Ontario, Canada, and moved to the United States in 1966 to study American literature with Penn State's Hemingway expert, Philip Young. After earning a Ph.D., he taught at the University of Iowa for sixteen years and eventually became an American citizen. All the while, he wrote fiction, inspired in his teenage years by the mix of action and ideas in Stirling Silliphant's scripts for the classic television series *Route 66*. Morrell's 1972 debut novel is probably his best known: *First Blood*. The character of Rambo (who has no first name, Hollywood bestowed the label "John") eventually earned a place in worldwide culture—an interesting evolution, considering that the character was christened after an apple, a delicious Pennsylvania type known as Rambo that Morrell's wife brought home from a roadside stand one day. Morrell has, so far, penned twenty-four novels, four nonfiction books, countless short stories, and a comic book series—many of them *New York Times* best sellers. His classic spy novel *The Brotherhood of the Rose* was a top-rated NBC miniseries that premiered after the Super Bowl in 1989. Many writers (myself included) regard him as one of the finest craftsmen working today, so knowledgeable that we respectfully refer to him as the "Professor."

In the summer of 1968, America was erupting. The Vietnam War was literally tearing the nation apart, riots and demonstrations so polarizing the country that one generation seemed utterly confounded by the other. Recently arrived in the United States on a guest visa was a twenty-five-year-old Canadian named David Morrell. He was married, with an infant daughter, preparing for a career as a teacher, fascinated by the United States, eager to learn about something he knew nothing about: the Vietnam War.

What he discovered deeply disturbed him. But something Socrates once said came to mind. *No one commits wrong intentionally.* For Morrell, that truism about how we rationalize everything we do became worth exploring, so he decided to write a novel that would allegorize the Vietnam War. Not to make a point. Or take sides. That could have been a problem since the terms of his guest visa specifically stated, on threat of deportation, that he should refrain from expressing political opinions. Instead, Morrell decided to tactfully objectify America's bitter philosophical and cultural divisions, transposing the brutality of Vietnam—and the radical conflicts that war generated at home—to a rural Kentucky town, creating a miniature version of the Vietnam War on American soil.

Instead of shotgunning the narrative with many points of view, he focused on only two. Rambo, the Vietnam vet, Green Beret, former POW, and Medal of Honor recipient. A man haunted by the war, repulsed by the violence he found in himself, embittered by the hostility he sometimes faced from those he fought to protect. In rebellion, he allowed his hair and beard to grow, shunned all possessions, and wandered the back roads of America, looking like a hippie. Searching. He represented those disaffected by the war.

Wilfred Teasle represented the establishment. A Korean War hero, recipient of the Distinguished Service Cross, Eisenhower Republican, chief of police in Madison, Kentucky. As troubled as Rambo, he's old enough to be Rambo's father, haunted by a different set of war memories, but equally as controlled by them.

By alternating back and forth between each man's anger, Morrell allowed the reader to identify with each man's motivations. As with Socrates—*no one commits wrong intentionally*—these two likewise draw from deep, well-meant convictions, making one mistake after another, their rationalized fury eventually guaranteeing a mutual destruction. Morrell was careful not to favor one character over the other. He wanted the reader to understand *both* sides and become dismayed as the two protagonists proved incapable of doing the same. At one point, Teasle sends for the Special Forces officer who trained Rambo—Colonel Sam Trautman, whose first name Morrell meant to echo that of Uncle Sam. In the end, after Rambo kills Teasle, Trautman kills Rambo, thus completing the allegory inasmuch as the representative of the system that created Rambo is the person who destroys him and turns out to be the only winner.

The palpable vividness of the prose in *First Blood* is matched by the book's unrelenting pace. Until its publication in 1972, few thrillers dram-

atized so much intense, continuous action. From the moment Rambo
breaks out of jail totally naked and hijacks a motorcycle, escaping into the
nearby mountains to fight a private war, the novel set a new standard for
unrelenting speed.

Often referred to as "the father of the modern action novel," Morrell's
First Blood has sold millions of copies around the world and remains in
print to this day. Inevitably, Hollywood discovered the tale and created
four films, not to mention a Saturday morning cartoon series. The fact that
the second and third films (and the cartoon) are patently false to Morrell's
initial concept is irrelevant. The films exist in worlds of their own and,
collectively, manufactured a pop-cultural icon—Rambo—one that aided
an emasculated America, in the 1980s, to again feel good about itself:
Ronald Reagan's so-called new morning.

Reagan himself elevated Rambo as his standard-bearer in numerous
press conferences, once remarking that, after watching a Rambo film the
night before, he knew what to do the next time there was a terrorist crisis.
Morrell himself experienced the phenomena when, one day in 1986, he
was on a publicity tour in England and picked up the *London Times* to find
a disturbing headline: US RAMBO JETS BOMB LIBYA.

Not exactly what he had in mind when he first manufactured that all-
too-real conflict between Rambo and Teasle. A novel that questioned war
and its devastating aftermath, a story that brought to life lingering cultural
wounds left by the Vietnam debacle, became a shorthand political
metaphor—a rallying cry for even more violence. Morrell himself com-
mented in 2000 that he thought it ironic that a 1970's novel about the political polarization of America (for or against the Vietnam War), became
the basis for films, in the 1980s, that resulted in a similar polarization (for
or against Ronald Reagan).

Eventually the *Oxford English Dictionary* cited *First Blood* as the source
for the creation of a new word. Rambo. Complicated, troubled, haunted,
too often misunderstood. Precisely like *First Blood* itself.

Steve Berry lives on the Georgia coast. After twenty-nine years, he no longer practices law, but continues to serve as one of five members of the Camden County
Board of Commissioners. He began writing in 1990, and though his undergraduate degree was in political science, it was Steve's interest in travel and history that
led him to write international suspense thrillers. His many books include *The
Amber Room, The Romanov Prophecy, The Third Secret, The Templar Legacy, The*

Alexandria Link, *The Venetian Betrayal*, *The Charlemagne Pursuit*, and *The Paris Vendettta*. Steve is an international best seller with books in forty-three languages, for a total of nearly eight million copies in print worldwide. He also served as co-president of International Thriller Writers.

63

Trevanian's

THE EIGER SANCTION (1972)

Lee Goldberg

The author known as Trevanian was as fictional a character as those he is credited with writing about. Trevanian was created by Rodney William Whitaker (1925–2005), a film professor at the University of Texas, for the purpose of writing his first novel, *The Eiger Sanction*. Whitaker told an interviewer that he came up with an idea for a novel, then created "the best writer to do the job. I build up the writer, giving him a voice, a style, a set of insights and prejudices, an educational and developmental background, a set of motivations, an age, a class, a culture, and sometimes a race. [Trevanian] was just the right persona to write spoofs on the shallow macho derring-do/superspy/hot crotch genre." He also wrote fiction as Nicholas Seare, Jean-Paul Morin, and Benat Le Cagot, among other names. Due to contractual requirements, some of the novels Whitaker initially intended to publish under other pseudonyms came out as Trevanian novels instead (*The Main*, *Summer of Katya*, *Incident at Twenty Mile*, and *The Crazy Ladies of Pearl Street*), causing some confusion and frustration among readers because of the disparate writing styles. Until Whitaker's death, the mysterious background and life of Trevanian, who many were convinced was a nom de plume for Robert Ludlum, remained nearly as compelling as the best-selling novels written under his name.

In 1972, Bond mania was waning and the spy craze it created had peaked. Sean Connery had just returned as 007 in *Diamonds Are Forever*, chubby and toupeed, driving a moon buggy in the Las Vegas desert. It was a toss-up who was more uncomfortable with Bond at that point, Connery or the audience. The pop-culture secret agent, portrayed as either an international playboy or a morose bureaucrat, seemed not just anachronistic but boring.

The genre was ready for a major shake-up, and it came from *The Eiger*

Sanction, though that certainly wasn't how Whitaker's first novel was intended. He'd set out to ridicule the genre.

His hero is Dr. Jonathan Hemlock, an art history professor and renowned mountain climber who lives in a converted church with a hidden, subterranean art gallery filled with works by the masters ("This isn't a house," one character says of the place, "it's a movie set." And it soon was. Clint Eastwood starred in and directed the 1975 film version of the book).

Hemlock finances his art collecting as an assassin, taking on "sanctions" for an ultrasecret intelligence organization. His mission is to hunt down an unknown, rival assassin who is believed to be one of several mountaineers about to climb the deadly Eiger.

It's an enticing premise that, on the surface, doesn't sound like a satire at all, but a rousing mix of espionage and Alistair MacLean-style adventure.

Perhaps to puncture that expectation, the book opens with the Inspector Clouseau of spies backing into a rose bush, running face-first into a streetlamp, and tugging his pants from between his buttocks before being ambushed and gutted by enemy agents.

Despite this comical introduction, an assassin/hero named after a poison, and a cast of characters with such overtly cartoonish names as Yurasis Dragon, Felicity Arse, Cherry Pitts, Randy Nickers, and Madame Bidet, the spoof is actually far more nuanced, written with such intelligence and respect for the conventions of the genre that the author and his readers soon forgot that it's all supposed to be a joke.

Naturally, every woman Hemlock meets instantly wants to bed him. But despite his "remarkable staying powers" and his expertise at lovemaking, his attitude toward sex is perfunctory. "It had been simple, uncomplicated, and temporarily satisfying: like urination. And that was the way he preferred his lovemaking to be."

Hemlock approaches the seduction of one particular woman with frank and startling pragmatism. "I'm just feeling tough and full of sperm. She happens to be around and looks capable."

Not only has he "never experienced that local physical ecstasy we associate with climax," but when he falls emotionally for the ludicrously named African-American spy Jemima Brown, he suffers premature ejaculation.

It all might have been meant as a joke, but it adds unintentional psychological depth to a character who has no conscience and yet values loyalty and friendship over all else. Betrayal, to him, is worse than murder. Not exactly the shadings you'd expect from a caricature.

Hemlock works for Mr. Dragon, whose secretary is the anti-Moneypenny, described as a squat, gray-haired nurse with sandpaper skin, a fat face, and a faint mustache. Dragon fears that Hemlock is suffering from an ailment known as "Tension Rot," which could also have been said about the spy genre itself at the time.

But there is no such rot in *The Eiger Sanction*, despite Whitaker's best efforts to create it. He becomes enamored by the conventions he intends to spoof, turning satire into a sly subversion and a clever reinvention of the genre. By the time Hemlock is on the mountain, Whitaker has forgotten the joke, and so have we. He explores serious themes about the meaning of friendship, the emotional vulnerability of trust, and turns the inanimate mountain into a truly terrifying character itself. Even the silly named, sexually voracious women evolve, almost against the author's will, into flesh-and-blood characters with an emotional depth that belies the increasingly halfhearted attempts at satire.

Ultimately *The Eiger Sanction* comes off as a darkly funny, exhilarating espionage adventure. Readers embraced it as a straight thriller, earning Whittaker huge sales and wide acclaim all over the world. It was hardly the reaction Whitaker-as-Trevanian was expecting.

Dismayed, Whitaker set out to spoof his spoof, bringing back Hemlock in *The Loo Sanction* (aka *The Toilet Assassination*), but readers and critics alike still missed or ignored the joke and once again took it seriously as a thrilling spy novel.

He later reimagined Hemlock as Nicholas Hel in his novel *Shibumi*, his final espionage tale, only now the assassin/spy was not only a deft lover, but he drove women to unimaginable heights of ecstasy by stroking them with razor blades. A footnote from the author warned readers not to try this advanced sexual technique at home unless you were well trained in the erotic arts. Sadly, I dropped out before getting my diploma.

Despite such ludicrous touches, even *Shibumi* was embraced as an espionage classic, some regarding it with greater admiration than *The Eiger Sanction*.

Trevanian would have appreciated the irony.

In creating the fictional author and his outrageous hero, Whitaker unwittingly reinvigorated a tired genre with wit and intelligence, while also paying homage to everything that makes spy novels irresistible.

Lee Goldberg is a two-time Edgar Award nominee whose many TV writing and producing credits include *Diagnosis Murder*, *Hunter*, *Martial Law*, *SeaQuest*, *Spenser: For Hire*, *Nero Wolfe*, *Missing*, and *Monk*. He's also the author of *My Gun Has Bullets*, *Beyond the Beyond*, and *Successful Television Writing* as well as the acclaimed *Diagnosis Murder* and *Monk* series of original mystery novels. He served on the board of the Mystery Writers of America and cofounded the International Association of Media Tie-in Writers.

64

Charles McCarry's
THE TEARS OF AUTUMN (1974)

Hank Wagner

Born in 1930 in Massachusetts, Charles McCarry served in the U.S. Army, where he was a correspondent for *Stars and Stripes*; later, he worked as a speechwriter in the Eisenhower administration. From 1958 to 1967, he was a CIA undercover operative in Europe, Asia, and Africa. McCarry was also editor-at-large for *National Geographic* and contributed pieces to the *New York Times*, the *Wall Street Journal*, the *Washington Post*, and other national publications. Besides writing about super spy Paul Christopher in novels like *The Secret Lovers* and *Second Sight*, McCarry wrote several other novels, including *The Better Angels*, *Shelley's Heart*, and *Lucky Bastard*. He is also the author of several works of nonfiction, including *Citizen Nader* and *The Great Southwest*.

Novels can turn into personal touchstones for readers, becoming part of their mental landscape, especially the books read in one's formative years: *The Tears of Autumn*, published in 1974, when I was fourteen, became one for me. The book had everything a teenage reader who had just devoured Ian Fleming's Bond books could want: a global scope, a stoic hero (Paul Christopher, who had played a key role in McCarry's brilliant first novel, *The Miernik Dossier*), sex, violence, action, and political intrigue. On top of that, it delved into the labyrinthine mystery surrounding what was perhaps the defining moment of the second half of the twentieth century, the assassination of President John Fitzgerald Kennedy.

As the novel begins in the early fall of 1963, it's truly a heady time for Americans. The initially shaky Kennedy administration has finally found its feet and is looking forward to conquering the new frontiers it sees ahead. A cockiness and arrogance pervade Camelot, an attitude that CIA operative Paul Christopher, on assignment in Vietnam, perceives in the Americans he associates with in that country—all too sure of themselves, they assume that things will inevitably go their way. Thus, when the uncooperative brothers Ngo Dinh Diem and Ngo Dinh Nhu of South Vietnam are assassinated as part of a coup on November 1, 1963, with the tacit approval of the U.S. president, many consider their deaths as acceptable collateral damage. But actions have consequences, and in this case, their deaths set in motion a complicated plot of revenge from beyond the grave that culminates in the tragic events of November 22, 1963.

Kennedy's assassination so shocks the country and its citizens that ten days pass before even Christopher realizes what truly occurred. When he does realize the truth, it comes as swiftly and surely as divine revelation. "The explanation struck like a bell in Christopher's mind." Suddenly, the brilliant operative knows exactly who killed the president and why. The difficulty of his task, he knows, lies in convincing his skeptical superiors that his theory is valid, and staying alive long enough to prove it. Undaunted, Christopher breaks with the CIA, and embarks on a relentless and perilous quest to bring the truth to light.

So, just what makes this book a must-read?

First, it provides a plausible solution to the riddle of who killed JFK, seizing on several theories (i.e., the involvement of the Vietnamese, the Soviets, the Cubans, even the American mob), blending them into a seamless whole that, given what readers experience vicariously through Christopher, seems to arrive at a stark core truth. This seems almost inevitable, when you recall that the book began life when McCarry, having used his journalistic talents to develop a theory on who ordered the assassination, proposed a nonfiction work on the subject to his publisher. The publisher thought the idea had merit, but urged McCarry to pursue the idea through his fiction.

Second, it offers a hero so compelling that some, such as *Washington Post* critic Patrick Anderson (the author of the insightful *The Triumph of the Thriller*), have accused McCarry of making his protagonist too perfect. The accusation has some merit, especially when you consider how "Renaissance man" Christopher is described by a superior early in the novel: "Three things: first, he's intelligent and entirely unsentimental. Second, he will go to any lengths to get the truth, he never gives up. Third, he is not subject to fear." All this is true, at least to those he associates with professionally. Readers, however, are privy to his secret, that he is somewhat less than mythic, a human being who is sentimental and regretful about events in his past, and fearful for those around him—the moment when he thinks his lover Molly might have been harmed in retaliation for his probe into the assassination is absolutely gut wrenching, and his relief in discovering he is wrong is palpable.

Third is McCarry's ability to make even the most outré elements in his tale seem absolutely normal. For instance, a key element of the plot hinges on several horoscopes drawn by a mysterious Vietnamese named Yu Lung—in fact, the assassination would never have taken place had these readings not been favorable. As rendered by McCarry, and experienced by Christopher, superstition and conjecture come to seem like science, at once adding an intriguing, alien element to the story, and emphasizing the extreme differences in the cultures involved. Another example is the presence of Dieter Dimpel, a Nazi-loving, mountain climbing, acrobatic dwarf, an expert in retrieving information from seeming impregnable spaces. Using Dimpel, McCarry injects some welcome humor into the proceedings, simultaneously making the potentially loathsome character sympathetic.

Finally, there's the beauty of McCarry's prose, and the literary allusions that add zest to his work. Reading McCarry, you might find yourself thinking of G. K. Chesterton (like Gabriel Syme, the hero of Chesterton's classic of paranoia *The Man Who Was Thursday*, Christopher is also a poet), of W. Somerset Maugham (*Ashenden or the Secret Agent* is a particular favorite of McCarry's), or even of Ernest Hemingway (in that McCarry's classic style often echoes that of the author of *To Have and Have Not*). A major allusion involves Shelley, as a key clandestine meeting takes place at his gravesite in Rome. You'll also find yourself reflecting on Fleming's Bond, Greene's Maurice Castle, le Carré's George Smiley, even Condon's Captain Bennett Marco. That McCarry, one of America's finest spy novelists, manages to evoke all these disparate elements so expertly is a tribute to his intelligence and skill.

Although McCarry would write about Christopher several more times, *The Tears of Autumn* is where you'll find both author and character at the height of their powers, providing readers with one of those rare reading experiences that you learn to treasure—a book that both enthralls and enriches those who read it.

Hank Wagner is the coeditor of *Thrillers: 100 Must-Reads*. He is a regular contributor to *Mystery Scene, Crimespree, Cemetery Dance, Hellnotes*, and numerous other genre magazines.

65

Peter Benchley's
JAWS (1974)

P.J. Parrish

Peter Benchley (1940–2006) was the son of children's book author Nathaniel Benchley and the grandson of Algonquin Round Table founder, humorist Robert Benchley. Educated at Phillips Exeter Academy and Harvard, he worked for the *Washington Post* as well as *Newsweek* and was a speechwriter for President Lyndon Johnson. The idea for his most famous book, *Jaws*, came after he read a newspaper story about a Long Island fisherman catching a 4,550-pound great white shark. Like *Jaws*, several of his other novels were adapted into films, including *The Deep* and *The Island*. Later in his life, Benchley became an advocate for shark protection.

It was twenty-five years after the publication of the book that catapulted him to fame and fortune, and Peter Benchley was being lowered into the waters off Australia in a shark cage. "One of these days, one of these fellows is going to take revenge for *Jaws*," he said.

Benchley probably should have feared the critics more than the sharks. They weren't kind to him when his book debuted, dismissing it as populist trash. And it doesn't help Benchley's legacy that his book eventually sank in the wake created by Steven Spielberg's landmark movie. The comparison is unavoidable and is symbolized in that iconic graphic of the fish rising from the deep toward the hapless woman swimmer that's become as well known as John Williams's *da-dum* sound track. On the dust jacket of the original *Jaws* hardcover (I've got a mildewed first edition on my shelf), there's the huge fish, rising out of the deep toward the hapless woman. But it looks like a toothless old dolphin, nothing like the fanged monster of the movie poster.

Is this one of those rare cases where the movie outshines the book? Alas, yes. While Spielberg's Oscar-nominated movie loops endlessly on cable, Benchley's slender paperback is readily available only via a mouse click on Amazon or else it is relegated to the bottom shelf in the back of

Barnes & Noble. (That's where I found it after the clerk confessed he didn't know there even was a book called *Jaws*.) Though it was a publishing phenomenon in its day, I'd guess few people today read *Jaws*. So what are we to make of Benchley's big fish story? Does it merit a place in the pantheon of great thrillers? Or it is just a rusty bucket of chum?

When *Jaws* came out in 1974, the critics chewed Benchley to bits, taking him to task for the "rubber-teeth plot," "lifeless characters," and "hollow portentousness." Sniffed the *Village Voice*: "If there's a trite turn to be made, *Jaws* will make it."

True, the book has its faults. Its craftsmanship is pulp level; its characters tend toward cardboard thin. And the story is burdened with ludicrous subplots featuring mobsters, ersatz-Cheever class warfare, supernatural omens, and gin-fueled adultery. An adulterous sex scene involving Chief Brody's wife in the booth of a seafood restaurant is just plain icky.

Ah, but back in its day, readers loved *Jaws*. It stayed on the hardcover best-seller list for forty-four weeks, selling twenty million copies. In a single day, one newsstand at O'Hare Airport sold 392 copies. Just seven days after *Jaws* finally disappeared from the hardcover list, it resurfaced on the paperback list at number 3, bumping off Erica Jong's *Fear of Flying*. It stayed on the paperback list for a year, rising and falling and fending off attacks from Richard Adams's *Watership Down* rabbits, selling an astounding nine million copies.

Jaws continued to be a phenomenon beyond its publication. The 1975 movie, backed by a massive history-making marketing campaign, became the highest grossing film up to that time (surpassed finally by *Star Wars*). It generated mass fear, causing a decline in beach attendance. And then there were the imitators. If a twenty-five-foot shark could generate all that money, what could a two hundred-footer do? First came *Megalodon* and then a self-published number called *Carcharodon* in which a giant prehistoric shark is freed when an iceberg melts. Others from the "gaping maw genre" were *Extinct* and *Meg*. You have to wonder if we'd have *Jurassic Park* without *Jaws*. Michael Crichton's book opens with a girl getting chewed up by a dinosaur on a beach. As Benchley himself said, "Every young man in the world is fascinated with sharks or dinosaurs."

But beyond the sheer numbers, there are good reasons why *Jaws* has earned its stripes as a seminal modern thriller.

First, the fish is a terrific character, undoubtedly the best-rendered character in the book (Benchley even gives the shark its own point of view). The story comes alive when the shark is on the page, pulling the narrative along in its wake, diverting our attention from the extraneous stuff. (Spielberg understood this and jettisoned the subplots).

Second, *Jaws* tapped into a primal but very believable fear. Benchley broke the realism barrier between fiction and nonfiction, giving us a predator from the real world—the beach no less, a place of fun and beauty on the surface, but a place of darkness and danger below. Chief Brody is all of us when he stares out at the ocean and thinks: "In his dreams, deep water was populated by slimy, savage things that rose from below and shredded his flesh, demons that cackled and moaned."

Lastly, at its basest level, Benchley's great white shark is one heck of a serial killer story. As one character tells Chief Brody: "Sharks are like ax murderers. People react to them with their guts."

And that is the bottom line. The greatest thrillers give us a fiend that taps into our deepest fears. The greatest thrillers deliver a visceral punch that stays with us long after we have turned off the light or folded up the beach blanket. With *Jaws*, Peter Benchley created a monster for the ages, the second most famous fish after Moby Dick.

As for his literary legacy, we'll let Benchley have the last word: "It's nice being a little rich and a little bit famous, but dammit, I didn't intend to rank with Melville."

P.J. Parrish is the *New York Times* best-selling author of two series about biracial police detective Louis Kincaid and his lover—female homicide detective, Joe Frye. Parrish is also a regular contributor to short story anthologies, among them *Detroit Noir, These Guns for Hire*, MWA's *Death Do Us Part*, and ITW's *The Chopin Manuscript*. Her titles include *A Thousand Bones, South of Hell, A Killing Rain, Thicker than Water*, and *Paint it Black*. She won ITW's Thriller Award, the Shamus Award, the Anthony Award, and was nominated for an Edgar.

66
William Goldman's
MARATHON MAN (1974)

Hank Wagner

Born in 1931, William Goldman grew up near Chicago. He received a B.A. from Oberlin College in 1952, and an M.A. in English from Columbia University in 1956. It's hard to pick a place to start a discussion about Goldman's lengthy, varied, and successful career. But surely you've heard of at least one of his sixteen novels, which include *No Way To Treat a Lady* (1964) and *The Princess Bride* (1973). Or screenplays he wrote for films as diverse as *Butch Cassidy and the Sundance Kid* (1969), *The Stepford Wives* (1975), *Misery* (1990), and *Maverick* (1994). Or read one of his memoirs, like *Adventures in the Screen Trade*, where he (in)famously summed up the entertainment industry with the phrase "Nobody knows anything." If not, you certainly should, as Goldman likely forgot more about writing and storytelling than most writers will ever know. Objective proof? Well, Goldman received two Academy Awards, one for *Butch Cassidy and the Sundance Kid* (original screenplay), and one for *All the President's Men* (adapted screenplay). He also received two Edgar Awards for Best Motion Picture Screenplay, one for *Harper* (1967), the other for *Magic* (1979).

Author Gene Wolfe defines good literature as "that which can be read with pleasure by an educated reader and reread with increased pleasure." That's certainly the case with William Goldman's *Marathon Man*. A classic thriller, it's also a class in thriller writing. Reading it, then rereading it, is as exciting as watching a skilled magician perform, then having him take you aside afterward to explain just how he accomplished his illusions.

Marathon Man is one of those novels that make you profoundly envious of those reading it for the first time. From its first pages, where readers are transported into the mind of a cranky old man named Rosenbaum, who's consumed by road rage against the driver of a VW ahead of him who is just . . . going . . . too . . . slow, to its oddly touching, bittersweet denouement, you realize that you've placed yourself in the hands of a master,

someone who is utterly ruthless about grabbing, then holding, your attention.

The book literally begins with a bang, as two cars careening through
the streets of mid-1970s Manhattan collide with a fuel tanker, resulting in
a terrific explosion. Certainly an attention-grabbing set piece, but the
events the explosion sets in motion lead to far more compelling reading.
From that moment on, a collision between profound evil and a seemingly
hapless Everyman becomes inevitable.

The driver of the VW is Kaspar Szell, father of Josef (The Angel of
Death) Mengele protégé Christian Szell, a Nazi dentist ironically labeled
by the Jews he tortured and stole from in Auschwitz as Der Weisse Engel,
the White Angel, due to his prematurely white hair. Ever since the end of
World War II, Kaspar has been channeling funds to his son through various (and surprising) means. His death forces the younger Szell to leave his
refuge in Paraguay and travel to the U.S., in order to recover the diamonds
that are the source of his ill-gotten wealth. Emerging from his lair, he has
one paramount thought: is it safe?

Meanwhile, Goldman introduces the young, brilliant, but insecure historian, Thomas Babington "Babe" Levy, and the ultralethal spy, code-
named Scylla, who works for a shadowy U.S. intelligence agency. Babe is
our stand-in, the Richard Hannay of this piece. Scylla is a man we instinctively fear, but whom we all want to be, a lethal, cunning, experienced master of tradecraft who stars in several tense set pieces overseas
before returning to America, where his path crosses those of Szell and Babe
Levy in thrilling and surprising ways. The resulting mayhem leaves two of
these players dead, and another deeply shaken and forever changed.

Most books are lucky if they have one memorable scene or plot twist;
Marathon Man has many. Indeed, if classic thrillers involve surprises, turn-
arounds, and reversals, then *Marathon Man* truly deserves the label. Among
its many stunning sequences:

The opening automobile "duel" between Rosenbaum and the elder
Szell;

Scylla's unplanned meeting with his opposing number "Ape" in an airport;

The stunning revelation of Scylla's true identity as Babe's beloved
brother, Doc;

Babe's torture at the hands of the sadistic dentist Szell, containing one of the most recognizable phrases in all of thriller literature (and of cinema, with Dustin Hoffman as Babe, and Sir Laurence Olivier as Szell), the infamous and chilling "Is it safe?"

Babe's escape from Szell's clutches, when he hallucinates running partners: fellow marathon men, Nurmi, and the barefoot marathoner, Bikila;

Babe's abrupt betrayal by Doc's associate, Janeway;

Szell being recognized by his former victims in New York's diamond district;

Babe's capture of Szell just as the ex-Nazi thinks he's going to get away (along with Babe's killer line, "It's not safe.");

The book's last scene, as Babe, shattered by all that has happened, contentedly skips the last of Szell's impressive hoard of diamonds across the Central Park reservoir.

Throughout, Goldman operates as methodically as a bricklayer in constructing his tale. Literally nothing is wasted. Seemingly disparate pieces of information ultimately tie together, just waiting for the right piece of exposition, or revelation, to explain it all coherently. If Goldman provides an early mention of a gun or a hidden knife (Szell's blade is dubbed "the cutter"), he's certain to use it later. If he mentions Babe's toothache or his obsession with running, it's sure to play a part in the subsequent action. The list goes on and on. The Puerto Rican stoop kids who live to taunt Babe play a surprising role in a later chapter, as does Babe's impossibly wonderful new girlfriend, Gretchen. The mention of Scylla's paramour, Janey, who we assume is a woman but turns out to be the man, Janeway. In the end, the book is a perfect example of the Butterfly Effect, with small things leading to bigger ones, one set piece building on another until the bloody crescendo of the final pages.

What else is notable? Well, a classic villain, a Nazi, when that idea wasn't grossly overused. The repeated, effective use of certain phrases, such as "Babe was candy," indicating extreme violence to come. The villains' comeuppance, brilliantly handled. The way Goldman gets into the heads of even the most minor of characters and brings you there too. The evocation of classic thrillers such as *The Thirty-Nine Steps*, or Goldman's subtle nod to Mickey Spillane's *I, the Jury* in Babe's last exchange with Szell. Finally, the fact that the hero is not some superman, but a human being who can be hurt—even though he emerges triumphant, Babe certainly doesn't emerge unscathed.

There are so many more things to discuss, but I think I'll end this here, to let you, Educated Reader, discover the remainder of this book's many wonders on your own—after all, I know that having read this book once, you're more than ready to dip into it again.

Hank Wagner, an attorney, lives in northwestern New Jersey with his wife and four daughters. Besides being coeditor of *Thrillers: 100 Must-Reads*, he is a coauthor of *The Complete Stephen King Universe* and *Prince of Stories: The Many Worlds of Neil Gaiman*.

67

James Grady's
SIX DAYS OF THE CONDOR (1974)

Mark Terry

James Grady (1949–) wrote his first novel, *Six Days of the Condor*, at the age of twenty-four. It became a monster success and was turned into a blockbuster film starring Robert Redford, titled *Three Days of the Condor*. Born and raised in Shelby, Montana, Grady worked various odd jobs including grave digger, farm tractor jockey, rock picker, hay bucker, janitor, and movie projectionist before he graduated from the University of Montana with a degree in journalism. In 1971, he took a position as a staff aide for the Constitutional Convention in Montana and spent a year fellowship with Senator Lee Metcalf's (D-Mont.) staff in Washington, DC. From there, Grady worked as an investigative reporter for syndicated columnist Jack Anderson. After four years, he left that position to concentrate on writing fiction and movies. Grady has had a successful writing career with a total of fourteen novels, mostly thrillers and mysteries, short fiction, and as a scriptwriter for film and TV. His script was the basis for the movie *Legacy*, and his short story, "Kiss The Sky," was the basis for an FX network project. Grady also served as a staff writer/story editor for a Stephen Cannell TV series in the 1980s, *Top of the Hill*, and created a police drama for CBS TV, *D.C. Cops*. He also received the French Grand Prix du Roman Noir, Italy's Raymond Chandler medal, and a Mystery Writers of America Edgar nomination.

It is almost impossible to divorce the novel, *Six Days of the Condor*, and the film, *Three Days of the Condor*, from the years in which they came out— 1974 and 1975, respectively. In 1974, the U.S. saw Richard Nixon resign from the presidency because of the Watergate scandal, and in 1975, Watergate continued with the trials and guilty verdicts against Mitchell, Haldeman, and Ehrlichman. The CIA was being investigated for domestic abuses, and Saigon fell to North Vietnamese forces. It was a period in which trust of the U.S. government was at a low and paranoia over what the government might be doing was at a high.

Six Days of the Condor drops into this environment a tightly structured thriller about a rogue CIA group that is smuggling drugs and murdering people in the U.S. to cover up for it. Every headline was an advertisement for the novel and the movie.

At this time, espionage novels fell into two broad camps—the over-the-top James Bond thrillers and the talky, brooding spy novels of John le Carré and Len Deighton. *Six Days of the Condor* cuts right through the middle. The book's main character, Ronald Malcolm (renamed Joe Turner in the film), is an Everyman. A bookish, sarcastic, mildly rebellious guy who finds himself pursued by extraordinary forces, relies on his brains, his wits, and more than a little luck to stay alive and uncover the conspiracy that surrounds him. His paranoia is real—everyone he knows is out to get him; even the people on his side are using him to their own ends.

It seems a little odd these days to consider that when *Condor* appeared in bookstores there were only a couple books published about the real workings and history of the CIA. Now entire sections of bookstores are dedicated to factual accounts of the agency. The novel is written with a distant, almost journalistic omniscient point of view, filled with descriptions of how the CIA is structured, how it works, and what legislation created it. In addition to providing a fairly riveting thriller narrative, the novel provides that basic of the thriller genre—esoteric information.

In a peculiar sidebar, *Condor* had an effect on the real world. The CIA division that Malcolm works for, Section 9, Department 17, CIAID, is tasked, the reader is told, with keeping "track of all espionage and related acts recorded in literature. In other words, the Department reads spy thrillers and murder mysteries. The antics and situations of thousands of volumes of mystery and mayhem are carefully detailed and analyzed in Department 17 files."

More than thirty years after writing the book, Grady learned that several KGB generals had seen the 1975 film and were convinced the CIA was spending more money and effort on analytical work than the KGB was. As a result, the KGB created—according to the book *Comrade J: The Untold Secrets of Russia's Master Spy in America after the End of the Cold War* by Pete Earley and Sergei Tretyakov—the NIIRP, or the Scientific Research Institute of Intelligence Problems of the First Chief Directorate of the

KGB. The NIIRP, they write in their book, was where, "Some two thousand employees there sifted through hundreds of newspapers and magazines each day from all over the world, looking for information that might prove helpful to the intelligence service."

As much as you can't separate the *Condor* novel and film from the era in which they were released, it's difficult to separate the novel from the film, partly because they came out so close to one another. Grady relates that his manuscript was pulled out of the W.W. Norton slush pile and the film rights were handled—on behalf of the publisher—by William Morris. The Sydney Pollack-directed film must have gone into almost immediate production, because it was released after the hardcover publication, but before the mass-market paperback publication.

Speaking about the novel and the film, Grady says, "*Condor* became like some existential stone thrown into our culture ponds. I'm so lucky to be the guy who got that stone dropped in his hand." As far as the film, he says, "I got to watch the best professionals in Hollywood turn my slim first novel into a far superior, classic, important movie. Few writers have been so lucky in Hollywood."

Three Days of the Condor makes significant changes to the book, but even there they resonate—at that time and today. Although in the novel the conspiracy involved a CIA cabal smuggling morphine, in the movie it was changed to a plot to overthrow Middle Eastern countries for oil—our first energy crisis was ongoing, although thirty-five plus years later this plot resonates stronger than ever. Grady originally planned for there to be five Condor novels, although only one follow-up was written, *Shadow of the Condor*, which Grady indicates was his least successful "literary" work, although it did hit the *New York Times* best-seller list and royalties continue to trickle in. "Midway through *Shadow*'s birth process, I realized that Redford had absorbed *Condor* so completely and that he was not going to do a series of movies like Sean Connery, and thus . . . I let *Condor* go."

That's probably a good thing. One of the most powerful things about *Six Days of the Condor* is how the Everyman uses his wits and guile to get out of trouble. It's a beautifully crafted character arc. Malcolm goes from being a naïve slacker to a brutal killer who's lost almost everything and can trust no one. It's doubtful, in retrospect, whether Malcolm could have been a successful recurring character. Still, Grady crafted a singular character and story that has stood out in popular culture ever since. It was even mentioned in the George Clooney/Elmore Leonard film *Out of Sight*, has appeared in spoofs on *The Simpsons* and on *Seinfeld* as "Three Days of the Condo," and was sampled on a Radiohead tune.

Author John le Carré said, "If you write one book that, for whatever reason, becomes iconic, it's an extraordinary blessing."

Grady echoes the sentiment. "For whatever reason—the convergence of time and circumstance and my imagination—I'm extraordinarily blessed. And awestruck."

Mark Terry was born in Flint, Michigan, and grew up in the neighboring suburb of Davison. He graduated from Michigan State University with a degree in microbiology and public health and spent eighteen years working in clinical and research genetics at Henry Ford Hospital in Detroit before turning to full-time freelance writing and editing. He has published five novels, including three that feature Department of Homeland Security biological and chemical terrorism troubleshooter Derek Stillwater: *The Devil's Pitchfork*, *The Serpent's Kiss*, and *The Fallen*. Several of his novels have been reprinted in French, German, and Slovak. He has written literally hundreds of articles, book reviews, white papers, and market research reports focusing on the U.S. healthcare system and biotechnology.

68
Jack Higgins's
THE EAGLE HAS LANDED (1975)

Zoë Sharp

Jack Higgins is the pseudonym of prolific British thriller writer Harry Patterson (1929–). Born in the northeast of England, he moved to Northern Ireland at an early age and was raised in Belfast during the turbulent 1940s. He left school without qualifications and joined the army, where he served as a noncommissioned officer on the East German border. Later, he took evening classes to gain a degree and became a teacher, but always wanted to write. He is now the author of more than sixty novels, translated into fifty-five languages, and sells hundreds of millions of copies worldwide.

Patterson's first novel, *Sad Wind from the Sea*, was published under his own name in 1959. He used various pseudonyms, starting with Martin Fallon for *The Testament of Caspar Shultz* (originally *The Bormann Testament*) in 1962; Hugh Marlowe for *Seven Pillars to Hell* in 1963; and James Graham for *A Game for Heroes* in 1970. Under these and his own name, Patterson wrote a remarkable thirty-five novels by 1974, all of which were fast paced and had the right ingredients, but none of which elevated him to stardom. Then 1975 brought the advent of his most successful pseudonym, Jack Higgins, and *The Eagle Has Landed*.

I vividly recall seeing a television interview with Higgins many years ago in which he recounted a chance encounter with an old teacher in the early seventies, whose counsel had a far-reaching effect on his writing. Basically, Higgins was told to concentrate far more on character. Higgins heeded this advice with a vengeance, creating not only one of his most enduring characters—Irish gunman and poet, Liam Devlin—but also the Boer spy, Joanna Grey; the half-American, half-German paratrooper Lieutenant Colonel Kurt Steiner; and crippled Winter War veteran Colonel Max Radl of the Abwehr. With these fascinating fictional creations, Higgins intersperses genuine historical figures: Winston Churchill, Adolf Hitler, Heinrich Himmler, and Admiral Wilhelm Canaris.

The plot of *The Eagle Has Landed* extrapolates from Hitler's delight at the success of Otto Skorzeny's 1943 "Operation Oak," which involved rescuing the Italian dictator Benito Mussolini from his prison cell at the top of the ten-thousand-foot Gran Sasso. Higgins imagines that, with a little careful political maneuvering from Himmler, Hitler then gave the order, "Bring me Churchill out of England."

From this simple, high-concept starting point, Higgins presents his story as a thinly disguised exposé: "At precisely one o'clock on the morning of Saturday 6 November 1943, Heinrich Himmler, Reichsführer of the SS and Chief of State Police, received a simple message. *The Eagle has landed.* It meant a small force of German paratroops were at that moment safely in England and poised to snatch the British Prime Minister, Winston Churchill. . . . This book is an attempt to recreate the events surrounding that astonishing exploit. At least fifty percent of it is documented historical fact. The reader must decide for himself how much of the rest is a matter of speculation."

This false document technique is further enhanced by the way Higgins begins the novel with his own first-person narrative, in which he explains how he first stumbled on the story of the German paratroopers buried in a Norfolk churchyard. The book then switches to a third-person, fairly linear narrative, in which Higgins rejects the opportunities for minor characters to play a more significant role—the Special Branch detectives on Devlin's trail, for instance—in order to drive the story toward its ultimate conclusion. In this, the writer really shows his skill, because although we know from the outset that Churchill was never snatched out of England—just as de Gaulle was not assassinated by a lone hitman in Frederick Forsyth's earlier novel, *The Day of the Jackal* (1971)—we quickly become caught up in just how close the operation came to success.

The real strength of the novel is the characterization. Apart from the unmitigatingly evil Himmler, most of the major characters are satisfyingly complex in their motivations. Higgins paints the hero, Steiner, with particular care. His bravery was displayed on the Eastern Front (the book was written when the Cold War was at its height) not the Western. Steiner's mother was American, giving him the possibility of mixed loyalties. He behaves honorably in a dishonorable situation—the rescue of a Jewish girl during a ghetto clearance in Poland—after which he and his men are condemned to a suicide posting, destroying Allied shipping in the Channel. Steiner's father has been arrested by Himmler, and his life hangs in the balance, depending on the success of Steiner's mission. He is a man with few options. Later, in Norfolk, his men break their cover as Polish paratroopers to save the lives of two village children.

The other enigmatic character is Liam Devlin, IRA gunman, philosopher, and general rogue, who should be a villain but again behaves with honor, taking an instant dislike to a British traitor, and earning the undying love of local girl, Molly Prior, by protecting her from violent assault, acting against his orders to keep a low profile. Higgins returned to the character of Devlin for several later books, starting with *Touch the Devil* in 1982, and even constructed a direct sequel, called *The Eagle Has Flown*, in which Steiner is resurrected as a pawn in another of Himmler's schemes.

The rest of the cast is large. Inevitably most of them need to be lightly sketched, but the interactions of the main characters are what help make the book a winner. It is still regarded by many as Jack Higgins's finest thriller. A fascinating work that expertly blends fact and fiction, it manages the neat trick of making the reader thoroughly root for the "wrong" people.

Like Jack Higgins, Zoë Sharp left school early. She spent her formative years living aboard a catamaran on the northwest coast of England and went through a variety of jobs in her teenage years before becoming a freelance photojournalist in 1988. Sharp began her thriller writing career after receiving death threat letters in the course of her work. Her ex-Special Forces turned bodyguard heroine, Charlotte "Charlie" Fox, was praised by the *Chicago Tribune*: "Ill-tempered, aggressive, and borderline psychotic, Fox is also compassionate, introspective, and highly principled: arguably one of the most enigmatic—and coolest—heroines in contemporary genre fiction." The first of Sharp's books to be published in the U.S. was *First Drop*, which was nominated for the Barry Award. Others followed, including *Third Strike*.

69

Joseph Wambaugh's
THE CHOIRBOYS (1975)

James O. Born

Joseph Wambaugh (1937–) is the best known of all cops turned writers. Born in Pittsburgh to a police officer and a homemaker, Wambaugh did a hitch in the U.S. Marines, giving him insight into the military culture as well as the discipline needed to write while holding down a job and raising a family. Wambaugh joined the LAPD as a patrolman in 1960, continuing his education, earning first a bachelor's degree, then a master's in literature. His first novel, *The New Centurions*, was published in 1971 and became an instant bestseller. He has since published fifteen novels and nonfiction books. Several of his works, including *The Onion Field*, *The New Centurions*, and *The Choirboys* were adapted into major motion pictures. Wambaugh also created the critically acclaimed 1970s TV series, *Police Story*. His books are continually on the best-seller lists and highly regarded. Two of his recent novels are *Hollywood Station* and *Hollywood Crows*.

The Choirboys, Wambaugh's third novel, was published in 1975. It was the first novel he wrote after leaving the LAPD, and it gave him the freedom to let go and show police work, warts and all. In the novel, he takes deadly aim on administrators and some of the ridiculous programs thought up by command staff who are so disconnected from actual life on the street that the programs are not only costly but counterproductive. His observations of drunken police officers are endearing compared to his disdain for administrators. The entire story starts with allusions to the "MacArthur Park incident," references made by supervisors who are essentially the villains in the story. In effect, the novel moves backward, ending with the actual event at MacArthur Park.

The bulk of the story centers around a group of patrolmen working the night shift in Wilshire Division of Los Angeles. The station is located close to MacArthur Park, which was technically located in the Rampart Division. The cops didn't want to cause problems in their own patrol area, or

as Wambaugh so poetically put it, "One does not shit in one's own nest."
Each segment of the novel focuses on a different pair of partners and the
wild adventures they live out on the street. These anecdotes reflect the
distinct personalities and frailties of the cops involved. For example,
Roscoe Rules is a violent bully with a serious inferiority complex that is exposed time and time again. His ego won't allow a slight to go unpunished
or a story of his courage to be told without exaggeration.

The de facto leader of the group and senior officer is Herbert "Sperm
Whale" Whalen, a nineteen-year vet of the LAPD who is also an Air Force
reservist who flew in World War II, Korea, and Vietnam. Sperm Whale
would work straight shifts until he had enough days off to fly transports to
Vietnam in the late sixties and qualify for combat flight pay. Whalen, like
all the characters and most events in the novel, is based on reality.
Wambaugh knew an officer who flew missions in Vietnam on his days off.
Whalen is the heart and soul of the squad as well as the conscience of the
book, and when he is forced to make tough choices, the reader feels them
like blunt trauma.

The novel was groundbreaking on several levels. Wambaugh provided
a glimpse into realistic lives of average police officers and used a number
of different story lines to merge into the final scenes. He used his unique
position as an actual police officer to offer insights that ran counter to the
image of the police work portrayed in TV shows and movies. The novel
also introduced a phrase to police work that is still used: "Choir Practice,"
meaning to share a drink after work and complain about the pressures of
administration, the dangers of the job, and the futility of life. The time period of the early seventies still lacked the unending parade of reality shows
presenting how cops work and live. At the time, if you didn't know a
police officer, you had virtually no idea what they faced on a day-to-day
basis unless you watched *Dragnet* or *Adam-12*, which sanitized every encounter with street people. Wambaugh went out on a limb to really present cops as humans in the most difficult of professions. The use of profanity
and ethnic slurs flew in the face of the image that the LAPD had tried to
cultivate by cooperating with the mild TV shows of the time.

In 1975, the profession was not viewed in the same way as it is today.
Just as the military at the time was seen in a negative light, cops were seen
as the muscle of a corrupt government. Wambaugh didn't make excuses
or value judgments about the actions of his cops in *The Choirboys*. He allowed readers to see firsthand the humor as well as the terror inherent in

police work. This was unusual and original. The truth of *The Choirboys* is evident in the fact that even thirty-five years after its publication the story and characters remain fresh and powerful.

Joseph Wambaugh holds a unique position of influence among modern crime writers as well as cops. His books and the TV show he created, *Police Story*, provided a glimpse of police work to a generation of young people looking to break out of traditional professions. A chance to experience something besides a nine-to-five office job, increasing pay and benefits as well as finding excitement, led a new crop of college-educated candidates to apply for police jobs across the country. Wambaugh saw this trend early and uses it in *The Choirboys*. All of the younger officers in the novel have college degrees whereas Sperm Whale Whalen, the fifty-two-year-old veteran, scoffs at the need to go to college.

The best of the Los Angeles-based crime writers, Michael Connelly, made this comment in a 2008 *Mystery Scene Magazine* article about Wambaugh:

> I think his recent books are just as strong as those books he changed the world with. He continues his unique style of weaving anecdotal vignettes into the mosaic of the story. But the story has a point and they are as much reports from the frontlines of modern police work and politics and the city of Los Angeles, as they are full-blooded novels. What Wambaugh never loses sight of is the difficulty in doing the job right and the underlying nobility of going against the odds. It's what makes police work a calling, not a job, and Wambaugh never forgets this.

From cops on the beat to phenomenal crime writers, Joseph Wambaugh has influenced generations of people with his honest observations, grand storytelling style, and sense of justice. His unflinching look at life on the street has served as the standard for police novels and TV shows. *The Choirboys* is Wambaugh's magnum opus of police work that continues to entertain, educate, and shock.

James O. Born is a former federal drug agent and novelist who credits Wambaugh with influencing both his career choices. Born's first novel, *Walking Money*, was published in 2004. He has four more police thrillers based on realistic law-enforcement procedure. He was the winner of the Florida Book Award for his third novel, *Escape Clause*. In 2009, the first in a series of police thrillers set in the near future was released under the pseudonym James O'Neal—*The Human Disguise* follows the life of a state cop in Florida after the world has been drastically changed by war, terrorism, and disease.

70

Clive Cussler's
RAISE THE TITANIC! (1976)

Grant Blackwood

Clive Cussler (1931–) began his writing career when his wife, Barbara, took a night job at the local police department. With the kids fed and put to bed, Cussler found himself alone in a quiet house with time on his hands and an imagination honed by working as an "idea man" at an advertising agency during the day. The protagonist he created, Dirk Pitt (named after his then toddler son, Dirk), was something of a split literary personality: one part contemporary hero—a high-school quarterback, Air Force Academy graduate, decorated pilot, and a marine engineer for the National Underwater Marine Agency—and one part swashbuckler: mannered but dangerous, more comfortable out-of-doors than in, at ease with greasy-handed mechanics and royalty alike, a hero who restlessly scans the horizon for that next indecipherable mystery or astounding adventure. In his spare time, Cussler pursues real-life nautical mysteries, participating in the discovery of over sixty shipwrecks, including *Carpathia* (the first ship to respond to the foundering HMS *Titanic*), the famed ghost ship *Mary Celeste*, and the Confederate submarine *Hunley*.

Cussler took his first steps into the fiction world with a clear vision of the kind of book he wanted to write and the kind of hero who would star in it. An avid outdoorsman and scuba diver, Cussler's "he who dares wins" attitude asserted itself early when in 1969, posing as a fellow literary agent, he sent a letter to his now longtime agent, Peter Lampack. Written on stationery Cussler himself created and styled in near-perfect "agent-ese," the letter asked Lampack to consider two manuscripts written by the son of his best friend. If not for his own impending retirement, the phantom agent explained, he would've already signed the writer. Though he didn't recognize the agent's name, Lampack assumed they'd met in passing at one event or another, so he agreed to take a look at this son-of-a-friend-of-a-colleague's work.

Cussler's first book, *Pacific Vortex*, which would eventually be published in 1983 after a trio of best sellers, was shelved by Cussler and Lampack in favor of his next effort, *The Mediterranean Caper*, which found a home at Pyramid Books and met with moderate success, garnering Cussler an Edgar Award nomination by the Mystery Writers of America for Best Paperback Original Novel of 1973. *Iceberg*, published in 1975 by Dodd, Mead, is a sentimental favorite of Cussler, marking a transition between the linear story lines of *Pacific Vortex* and *The Mediterranean Caper* to one with a greater cast of characters, multiple plot twists, and a ruthless, powerful villain bent on changing the course of history.

Turning his mind to the book that would eventually become *Raise the Titanic!*, Cussler found himself already forearmed with arguably the most important ingredient in commercially successful thrillers: a larger-than-life protagonist. Backed up by his stalwart sidekick Al Giordino, Dirk Pitt had already racked up what most real-life adventurers would consider a lifetime of challenges: going nose-to-nose with a World War I biplane terrorizing an air force base on the Greek island of Thásos, narrowly escaping from a labyrinth known as the Pit of Hades, salvaging German U-Boats and Japanese I-Boats converted into automated heroin-smuggling vehicles, finding a missing billionaire's yacht gutted by fire and embedded in a massive iceberg, trekking across the blasted moonscape of Iceland, and fighting a shadowy organization determined to topple the governments of an entire continent.

With his first two books, Cussler had charted relatively unknown territory in the literary world of that time. His brand of high-concept, high-stakes maritime action had gone unrepresented in the thriller genre for two decades since Hammond Innes and Alistair MacLean (one of Cussler's models) in the 1950s. During the two years leading up to *Raise the Titanic!*'s publication, best-selling thrillers had been dominated by a man-eating shark (*Jaws* by Peter Benchley), Cold War spies and mercenaries (*Tinker, Tailor, Soldier, Spy* by John le Carré, and *The Dogs of War* by Frederick Forsyth), World War II intrigue (*The Eagle Has Landed* by Jack Higgins), and a historical caper (*The Great Train Robbery* by Michael Crichton). In fact, so atypical were Cussler's first two books that he and Lampack were encouraged by industry insiders to steer the next book into more familiar genre categories. Trusting his instinct, Cussler declined. Still, he understood the crux of the issue: how to fuse Dirk Pitt and his swash-buckling adventures with a topic that would grab the attention of the reading public. At the time, the U.S. and the Soviet Union were engaged in not only a Cold War but also an arms race that had packed their respective arsenals with enough nuclear weapons to destroy the planet many times over.

Raise the Titanic! started with a series of what-if questions. Cussler asked himself: What if the US government developed a sound-based shield able to obliterate incoming ballistic missiles? What if the shield's power source, a mineral known as byzanium, existed in only one accessible place on Earth, a tiny island off the northern coast of the Soviet Union? What if the government discovered that the byzanium had long ago been spirited from the island by a mysterious mining concern known as The Coloradans? And finally, what if the missing byzanium was now in a place no one could reach? Cussler's answer to the last question reflected both his and Pitt's nautical leanings, as well as their drive to explore the unknown. The byzanium, Cussler decided, had been placed in the hold of the HMS *Titanic*, only to be lost when the supposedly unsinkable ship struck an iceberg and sank to the bottom of the Atlantic Ocean. Enter Dirk Pitt and the National Underwater Marine Agency.

Published in the late fall of 1976, *Raise the Titanic!* landed on the *New York Times* best-seller list just before Christmas and stayed there for the next twenty-six weeks, making Cussler, Dirk Pitt, and NUMA household names to readers across the country.

In the forty-five years since Cussler began writing, his best-selling books have been published in over forty languages in more than one hundred countries. He has 160 million copies of his thrillers in print and has inspired a genre he continues to lead and shape to this day.

In 2006, at the International Thriller Writers yearly gathering—aptly named ThrillerFest—Cussler was presented with the first-ever Thriller Master Award. Before he was brought on stage, the host conducted an experiment: Would those of the three hundred author attendees who had been either influenced, inspired, or helped by Clive Cussler please stand up?

Not a chair remained occupied.

Grant Blackwood, a U.S. Navy veteran, spent three years aboard a guided missile frigate as an Operations Specialist and a Pilot Rescue Swimmer. His high-action credentials are amply demonstrated in his Briggs Tanner international thriller series (*The End of Enemies*, *The Wall of Night*, and *An Echo of War*), as well as the short story "Sacrificial Lion" from the anthology *Thriller: Stories to Keep You Up All Night*. Blackwood lives in Colorado. His first book cowritten with Clive Cussler, *Spartan Gold* (featuring the treasure-hunting team of Sam and Remi Fargo) debuted in 2009.

71

Ira Levin's
THE BOYS FROM BRAZIL (1976)

Daniel Kalla

As versatile as writers come, Ira Levin (1929–2007) demonstrated the breadth of genres that a talented thriller writer can conquer. In fact, as a novelist, playwright, television writer, and Broadway lyricist, he exceeded the bounds that limit most of us. He achieved critical acclaim early with his Edgar-winning debut novel, A *Kiss Before Dying* (1954). His play, *Death-trap* (1977), earned him a second Edgar and has the distinction of being the longest running comedy-thriller ever on Broadway. Although not prolific (only seven novels in an extremely long career), he wrote best-selling books in multiple genres, including the science fiction satire, *The Stepford Wives* (1972), the horror classic, *Rosemary's Baby* (1967), and of course the thriller, *The Boys from Brazil* (1976). The expression "a Stepford wife" became common in the English language. Most of his works have been adapted as films, often more than once. His other titles include *This Perfect Day*, *Sliver*, and *Son of Rosemary*. In 2003, the Mystery Writers of America honored him with its Grandmaster award.

People familiar with *The Boys from Brazil*, the book or the movie, realize the story concerns cloning modern-day Hitlers. But for those who read it unaware, the novel begins far more obliquely. At a mysterious meeting inside a Brazilian restaurant, the leader of an all-German cabal disperses a group of six middle-aged men across Europe and North America to assassinate ninety-four low-level civil servants, all of whom are approaching the age of sixty-five. A young amateur investigator manages to tape the meeting and replay part of it over the phone for famed Nazi hunter, Yakov Lieberman, before being cut off (and cut up) by the plotters. Half a world away, Lieberman—who faces the daunting prospect of a Cold War world that would just as soon forget about aging Nazis—doesn't know whether or not the call is a hoax.

Deciding to kick the tires, at first he finds nothing to substantiate the caller's claim. But that changes when he visits the family of a recently deceased civil servant and meets his son who is an exact replica of another dead official's child. Lieberman and his ragtag associates soon piece the conspiracy together, realizing they are facing thirteen-year-old clones of history's most infamous leader. Not only are the ninety-four boys from Brazil cloned from Adolf Hitler; they are being raised under identical circumstances, down to the younger mother and older civil servant father who conveniently dies when the boys hit thirteen (to maximize the chance that at least a few of them will grow up just like the führer.) This puts Lieberman on a crash course with the cabal's leader, Dr. Josef Mengele (the most famous Nazi to elude postwar justice), and leads to a memorable climax and an ethically ambiguous ending.

The Boys from Brazil epitomizes the high-concept thriller. In this relatively short novel, Levin manages to toss in more themes, issues, subplots, and characters than most books twice its size. The story could be categorized as science fiction, suspense, thriller, or even historical. And in terms of subgenres, it contains elements of espionage, medicine, war, science, and political thriller.

Levin offers the reader a global thrill ride with massive stakes and larger-than-life heroes and, especially, villains. His protagonist, Lieberman (obviously based on Simon Wiesenthal), makes for a wildly sympathetic and flawed hero. As a Holocaust survivor, he is already the ultimate victim. But when we meet him, Lieberman is coping with the recent loss of his wife, the maladies of aging, financial setbacks, and a world largely indifferent to his raison d'être. Then he comes to face a horrific dilemma in what to do about the young Hitler clones.

Who could envision a more despicable antagonist than Dr. Josef Mengele, whose greatest interest lay in performing unspeakably inhuman experiments on identical twin children? Levin ingeniously combines Mengele's real-life passion for genetics (more accurately, eugenics) with the fictional breakthrough in cloning humans.

In lesser hands, this ambitious story could have wound up as cartoonish—Dr. Evil run amok in a laboratory cranking out more and more Hitlers. But Levin's clever story structure encourages the reader to suspend disbelief. First, he does not focus on the technology of cloning that even now, more than thirty years after the book was written, still has not produced a successful human clone (that we know of). Instead, he merely touches on the principle of the technology and starts the story thirteen years later, concentrating on the morality and ethical questions that might arise, after the fact. Second, he embeds fascinating philosophical questions such as: What ingredients could lead to another Holocaust? And would identical DNA and a very similar upbringing create a true replica of the original person?

But like any successful novel, *The Boys from Brazil* works primarily because of Levin's brilliant characterization. The characters, particularly the emotionally spent and ethically conflicted Lieberman, spring off the page as three-dimensional people with their own identities, conflicts, and history. Lovable or loathsome, they are fascinating individuals whose motivations keep the pages flying to the very end.

Writers before him (for example Philip K. Dick) have brilliantly intertwined history and fantasy, but Levin accomplishes it in a way that feels immediate and contemporary; in short, it reads like a damn good thriller. Though not the first, his groundbreaking merger of science thriller and historical suspense is one of the best examples of its kind.

Born and raised in Vancouver, Daniel Kalla is a practicing emergency room physician and the author of five suspense novels and medical thrillers. His works have been translated into ten languages, and two of his novels, *Resistance* and *Pandemic*, have been optioned for film. Two years in a row, his novels, *Rage Therapy* (2007) and *Blood Lies* (2008), have been runners up for the Spotted Owl Award for Best Mystery novel by a Pacific Northwest writer. His latest is an epic multigenerational novel, *Of Flesh and Blood*. Dan is married and the father of two girls. When not doctoring or writing, he is an avid skier and hockey player.

72
Robin Cook's
COMA (1977)
CJ Lyons

Dr. Robin Cook (1940–) has been on the best-seller lists for over thirty years and has published twenty-eight books, several of which were made into movies and TV miniseries. His work has been translated into forty languages, and he has sold over a hundred million copies of his books. After graduating from Wesleyan University and Columbia University School of Medicine, Cook did his ophthalmology residency training at Harvard. His first novel, *The Year of the Intern* (1972), dealt with issues Cook faced in medical school. His next novel was the medical thriller, *Coma*, which went on to become a *New York Times* best seller and a blockbuster film. Despite his literary success, Cook is still on the staff of Massachusetts Eye and Ear Infirmary and advises medical students, thinking of himself more as a doctor than a best-selling author. Cook's novels are credited with popularizing the medical thriller genre. In them, he explores a variety of subjects of social relevance, including organ transplantation, stem cell research, genetic engineering, managed health care, pharmaceutical research, and bioterrorism.

Robin Cook's *Coma* was published in 1977. The movie based on it appeared in 1978. I was a child then, but I can remember the passionate arguments regarding a patient's right to die brought about when Karen Quinlan was removed from life support in 1976. This was also only a decade after Dr. Thomas Starzl performed the first successful human liver transplant.

Economically, the times were tumultuous. Our family conserved everything from toilet paper to lightbulbs, and my favorite T-shirt was one espousing President Ford's "Whip Inflation Now" slogan. Urban legends of people selling their organs to black market profiteers were popular enough that they spread through my small-town elementary school.

It was an era where real life was so scary that we looked for our entertainment to be even more frightening—as if the adrenalin rush of being terrified by novels and the big screen made our daily worries seem small in comparison. The *Godfather* saga (1972, 1974) reminded us that no matter how crazy and violent the world around us was, family was everything. *Jaws* (1975) taught us not to go into the water. *Star Wars* (1977) showed us that entire worlds can be wiped out, but there's always hope. *Alien* (1979) reminded us that as horrifying as technology can be, humanity could always go it one better (or worse.)

In the midst of all this was one chilling, subtly terrifying novel and movie about normal, everyday people who go into a trusted hospital, place themselves under the care of their godlike surgeons, undergo routine, minor surgery—and never wake up.

I once asked Robin Cook why he felt compelled to write *Coma*. He said that while he was an ophthalmology resident he realized that corneal transplants were becoming commonplace but also noticed that "no one was paying attention to the supply side of the operation. It didn't take a genius to realize that medicine was creating its own horror show."

It was a horror show that struck a chord in Cook's audience. Suddenly there was nothing routine about going into a hospital. Doctors, once regarded as "minor deities," were now objects of suspicion—were they profiting from patient's tragedies? What about the corporations who were now intruding themselves into medicine, buying hospitals, running clinics, developing the drugs and equipment used on patients? Was there a conspiracy brewing in health care, and if so, how far up did it go? What was really going on in a surgeon's mind behind the mask?

These questions provided subject matter for many of Cook's subsequent novels as he turned the spotlight onto the once hallowed halls of medicine and illuminated its many unsavory, hidden flaws.

Coma was his first thriller (his previous novel, *The Year of the Intern*, was a semiautobiographical account of the travails of a medical student) and broke ground by popularizing the medical thriller genre.

I first read *Coma* (and saw the movie) almost a decade after its publication. As a first-year medical student practically living in the lecture hall and labs, I was drawn to any depiction of how "real" doctors treating "real" patients lived.

Although most of *Coma*'s audience was captivated by the conspiracy theories and the creepy long-term care institution (all those bodies strung up like marionettes!), what interested me was the depiction of a woman medical student as the main character. After all, I was a woman in a male-dominated field about to encounter the same challenges that Susan Wheeler was facing: her fear of losing her femininity, her uncertainty about how to approach handsome male patients, her need to assert herself—and the repercussions she suffered after being too frank. As Cook notes, "She felt that she was entering a male club; she was an outsider forced to adapt, to compromise."

I loved the scene where Susan rejects the nurses' scrub dresses and enters the doctors' lounge (male only), surprising her male classmates and the surgical resident in charge of them. Even a decade later, when I was in medical school, similar attitudes prevailed. Seeing a woman—even a fictional character—meet and overcome those attitudes with a sense of humor, fast thinking, and sheer perseverance was inspiring.

The medical professionals in *Coma*, both heroes and villains, are well drawn and share the same motivation. They each want to play God and save the world—but on their terms. At one point, Susan berates the resident in charge of her as being an "invertebrate" for not standing up to the powers that be and challenging their assumptions about why patients are succumbing to mysterious comas. His answer is that he "just wants to be a surgeon," to which she replies: "That, Mark, in a nutshell, is probably your tragic flaw."

Even the villain wants to save humanity—despite his attempts to kill Susan, murder innocent patients, and profit from the sale of his bootlegged human organs. When Susan confronts him at the end, he answers her accusations by saying, "Breakthroughs do not come easy, not without hard work and sacrifice. Not without a price." Then he goes on to compare himself to Leonardo da Vinci and Copernicus.

Isn't that the heart of a good thriller? Both good and evil striving to rule the world—not solely for personal gain but because they each feel they know how best to save humanity. With stakes that high, and danger lurking in places like hospitals where we all are at our most vulnerable, compelling fiction is certain to follow.

Award-winning medical suspense author CJ Lyons is a physician trained in pediatric emergency medicine. She has assisted police and prosecutors with cases involving child abuse, rape, homicide, and Munchausen by proxy and has worked in numerous trauma centers as a crisis counselor, victim advocate, and a flight physician for Life Flight. Her medical suspense novel, *Lifelines*, debuted in 2008 and became a national best seller. The second in the series, *Warning Signs*, was released in 2009.

73

Ken Follett's
EYE OF THE NEEDLE (1978)

Tess Gerritsen

Ken Follett (1949–) was still a relatively unknown novelist when he became intrigued by the history of "Operation Fortitude," a war-time deception hatched by Allied forces to convince Germany that the invasion of France would occur at Calais, not Normandy. This obscure bit of World War II history was what inspired his spy thriller, *Eye of the Needle*. Released in 1978, *Needle* received the Mystery Writers of America Best Novel Edgar Award and rocketed Follett into the rarefied world of international bestsellerdom. In the span of his literary career, Follett has produced nearly thirty novels, including several that were written under pseudonyms. The length of his bibliography is impressive enough, but his versatility truly astonishes. He has written children's books, science fiction, spy thrillers, medical thrillers, and sweeping historical epics. His settings have ranged from war-torn England to North Africa to Afghanistan. Undaunted by the challenges of moving across genres, Follett has established a reputation as a fearless storyteller capable of surprising even his longtime readers who think they know what to expect of him.

By the time I got around to reading *Eye of the Needle*, it was already a huge best seller. In those days, I was working as a physician on a remote island in Micronesia, and the house I lived in came with a library of battered paperbacks, left behind by previous tenants. I recall the hot tropical evening when I cracked open the book, and how quickly I felt chilled, as though I'd been plunged into the North Sea. It was my first taste of literary "faction," a thriller made all the more intriguing because it was based on real history. And the history alone was frightening enough.

In 1944, the war between Germany and Allied forces was building toward one of its bloodiest confrontations. The question was, where would the invasion of France take place? Would the Allies land on the beaches of Normandy, or would they invade via the Pas de Calais? Germany was desperate to learn this information ahead of time, so they could position their troops in defense. The Allies were just as desperate to hide their plans and catch the enemy unprepared. To trick the Germans into believing the attack would come at Calais, the Allies created a fictional army in East Anglia, complete with inflatable tanks, cardboard airplanes, and fake barracks, which they knew the Germans would photograph from the air. But if any German spy on the ground discovered the deception and transmitted this vital intelligence to Germany, the D-day invasion—and history itself—could be drastically altered.

Enter Follett's main character, Henry Faber, a quiet and unassuming gentleman who lives in a London lodging house. Though Faber claims to be a traveling salesman, he is in fact Germany's most valuable spy, known as The Needle because of his peculiar choice of weapon: a stiletto.

That stiletto proves useful in the very first chapter when Faber is forced to brutally kill his landlady. The murder is shocking not just because of its sudden violence, but also because of the utterly dispassionate logic with which Faber considers his next moves. How to stage the scene to make it look like an ordinary lust crime? How will it complicate his mission? Every detail is coldly considered, every consequence weighed, in a scene that tells the reader exactly what kind of man Henry Faber is—and what he is capable of doing. Heartless and brilliant, he is both villain and, strangely, a hero, whose ingenuity one cannot help but admire, even as his actions repel.

Such a powerful antagonist demands an equally powerful protagonist, but the first appearance of Lucy Rose is not particularly heroic. We meet her on her wedding day as she marries a handsome young RAF officer, her focus on dresses and hairstyles, champagne and honeymoons. With war closing in around them, the wedding seems a distraction from the truly important business of the day. Lucy could be any young bride, neither heroic nor remarkable, as she and her new husband drive away to start a new life.

But tragedy marks the couple for a grim fate. A car accident maims her husband, David, forcing the amputation of both his legs and leaving him embittered and resentful. He and his now-pregnant wife retreat to remote Storm Island, where they live in unhappy and self-imposed exile. Her marriage in shambles, isolated from the outside world, she would seem to have a bleak future indeed, with no opportunity for happiness—or heroism.

In the meantime, Henry Faber has not been idle. His exploits leave a trail of bodies as he uncovers the secret behind Operation Fortitude. Disguised as a boater on holiday, he takes photographs that prove the "British Fourth Army" is pure fiction, complete with fake aircraft and shell barracks. This is explosive information vital to Germany, and he must get it out of the country, but it requires him to travel the length of England to rendezvous with a submarine.

His mission is complicated by two pursuers, Percival Godliman and Frederick Bloggs, both employed by MI5, which is hot on Faber's trail. Bloggs and Godliman have uncovered "The Needle's" identity, and in a tense game of cat and mouse, they pursue him north toward Faber's rendezvous point. But they are always one excruciating step behind him, and when Faber steals a boat and vanishes, they fear they have lost their quarry—and perhaps the war itself.

But Faber has not escaped. A fierce gale at sea destroys his boat and washes him ashore on Storm Island, where he will encounter his most formidable opponent yet: not MI5, not a skilled Allied agent, but an unhappy housewife starved for affection and eager for company.

Nearly drowned, shaking with cold, Faber is taken in by Lucy and David Rose, who assume the spy is merely an unfortunate boater. Lucy finds the shipwrecked stranger both fascinating and attractive. And Faber, who has so easily dispatched countless victims with his stiletto, is surprised to feel stirrings of affection for Lucy. Their affair, given the circumstances, is inevitable. But plagued by guilt over betraying her husband, Lucy soon finds reasons to regret the affair. Little by little, she uncovers clues that her new lover is an enemy agent and a dangerous man. When Faber murders both David as well as the elderly caretaker on the island, Lucy is the only one left who can stop him.

The fate of England now lies in the hands of one frightened, lonely woman who must discover depths of courage she doesn't know she has.

This battle between such starkly unequal opponents is what makes the climax so powerful—and exhilarating. It encourages the reader to think: *Although I may be utterly ordinary, I could be the one to save my country.*

Most of us will never be able to identify with James Bond or the other dashing supermen who populate most thriller novels. But in the character of Lucy Rose, we can recognize ourselves. Watching a mere housewife bring down a master spy gives every reader the chance to imagine being a hero. *Eye of the Needle* celebrates the courage of Everyman —and Everywoman.

Internationally best-selling author Tess Gerritsen took an unusual route to a writing career. A graduate of Stanford University, Tess went on to medical school at the University of California, San Francisco, where she was awarded her M.D. While on maternity leave from her work as a physician, she began to write fiction. In 1987, her first novel was published. *Call After Midnight*, a romantic thriller, was followed by eight more romantic suspense novels. She also wrote a screenplay, *Adrift*, which aired as a 1993 CBS Movie of the Week starring Kate Jackson. Tess's first medical thriller, *Harvest*, was released in hardcover in 1996 and marked her debut on the *New York Times* best-seller list. Other best-selling novels followed, including *Life Support*, *The Mephisto Club*, *The Bone Garden*, *The Keepsake*, and *Ice Cold*, the main characters of which (Jane Rizzoli and Maura Isles) are featured in a TNT television series. Her books have been translated into thirty-three languages, and more than 18 million copies have been sold around the world. She received the Nero Wolfe Award (for *Vanish*) and the Rita Award (for *The Surgeon*). Now retired from medicine, she writes full time. She lives in Maine.

74

Ross Thomas's
CHINAMAN'S CHANCE (1978)

David J. Montgomery

Ross Thomas (1926–1995) was born in Oklahoma City, less than twenty years after Oklahoma was admitted to the Union as the forty-sixth state. He grew up in the West when it was still more frontier than cosmopolitan society. The effect of that experience can be seen in Thomas's writing, as he often set his stories in places on the edge of civilization, either physically or metaphorically. He left home at a young age to join the United States Army, fighting with the infantry in the Philippines during the Second World War. That formative experience would likewise influence the development of his fiction, most notably in his use of Asian locations in several of his novels. Thomas pursued a handful of careers over the next two decades, including journalist, union man, and public relations flack; he even gained a reputation as a political operative. He managed campaigns for labor leaders, senatorial and gubernatorial hopefuls, and once advised a tribal chief trying to become the first postcolonial prime minister of a newly independent African state. All of that was grist for the mill when he finally turned to his true calling as a writer of fiction, eventually producing twenty-five thrilling novels of adventure and wit, nearly all of which were outstanding.

It wasn't until the age of forty that Ross Thomas wrote his first novel, *The Cold War Swap*. As legend has it, the process took him but six weeks. He boxed up the manuscript and sent it off to New York. William Morrow purchased it and published the novel in 1966 to some acclaim. The following year *The Cold War Swap* was awarded the Edgar Award for Best First Novel. (Almost two decades later in 1985, Thomas won the Edgar Award for Best Novel for his book *Briarpatch*.) His pathway to success was seemingly as effortless as his prose. Whether in the business or the art of writing, Thomas simply had a way of making it look easy.

Despite such recognition, accompanied by reviews the likes of which most authors would kill for—the *New York Times* once called him "America's best storyteller" while the *Washington Post* touted him as "a writer of brilliant thrillers"—Thomas's books were modest sellers, not blockbusters. After his death in 1995, twenty-four of his novels soon went out of print. The only one available in a current edition, *Chinaman's Chance*, was perhaps his best. (A few years back, St. Martin's Press undertook a program to return Thomas's novels to print. Sadly, it was discontinued after less than half the titles were republished.)

Chinaman's Chance introduced readers to Artie Woo and Quincy Durant, two of the most memorable and unique characters in all of thriller fiction. (They would subsequently appear in the equally fine *Out on the Rim* and *Voodoo, Ltd.*) Lifelong pals since they teamed up in a San Francisco orphanage, Durant, a former covert operative with a shadowy past, and Woo, the pretender to the Chinese throne, were lovable grifters, con men with hearts of gold ever searching for their next big score.

The duo usually plied their trade somewhere on the Pacific Rim, and *Chinaman's Chance* finds them in Pelican Bay, a small, down-at-the-heels (fictional) town south of Los Angeles. You wouldn't know it at first glance, but Pelican Bay is the most corrupt American city outside of Washington, D.C. Crooked politicians, bent cops, shadowy Company rejects and the Mob are all up for a piece of the action. In other words, it's the perfect setting for Woo and Durant to work their magic.

This juicy, twisted tale of opportunists on the make was tailor-made for Ross Thomas's fast-paced and witty style. He had a remarkable ability to make cynical characters likable and complex plots believable. His novels are "page-turners," but they're also insightful and poignant sketches of human nature.

Thomas was often described as an author of "political thrillers," but that label is too limiting. His books were thrillers, and they often did involve politics in one way or another, but they encompassed a myriad of plots, ranging from spy stories to kidnappings, fixed elections to financial shenanigans. The settings and characters of Thomas's books were as varied as the stories: Hong Kong, Singapore, Washington, D.C., Germany, the Deep South; congressmen, writers, union organizers, historians, advertising men. Few authors have managed to tackle such a diversity of stories with such panache.

Thomas wrote about the people behind the headlines; the men—and they were usually men, reflecting the times in which they were written—

who keep the games of politics and commerce moving. They are ordinary people—perhaps a bit smarter, a bit greedier, with a touch more wit, but still essentially ordinary—who participate in extraordinary events. They aren't that different from the rest of us, which makes them all the more enjoyable and fascinating to observe.

One of the things that Thomas did better than anyone else was lead his readers through the labyrinthine world of politics, treachery, and deceit, all while keeping them entertained and perched at the edge of their seats. The power brokers, the intelligence community, the military-industrial complex, the shadowy world of mercenaries, thieves and guns for hire all come alive in an interwoven tapestry of intrigue that stretches throughout Thomas's books.

In lesser hands, such plots might become tedious, confusing, and improbable; flowing from the pen of the master, they were damn near perfect. With his commitment to sharp and precise prose, Thomas raised the stakes for thriller authors, showing a generation of readers and writers that suspenseful writing could be lean, but still meaty. His keen eye for chicanery and insight into the devious side of human nature helped him create stories that are as delightful to experience on the fifth reading as they were on the first, a quality that makes him among the rarest of genre writers.

Otto Penzler, the famed bookseller, editor, and critic, once described Thomas, and more specifically *Chinaman's Chance*, as his "secret weapon." When customers came into his store (the Mysterious Bookshop in New York City) asking for a recommendation for a good book, Penzler would press *Chinaman's Chance* into their hands. Invariably, he said, they would come back, praising the brilliance of his selection. As Penzler put it, the book was "drop-dead perfect." I couldn't agree more.

David J. Montgomery has written about authors and books for many of the country's largest newspapers, including the *New York Times*, *Washington Post*, *USA Today*, *Boston Globe*, and several others. He currently holds the position of mystery/thriller columnist for the *Chicago Sun-Times* and maintains a popular Web site, the Crime Fiction Dossier. Montgomery is an original member of ITW and an occasional writer of fiction. His story "Bedtime for Mr. Li" appeared in ITW's second *Thriller 2* anthology in 2009.

75

John D. MacDonald's
THE GREEN RIPPER (1979)

J. A. Konrath

John D. MacDonald (1916–1986) was an amazingly productive author of more than sixty novels, plus almost five hundred short stories and a handful of nonfiction books. Although he worked in several genres (science fiction, westerns, sports), the bulk of his work involved crime and suspense. In 1939, he graduated from Harvard University with an MBA and a year later joined the army, eventually serving in the OSS during World War II. In 1945, to amuse himself, he wrote a short story that his wife submitted to *Story* magazine without telling him. When it was accepted, he plunged into a writing career with an energy that most authors can only dream of— he once wrote eight hundred thousand words in four months. In the 1950s, the pulp short story market gave way to the paperback novel, and during this period, he wrote several classics, especially *The Executioners* (1957), which became the much admired 1962 suspense film, *Cape Fear*, and later a 1991 remake directed by Martin Scorsese. In 1972 the Mystery Writers of America honored him with its Grandmaster award. In 1980, he received an American Book Award for *The Green Ripper*.

> I was an artifact, genus boat bum, a pale-eyed, shambling, gangling, knuckly man, without enough unscarred hide left to make a decent lampshade. Creaking knight errant, yawning at the thought of the next dragon. They don't make grails like they used to.
>
> —*The Green Ripper*, John D. MacDonald

For his eighteenth Travis McGee novel, John D. MacDonald propelled the series hero, and the thriller genre, into complex new territory.

MacDonald published his first book in 1950, after spending the latter half of the 1940s honing his prose in pulp magazines. In 1964, more than three dozen novels later, he penned the first Travis McGee adventure, *The Deep Blue Goodbye*. There would eventually be twenty-one books in the series, all of them with a color in the title.

McGee was unlike most of his mystery ancestors. He wasn't a grizzled, hard-boiled detective, or a tough cop with a drinking problem, or a dandy sleuth who uncovered clues while keeping his hands clean of blood.

Travis called himself a salvage expert. His Florida home was a houseboat, *The Busted Flush*, so called because he won it in a poker game. He lived his retirement in sections, choosing to do so while still young enough to enjoy it. When McGee had money, he was a man of leisure. When he needed money, he "recovered" things for people in need, taking half of the salvage as his fee.

McGee was a sexual being and usually wound up in a physical relationship with a different woman in every book. He used his brain and his fists equally well, and the series presented thought-provoking mysteries mixed with nail-biting action. But McGee would also philosophize about his life, man's nature, and the acts he and others committed. This was a hero with a conscience, showing depth not seen before in this genre.

The Green Ripper is a departure for both McGee and MacDonald. This isn't a whodunit. It isn't McGee uncovering some crime, then hopping on his figurative white steed to find out who's responsible.

The Green Ripper is about revenge.

It begins on Pearl Harbor Day in 1979, with a conversation between our favorite beach bum and his economist best friend and neighbor, Meyer. It's revealed that Gretel, whom McGee rescued in the previous book, *The Empty Copper Sea*, has moved out of *The Busted Flush*. This isn't a surprise to McGee readers—the women usually leave him by the end of the book. But it is a surprise here, because Gretel hasn't moved out of McGee's life, and their relationship is stronger than ever.

The world's most eligible bachelor, settling for just one woman? It appears so. McGee is in love, and happy with the relationship. Meyer, on the other hand, is depressed. Having just returned from a conference, he fears the world is very close to collapsing.

His prophecy proves true, not for the whole world, but for McGee's. Gretel soon joins the duo, cheering Meyer up with her mere presence. She talks of her new job, and a strange man she met at work, someone involved in a cult. She and McGee make love, and the next day he's called to the hospital. Gretel has come down with some sudden, serious illness.

By the end of chapter two, Gretel is dead. The "green ripper," a child's misinterpretation of "grim reaper," claimed her.

McGee, devastated, is visited by two government men who ask cryptic questions about Gretel. Curious, he and Meyer begin to poke around and come to the realization that Gretel was murdered and that a mysterious cult is involved.

So our hero writes Meyer a letter, leaving him in charge of his affairs, uncertain if he'll make it back. He buries Gretel's ashes, says a poem over her grave, and then adopts the fictional identification and persona of Tom McGraw, an unemployed commercial fisherman, supposedly searching for his runaway daughter.

Then he goes looking for the cult that killed the woman he loved.

Of course, he finds them. A terrorist cell, brainwashing a small group of men and women to turn them into weapons. (Bear in mind that terrorists weren't a common plot device back in 1979. Eerily, much of what they say anticipates actual events, such as 9/11.) McGee/McGraw plays along, pretending to become indoctrinated, even superficially befriending a few of the cultists.

Then he kills everyone. Twelve people in all.

It's not quite that cold. When the moment arrives, McGee has no real choice in the matter—he's fighting for his life. This cell is obviously a danger to the world, and dispatching it is for the good of humanity. But even though the cult's destruction is ultimately the result of revenge and is as necessary as killing predators that prey on livestock, there's no place for philosophy on the battlefield. It's kill or be killed, and McGee goes into commando mode, acting more out of self-preservation than the need to make things right.

This is a quantum leap forward in the evolution of the thriller hero. McGee has been forced to defend himself in previous books, and the villain usually meets an appropriate demise at his hands. But *The Green Ripper* has an ambiguity to the violence, especially considering that the hero has, time and again, shown himself to have a conscience.

It's almost as if Superman suddenly killed Lex Luthor, rather than just putting him in jail for the hundredth time.

Of course, McGee doesn't breeze through this slaughter with his psyche intact. After the violence is over, he shows obvious signs of posttraumatic stress disorder, barely able to hold it together, obsessing about being unable to find the severed arm of one of the dead.

In the hands of a lesser writer, this climax could have been played for all of its schadenfreude potential, making the audience cheer McGee's violent acts and savor the revenge he so deserves.

But MacDonald prefers to dwell on the ugliness of violence, and the scars it leaves on those forced to commit violent deeds. McGee doesn't celebrate his victory over evil. He isn't even sure it is a victory at all. While the action scenes, with McGee fighting for his life and eliminating cultists one at a time, are incredibly suspenseful, MacDonald spends almost as much time on the aftermath of the massacre, following McGee as he gathers up the dead and reports the incident to the authorities. For a revenge novel, it's a melancholy, oddly poignant triumph.

In the epilogue, McGee comes full circle. He makes peace with himself and is able to pick up his life. But the book's readers aren't as resilient as McGee. We end this book with more questions than answers. We've been shown that our heroes can express doubts, that violence affects everyone, and that the classic murder and vengeance plot so common in thrillers isn't as black-and-white as we thought it to be.

In 1979, John D. MacDonald showed us that a series protagonist can be flawed, and vulnerable, and forced to commit deeds that weigh hard on his conscience, and on ours. In other words, with *The Green Ripper*, MacDonald created the template for the modern-day thriller hero.

J. A. Konrath is the author of six thrillers in the Jacqueline "Jack" Daniels series: *Whiskey Sour, Bloody Mary, Rusty Nail, Dirty Martini, Fuzzy Navel,* and *Cherry Bomb.* Joe also wrote the technohorror novels, *Afraid* and *Trapped,* under the pen name Jack Kilborn. His short fiction and articles have appeared in over seventy publications. His Web site features a blog about publishing that many authors find useful (www.JAKonrath.com).

76

Justin Scott's
THE SHIPKILLER (1979)

Lawrence Light

Justin Scott (1944–) wrote the perfect seafaring thriller animated by revenge. *The Shipkiller*, published in 1978 to great acclaim, paid homage to the heart-pounding sea sagas of Herman Melville and Nicholas Monsarrat, then brought that tradition into the age of modern technology. Scott came from a writing background. His father, Alexander Leslie Scott, was a celebrated author of two hundred Western pulp novels, produced under several pseudonyms. The son has written more than twenty-four novels, half of them in his own name, and many set on land, such as the Ben Abbott mysteries, about a small-town realtor. He also has penned a novel with Clive Cussler, a Western-themed detective yarn set in 1907, called *The Wrecker*, published in late 2009. In his youth, Scott had sailed on Long Island's Great South Bay, but he knew he lacked sufficient nautical knowledge to write *The Shipkiller*. As research for the book, he had a proficient sailor tutor him about sailboats, made a rough Atlantic winter crossing aboard a ten thousand-ton Polish freighter, and rode on a two hundred forty-ton supertanker. Following the success of the novel, Scott was invited socially onto various craft by folks who thought he had a daunting maritime prowess. "I didn't fool them for long," he said.

The sea is a place of great beauty and great peril, a moody thing that can turn in a moment from a lush, sparkling serenity to a howling hell. This duality underlies any good story about sailing. For Justin Scott, a long-time fan of C. S. Forester's Hornblower series and other seagoing yarns, setting his masterwork on the bounding main was a can't miss move. Pitting man against the elements is inherently exciting.

Perhaps because most people nowadays fly over oceans instead of sailing on them, the sea story has become an anachronism, as familiar to readers as walking on the moon. Apart from Clive Cussler, few thriller writers use the sea as a setting any longer. This was as true three decades ago, when

Scott published *The Shipkiller*, as it is today. A pity and a lost opportunity for dramatic storytelling. Example: One of the most striking passages in Nicholas Monsarrat's gripping World War II novel, *The Cruel Sea* (1951), has his Royal Navy sailors encountering a floating chain of grinning skeletons, tied together in their life jackets.

Scott updates the genre cleverly with *The Shipkiller*'s choice of a nemesis—a huge oil supertanker that's a force of nature to rival the relentlessly powerful ocean. A third of a mile long, carrying a million tons of oil, it takes four miles to stop and blindly smashes anything in its way. Scott got his inspiration from news stories in the 1970s about how massive oil carriers were sinking small trawlers off Africa. Supertankers came into even worse repute later with the *Exxon Valdez* oil spill. Scott calls his foe LEVIATHAN (he uses capital letters on every mention to evoke the tanker's enormous size), after the biblical sea monster likely inspired by whales.

As a sea story about obsessive revenge, this book is akin to Herman Melville's *Moby-Dick* with one key difference. The crazed Captain Ahab, who lost his leg to the white whale, is a mean and odious fellow who cares about no one. But Scott's monster hunter is a likable doctor, hence a healer of others, who is suffering the loss of a loved one. Hardin loses his wife to the supertanker, and he is wracked with grief and guilt.

Hardin is crossing the Atlantic on his forty-foot ketch when, during a squall, the gargantuan vessel appears from nowhere and "trampled *Siren* into the sea." With his sailboat, *Siren*, shattered into fiberglass splinters and his wife, Carolyn, dead, Hardin eventually washes up on the English coast. After he gets no legal redress against the supertanker or its arrogant captain, Cedric Ogilvy, Hardin vows a more violent form of vengeance. At the core of his soul, he needs to kill a ship, a very large ship.

Hardin fits out a new, very speedy sailboat with state-of-the-art radar and a purloined military missile launcher, then sets forth to destroy LEVIATHAN. Captain Ogilvy learns that Hardin is after the tanker, and the shipping company provides an armed helicopter to blow the ship's pursuer out of the water. What follows is a fascinating cat-and-mouse game—with the mouse a massive steel juggernaut—and the wickedly fickle weather an ever-present danger. Amid these deadly surroundings, the kinetic suspense of this brilliantly rendered narrative makes you glad to be sitting at home, safe and dry.

The best thrillers introduce you to a new and scary world and teach what it takes to function and survive there. That the hero has this specialized expertise adds to his allure. So you may read how a spy tails an enemy undetected, how a sniper successfully aims at a target, how a stranded explorer lives through a killing snowstorm. Scott does the same for the sea, telling what to do with the different sails and the rudder in evil weather. His narrative is peppered with the jib halyards, fixed keels, and spinnakers that Hardin the hero uses to master the waves. The illusion is complete that Hardin has a fighting chance of surmounting the worst hazards that nature can churn up.

Scott's writing has a poetic elegance that serves the story well. Always, the sea is a majestic presence requiring painterly description. As he sails over the vast water, Hardin braces "when a sudden wave rose higher than the rest in a long trough, [and] the wind knocked it down for its impertinence." Coming into a peaceful stretch after a rough passage, Hardin yearns to hear a human voice to know that "he had not, by a quirk of navigation, sailed into a dream sea at the end of the world."

At the same time, the fine writing conveys the harrowing tension of this perilous voyage. When his sailboat is snagged and Hardin must swim down deep to try freeing it, a poisonous sea snake attacks: "A serrated row of teeth, silvery as fishbones, gleamed in the yellow light. It hit repeatedly, with the rhythmic speed of a jackhammer, its venom fangs reaching greedily beyond its needle teeth."

On the track of his quarry, Hardin and his sailboat, the *Swan*, run into a horrendous winter storm off the Cape of Good Hope. Mountainous swells, called "rollers," chase him:

> [T]he only way to survive their awesome power was to hold the *Swan*'s stern to the advancing rollers so she would rise with them before they broke over her. But when she climbed their steep faces, her sleek racing hull betrayed her ... she rushed along the steepening slope so fast that she was in danger of ramming her nose under water and pitchpoling end over end.

Also remarkable is how skillfully Scott draws the main characters, Hardin and the vile Captain Ogilvy. As the chase intensifies, Hardin becomes grimmer and more obsessed. But his budding affection for a female doctor, who accompanies him on the voyage, keeps him from turning into another Ahab and cements our sympathies for him. Ogilvy is a fine bad guy: nasty, tyrannical, and power-mad. He is a fitting personification of the ship he commands. You can't wait for him to get his.

The foremost character is the sea, of course. After the novel's cataclysmic climax, it is once again calm. But from all that has happened before, you get the sense that this is temporary. The lingering suspicion is a graceful end note to what makes *The Shipkiller* a memorable jewel in the thriller canon.

Lawrence Light, Executive Vice President of Mystery Writers of America, is the author of the Karen Glick mystery series set on Wall Street (*Too Rich to Live* and *Fear & Greed*) and with his wife, Meredith Anthony, the dark thriller *Ladykiller*. His short stories have appeared in the anthologies *Wall Street Noir* and *Thriller 2*. Larry is a finance editor at the *Wall Street Journal* and has won many journalism awards. He previously worked at *Forbes, Business Week, Newsday*, and *Congressional Quarterly*. He lives in Manhattan.

77

Robert Ludlum's
THE BOURNE IDENTITY (1980)

Linda L. Richards

Before beginning his second career as a novelist when he was in his forties, Robert Ludlum (1927–2001) was a stage and television actor (*Kraft Theater, Studio One*) as well as a theatrical producer. More than thirty-four novels are attributed to him. The majority were written by him under his own name; a few were written as either Michael Shepherd or Jonathan Ryder; and some later novels were collaborations or else written by others. Nearly three hundred million Robert Ludlum novels are in print in thirty-two languages. He was born in New York City, raised in Short Hills, New Jersey, and educated in Connecticut, studying fine arts at Wesleyan University. He became a professional actor in 1951 and in 1960 started the Playhouse-on-the-Mall in New Jersey. Eventually he developed an interest in writing novels. He was the first author to have two #1 *New York Times* best-selling novels at the same time. On March 30, 1980, his *The Bourne Identity* led the hardback list while his previous novel, *The Materese Circle*, led the paperback list. Though he maintained a home in Connecticut, after 1984 he began spending the winter months in Naples, Florida. He died there in 2001 from heart failure.

By the time the book he is most strongly identified with was published in 1980, Robert Ludlum was at the peak of his inventive powers. *The Bourne Identity* was the twelfth book of an astonishing second career. Partially inspired by events in Ludlum's own life, including a bout of short-term memory loss, it is a powerful, influential work and a good starting point when coming to either Ludlum or thrillers.

Almost three decades after publication, there is more about *The Bourne Identity* that feels fresh and au courant than that which feels dated. While the 2002 film version starring Matt Damon reduces the size and spirit of the female costar's role, in Ludlum's novel Marie St. Jacques, a Canadian economist, is a fully developed character rather than merely a love interest. In fact, it seems unlikely that Bourne would have survived his first fictional outing had their paths not crossed: she saves his bacon so elegantly and so often. There is perhaps a bit more smoking and drinking than one would encounter in a contemporary tale, and it's possible that the main characters expend more emotional energy on suitable attire for each situation than would be the case these days, but most of the story is perfect just as it stands: a sharp-edged knife poised for danger.

> He felt rushing cold water envelop him, swallowing him, sucking him under, and twisting him in circles, then propelling him up to the surface—only to gasp a single breath of air. A gasp and he was under again.
> And there was heat, a strange moist heat at his temple that seared through the freezing water that kept swallowing him, a fire where no fire should burn.

When we meet the title character, he has lost his memory after a mishap at sea. The crew of a commercial vessel finds him clinging to life and to a slender board. The crew takes him to their home port and deposits him with the local doctor, a wasted Englishman who seems determined to kill himself slowly with alcohol. He nurses the man whom he calls "The Patient," removing bullets, trying to help him recover his memory. It's no use: in some ways, The Patient is newly arrived in the world. He has instinct, but he possesses no knowledge. Spiritually, then, he is newly born. And later, when we discover that his name is Jason Bourne, we understand that this was probably not unintentional.

The Patient is a dangerous newborn, possessed of deadly skills and abilities he is not aware of. At the same time, like that famous Argonaut, *this* Jason has a mission, an intense journey, although at first its shape is unclear.

This is where Ludlum achieves a lot of the joy and fascination that goes with *The Bourne Identity*. We are with The Patient on his journey of self and rediscovery. So much has been lost. But while we watch, he recovers tiny pieces, one at a time. And each new discovery seems to ask an even greater question than the one just answered: Is he an assassin? A thief? A secret agent? Or something altogether more base and mundane? We accompany Jason Bourne while he uncovers the pieces, and we are just as mystified and misdirected as our unwitting host.

The Bourne Identity is typical of Ludlum's writing in several ways. Ludlum consistently delivered an iconic figure or group of underdogs struggling against an evil foe, be it governments, international corporations, or terrorists. And no matter what might seem to be going on in a Ludlum novel, we can always be confident that whatever appears to be the case is most likely not. Influenced by rumors about powerful organizations like the Trilateral Commission, Ludlum specialized in conspiracy theories and did it with enthusiasm (not to mention exclamation marks), beginning with his debut novel, *The Scarlatti Inheritance*, a tale of intrigue and conspiracy set in Washington during World War II with schemes concerning Nazis and secret files. Contemporary critics have occasionally said that the novel is formulaic. It's worth remembering, though, that the book was published in 1971: if there is a formula, Ludlum was creating it. Moreover, he brought an actor's understanding of pace and suspense to his work, one that future generations of thriller writers still try to emulate. As the author once said, "A theater person should know what holds an audience and what does not."

Ludlum would never again put the pieces together as successfully as he did for his first Bourne book and the novel that preceded it, *The Materese Circle* (1979). Their impact is immense. While earlier thriller writers such as Helen MacInnes emphasized international locales, Ludlum was a master at crosscutting among an amazing variety of colorful settings, using precise details based on his personal travels. He added a new level of action to the spy genre, and his emphasis on conspiracies created a genre of its own.

Nearly a decade after his death, his influence keeps growing. The Bourne movies have been widely imitated, and at the time of this writing, four new film projects based on Ludlum novels are in various stages of development, with some of the biggest Hollywood names attached. Gaming giant Electronic Arts has signed a deal with the Ludlum estate that will see EA creating games based on Ludlum books for at least the next decade. Directly or indirectly, Robert Ludlum's hand is a major force in the heritage of the modern thriller.

Author and journalist Linda L. Richards is the founding editor of *January Magazine*, one of the founders of the blog The Rap Sheet, and the author of five novels, including *Death Was the Other Woman*. The most recent, *Death Was in the Picture*, is classic noir from a woman's perspective. It takes place in Los Angeles in 1931 against the backdrop of the end of Prohibition and the beginning of the Depression. Richards is currently at work on a contemporary thriller set in Vancouver as well as several film projects.

78
Eric Van Lustbader's
THE NINJA (1980)

J. D. Rhoades

Eric Van Lustbader is the author of over thirty best-selling novels and has been translated into more than twenty languages. A native of New York City, and graduate of Columbia College, he worked as a child educator and music journalist (the first in the U.S. to predict Elton John's success) before writing fiction full time. He is not only one of the biggest names in the thriller genre (*Sirens, Black Heart, The Miko, French Kiss, The Testament, First Daughter*, and *Last Snow*); he has also written a fascinating fantasy epic: *The Pearl Saga (The Ring of Five Dragons, The Veil of a Thousand Tears*, and *The Mistress of the Pearl*). In 2004, he was picked by the Robert Ludlum estate to continue Ludlum's Jason Bourne series, beginning with *The Bourne Legacy*. Lustbader and his wife live on the South Fork of Long Island. He is a second-level *Reiki* master.

Who among us does not love ninjas?

From books, to movies, to comics (particularly the Japanese graphic novels known as *manga*) to cartoon series about ninja turtles, to one particularly hilarious *South Park* episode, the shadowy warrior/assassins of feudal Japan have become stock figures in American, as well as Asian, pop culture. Even Thomas Pynchon put a society of *kunoichi* (female ninjas) into his 1990 postmodern novel, *Vineland*. And who could forget the Tom Cruise epic, *The Last Samurai*, wherein the writer felt obligated to shoehorn a ninja attack into the movie, even though the ninja had not been seen in Japan for years. After all, how can you have a movie about samurai unless you put in ninjas as well? Go online or browse any martial arts magazine, and you'll find dozens of places to buy ninja swords, ninja throwing stars, ninja black jammies, and books on how to be a real sure 'nuff ninja.

Yes, we do love our ninjas. So it's no great surprise that when Eric Van Lustbader's groundbreaking thriller, *The Ninja*, came out in 1980, it shot to

the top of the *New York Times* best-seller list, where it spent five months
and eventually spawned five equally successful sequels. It was at the fore-
front of current interest in ninja and arguably was a major force in creating that interest. With intense vividness, the book tells the story of
Nicholas Linnear, a half-Asian, half-Caucasian man living a somewhat
restless life in New York City. As we learn through flashbacks, Nicholas,
raised in Japan by a British father and a Chinese mother, is also adept in a
variety of Asian martial arts, including ninjutsu.

At the beginning of the story, Nicholas is called in as a consultant on
a murder case because his friend, the medical examiner, knows about his
background. He quickly determines that what the M.E. suspects is true:
the victim was killed by an exotic poison distilled from chrysanthemums
and only used by ninjas. As Nicholas is drawn deeper into the investigation, he also becomes more and more romantically entangled with a beautiful, enigmatic, and mentally disturbed woman named Justine. This leads
to lots of hot and occasionally kinky sex scenes, about which more anon.

As members of Nicholas's circle of friends are killed one by one using
arcane ninja techniques, he eventually realizes that the ninja behind the
killings is his old nemesis from Japan, his cousin Saigo. Saigo's a particularly nasty piece of work; his last encounter with Nicholas ended with
Saigo raping both Nicholas and his beautiful Japanese girlfriend, Yukio,
then enslaving and later killing Yukio. Nicholas also divines that Saigo's
ultimate target is Justine's wealthy and powerful father. I think we can all
see where this is going, and Lustbader doesn't disappoint; the final confrontation is as full of sword-swinging, head-rolling goodness as any thriller
fan could hope for.

So what is it about *The Ninja*, and about ninjas in general, that's so
appealing? Well, there are the aforementioned sex scenes. One of the conventions of modern ninja mania, at least for adult literature, is the idea
that Asian martial arts disciplines make you hell on wheels in the sack.
"As lethal in the arts of love as in the rites of death!" blares the copy on
my tattered paperback.

For those folks like me who enjoy a little learning with our thrills, *The
Ninja* also contains a large amount of interesting material about Oriental
philosophy, especially *The Book of Five Rings*. A classic by the legendary
Japanese "Sword Saint" Miyamoto Musashi, it analyses the nature of conflict in its various forms. Musashi was a warrior whose unique style was
based on fighting with a long sword in each hand and who was so expert

that in later life he started taking on challengers, using only a pair of wooden swords or even sticks just so it'd be interesting.

Another attraction of the ninja character is that the ninja is basically a superhero. Ninjas are able to scale tall buildings, slip through hundreds of enemies like the Invisible Man, do their work, and then get away clean in a puff of smoke. They also get some extremely cool toys. It's not a coincidence that one of the films in the Batman mythos has Bruce Wayne in *Batman Begins* getting his stealth and combat training from the Brotherhood of Shadows, a secret society who are ninjas in all but name.

Notably, however, when ninjas attack in force as in *The Last Samurai* and *Shogun*, their effectiveness is usually greatly reduced. Ninja armies often fail, especially when opposed by a single rogue ninja, as when Elektra in the Marvel comics takes on her erstwhile buddies The Hand, or when the Teenage Mutant Ninja Turtles dispatch dozens of soldiers in the evil Foot Clan, but can never seem to close the deal when fighting their leader Shredder, even when it's four on one. This has led some jokers to hypothesize that there is an Inverse Ninja Law: the effectiveness of a group of ninjas is inversely proportional to the number of ninjas in the group.

Like most jokes, the Inverse Ninja Law has a kernel of truth that illustrates the final appeal of the ninja. He's a man alone, using his wits and his training against impossible odds. He's a man apart as well, separated from the rest of us by his esoteric knowledge and the darkness in his soul, a darkness symbolized by his black clothing and hidden face. When he can overcome it, as Nicholas Linnear manages to do, he's a hero; when he lets the darkness overcome him, as Saigo does, he's the villain. Either way, he's totally badass. And that's why we love *The Ninja*. Beginning with its starkly arresting first sentence, "In darkness, there is death," it is a thriller whose influence continues to be felt in popular culture.

J. D. Rhoades is the author of *Breaking Cover*, which the *Chicago Tribune* called "the perfectly crafted hard-edged thriller," and of three novels featuring bounty hunter Jack Keller: *The Devil's Right Hand* (nominated for a Shamus award), *Good Day in Hell*, and *Safe and Sound*. J. D. was born and raised in North Carolina, and worked as a radio news reporter, club DJ, television cameraman, ad salesman, waiter, trial attorney, and newspaper columnist. He blogs at the Anthony-nominated Murderati.com and at his own blog, What Fresh Hell Is This? He currently lives, writes, and practices law in Carthage, North Carolina.

79
Thomas Harris's
RED DRAGON (1981)

Bev Vincent

William Thomas Harris III (1940–), creator of Hannibal (the Cannibal) Lecter, doesn't give interviews or attend signings. The biography on his Web site states only that he was a reporter and editor for AP, and covered crime stories in the U.S. and Mexico. While at university, he reportedly submitted "macabre" stories to pulp magazines like *True* and *Argosy*. The sale of film rights to his 1975 debut novel, *Black Sunday*—inspired by the Munich Olympics terrorist attacks and initially outlined as a collaboration with two colleagues—allowed him to write full time. Since then, his novels have focused on serial killers like Lecter, who first appeared in *Red Dragon* (1981) and became a household name after the Oscar-winning adaptation of *The Silence of the Lambs* (1988). To research serial killers, Harris visited the FBI's Behavioral Science Unit, where he was given access to the case files of Edmund Kemper, Richard Chase, and Ed Gein. He attended the trial of the alleged "Monster of Florence" while preparing *Hannibal* (1999). Lecter's backstory is exposed in *Hannibal Rising* (2006), and Harris is contracted for one more novel featuring Lecter. However, since he has averaged eight years between books, it may not appear soon.

An FBI agent descends into the bowels of a maximum-security prison to seek advice from a legendary serial killer. It is impossible to hear the name Hannibal Lecter without imagining Anthony Hopkins in that scene from *The Silence of the Lambs*. However, long before Clarice Starling entered the Chesapeake State Hospital for the Criminally Insane, with her good bag and cheap shoes, Special Agent Will Graham was there first.

Hannibal Lecter is urbane, erudite, witty, charming, egotistical . . . and monstrous. He kills—and, oh yes, eats—incompetent and stupid people. Perhaps the first cannibal antihero, he is a clear antecedent to Jeff Lindsay's Dexter Morgan, who murders killers that have escaped prosecution.

In *Red Dragon*, Lecter is an enigma, labeled a sociopath because that is the only psychiatric term available to describe him. The few details known about his origins (sadism towards animals as a child, for example) are contradicted in later books. In a rare promotional statement, Harris says that, from a writer's perspective, Lecter is both amusing and difficult company. "He's the dark side of the world. He's probably the wickedest man I've ever heard of—at the same time he tells the truth and he says some things that I suppose we would all like to say."

Besides being the debut of an iconic villain, Red Dragon is the book in which Thomas Harris creates the formula for modern serial-killer fiction. While spending time with the FBI studying the case files of famous mass murderers, Harris also observed the behaviorists who pursue them. His research allowed him to develop scenes like the one where Will Graham interviews a reluctant—almost hostile—witness and expertly extracts information the man didn't know he possessed. Though Graham's use of observation to piece together disparate clues and arrive at accurate conclusions about killers may feel clichéd now, this book is where many contemporary behaviorist clichés originated.

Red Dragon is much more than a procedural novel, though. Conflicted by his skills, Will Graham is as fascinating as his nemesis. Despite what he claims, Graham isn't seeking advice or insight from Lecter. He visits to "get the old scent" of a killer so he can start thinking like one again. "Why don't you just smell yourself?" Lecter asks him. Palpable tension arises from their awareness that they are more alike than Graham could ever admit. "He understood murder uncomfortably well," Harris writes in the final page.

However, Graham doesn't anticipate the risks of drawing Lecter's undivided attention. As the man responsible for ending his reign of terror, Graham is seen by Lecter as an intellectual equal and a worthy adversary. Though onstage for only eleven pages, Lecter's influence is felt throughout the rest of the book. By revealing Graham's address to the serial killer known as the Tooth Fairy, Lecter puts Graham in a position where he can't simply evaluate the evidence and go back home to his wife and stepson. To remove the target Lecter placed on his family's back, Graham must become bait for the murderer. Even from his high-security prison cell, Lecter manipulates events in the outside world.

Lecter isn't the only fascinating villain in Red Dragon. Whereas Graham's empathy allows him to think like a monster, Francis Dolarhyde (whose name brings to mind Edward Hyde of Robert Louis Stevenson's famous novel) is a monster who yearns to feel like a human being. Harris stops the forward momentum of the novel to devote several chapters to Dolarhyde's origins. While the author's attempts to explain the genesis of Lecter in subsequent books tend to undermine his potency, Dolarhyde benefits greatly from an exploration of his backstory (though it was decried as a typically knee-jerk liberal mind-set by a *New York Times* reviewer at the time).

The novel was filmed twice, first by Michael Mann as *Manhunter* (1986) and again by Brett Ratner as *Red Dragon* (2002) with Anthony Hopkins reprising his Academy-Award-winning role. The first movie robs Dolarhyde of any humanity. Because Harris shows what made him the way he is, readers empathize when he meets Reba and, for the first time in his life, makes a real human connection and begins to doubt his "mission." His story is as tragic as that of Frankenstein's monster—created against his will and unable to find a place in society. Though the killings he committed are monstrous, when he thinks that Reba has turned against him, Dolarhyde's rage is understandable. He's not a superman like Lecter, just a broken man engaged in a futile search for something better. Humanizing both sides of the equation gives *Red Dragon* the depth that formulaic serial-killer stories often lack.

As a former reporter, Harris is a master at showing versus telling. He reports every furrow in Graham's brow, every crease in Dolarhyde's forehead, and leaves it to the reader to understand why. He often establishes setting through the use of terse sentence fragments. Expository sections switch tense or use the second person. "Dr. Lecter's eyes are maroon," he writes, though everything else in the scene is in past tense. When Dolarhyde watches film of his next victim while Reba pleasures him, Harris again switches to present tense.

The story's inertia drives it to an inevitable confrontation—except that Harris doesn't follow the predictable path. He plays with the familiar horror cliché of the supposedly dead monster reappearing, using a prestidigitator's skill to misdirect. By creating a false denouement that focuses on how everything *isn't* fine with Graham when he returns to his family, he catches even the most jaded reader off guard.

Bev Vincent is the author of *The Road to the Dark Tower*, an authorized companion to Stephen King's Dark Tower series and a nominee for the 2004 nonfiction Bram Stoker Award from the Horror Writers Association. His column "News From the Dead Zone" has appeared in *Cemetery Dance* magazine since 2001. Some of his fifty short stories have appeared in anthologies like Bram Stoker Award winner *From the Borderlands*, the Mystery Writers of America anthology *The Blue Religion*, and *Doctor Who: Destination Prague*. He coedited *The Illustrated Stephen King Trivia Book*, writes for *Onyx Reviews*, and contributes a monthly essay to *Storytellers Unplugged*. His script for Stephen King's *Gotham Café* won the Best Adaptation Award at the International Horror and Sci-Fi Film Festival.

80
Jack Ketchum's
OFF SEASON (1981)

Blake Crouch

Jack Ketchum, a pseudonym for Dallas Mayr (1946–), owns some of the blackest real estate in the world of thriller fiction. A former literary agent and actor, Ketchum published his first novel, *Off Season*, to the dismay of the mainstream literary establishment and the delight of what would grow into a cult following. Over the last quarter of a century, he has published numerous novels, novellas, and works of short fiction. However, only in the last five years has he gained notoriety, largely due to the praises of Stephen King. In 2003, while accepting the National Book Foundation's Medal for Distinguished Contribution to American Letters, King said, "There's another writer here tonight who writes under the name of Jack Ketchum and he has also written what may be the best book of his career, a long novella called *The Crossings*. Have you read it? Have any of the judges read it?" In his approach to thrillers, as typified by *The Lost*, *Red*, *She Wakes*, and *The Girl Next Door*, Ketchum defines fearless and unflinching.

Off Season isn't Jack Ketchum's best book or even his most disturbing. It is, however, his first and his most important, since it remapped the boundaries of where writers could go in the name of suspense.

But as often happens when something different arrives, the critics didn't understand. The *Village Voice* condemned *Off Season* as violent pornography, and even Ketchum's publisher and distributors were stricken with a late case of buyer's remorse, finally losing their nerve about giving the book the full marketing and publicity push they had originally intended. Then there were the edits Ketchum was strong-armed into making—the toning down of the most brutal scenes (no recipe for man-meat jerky or cock-stump spitting), and an absolute ultimatum from his publisher to let a character live whom he had every intention of killing—so that the 1981 publication, while still chock-full of groundbreaking unpleasantness, did not embody Ketchum's initial vision, which was to write, in his words, something with the "kind of teeth pretty much unseen before in mass-market fiction." Following its initial 1981 publication, the book promptly went out of print until Leisure Press finally released Ketchum's uncut, uncensored version of the novel a quarter of a century later in 2006.

Enviably accomplished for a debut novel, *Off Season* draws its inspiration from the legend of Sawney Bean, the Scottish leader of a fifteenth- or sixteenth-century clan that engaged in mass murder and cannibalism until their capture, torture, and execution. *Off Season's* narrative structure, while by no means revolutionary, is deceptively simple and ingenious. Six friends meet at a remote cabin in the Maine woods, not far from the coast—Nick, Marjie, Dan, Laura, Carla, and Jim. One of the most intelligent choices Ketchum makes is not to rush anything. The first 130 pages are essentially violence free and dedicated to the introduction of the six main characters, along with foreshadowing of the horrible events to come. The sense of increasing dread is palpable, and by the time the family of cannibals gets around to attacking the vacationers at the cabin, the suspense has been ratcheted to an unbearable degree.

If the first 130 pages are prelude, the last 140 are the roughest, nastiest, and most brutal you will ever read. "Unflinching" is thrown around liberally these days, to the point where the word has lost its impact. But Ketchum truly is unflinching in a way that few other writers have dared to be, and this is what sets him and his debut novel apart. The author's chief talent lies in creating scenes of overwhelming violence in such a lean, straightforward, and disinterested style, that it is simultaneously torture to read but impossible to look away.

Witness Ketchum's portrayal of the second character's death:

> In a slow, deliberate motion he reached into the chest and touched the heart. It was still warm, still beating. He severed the veins and arteries with the knife and lifted the muscle into the light, and still it beat, steaming in the cool air. For the man this moment was the nexus of all mystery and wonder, the closest thing he knew to worship. He stared until finally the heart was still.

At the center of the carnage and mayhem stands the character of George Peters, the decent lawman, appalled and disgusted by what he sees, an early incarnation of Sheriff Bell from Cormac McCarthy's *No Country for Old Men*, and Police Chief Marge Gunderson of *Fargo* fame. Sheriff Peters is order, or the *attempt* to restore order in the face of pure depravity, and like the reader, if he escapes harm, it is only a physical escape. His and our psyches will never recover.

Though *Off Season* was published at a time when such independent slasher films as *Halloween* (1978) and *Friday the 13th* (1980) were challenging the shock value of *Psycho*, there is little to compare. Those films are comical, cheap, even childish in their treatment of violence, in a way that is completely diametric to the very adult study of violence that is the foundation of *Off Season*. If anything, the novel was a nod to *The Texas Chain Saw Massacre* (1974), *The Hills Have Eyes* (1977), and a precursor to Bret Easton Ellis's controversial novel, *American Psycho* (1991), Park Chan-wook's *Oldboy* (2003), and the best work of Takashi Miike, the prolific Japanese director of such ultraviolent films as *Audition* (1999) and *Ichi the Killer* (2001).

What makes *Off Season* so effective and important is Ketchum's masterful manipulation of the reader. Just as in *Psycho*, *Off Season's* erstwhile hero, Carla, is killed first and most horribly. This is Ketchum grabbing the bullhorn and screaming at the reader: "No one is safe or off-limits in this book! Not even you!" And while *Off Season* muses on such "big ideas" as the rational vs. the natural, the family unit, and urban vs. rural, its most enduring message concerns the abrupt ugliness of human violence, and how people face such extreme situations and horrors that come out of nowhere. The violence that occurs in this book touches us so profoundly because it is perfectly reminiscent of the awful and sudden turns that life can take. It is ultimately the unpredictable, uncompromising way Ketchum rains his terrors down upon his characters and the reader that earns *Off Season* a place in the canon of classic thriller fiction.

Off Season may upset you. It may even make you sick. But it won't make you feel cheap. Whether you have the nerve to experience what Ketchum has to say about violence and the human condition is another matter. Just don't say I didn't warn you.

Blake Crouch was born near the Piedmont town of Statesville, North Carolina, in 1978. He attended the University of North Carolina at Chapel Hill and graduated in 2000 with degrees in English and creative writing. His first two novels, *Desert Places* and *Locked Doors*, were published in 2004 and 2005. Inspired by his relocation to Durango, Colorado, he wrote *Abandon* (2009), a novel set in the past and present in a remote mining town high in the San Juan Mountains. His short stories have appeared in *Ellery Queen's Mystery Magazine*, an anthology from Bleak House Books titled *Uncage Me*, and ITW's *Thriller 2* anthology. David Morrell called him, "One of the most exciting new thriller writers I've read in years."

81
Thomas Perry's
THE BUTCHER'S BOY (1982)
Robert Liparulo

Thomas Perry (1947–) was born in Tonawanda, New York. After earning a B.A. from Cornell University and a Ph.D. in English Literature from the University of Rochester, he banged around in a variety of jobs: commercial fisherman, weapons mechanic, university administrator, and teacher. Then he began honing his skills as a writer on such television shows as *Simon and Simon*, *21 Jump Street*, and *Star Trek: The Next Generation*. His first novel, *The Butcher's Boy*, was published in 1982. The thriller garnered a bevy of critical praise (the *Washington Post* called it "a stunning debut") and an Edgar Award from the Mystery Writers of America for Best First Novel. Each of his subsequent novels—such as *Metzger's Dog* (1983), *Big Fish* (1985), and *Island* (1987)—pulled in more fans. But it wasn't until 1995's *Vanishing Act* that Perry became a blip on seemingly every thriller buff's radar. The book introduced the character of Jane Whitefield, an unofficial one-woman witness protection program, who became so popular that Perry continued her saga through four back-to-back sequels. (After ten years and five stand-alone novels, Perry gave Jane a long-awaited comeback in 2009's *Runner*.) Still, many thriller aficionados—including Michael Connelly, who sang the book's praises in an introduction to the 2003 reissue—consider *The Butcher's Boy* perhaps the best of Perry's seventeen novels. It shattered their expectations of what a "thriller" meant.

Like the characters that people his stories, Thomas Perry is a master rule breaker. And he didn't waste time proving it. His first novel, *The Butcher's Boy*, turned thriller conventions on their heads, starting with its unlikely principal protagonist, a cold-blooded killer. As if making readers side with such an apparently unsympathetic character wasn't enough of a challenge, Perry eschews typical gimmicks often used to soften readers' hearts. He refuses to divulge the assassin's name, forcing us to think of him only as the titular Butcher's Boy, whose mentor was a Latvian butcher and brilliant

299

assassin. He has no extraordinary physical features with which we can identify; rather, he is "a man not fat, not thin, not young, not old, not tall, not short, not dark, not light." We can't even sympathize with his choice of victims. The promise of a paycheck drives him to murder a grandfatherly senator, and he kills two muggers after rendering them unconscious.

It's a testament to Perry's skill that we *do* start to like the guy. As Perry says in an interview, "Slowly, we begin to appreciate his competence, his courage, his cunning, and his sheer tenacity, his determination to live. Soon we realize that, while he is a bad man, he is up against adversaries who are much, much worse."

Looking at thrillers published before and since *The Butcher's Boy*, it's not difficult to believe the novel ushered in a new era of the antihero— the flawed, even amoral protagonist readers find themselves grudgingly rooting for. Not that criminal protagonists are new (think Shakespeare's Macbeth, Patricia Highsmith's Tom Ripley, and Richard Stark's Parker), but their presence seems stronger today than ever before (Thomas Harris's Hannibal Lecter, Andrew Vachss's Burke, Michael Connelly's Cassie Black, Barry Eisler's John Rain, Jeff Lindsay's Dexter Morgan).

The story opens with the Butcher's Boy assassinating a small-time machinist in California. This draws the attention of Elizabeth Waring, a young employee in the Justice Department's organized crime unit. She's a brilliant analyst, but lacks the field experience required to move up, so her supervisor helps her by sending her to investigate. Upon the death of that aforementioned grandfatherly senator, Waring is ordered to Denver to represent her agency in the inquiry.

The Boy travels to Las Vegas to collect his fee. Instead, his Mafia employers decide he knows too much and make a botched attempt to kill him. With mob goons and federal investigators closing in on him, the Boy sets out to settle the score. As capos begin dropping like slot machine coins, Waring "correctly perceives the patterns and goes in the right directions," Perry explains, "but can never persuade her superiors to believe her theories, much less to act on them in time." She is always one step behind the Boy.

Whether describing firefights or the thrill of discovering a link between two seemingly unrelated crimes, Perry manages to give the story near-constant breathtaking momentum. Like the clank-clank-clank of a roller coaster climbing the first steep hill, short, tightly constructed scenes at the beginning portent the ride to come. You can almost feel your head snap one way then the other as you read.

But it's not always a sudden twist or rushing action that exhilarates. Through the use of dramatic irony—that is, our knowing something the characters don't—Perry gives readers additional layers of insight and emotion. How can we not smile or groan in pleasant frustration at Waring's sometimes faulty reconstruction of crimes we as readers witnessed? Rather than unraveling mysteries in sync with the characters, the fun lies in watching them try to catch up with what we already know. And as this catching up grows quicker, we realize the characters are *learning*; they're adjusting their thinking to better understand their adversaries.

Careful readers can catch subtle hints of Perry's disregard for "rules." Take, for instance, the mid-scene point of view shifts that would have English profs and editors reaching for their red pens. But Perry pulls them off so gracefully, they're almost impossible to notice.

In at least one area, Perry never plays it fast and loose: the facts. When he writes, as he does in *The Butcher's Boy*, that the drive from Denver to Cheyenne takes two hours, you can bet your watch it does. By being meticulous in verifiable details like that, readers take him at his word when he describes things that are harder to prove, like the way in which the mob launders money and how many pounds of pressure it takes to crush a windpipe. Because of this verisimilitude, readers feel they have been on the Las Vegas Strip without actually having walked it, or think they know how to work a crime scene as well as any investigator.

Years ago, I satiated my fiction cravings with a steady diet of horror. Then a friend convinced me to read *The Butcher's Boy*. I was hooked. I hadn't realized that thrillers could be so—*thrilling*. My bookshelves are now crammed with hundreds of thrillers I've read over the years. Perry's novels occupy a special shelf in my office.

In writing my own novels, I have no doubt that I am influenced by Perry's bold style of telling stories: his tackling heady challenges, such as creating likeable bad guys, using dramatic irony to build suspense and show character growth, ignoring traditions and formulas and rules—in short, his doing whatever it takes to tell a damn good story. Call it a guilty pleasure, liking a book about a nasty assassin so much that it changed my reading life—and career—forever. But a pleasure it is.

Robert Liparulo is a former journalist, with over a thousand articles and multiple writing awards to his name. He is the author of the thrillers *Comes a Horseman*, *Germ*, *Deadfall*, *Deadlock*, and *Lunatic Fringe* as well as the best-selling young adult series, Dreamhouse Kings. He is currently working on a trilogy of sniper novels, based on the critically acclaimed short story, "Kill Zone," that he contributed to James Patterson's ITW *Thriller* anthology. In addition, he is penning a novel and script of a political thriller with the director Andrew Davis. He lives with his family in Colorado.

82
Tom Clancy's
THE HUNT FOR RED OCTOBER (1984)

Chris Kuzneski

Tom Clancy (1947–) grew up in Baltimore, and received an English degree from Loyola College. Attracted to the armed forces since he was a boy, he turned his attention to writing when poor eyesight kept him from a military career. While working full time as an insurance salesman, Clancy wrote *The Hunt for Red October* at night on his dining room table. He finished it on February 28, 1983. Knowing no better, he drove the manuscript to his editor instead of mailing it. A year and a half later, it was published in October 1984. The book introduced the character of Jack Ryan, who would later be featured in several of Clancy's other novels, including *Patriot Games, Clear and Present Danger,* and *The Sum of All Fears.* These books have another thing in common: they were adapted into major motion pictures. In 1996, Clancy aimed his expertise in a different direction. He cofounded Red Storm Entertainment, a computer game company that launched the *Rainbow Six* and *Ghost Recon* franchises. In addition, he licensed his name and the *Splinter Cell* brand to Ubisoft Entertainment. Less than a decade later, Tom Clancy is more than a best-selling author. He is a multimedia giant, whose name is synonymous with military action.

In early 1985, President Ronald Reagan stepped off Marine One with a book tucked under his arm. A reporter asked him what he was reading, and Reagan held up a copy of *The Hunt for Red October* for the world media to see. The book jacket was a memorable one. It featured a black submarine, stamped with a red hammer and sickle—a symbol that appeared on the Soviet flag. This was during the Cold War, shortly after Reagan had labeled the U.S.S.R. as the "evil empire," so reporters were intrigued by the cover image and asked him about the book. When Reagan called the novel "unputdownable" and referred to it as "the perfect yarn," it made international news.

"I'm a storyteller who got very lucky," Clancy told me. "President Reagan got it for Christmas 1984. People noticed it and asked the President about it, and SHAZAM, I became a best-selling author. Quite a jump from insurance agent. Rather like an instant cure for leprosy. I never looked back."

Casper Weinberger, Reagan's secretary of defense, was another fan of the novel. He reviewed it for *The Times Literary Supplement*, calling it "a splendid and riveting story" and praising the technical descriptions as "vast and accurate." Of course, this shouldn't be surprising since *The Hunt for Red October* was released by the Naval Institute Press, a noncommercial publisher based at the U.S. Naval Academy in Annapolis, specializing in naval and military history. *The Hunt for Red October* was the first fictional work it had ever published, and to this day it is still its most successful book, based on total sales and its impact on contemporary writing. Clancy's debut novel ushered in a brand-new, extremely popular genre: the modern techno-thriller, books that included a massive amount of technical details and cutting-edge technology while maintaining action and suspense. And *The Hunt for Red October* does it better than most, taking readers into the middle of the Cold War during a nautical game of hide-and-seek.

"*Red October* was based on a true story, the attempted defection of the Soviet Krivak-class missile frigate, *Storozhevoy*," Clancy revealed. "I had read about it in the *Washington Post* in 1976 or so, and it germinated in my head. I decided to up the ante, as it were, by making the ship a missile submarine instead of a surface warship."

One glance at the book's synopsis, and Clancy will have you hooked:

> When Jack Ryan, a young analyst at the CIA, gets word that an unexpected Red Fleet operation is in progress, he thinks he knows the cause: The Soviets' most-valuable ship, a new ballistic-missile submarine, is attempting to defect to the United States, and the Soviet Atlantic fleet has been ordered to destroy her. Ryan reasons that if the U.S. can find the submarine first, it would be the intelligence coup of all time. But *Red October* has the entire Atlantic to hide in and a new silent propulsion system that makes it impossible for either side to detect. Or does it? Captain Marko Ramius has plotted his escape with the cunning of a lifelong submariner. Viktor Tupolev, who commands the Soviets' fastest attack sub, is counting on his boat's new

sonar system to guide him to his prey. And Bart Mancuso, the commander of the U.S. Navy's new attack sub *Dallas*, is banking on the sensitive ears of "Jonesy," his resourceful sonar operator, to identify *Red October*'s unique sound print and track her down.

The first time I read *The Hunt for Red October*, I was still in high school. My father had purchased the book based on the president's recommendation and because Clancy, like my father, was a successful insurance agent. As soon as my dad finished reading it, I borrowed his copy and dove right in. Within seconds, I was underwater with the Northern Fleet, exploring the Murmansk coast and the bluffs of the Kolo Fjord. But unlike all the books that I had read previously—where Soviet military personnel were portrayed as maniacal bad guys—I actually found myself rooting for the *Red October*. I wanted Ramius and his crew to escape the clutches of evil and experience the simple joy of shopping for fresh fruit in a supermarket. Or as Visily Borodin (Sam Neill) mentioned in the film version, to buy a recreational vehicle and live in Montana, where he could marry "a round American woman and raise rabbits." It didn't matter that most of the technical details about the submarine were over my head. Heck, some of Clancy's information would have confused an admiral. In the end, all that mattered was that I believed the world that Clancy had created. To me, there was nothing more important than capturing the *Red October* so the U.S. Navy could examine the new "Caterpillar Drive" system. Why? It was the only way we could stop those Commie bastards from parking an undetected nuclear submarine off the coast of our most important cities. And let's face it, what was more important than that?

The story had such an impact on me, I found myself paying tribute to it when I wrote my first novel, *The Plantation*. As an author, I've always had trouble picking the right name for my characters. I know the process should be a simple one since there are thousands of names to chose from, but for some reason it's always been a struggle for me. And I mean, *always*. In this case, I knew everything about one of my main characters—ex-military, extremely intelligent, cultured and well read, yet somewhat of a jokester—except what to call him. Then it dawned on me, my character sounded a lot like "Jonesy" from *The Hunt for Red October*. In fact, the men sounded like brothers. So I thought, what the hell? I took the surname and ran with it, an homage to the father of the techno-thriller.

Four best sellers later, David Jones and his best friend Jonathon Payne are still kicking butt in countries around the world. If they're lucky, maybe one of these days they'll get to meet Jack Ryan. I'm sure the three of them would hit it off.

Chris Kuzneski is the *New York Times* best-selling author of *The Lost Throne*, *Sword of God*, *Sign of the Cross*, and *The Plantation*. His thrillers have been translated into more than twenty languages and have been praised by James Patterson, Clive Cussler, Nelson DeMille, Lee Child, James Rollins, Vince Flynn, Steve Berry, and many others. Although he currently lives on the Gulf Coast of Florida, he grew up in western Pennsylvania where he played football at the University of Pittsburgh and passed most of his classes. He is currently working on his golf swing, his social life, and his next book.

83

F. Paul Wilson's
THE TOMB (1984)

Heather Graham

F. Paul Wilson (1946–) might be called a renaissance man. Born and raised in New Jersey, he says "he misspent his youth playing with matches, pouring over Uncle Scrooge and E.C. comics, reading Lovecraft, Matheson, Bradbury, and Heinlein, listening to Chuck Berry and Alan Freed on the radio, and watching Soupy Sales and Shock Theatre with Zacherley." A medical doctor, Paul continued with his practice even after finding success as a writer; after all, he had patients who depended on him. While still a student, he began his writing career with science fiction. In 1981, he received acclaim and *New York Times* best-selling status with his novel *The Keep*; in 1984, he repeated that success with *The Tomb*, and Repairman Jack came onto the scene as an engaging antihero with whom decades of readers would fall in love. Paul's affection for New York is clearly apparent in his descriptions of it. In *The Tomb*, the city lives and breathes and is an integral part of the complex plot that made it a landmark novel. He initially called the book, *Rakoshi*—the name of Jack's adversaries in the story. But the publisher wasn't sure that people would be attracted to a novel with that title and decided arbitrarily to call it *The Tomb*. Paul is still curious why, given that there isn't a tomb in the story.

To me, F. Paul Wilson's *The Tomb* is the perfect book. It has everything: history, suspense, mystery, romance, adventure, and a touch of the occult. It's an exciting story, well written, and masterfully told—a thriller that defies genre.

I read it the year it came out, 1984. I marveled that any book could encompass so much, captivate the reader, and build momentum steadily throughout. *The Tomb* was fresh; it was different; I had never read anything before that brought so many diverse elements to a single novel.

From that day on, I grabbed everything I saw with the name F. Paul Wilson on it. Years later, when I was finally able to meet Paul, I was with my family, who felt the way I did. We must have looked pathetically silly to him, all of us just staring at him, wide-eyed and gaping. It was somehow reinforcing to find out that the brilliant writer was also an extraordinary man, as down to earth and as essentially kind as his character, Repairman Jack. And why not? The author's voice displays a remarkably witty sense of humor.

Let me tell you why this is one of the best thrillers ever written. First, there are those who are excellent writers. They know the language well, know what words to use when and where. Enough metaphors, and yet not too many. Words that form sketches that create vivid scenes in the mind. No clichés. Then, there are storytellers. Perhaps they don't use language with as much skill, but they tell a story that seduces, amuses, entrances, or creates states of deep thought that linger long after the last page.

Therein lies one of the beauties of *The Tomb*. Paul is both a writer *and* a storyteller. His words create a vital world that enters the mind and remains in the soul. If you have been to a location he's describing, you agree with his description, and your agreement is often wry, as if you are sharing a joke. If you're never been there, you still feel that you know the place; you feel the heat, the sweat, the touch of the sun, or the cold of snow. It's not just reading. It's experiencing.

Perhaps most importantly, what Paul did with *The Tomb* was create characters who are real. I know exactly what they look like. I know why they feel what they do, and I sympathize with what they're thinking. He manages to create people we love, hate, resent, and fear, and thus we live the emotions of these fascinating friends and acquaintances.

Repairman Jack is the perfect protagonist. A relentless righter of wrongs, he is also vulnerable. He isn't the tallest, strongest, or most handsome. In a way, he is Everyman, and in a way, he is the most extraordinary. He has a deep fiber of morality. I would walk through any dark alley with him. He knows the streets and loves them. He will not kill—unless there is no other way. Punishment fits the crime. His methods are possible (finding someone who beat up an old lady and beating him up in turn, breaking his hands) because he exists in nonexistence—a shadow man, he has no social security number and doesn't file taxes. He isn't the law—he is a repairman. "He didn't have a bad face. Brown eyes, dark brown hair growing perhaps a little too low on his forehead. A nose neither too big nor too small . . . the teeth could have been whiter and straighter, and the lips were on the thin side. An inoffensive face. As an added bonus, a wiry, well-

muscled, five-eleven frame went along with the face at no extra charge."
Jack fits in with the crowd while rising above it.

Then there is Gia, not just the love interest, but the woman who will
bring many of the plot elements into play. Through the early part of the
book, I simply want to shake her. What is the matter with this woman?
Jack cares for her so deeply, and she makes his heart bleed. And yet I understand her as well. I can see her fears for herself, her daughter, and her
future. She, too, has wounds and scars.

Numerous plotlines come together in *The Tomb*. Repairman Jack must
search for the aunt-in-law of his beloved Gia, who is trying to distance
herself from him, afraid after discovering weapons in his home and learning what he "repairs." Meanwhile, he's also hired to find the mugger who
stole the necklace of an elderly Indian woman—an impossible task in the
labyrinth of New York City. But he knows the streets, knows how to lure
a crook, and he's not above using a disguise. In an alley he changes into
women's clothing, and sets his trap. Amazingly, he finds the crook, and
here the first hints of something beyond the ordinary appear—the crook
hadn't tried to pawn the necklace. He had thrown it away because of the
unpleasant sensation he experienced when holding it. The necklace is returned, and a bizarre death befalls the crook. Jack thinks he's finished with
the job, but he's not. History comes into play, intricately woven into the
plot. What had appeared totally unrelated to Repairman Jack suddenly begins to meld together and Jack is left not just to "repair" but to fight a battle for the lives of those he loves. Each page reveals more twists, more clues.
Hints are delicately braided into a story that moves eerily into the unbe-
lievable that we believe. Its real; it's surreal.

The Tomb combined the thriller, the horror novel, the mystery, and
even the romance, opening the door for scores of writers to follow.

F. Paul Wilson didn't actually intend to write a continuing character.
The Tomb stood alone for many years before Paul brought Repairman Jack
back with *Legacies* in 1998. Jack now has many adventures in print. Thank
God F. Paul Wilson delivered more. What makes a book truly brilliant after
all the analysis? The writer's voice. And in every story, with every character, Paul's voice continues to enchant, thrill, chill, and seduce.

New York Times best-selling author Heather Graham majored in theater arts at
the University of South Florida. After several years of performing in dinner theater, providing back-up vocals, and bartending, she stayed home after the birth of

her third child and began to write. Since then, she has authored over 150 novels and novellas, including suspense, thriller, historical romance, vampire fiction, time travel, occult, horror, category, and Christmas family fare. She has been translated into twenty-five languages and has over seventy-five million books in print. Her honors include awards from Walden Books, B. Dalton, Georgia Romance Writers, Affaire de Coeur, Romantic Times, the Lifetime Achievement Award from RWA, and the Silver Bullet award from the International Thriller Writers organization. She has been featured in *The Nation, Redbook, People,* and *USA Today,* and appeared on many television shows such as *Today* and *Entertainment Tonight.* She thanks God for her career and nominally runs the Slush Pile players, a varied group "performing something like entertainment" at various venues to benefit children's AIDS societies.

84
Andrew Vachss's
FLOOD (1985)

Barry Eisler

For over thirty years, Andrew Vachss (1942–) has dedicated himself to the protection of children: as an attorney, a consultant, a prison supervisor, and, most prominently, as a novelist. His award-winning Burke novels (*Strega*), graphic novels (*Batman: The Ultimate Evil*), and stand-alones (*The Getaway Man*)—more than thirty—draw on his long and dark experience in battling child predators. They're not just gripping fiction; they're a call to arms to anyone who cares about protecting, and preventing evil from infecting, the most innocent among us.

The only thing fictional about Andrew Vachss's ultrahard-boiled novels is the dark, damaged characters populating them, and even these, it's clear, are based on people Vachss has known. But the settings—typically the rancid underbelly of New York City—and the plots—typically involving sociopaths who prey on children, and their familiars in the civilian world—are all from the hard path walked by Vachss himself, a former juvenile prison director and lawyer specializing in advocacy for, and protection of, abused children.

I first heard of Vachss in 1989, when, as a new covert recruit with the CIA, I was reading a lot about crime, violence, and the street. Vachss was mentioned in the bibliography of what remains one of the best self-defense books I've ever read, *Cheap Shots, Ambushes, and Other Lessons*, by Marc "Animal" MacYoung. MacYoung praised Vachss as one of the few novelists who really understood and was able to accurately portray the way the street works: the hits, the scams, the freaks, the whole ugly symbiosis between the criminal world and the civilian. Because MacYoung was clearly a man with his own intimate acquaintance with Vachss's world, I decided to give Vachss a try.

I found *Flood* at my local library and couldn't put it down. Vachss had created an unforgettable antihero—a man known only as Burke, a criminal living like a ghost in the underbelly of New York, preying on other criminals. Burke was a loner, but he wasn't alone: in place of the family he never had, there was his clan, a collection of people as damaged and dangerous as he, and together, probably the most lethal underground outfit in fiction. There was Max the Silent, a stone-reliable courier and expert karate-ka whose name was a reference more to his stealth than to his being a deaf/mute; the Prof, short for professor, or maybe prophet, an ex-con who knew every street move ever invented and communicated them in slang; the Mole, who ran his junkyard like an underground castle, his dog pack protecting it like a vicious, moving moat; and Mama, whose Chinese restaurant was a front for her own criminal enterprises and who served as Burke's cutout to the rest of the world. I'd never read anything like it and devoured the other then-available books in the Burke series—*Strega*, *Blue Belle*, and *Hard Candy*—in a matter of days.

What struck me most about the books was their unflinching realism. Reading Vachss, you didn't sense mere verisimilitude; you sensed reality. The places were real; the events were horrors you could read about in the headlines, if you could bear it; and the characters, hard as they were, were also all too human—men who'd learned from brutal experience to trust no one, and yet who found a way to trust each other. More than the gripping plots, more even than the razored-down prose, it was the *reality* of Burke's world that set the books apart and made them so affecting.

Today, when people ask me to name some of my literary influences, Vachss is always on the shortlist. He's the author who opened my eyes to the dramatic possibilities of dropping fictional characters into nonfictional settings and circumstances. He awakened a latent love of clipped dialogue and bleak prose. He implicitly instructed me on how to make the bad guy good: understand him profoundly, make sure that beneath his dark carapace lie certain core qualities the reader can respect and even admire, drop him into a world whose moral palette consists only of the bleakest shades of gray, and populate that world with people even worse than he.

You can't like thrillers and not love Vachss's books—not only the Burke books, but also the stand-alones and short story collections. It's an oeuvre without equal, adding depth and darkness to a genre I love and changing the trajectory of that genre in the process. And though there's much to be learned from them, these books weren't written to be studied. They were written to be read. Pick one up and you'll instantly understand why.

Barry Eisler spent three years in a covert position with the CIA's Directorate of Operations, then worked as a technology lawyer and start-up executive in Silicon Valley and Japan, earning his black belt at the Kodokan International Judo Center along the way. Eisler's best-selling thrillers have won the Barry Award and the Gumshoe Award for Best Thriller of the Year, have been included in numerous "Best Of" lists, and have been translated into nearly twenty languages. The first book in Eisler's assassin John Rain series, *Rain Fall,* was made into a movie starring Gary Oldman, released by Sony Pictures Japan in 2009. His other titles include *Killing Rain, Requiem for an Assassin*, and *Fault Line*. Eisler lives in the San Francisco Bay Area and Tokyo.

85
Stephen King's
MISERY (1987)

Chris Mooney

Stephen King (1947–) is an astonishingly prolific, international best-selling author of more than fifty novels, short story collections, and novellas, many of which are set in his native state of Maine. Almost all of his works have been adapted for film or TV, some of which he scripted and one of which, *Maximum Overdrive*, he directed. Because of his immense popularity, his early novels—horror classics such as *Carrie*, *'Salem's Lot*, and *The Shining*—were dismissed by critics. But in 2003, the National Book Foundation honored King with their prestigious Medal for Distinguished Contribution to American Letters—a first for a "popular" author of successful commercial fiction.

I spent a good portion of my childhood every Saturday afternoon watching old black-and-white horror movies on a terrific (and now defunct) Boston television program called *Creature Double Feature*. The good stuff—the color flicks full of blood and gore—were shown later at night. None of them scared me half as much as the movie trailer for *The Shining*. I *had* to see it.

Despite my persistent begging, my parents refused to take me. Then I found out the movie was based on a book and somehow managed to convince my father to allow me to read it. After a particularly heated exchange with a blue-haired librarian whom I'm sure babysat Moses (she told my father he shouldn't allow his eleven-year-old son to read "such filth"), I took the book home. Convinced I had something magical in my hands, I read it through the night. That moment not only began my love affair of reading (and as Stephen King's #1 Fan), but it also marked a turning point in my life: I wanted to be a writer.

A whole new world opened up for me. I learned that King was influenced by a Golden Age of horror in the 1950s, typified by the works of Richard Matheson, Robert Bloch, and Jack Finney. As critic Douglas E

Winter noted, these writers shifted fright from "misty moors and haunted mansions to the American suburbs." They "invited terror into our shopping malls and peaceful neighborhoods—into the house next door."

King built on their contributions, using an extremely expansive style crammed with minute descriptive details and plentiful cultural references in an effort to make the reader identify with the story as well as to establish a feeling of normalcy and reality. As soon as the groundwork was set, King was then able to gradually introduce paranormal or even supernatural elements while continuing to retain the reader's suspension of disbelief. His settings were high schools, coffee shops, and supermarkets, the stuff of common daily life, with characters who were often ordinary people forced to behave in extraordinary ways.

Preceded by Ira Levin's *Rosemary's Baby* (1968), William Peter Blatty's *The Exorcist* (1971), and Thomas Tryon's *The Other* (1971), King pioneered a second Golden Age of horror in the 1970s and 1980s. That era ended as publishers tried too hard to fill demand and opportunistic authors jumped on the trend, failing to understand the elements that made King's books effective. Readers turned from a genre that, with exceptions, had become predictable and formulaic.

But King, a master storyteller with an immense gift for creating memorable characters, remained as popular as ever and showed his versatility by writing various kinds of thrillers, often avoiding the supernatural in works like *Cujo* and the prison novella "Rita Hayworth and the Shawshank Redemption." One of the best and most famous examples of his non-supernatural fiction is 1987's *Misery*, a book that marked another turning point in my writing development. This time, the horrors were solidly rooted in the real world, and the result, to this day, still frightens me to the core.

On the surface, the book is deceptively simple: what if a best-selling romance writer suffers a nasty car accident and wakes up crippled and in unimaginable pain inside the remote farmhouse of a psychotic ex-nurse who considers herself to be the writer's #1 fan? The plot alone had me hooked. What fascinated me was the complicated, almost symbiotic relationship between Paul Sheldon and Annie Wilkes.

Paul is entirely dependent on the manic-depressive ex-nurse to give him a highly addictive codeine-based medication to take away his pain. Annie needs her favorite writer to resurrect from the dead his famous character, a dimwitted but loveable heroine named Misery Chastain, in a new

novel she has titled *Misery's Return*. Not only is Paul forced to work under
intense physical and mental pressure (and on a literal deadline) using a
manual typewriter with missing keys, but also the pages must meet Annie's
approval.

In Annie Wilkes, King develops one of the most complex and terrifying villains in popular culture. He doles out the depths of her psychosis—
and the ensuing terror—in slow, maddening increments. In one early
scene, she forces Paul to swallow his Novril pills, using a bucket full of
soapy rinse water as punishment for making her angry. Yet she's also prim
and proper. When she finds a manuscript in Paul's briefcase, she asks his
permission to read it. She considers herself a good Christian woman. She
prays to God for guidance and won't swear, choosing to use the now-famous
words "cockadoodie" and "dirty-bird." Annie is also crafty and cunning.
After suffering one of her manic-depressive episodes, she is afraid she'll
hurt Paul and decides to leave him locked inside the bedroom while she
cools off at her "Laughing Place." She sets little traps throughout her house
to alert her if Paul strays from his bedroom.

During one of these outings, Paul discovers a scrapbook Annie has labeled "Memory Lane," the pages stuffed with yellowed newspaper clippings
highlighting her decades-long career as a serial killer. At this moment, Paul
realizes just how dire his situation really is. He is crippled, bound to a
wheelchair, and locked inside a house with no phone or any means of escape. No one is coming to rescue him. He's a prisoner. Writing the book,
he discovers in a Scheherazade moment, is the *only* way he can stay alive.

Annie's complexity and unpredictability kept me glued to the pages.
One moment she's chopping off Paul's foot. ("Don't worry," she tells him
as she raises the axe. "I'm a trained nurse.") Next she's smiling and humming while spoon-feeding him an ice-cream sundae. With each turn of the
page, I couldn't stop wondering if Sheldon *could* find a way to escape his
bedroom-turned-torture chamber. No sooner would I put down the book
than I'd have to pick it up again, needing to know what new horror Annie
had in store for Paul—and whether or not he'd survive it.

Equally compelling are King's ruminations on the craft of writing and
his mixed feelings about being a popular writer—a recurring theme in several King books and novellas. Like Thad Beaumont in *The Dark Half*, Paul
Sheldon "wrote novels of two kinds, good ones and best sellers." Sheldon
wants to write serious books that are given respect by the literary community and its critics. In one memorable scene, Annie makes him burn the

sole manuscript copy of his first literary novel, *Fast Cars*, on a charcoal grill because "It's filthy. That aside, it's also no good." In addition to becoming Paul's editor-from-hell, Annie has become his ultimate critic.

For much of his career, King—like Sheldon—was given credit for being nothing more than a highly successful commercial writer. In recent years, many critics have taken another look at the prolific writer and, as evidenced by his National Book Foundation Award, recognized that King is also an immensely talented artist. As Ted Brautigan tells eleven-year-old Bobby Garfield in the novella "Low Men in Yellow Coats" (the basis for the film *Hearts in Atlantis*), "There are books full of great writing that don't have great stories. Read sometimes for the story, Bobby. Read sometimes for the words—the language. Don't be like the play-it-safers that won't do *that*. But when you find a book that has both a good story and good words, treasure that book." Within King's body of work, there is much to treasure.

Chris Mooney is the international best-selling author of *Deviant Ways*, *World Without End*, and *Remembering Sarah*, which was nominated by the Mystery Writers of America for its Best Novel Award. *The Missing*, the first book in the Darby McCormick series (which also includes *The Dead Room*) was selected as the International Book of the Month and published in twenty-two languages. His short story, "Falling," appeared in ITW's *Thriller* anthology. He lives outside Boston with his wife and son.

86
Nelson DeMille's
THE CHARM SCHOOL (1988)

J.T. Ellison

Nelson Richard DeMille (1943–) was born in New York City. He spent three years at Hofstra University, then joined the army and attended Officer Candidate School. He was a first lieutenant in the United States Army (1966–69) and saw action as an infantry platoon leader with the First Cavalry Division in Vietnam. He was decorated with the Air Medal, Bronze Star, and the Vietnamese Cross of Gallantry. DeMille returned to the States and went back to Hofstra University, where he received his degree in political science and history. DeMille's earlier books were paperback original NYPD detective novels. Desiring more from his writing career, he decided to write a book that would command the attention of the publishing community. That novel was *By the Rivers of Babylon*, an ambitious international thriller about a team of Middle East peace envoys whose plane crashes in the desert, where the peacemakers are forced to take up arms to defend themselves against Palestinian gunmen. Published in 1978, it is still in print, as are all DeMille's succeeding novels. He holds three honorary doctorates: Doctor of Humane Letters from Hofstra University, Doctor of Literature from Long Island University, and Doctor of Humane Letters from Dowling College. His numerous thrillers, including *Cathedral*, *Word of Honor*, *The Gold Coast*, *The General's Daughter*, *Plum Island*, *The Lion's Game*, *Up Country*, *Night Fall*, *Wild Fire*, and *The Gate House*, delve into timely subjects such as germ-warfare research, war crimes, terrorist tactics, and spouse abuse.

When Nelson DeMille's *The Charm School* was published in 1988, America was still embroiled in the last vestiges of the Cold War. The U.S.S.R. remained our enemy, a tangible opponent. Although the Iron Curtain was beginning to crumble, spies on both sides ran rampant.

I was working on a presidential campaign, planning a career in public service, when I first read *The Charm School*. I lived in Washington, D.C. for fifteen years, every day driving past the monuments that are the markers of our country, the identifying features of postcards and movies. I lived inside the beltway, a transient, intense place where you were only as good as your last quote in the *Washington Post* or *Congressional Quarterly*. I worked in politics, on the Hill, on campaigns.

None of those experiences affected me as much as this book. After finishing it, I knew I needed a different path. I went to the State Department and got the paperwork I needed to take the Foreign Service exam. I decided I wanted to be a spy.

Why did *The Charm School* impact me so much? The frightening concept of a school where American POWs are forced to train Russian spies to be Americans. In a carefully hidden compound in Russia, every effort has been made to recreate an American community, where the spies are taught to feel completely at ease in American culture. The concept seemed so unreal, and yet so possible. It scared me. I wanted to do something to make sure that it could never happen in actuality.

DeMille creates a credible threat to the United States. His main characters Colonel Sam Hollis, a U.S. Air Force attaché/intelligence officer; Lisa Rhodes, a State Department liaison officer; and Seth Alevy, a CIA station chief, all working in Moscow, embody the spirit of everything that was right, and everything that was wrong, with the Cold War intelligence community. The book begins with an American tourist who drives into a restricted area and encounters a man who claims to be a U.S. pilot shot down during the Vietnam War, held captive ever since. After reporting this to the U.S. embassy, the tourist disappears.

In the subsequent investigation, Hollis and Rhodes find themselves trapped in a nightmare, and their struggle is so believable, so real, that it feels like you're reading a newspaper instead of a novel. That's what De-Mille does—he teaches. All of his novels have a deeper lesson, but it's more than that. I learned about the intelligence service from a whole different perspective, one that made me angry about political compromises. My emotions made me want to join the State Department, to become a foreign attaché. Because of this book, I wanted to help change the world.

Yes, that's idealistic. But there are passages that resonate for me, even all these years later. The most important and cynical of these involved the CIA station chief talking about his job. It always stuck in my mind. "I don't have time for moral abstractions. My job is to try to fuck the Soviets, and they respect me for it."

Yes, the language is blunt, but the message is clear. The Russians and the Americans knew the game that was being played. DeMille takes a slice of history and gives us a true and honest account of what happened behind the Iron Curtain, showing what our people faced day in and day out as they tried to end the Cold War.

The whole concept of Miss Ivanova's Charm School is terrifying and especially relevant in our current war on terror. But could it really work? Could something like this actually happen? I'm afraid the answer is yes.

Once Colonel Hollis is held captive in the school, he has a conversation with one of the American POWs, a former instructor at the school who explains the essential and existential theme of this book: "[The Charm School] took the spycraft ideal of deep cover to its ultimate realization; it assaulted the very notion of identity that all human beings took for granted."

The concept is simple: by teaching Russian spies to become Americans and slipping them into our society, the Russians could at last win the Cold War. Yet elements of the U.S. government want to keep the discovery of the Charm School a secret lest improving relations between the United States and the U.S.S.R. be compromised. The terror of DeMille's novel is not in the idea that a Charm School could be created, but that one already had been and that nothing was being done about it. Could it happen? Of course it could.

The vividness of *The Charm School*'s setting must be mentioned. Russia is, for many of us, a foreign place and was especially so when this book was written. The average American citizen wasn't taking vacations in Moscow; travel was limited to official business. The Russian people were starved—physically, emotionally, spiritually—and DeMille captures their heartache so eloquently, so perfectly, that you feel you're on the streets of Moscow.

Nelson DeMille is an author who isn't afraid to move readers toward great heights and dark abysses. A master of extended action sequences, he is also a beacon of intellectual stimulation through the thriller form, and an author whose work makes a lasting impression on the reader.

J.T. Ellison is the best-selling author of the critically acclaimed Taylor Jackson series, including *All the Pretty Girls*, *14*, *Judas Kiss*, and *The Cold Room*. A former White House staffer, she moved to Nashville, and began research on her passions: forensics and crime. She has worked extensively with the Metro Nashville Police, the FBI, and various other law enforcement organizations to research her novels. She lives with her husband and a poorly trained cat. Her short story, "Prodigal Me," appeared in the ITW-sponsored anthology, *Killer Year: Stories to Die For*.

87
Dean Koontz's
WATCHERS (1988)

Lee Thomas

Dean Koontz (1945–) is one of the most prolific and popular of contemporary American authors. In a career spanning four decades, he has published over ninety novels under his name and a variety of pseudonyms. As a senior in college, he won an *Atlantic Monthly* fiction competition and became determined to make a living from storytelling. Early on, he worked a variety of day jobs, refining his craft evenings and weekends, until his wife, Gerda, offered to support him while he pursued a writing career in earnest. His first novel, *Star Quest*, was published in 1968, and he published extensively since with as many as nine novels released in a single year. His books have been translated into thirty-eight languages and have sold 375,000,000 copies to date. Eleven of his novels rose to number one on the *New York Times* hardcover best-seller list, and fourteen of his books rose to the top spot on the paperback list. He and Gerda maintain a home in Southern California, where many of his novels are set.

Nearly two decades after the publication of his first novel, Dean Koontz released *Watchers*, which many fans and critics consider his finest book. Not only did *Watchers* successfully incorporate elements from the varied genres Koontz had written in over the years—science fiction, mystery, suspense, and even romance—but it also defined his unique place in modern storytelling, setting a standard for the wave of best-selling novels to follow, including *The Bad Place*, *Hideaway*, and *Velocity*.

    Choosing a single Koontz title to recommend is certainly a difficult task, as he has produced an uncommon breadth of work. A reader can pick up any of his novels and enjoy rich, detailed descriptions, nuanced and fully realized characterizations, and complexity of plot. But few of his books so thoroughly and effectively explore the themes for which he is known, while grabbing the reader with such an engrossing tale of suspense. Koontz himself says that while he believes he has written a few books he likes as well as *Watchers*, he's never written one he liked better.

Watchers begins with Travis Cornell, a former Delta Force soldier and widower, who takes a day trip to the foothills of the Santa Ana Mountains, a place he remembers fondly from his youth. Consumed by loneliness and depression, Travis thinks the trip will help him recapture the hope and wonder of his childhood. Along the way, he encounters a golden retriever that seems to be warning him of impending danger, and though Travis cannot see this threat, he senses it and flees with the dog. Travis and the retriever, which he later names Einstein (for its obvious intelligence), form a bond. While in the park one day, they encounter Nora Devon, a woman emotionally damaged by an abusive aunt. Einstein acts as matchmaker, eventually bringing the two lonely people together.

Travis and Nora spend the first half of the book building a relationship and working with Einstein to test the limits of his intelligence. Meanwhile, the reader is introduced to the antagonists of the piece. A Mafia hit man by the name of Vincent Nasco is dispatched to murder a group of scientists, all of whom were employed by a genetic research facility. Koontz also introduces readers to the Outsider, a genetically enhanced monstrosity that escaped the research facility (soon after Einstein made his own escape). The Outsider shares Einstein's advanced intellect, but was designed as an instrument of violence with unbridled savagery and a deep-seated loathing for the dog.

Discovering that they are targets, not only of Nasco and the Outsider, but also the U.S. government, Travis and Nora assume new identities and go into hiding. Though their ruse successfully throws their government pursuers off track, both Nasco and the Outsider find them, and a final confrontation ensues.

Watchers, like many of Koontz's novels, expresses the author's belief in the power to overcome the tragedies and obstacles of the past, particularly when one opens up emotionally and allows new relationships to form. Though both Travis Cornell and Nora Devon begin in very dark emotional territory, neither believing they can attain happiness, it is through the process of trusting, befriending, and eventually loving that they find hope, allowing them to transcend their insecurities and fears.

Additionally, Koontz celebrates the strength of the individual over acknowledged power institutions, a very common theme in his work. In

Watchers, such diverse groups as family (Nora's bitter, manipulative aunt), the Mafia, and the government are representative of these coercive institutions. Koontz puts his popular theme into concrete terms during an exchange Travis has with the intellectually enhanced golden retriever when he summarizes A *Tale of Two Cities*, saying in part, ". . . well, it's all about the importance of valuing individuals over groups, about the need to place a far greater value on one man's or woman's life than on the advancement of the masses."

Any reader with knowledge of Koontz's private life is well aware of his affinity for dogs. His belief in the fundamental loyalty, nobility, and integrity of canines is nowhere better shown than in his memorable and much-praised depiction of the golden retriever, Einstein, who maintains these admirable traits, despite having intellectually transcended his species. As such, Einstein serves as the perfect Koontz hero, suffering neither the moral ambiguity nor the internal dissonance of a human.

The lines of good and evil are clearly drawn in Koontz's novels. Heroic figures endure tragedy, and some are even martyred, but the author conveys an unerring message of right over wrong. Rarely do Koontz's characters face strictly supernatural menace. Though otherworldly events may be implied (generally the result of a villain's delusional state), often the true evils his heroes face are man made, whether they are inspired by technological, scientific, or physiological aberrations.

Vince Nasco is the quintessential Koontz villain. He suffers delusions of grandeur, believing his murders serve a higher purpose: the life energy of his victims fueling his own immortality. Nasco is ruthless, selfish, and beyond redemption, as are many of Koontz's villains. That noted, the author is far kinder in his depiction of the genetically designed monster. In fact, the Outsider serves to further point out Koontz's belief that all true evil stems from human hands. As in Mary Shelley's *Frankenstein*, Koontz imbues his man-made creation with pathos, generating understanding and sympathy for the creature. In this way, Koontz suggests a victimization of the natural order by man; the Outsider is merely an instrument of human cruelty. It cannot help its violent tendencies, but even so, by the novel's end, it acknowledges its own evil and manages redemption in a way its human counterpart, Nasco, never would.

Koontz has such a vast body of work that it's difficult to select any single novel to illustrate all he has to offer, but *Watchers* is an excellent point of entry. It's a model of what a thriller can be, intense action matched by strong emotions and insistent themes. Koontz's use of multiple genres is extraordinary and proves again that the spirit of a thriller isn't limited to any one type of book.

Lee Thomas is the Bram Stoker Award and Lambda Literary Award-winning author of the supernatural thrillers *Stained*, *Damage*, *Parish Damned*, and *The Dust of Wonderland*. His short fiction has appeared in dozens of magazines, both print and electronic, and in the anthologies A *Walk on the Darkside*, *Unspeakable Horror*, and *Inferno*, among others. Writing as Thomas Pendleton, he is the author of *Mason* and coauthor (with Stefan Petrucha) of *Wicked Dead*, a series of edgy horror novels for young adult readers. His other titles for teens, under the pseudonym Dallas Reed, include the suspense thrillers *Shimmer* and *The Calling*.

88

Katherine Neville's
THE EIGHT (1988)

Shirley Kennett

Katherine Neville (1945–) was born in St. Louis, and developed a passion for writing as a young girl, completing her first novel when she was eight. After she graduated from college, the only job she could find was in the burgeoning new computer industry. Neville became an international consultant and executive, specializing in energy, a career that took her around the world. She never stopped writing, working at it on nights and weekends. But it wasn't until she was forty that she sold her first two books and was able to quit her career and retire full time to her California tree house, free of distractions (including computers) to write full time. She poured her varied experiences into her first published book, *The Eight*, and created a multigenre story steeped in the terminology and symbolism of a chess game. The book is part historical realism, big-stakes thriller, suspense novel, puzzle mystery, cautionary political tale, conspiracy theory, and adventure quest with occult underpinnings—and all genius. *The Eight*, published in 1988, has been translated into forty languages and is a cult classic. Its innovative elements have influenced writers and delighted readers. Neville's other novels are *A Calculated Risk*, *The Magic Circle*, and *The Fire*, the sequel to *The Eight*.

Opening *The Eight* is a bit like taking Alice's hand for a trip through Lewis Carroll's Wonderland. Very little is what it seems on the surface, puzzles abound, and the game can result in losing one's head.

The novel begins in France in the 1790s. The French Revolution is on the horizon, but for two young nuns in the Abbey of Montglane, cousins Mireille and Valentine, politics seems remote. The abbess, though, sees blood and chaos coming after seizures of church properties begin.

For centuries, the abbey has hidden the pieces of the Montglane Service, a chess set said to contain mystical powers. The service was presented to Charlemagne a thousand years ago. The chessboard is a section of the abbey floor, hidden in plain sight. The pieces, heavily crusted with precious gems, are concealed in the walls.

To keep the Service safe, the nuns abandon the abbey and scatter into the world, some of them carrying chess pieces. Plunging into a radically different life in Paris, Mireille and Valentine try to adjust to rapidly changing conditions.

> Alice: I know who I was when I got up this morning, but I think
> I must have been changed several times since then.

A parallel story unfolds in the 1970s. Catherine Velis, a computer specialist, is transferred to Algiers to work for OPEC. At her farewell party, a fortune-teller gives her a warning of danger, including "On the fourth day of the fourth month, then will come the Eight." Before Catherine leaves, she reluctantly agrees to search for pieces of a jeweled chess set on behalf of a collector. At least, that's the cover story—she's been convinced by a close friend that she has a major role to play concerning the Montglane Service.

The fortune-teller's dire prediction begins a series of references to April 4th, Catherine's birthday (and Katherine Neville's). The month and day are 4 + 4 = 8. On its side, the numeral eight is the symbol for infinity ∞. Standing upright, it is a representation of the double-helical structure of DNA. In the novel, it represents universal connectedness and timelessness. The chess pieces and the board embody ∞ because they contain a coded formula for immortality: the Elixir of Life, the ultimate goal of alchemy.

Alternating between the two timelines, the women's stories weave together like two ribbons forming the number eight, a cycle endlessly repeating. Semiotics, the study of signs and symbols, is a tool that allows the reader to take part in the puzzle solving. High adventure, suspense, misdirection, violence, sex—it's all here.

> The Gryphon: The adventures first . . . explanations take such
> a dreadful time.

Mireille and Catherine both end up in Algiers, separated by roughly 180 years. Mireille takes up her role as Black Queen and decodes the formula for the Elixir of Life. Catherine treks through the desert, enters hidden caves, and has other adventures as she unravels the puzzles surrounding the Service. Finally she realizes that she is to be the next Black Queen.

> Alice: But it's no use going back to yesterday, because I was a
> different person then.

Katherine Neville blended several writing techniques in a book that is truly greater than the sum of its parts. Dual timelines, misdirection, suspense, the incorporation of historical figures, powerful female leads, a quest format, and a grand theme played out over centuries are brilliantly combined.

Nearly every chapter ends with a cliffhanger. While *The Eight* isn't the first to use cliffhangers (think of the 1914 movie serial *The Perils of Pauline* or Thomas Hardy's serial novel *A Pair of Blue Eyes* in 1873), they're particularly effective in this book. The end of a chapter not only leaves a character or situation at a suspenseful point, it also vaults the reader from one timeline to the other when the page is turned.

Neville portrays a number of historical figures in the book, among them Robespierre, Bach, Catherine the Great, Marat, Napoleon, Isaac Newton, Benjamin Franklin, and Muammar Khaddafi. These people interact with the book's characters in plausible ways, creating an increased sense of believability. A particularly skillful interweaving occurs with Jean-Paul Marat, murdered in real life by Charlotte Corday in 1793. In Neville's book, Marat is stabbed to death by Mireille, but Corday, who'd been planning the same crime, comes to Mireille in prison. The two women exchange clothing, and Mireille walks free. Corday goes to the guillotine not for having done the deed but as a willing sacrifice.

Mireille and Catherine are strong heroines, solving the puzzles and dealing with violence and dangerous journeys. They are the Black Queens, and in chess, the queen is the most powerful piece. While the capture of the king ends the game, the king is weak and needs protection by the queen and the other pieces. No man comes to the rescue of Mireille or Catherine, who power through quests with the same flare and audacity Indiana Jones displays. Neville established that women could hold their own in adventure tales, as Sue Grafton and Sara Paretsky had done a few years earlier in the crime-solving field.

The Eight had a considerable effect on thrillers, likely paving the way for Dan Brown's *The Da Vinci Code* published fifteen years later. Neville's influence and the popularity of Brown's book led other authors to write quest-driven thrillers with historical backgrounds, notably William Dietrich's *Napoleon's Pyramids* and Steve Berry's *The Templar Legacy*.

> Alice: When I get home I shall write a book about this
> place. . . . if I ever do get home.

Shirley Kennett's life parallels Katherine Neville's to some extent. Kennett was born in St. Louis, wrote her first short story at the age of eight, and studied computer science. She rose from programmer to top-level manager in the field of hospital systems, and then became an independent computer consultant in clinical applications. In her forties, Kennett returned to her first passion, writing. She published a series of techno-thrillers (*Time of Death* and *Gray Matter*, among them) about a female computer expert, PJ Gray, who uses virtual reality to recreate homicides and then enters the simulations for harrowing experiences that provide insight into the killer's mind. As Dakota Banks, Kennett also publishes quest thrillers with a paranormal twist (*Dark Time*).

89
Peter Straub's
KOKO (1988)

Hank Wagner

After writing two literary novels in the mid-1970s (*Marriages* and *Under Venus*), Peter Straub (1943–) composed *Julia*, his first novel of the supernatural, in 1976, and his second, *If You Could See Me Now*, in 1977. He came to prominence in the genre, however, with his fifth novel, *Ghost Story*, in 1979. Other horror novels followed, including *Floating Dragon*, as well as his collaborations with kindred spirit Stephen King: *The Talisman* and *Black House*. Departing from supernatural themes, Straub published *Koko* in 1988, which he followed with *Mystery*, *The Throat*, and *The Hellfire Club*. His other thrillers include *Mr. X.*, *lost boy lost girl*, and *In the Night Room*. Straub edited the Library of America volume *H. P. Lovecraft: Tales*, the "New Wave Fabulists" issue of *Conjunctions* magazine, and the anthology *Poe's Children*. He also published several volumes of poetry, the most notable being the collection, *Leeson Park and Belsize Square: Poems 1970–1975*. Straub's talent has been recognized many times over, earning him numerous World Fantasy, British Fantasy, International Horror Guild, and HWA Bram Stoker awards, as well a Lifetime Achievement Award from the Horror Writers Association, proving once again that thrillers span many genres.

Few would deny that the Vietnam War indelibly imprinted itself on the psyches of those who came of age in the 1960s, both those who traveled to that far-off land and those who stayed home. Author Jack Ketchum once wrote, "There's nobody in my generation of U.S. citizens who doesn't know somebody—or for that matter hasn't lost somebody—in that goddamn war. And I doubt there's a writer of my generation who hasn't wanted to address the subject in one way or another."

Peter Straub addresses that subject head-on in the meticulously researched *Koko*, along with one other theme that preoccupied him over the years: the majestic power of stories, their effect on their tellers and

listeners, their ability to define and redefine individual realities and histories, and their effectiveness in probing the truth of any situation. As one
of his characters notes, "Deep down, the things that happened to you never
stop happening." Straub's basic underlying point seems simple but is actually very complex: we are all the sum of our experiences, bad and good.
When the bad dramatically outweigh the good, our essence can be perverted. We all try to cope, but some of us are pushed too far, as is the case
with Straub's title character in Koko. Then, nightmare becomes reality.

For the author, Koko represented a rigorous, arduous experiment with
style, transparency, and precision. It also represented an exploration of horror through the vehicle of realism, rather than through the fantastic, as he
had done in previous works. For readers, it's a vivid, disquieting sojourn, a
visceral, engaging, painstakingly crafted thriller that disturbs and excites.

In Koko, the immediate journey begins in 1982 at the Vietnam War
Memorial in Washington D.C., as several veterans gather at the monu-
ment ostensibly to pay tribute to their fallen comrades. But they are actually assembling for another reason. A string of brutal murders committed
by a killer who leaves a playing card signed "Koko" on his victims leads
them to conclude that one of their fellows is responsible. As only they
have put the clues together, only they can stop him. For this reason, and
personal reasons of their own, comrades Michael Poole, Conor Linklater,
and Harry Beevers embark on a trip to the Far East in search of writer Tim
Underhill. Their mission takes them from Bangkok to Singapore to New
York, and finally to Milwaukee, where they finally uncover the real narrative thread that has been driving events, a story so bleak and sordid it
makes the battle-hardened veterans shiver in fear and sympathy.

The shared story of their experiences in Vietnam binds these men together, a story whose end only they are capable of writing, one only they
are capable of completely understanding. It's a story about staring into the
abyss, about exploring the dark recesses of the human mind and behavior
(Straub is constantly leading his characters into and out of caves and cave-
like structures, playing on the reader's instinctive fear of the dark and
closed, tight spaces). It's a story about monsters, the human kind who lose
their way. It's a story about ghosts, in the sense that memories haunt all the
participants. It's a horror story, not in the supernatural sense (although
there are supernatural elements to be found), but in the sense that it chronicles man's irrational excesses, his often inhuman behavior toward his fellow man. And, most importantly, from the thriller point of view, it's a

desperate race against time, as Koko has embarked on a killing spree that will not cease anytime soon unless his former comrades intervene.

Koko was a big hit, joining (significantly in hindsight) *The Silence of the Lambs* on the *New York Times* best-seller list, for *Koko*, like Thomas Harris's smash hit, signaled the beginning of a new era in thriller fiction, that of the serial killer as enigmatic antihero. Like Hannibal Lecter, Koko is frightening because he often seems superhuman, blessed with almost supernatural gifts that enable him to stalk and dispatch his prey, all the while eluding discovery. It was the dawning of the age of a new bogeyman, one who might be standing next to you in line at the supermarket, or sitting across the table from you at dinner.

As was the case with Harris, Straub had not yet finished wringing the last ounce of story value from his situations and characters, but unlike Harris, Straub's subsequent forays into this strange landscape proved just as intriguing as their predecessor. Like the classic jazz artists he favors, Straub, a remarkably deft and versatile writer, found numerous and creative ways to riff on the situations he set up in *Koko*, penning two additional novels (*Mystery* and *The Throat*) in what came to be known as his Blue Rose trilogy, and writing several striking short stories that gave insight into the characters featured therein (including "Blue Rose," "The Juniper Tree," "The Ghost Village," and "Bunny Makes Good Bread"). Tim Underhill became a sort of doppelgänger/colleague of Straub, appearing in two of the author's non-Blue Rose works, *lost boy lost girl* and *In the Night Room*. As did *Koko*, each successive work, in its own way, continued to probe what Joseph Conrad labeled "the heart of darkness" or, as his character Kurtz said, "The horror."

Hank Wagner lives in northwestern New Jersey with his wife and four daughters. Hank's reviews and interviews have appeared in *Jazz Improv*, *Mystery Scene*, *Cemetery Dance*, *Hellnotes*, *Dead Reckonings*, *Nova Express*, and *The New York Review of Science Fiction*. Besides being coeditor of *Thrillers: 100 Must-Reads*, Wagner is a coauthor of *The Complete Stephen King Universe* and *Prince of Stories: The Many Worlds of Neil Gaiman*. He is currently at work on *The Repairman Jack Companion*, a book about F. Paul Wilson's popular series character.

90
John Grisham's
THE FIRM (1991)

M. Diane Vogt

In 1991, an explosive new talent conquered the best-seller lists, reinventing the legal thriller. *The Firm* was Mississippi small-town lawyer John Grisham's (1955–) second novel. In its wake, Grisham's books, including legal thrillers, nonfiction, and other novels, have sold more than 235 million copies worldwide. Prior to *The Firm*, Grisham spent ten years in his first career as a small-town lawyer and Mississippi legislator. The passion to write his first novel, *A Time to Kill*, was ignited by an incident he witnessed while waiting his turn in court. The disturbing testimony of a twelve-year-old rape victim made him imagine the consequences if the victim's father had killed her assailants. That first novel was published by a small press and had a printing of five thousand copies. Grisham then began writing *The Firm*, combining Faust's mythical devil deal with high-octane David vs. Goliath, an unrivaled combination that became his forte. Grisham's other thrillers include *The Pelican Brief* and *The Client*, two of his many books that were adapted into movies.

Ten years after the unlikely anthropology professor Indiana Jones defeated the Nazis with a lot of help from God (and considerable suspension of disbelief), rookie tax lawyer cum action hero Mitch McDeere spectacularly defeated modern-day Mafia and government manipulators, using only his wits and his Harvard law degree.

Certainly lawyers had been inspirational literary heroes, triumphant in mythic David and Goliath battles before *The Firm* was published in 1991. But this was no courtroom drama and McDeere was not our father's Perry Mason or even Scott Turow's worthy but flawed *Presumed Innocent* (1987) prosecutor, Rusty Sabich. Rather, *The Firm* dramatizes a minimum of lawyering and instead emphasizes McDeere's race to save himself before his government or his employer terminate his life.

The Firm captures the despair of gray-flannel-suited lawyers who felt shackled by golden handcuffs to their lavish lifestyles. Its emblematic cover depicted an attorney clutching a briefcase while being manipulated by the strings of a puppeteer. The book energized the legal thriller, which heretofore every working lawyer knew was an oxymoron on steroids. Grisham's ability to make the genre exciting and suspenseful by featuring larger-than-life lawyer heroes propelled The Firm and Grisham to the top of the charts where he has remained for almost two decades.

At the end of the 1980s, a decade of conspicuous consumption and excessive spending, workaholism reigned in all sectors of the economy. Lawyers were commanding salaries beyond their wildest dreams. Megafirms launched, the number of lawyers skyrocketed, and the competition to hire the best and the brightest intensified. What was once a genteel, collegiate, underpaid profession became a cold, profit-driven business supported by billable time.

Against this backdrop, The Firm opens with the hazing ritual all law students must endure: the first law job interview. The uninitiated reader might assume job interviews lack even quiet drama, let alone thrills. Yet, a typical law student feels more nausea during the process than panicked passengers escaping the half-submerged Titanic. Following years of hefty debt accumulation and daily Socratic inquisitions during which students consume thousand-page casebooks digested and regurgitated into a three-hour essay exam upon which the entire grade for the course and subsequent employment depend, exhausted students compete for work. Making the best choice is yet another angst-producing hurdle. The tension of the interview process lasts most of the fall and into the spring of the final year.

More determined, better credentialed, desperately motivated by personal struggles, and closer to the brink of financial ruin is Grisham's Mitch McDeere. Third in his class at Harvard, Mitch receives offers from prestigious firms in New York and Chicago. But when he's seduced by an elite Memphis law firm's extravagant offer, he proves his mettle by interrogating the hiring partner. He's assured that no lawyer has ever voluntarily resigned from the firm.

Wanting to believe the firm is that good, Mitch decides he has no choice; he must take the lavish offer. After all, like all law students on the brink of licensure, he is confident that he can handle whatever comes his way. But his bravado soon evaporates—the coming challenges far exceed his practical risk analysis. Early on, every reader knows the job is not what it seems, but like Mitch, they're already hooked.

Before *The Firm*, lawyer readers had already made the same bargain Mitch did. They knew that despite the astronomical salary, new BMW, low-interest home mortgage, repaid student loans, and beyond-the-call support in passing the dreaded bar exam, the job would be hell on earth. And so it is with Mitch.

What follows is a brief period of calm before he realizes that the limitless job he's accepted with the Mafia-controlled firm can have only one possible outcome. Like his colleagues, he is literally tethered to the firm. He will work until death.

Grisham crafts his story expertly. Readers fear that Goliath will win and that Mitch will either conform to the firm's policies or die. But despite the forces opposing him, Mitch McDeere is not your average David, as we've suspected from the outset. The Mafia and the FBI are no match for him.

Lawyers can be heroes, too, Grisham reminds us, not just in *The Firm*, but in each of his many books about the legal profession that followed. In Grisham's world, attorneys are a force to be reckoned with. They lead lives not of quiet desperation, but of noisy, active, responsible accomplishment in the face of powerful opposition. The practice of law, at least on the page, has never been the same since Grisham's debut.

M. Diane Vogt was an associate and a partner in a large Detroit law firm where she and her colleagues were living Mitch McDeere's Faustian bargain themselves when *Presumed Innocent* ignited and later *The Firm* inflamed her passion to write lawyer-hero stories of her own. One of the country's top attorneys for more than twenty-nine years, Diane is the author of several novels featuring Judge Wilhelmina Carson (*Silicone Solution*, *Justice Denied*, *Gasparilla Gold*, and *Six Bills*) as well as two nonfiction titles, a book of crime puzzles, short stories, book reviews, and countless nonfiction articles. Her short story, "Surviving Toronto," appeared in ITW's *Thriller* anthology.

91

R.L. Stine's

SILENT NIGHT (1991)

Jon Land

"My job," says R.L. Stine (1943–), "is to make kids laugh and give them the CREEPS!" Toward that end, Stine has become one of the best selling authors of all time. Never a great student, he found an old typewriter in his attic at the age of nine, and his career began, literally, the next day with the penning of stories and joke books. But it wasn't until 1989, when he created the *Fear Street* series, that the world discovered Stine's work. *Fear Street* went on to become the best-selling young adult book series in history and was followed by the *Goosebumps* series in 1992. Recently, he developed two new series, *Rotten School* and *Goosebumps Horrorland*. In 2007, the International Thriller Writers organization gave him its Silver Bullet award.

"The burgeoning interest in literature for teenagers took a giant leap forward when government money became available to libraries in the 1960s under Lyndon Johnson's presidency," writes K.L. Going in *Writing and Selling the YA Novel*.

If that era didn't mark the official beginning of young adult literature, it came close enough, giving birth to works by S. E. Hinton, Paul Zindel, and, in the 1970s, Judy Blume. Going credits these and other authors, "who consistently wrote amazing, literary novels through these decades," with introducing scores of young readers to fiction. But it took a bit more time for the thriller form to make its way into young adult literature. Christopher Pike and Robert Cormier started that ball rolling, but in 1989, it was R.L. Stine, who turned the ball into a steamroller, defining the YA thriller for generations while introducing millions of teenagers to the genre.

What's next? Riva wondered with a cold shudder. What's next?

That question forms the heart of *Silent Night* and pretty much all one hundred-plus thrillers by R.L. Stine that between them have sold over 350 million copies. And wanting to know the answer to it is what has kept young adults turning the pages for decades. For millions of them, R.L. Stine's *Fear Street* series represents their first exposure to a genre with which they ultimately fell in love.

Silent Night is typical of the structure found in all of them, distinguished by its consistency of theme across the gamut of Stine's prolific bibliography. A young protagonist, in this case seventeen-year-old Reva Dalby, finds herself embroiled in a web of her own deception and deceit after she lands jobs for a number of her friends at her father's Macy's-like department store for the Christmas rush. Reva is self-centered and bitingly cruel, the residue of her mother's death and her mostly absent father. The book opens with her disinterestedly working behind a cosmetics counter. She's smoothing her own lipstick into place when a sharp pain strikes her and she tastes blood. Reva realizes in horror that someone has stuck part of a razor blade into her lipstick and she's just sliced her own lip.

Sounds like something more suitable for Robert Bloch's *Psycho* or a scene from an early Brian De Palma movie. *Silent Night*, like virtually all of the entries in the voluminous *Fear Street* series, succeeds by confronting its young protagonists with adult problems they must solve for themselves. The journey is never direct and obstacles are everywhere along the way. But the journey is also one steeped in self-discovery, the protagonists becoming different people than when he or she began.

In *Silent Night*, Reva's various mechanizations and manipulations have tragic consequences for her friends and estranged cousin Pam. The ending, though, provides hope that she has at last learned her lesson.

I feel so warm, Reva thought, so light, as if a layer of ice had melted away from me. If I hadn't been so cold, so bottled up, so hateful, maybe none of this would have happened. What a shame such horrors had to take place before I could feel again.

A shame for her, perhaps, but not for the readers. Because the moral dilemma Reva must confront in her evolution as a character forms the heart of *Silent Night*. Stine rotates his chapters among varying points of view, mostly Reva's and her cousin Pam's. This has the effect of giving us not just Reva's conniving, twisted actions, but also the ultimate upshot of those actions, leading to both death and incarceration. The answers aren't easy. Redemption comes with a price.

Contemporary adult thrillers are no different. The heroes that keep us reading late into the night are often tortured figures haunted by pasts that define their quests for redemption. And for many the road to understanding these heroes was paved by R.L. Stine. It's not hard to make the argument that the most successful thriller writers of today have survived, even thrived, by reverting to or reinventing, a structure to which their current audience was introduced by Stine.

Silent Night builds to a climax inside a cavernous department store on Christmas Eve. The store is closed and deserted, leaving Reva to confront her nemesis and her own moral failings. This comes in the aftermath of a botched robbery of the store by some friends for whom she secured jobs, with tragic consequences.

"You can't do this to people, Reva!" a boy she scorned accuses at one point.

In point of fact, she already has, but it's doubtful she'll do so again. She has succeeded in saving, at least salvaging, her own world. And, ultimately, that is what all thrillers are about.

"How do teenagers today view books?" Going asks in *Writing and Selling the YA Novel.* "And are we doing all we can to keep them reading?"

Well, R.L. Stine certainly is. Between the time I write this essay and when it's published, another ten million or so of his books will be sold to young people who will eventually turn to adult thrillers to keep them reading into the dark hours of the morning when the child in us all is free to run wild.

Jon Land is the author of twenty-five thrillers, fifteen of which have been national best sellers, including *The Seven Sins: The Tyrant Ascending.* He is published in over fifty countries. His latest series hero, female Texas Ranger Caitlin Strong, is featured in *Strong Enough to Die* and *Strong Justice.* Jon graduated from Brown University in 1979 Phi Beta Kappa and magna cum laude. He continues his association with Brown as alumni advisor to the Greek System and president of the Brown Faculty Club. He is an associate member of the Unites States Special Forces, volunteers frequently in schools to help young people learn to enjoy the process of writing, and served as Vice President of Marketing for the International Thriller Writers organization. He lives in Providence, Rhode Island.

92

James Patterson's
ALONG CAME A SPIDER (1992)

Mary SanGiovanni

James Patterson (1947–) has sold over 150 million copies of his books worldwide. He received a B.A. from Manhattan College and a master's degree from Vanderbilt University. After the huge success of *Along Came a Spider*, he resigned his chairmanship of the J. Walter Thompson advertising agency, and to date has gone on to write more than fourteen books in the Alex Cross series, eight in the *Women's Murder Club* series, five in the *Maximum Ride* series, and many others. His advertising expertise contributed new approaches that helped authors promote their fiction. His work has been adapted numerous times into movies and television programs. He is the recipient of the Edgar Best First Novel Award (*The Thomas Berryman Number*, 1976), the BCA Mystery Guild's Thriller of the Year Award, and ITW's ThrillerMaster Award. He holds the *New York Times* best-seller record with, so far, more than forty best-selling titles and nineteen consecutive #1 *New York Times* hardcovers.

In an interview, James Patterson once remarked that all his books are "about nightmares, not literal nightmares, but nightmares . . . about the world." His idea for his first thriller, *Along Came a Spider*, occurred to him after pondering the Lindbergh kidnapping and its sensational media coverage. At its root, both that case and the novel concern a missing child— and the nightmare that such a crime surely is to parents and teachers, to the child herself, and to all the hardworking law enforcement officials who spend tireless nights and thankless days racing against time and insanity and uncertainty to save the life of an innocent. What deepens the horror of the situation is the not knowing, the possibility of never knowing, of having no closure.

This novel pits a larger-than-life murderer and child kidnapper, someone so evil that he is deliciously hateful, against a hero, a single father, and protector of children, whose heroism is also larger than life. Alex Cross, a thirty-something police detective and forensic psychologist, is handsome, strong, fit, incredibly smart, indefatigably dedicated, and firm in his convictions of right and wrong. He generously gives back to his community, working the local soup kitchen, and giving pro bono counseling to those who need it. He chooses to live in the rougher part of Washington, D.C.'s, outskirts, even though he doesn't need to, even though so many neighbors and acquaintances distrust the police. Nonetheless, he still gets angry and loses his temper. He is vulnerable when it comes to his two young children, whom he loves very much, his grandmother, who has raised him since he was a young boy, and a certain sense of loneliness since the death of his wife.

Cross is often stymied by the red tape that is laid in his path by the officials above him, and he is acutely aware that his being African-American makes an impact, usually negative, on both his opportunities and his business and personal relationships. Cross is someone who has pulled himself up in his community, has achieved an education, financial security, and a career position that he still feels he has to fight to prove he earned.

I think what makes Cross likeable to the reader, and a good hero model for the thriller writer, is that careful balance in characterization—the reader does not put Cross on a pedestal or find him too conveniently superhuman because of his strengths, and is not put off by his flaws or insecurities. The first-person insight into Cross's thoughts and feelings allows readers to be inside his head, to be there with him for his victories and frustrations, his sympathies and pains and the uncomplicated love he shares with his family. Further, as the books progress, Alex Cross develops, grows, changes as a person—and readers develop and learn and grow alongside him.

In *Along Came a Spider*, Patterson isn't afraid to fully explore race issues, class issues, and family issues. He isn't afraid to hurt his characters. He isn't afraid to let them snap, or let them cry, or let them drink themselves into a hangover. And he isn't afraid to delve into the sinister meat of the criminal mind and really demonstrate the ugliness of its murderous rage. Patterson's characters are boldly, nakedly real. And they live in a world as scary and dangerous as the one just beyond our newspapers. We, as readers—as escapists, maybe—want someone to fix it, or at least to even things out. Regardless of race, economic class, or home situation, readers can't help but feel Alex Cross is one of our own, and one that we are relieved to have on the case, keeping at least our fictional world outside a little safer.

What also makes *Along Came a Spider* successful is the pace of the story. Patterson's understanding of the nature of the page-turner has allowed him to develop a winning structure for plot and atmosphere. He knows what the reader wants and what the reader will make time for. His language is intelligent but accessible and gives a clear, distinct picture of the scene and Cross's place in it. The chapters are short, and more often than not, end in cliffhangers. The action is quick and fluid. The characters are richly unique in their personalities and easy to identify and remember. There are twists and turns, red herrings, plot teases that make readers keep turning pages. Pop culture references put readers in a "real" and contemporary world.

The true mark of a magician is to make the magic look easy and effortless. And the mark of a good thriller is to make readers forget that they are reading a story, and instead to convince them that they are experiencing it, *living* it. *Along Came a Spider* delivers that kind of power and immediacy. For many subsequent thriller writers, it has been a textbook.

Mary SanGiovanni is the author of the Bram Stoker nominated *The Hollower* and its sequel, *Found You*. Mary's short fiction has appeared in periodicals, online magazines, and anthologies (*Dark Territories*) since 2002, and has been collected in her book *Under Cover of Night*. She has a master's in writing popular fiction from Seton Hill University. She lives in northern New Jersey with her son and is currently at work on a new supernatural thriller.

93

Stephen Hunter's
POINT OF IMPACT (1993)

Christopher Rice

Stephen Hunter (1946–) is one of only three film critics to have won the Pulitzer Prize for Criticism, and the author of multiple *New York Times* best-selling novels. Most of his novels are linked by the characters of Bob Lee Swagger, a former marine sniper first introduced in *Point of Impact*, and his father Earl Swagger, both war heroes from Vietnam and World War II respectively. His other novels include *Dirty White Boys, Black Light, Time to Hunt, Pale Horse Coming, Night of Thunder* and *I, Sniper*. In 2008, he retired as chief film critic for the *Washington Post*. That same year, he told an interviewer, "I have no idea how to write a book without violence in it." As a young man, he graduated from Northwestern University with a degree in journalism before spending two years in the U.S. Army.

I got the chance to meet novelist and distinguished film critic Stephen Hunter at a literary festival in Fort Lauderdale, where we were both featured guests. He seemed mildly taken aback by the high praise I heaped on his immensely popular novel, *Point of Impact*. It's possible he thought my wild affection for his hero Bob Lee Swagger was out of character; my own books are noted for their portrayals of young people in various states of sexual anguish, characters who wouldn't have the slightest idea how to handle any of the numerous rifles Hunter places at the center of his acclaimed fiction. Or maybe, just like "Bob the Nailer," he was accustomed to being approached by those who had a darker agenda at work beneath their compliments.

Published in 1993, *Point of Impact* contained all the essential elements of a post-Cold War thriller in which monolithic villains are replaced by ferocious, covert splinter groups with origins that are unnervingly close to home. There is a nomadic battle-scarred hero caught in a vast conspiracy that results in multiple sequences of dizzying gunplay. There is a diabolical private security firm called RamDyne—as effective a villain in the Blackwater days of 2008 as it was when the book was first published.

The plot in a nutshell: Bob Lee Swagger, a master sniper from the Vietnam era, is recruited by a shadowy private security contractor to determine the methodology an infamous and elusive Russian sniper might use to assassinate the president of the United States. The catch? The Russian would-be assassin is the same sniper believed to be responsible for the death of Swagger's beloved friend and spotter back in Vietnam. And the twist? Swagger isn't just being asked to figure out how the assassination will take place; he's being set up to take the fall for it, which he doesn't realize until one of his new employers has put a bullet in his chest and he's on the run from every law enforcement agency in the United States.

But to reduce *Point of Impact* to the machinations of its plot—as was done by the makers of the disappointing film adaptation, *Shooter*, starring Mark Wahlberg—is to miss its singular achievement in the landscape of contemporary action-driven thrillers. That achievement is the effortless manner in which Hunter peoples the intricate architecture of his story with robust, utterly human characters. (As someone who grew up in the Deep South, I found Bob Lee Swagger's Arkansas manner to be so convincing that I still have trouble believing his creator hails from Missouri.) Furthermore, in a story ripe with gunplay and government intrigue, Hunter deploys an assured narrative voice that can be as folksy and intimate as Stephen King's.

Too often in the thriller world, critics and readers draw a line between stories that are long on plot and those that go deep into their characters. For writers, this is about fear, pure and simple. If the characters show too much of themselves, if they allow themselves the emotional outpourings that Hunter's characters do, then the reader might slow down long enough to take an unforgiving magnifying glass to the high-concept plot the writer has been building for many pages. But Hunter either doesn't suffer from those fears, or he has successfully overcome them.

A fine example comes in the middle of the novel, when a desperate Bob Lee Swagger turns to the widow of his former spotter for help, and in a speech that goes on for almost a full page, she explains to him, and to us, the bewildering position that a hero like him occupies in American culture.

> You see, you make it terrible for us . . . For the women. Because normal men want to be like you, they learn about you from movie versions of you, and they try for that same laconic

spirit, that Hemingway stoicism. They manufacture themselves in your image but they don't have the guts to bring it off. So they exile themselves from us, pretending to be you and to have your power, and we can never reach them.

What could have been a stock "damaged-woman-helps-wounded-hero scene" is elevated by a moment of emotive, postmodern sophistication. Hunter treats his human characters as seriously as he treats his guns, and the passion with which he does so distinguishes *Point of Impact* from countless other thrillers in which the author displays a cold, mechanical allegiance to the weapons and cutting-edge technology his characters interact with like mindless robots.

In 2003, when Stephen Hunter became one of only three film critics in history to win the Pulitzer Prize for Criticism, the jury wrote, "He is forever suggesting that art can be a good, lusty, happy thing." Such praise could be applied just as easily to Hunter's novels. As both a storyteller and a critic, Stephen Hunter has the courage to employ passion and conviction in a genre often defined by hard-boiled irony or clinical detachment; *Point of Impact* is fine evidence of his bravery and his skill.

At age thirty, Christopher Rice is the author of four *New York Times* best sellers. In 2008, he was elected president of the Lambda Literary Foundation, which seeks to increase the visibility of lesbian, gay, bisexual, and transgender writers. (His second novel, *The Snow Garden*, received a Lambda Literary Award in 2002.) He is also a contributing columnist for *The Advocate*. His additional novels include A *Density of Souls*, *Light Before Day*, and the critically acclaimed, *Blind Fall*. He is the son of best-selling novelist, Anne Rice, and the award-winning poet, Stan Rice.

94
John Lescroart's
THE 13th JUROR (1994)
Karna Small Bodman

John Lescroart (1948–) performed songs as Johnny Capo of Johnny Capo and his Real Good Band at clubs and honky-tonks in San Francisco, but his real passion was writing. In 1978, when he finished his first novel, *Sunburn*, he sent it to his old high school English teacher who didn't like it and simply said, "You should write a different book." Then the teacher's wife found the manuscript on the bedside table, read it, and made the suggestion, "You should enter it for a literary award." "That's ridiculous," came the stunned response. She submitted it for him, and out of 280 entries, it won the Joseph Henry Jackson Award given by the San Francisco Foundation. The experience changed Lescroart's life. He quit the musical gigs, took on a succession of day jobs—legal secretary, fund-raiser, bartender at the Little Shamrock bar in San Francisco—and began to write novels. Five were published, but as Lescroart puts it, "There was no commercial success." Then another life-changing experience occurred in 1989 when he went body surfing in contaminated water off Seal Beach in Los Angeles. The next day, as he suffered from a high fever, a doctor told him he had spinal meningitis and had two hours to live. He went into a coma for eleven days. When he came out of it, he made the decision to change his life completely and write full time. Since those fateful days, John Lescroart has published more than twenty books. The majority featured young attorney, Dismas Hardy, and firmly established this author as a master of the legal thriller. His work has been translated into sixteen languages in over seventy-five countries.

"I'm a justice freak," Lescroart tells an interviewer. Though never having attended law school, he worked for many law firms, typed briefs and pleadings, and embedded his extensive legal research into the Dismas Hardy series. The "break-out" novel featuring this character along with Abe

Glitsky, the San Francisco homicide detective, was *The 13th Juror*, which changed the paradigm for legal thrillers.

In the story, Lescroart took a current social issue, battered woman syndrome, and created a character, Jennifer Witt, who was equal parts sympathetic and maddeningly rigid in her denial that she fit the mold. In 1990s San Francisco, the issue of "burning bed cases" in which a wife who had been beaten physically and psychologically by her husband kills him was becoming news at the Hall of Justice. Lescroart decided to make it headline news. Nobody had written a novel about it before. Many of the victims of such abuse often denied it ever took place, fearful not only of reprisals by their husbands but also of the stigma of shame, of being seen as weak.

When Jennifer Witt's abusive husband and son are murdered, she becomes the prime suspect and hires well-known San Francisco defense attorney, David Freeman, to defend her. He brings along young lawyer, Dismas Hardy, as an associate assigned to handle the penalty phase of the trial, pleading for life in prison instead of execution in the event that a jury were to find her guilty. But Jennifer maintains her innocence and refuses to allow her attorneys to use battered woman syndrome as a defense. After all, by using that defense, she would in effect be admitting that she committed the murders, even if such a defense offered mitigating circumstances.

The reader can see a few similarities between *The 13th Juror* and some traditional lawyer stories where the older seasoned defense attorney begins the trial without enough evidence to help his client and relies increasingly on a younger associate. But in those traditional approaches, the private lives of the older attorney and his younger counterpart are seldom examined.

In Lescroart's stories, however, private lives matter as much as the courtroom drama. As the trial comes to dominate Hardy's life, *The 13th Juror* emphasizes what happens to his marriage and his relationship to his children. It also dramatizes his strained friendship with former beat cop, Abe Glitsky, who can help Hardy figure out the guilt or innocence of his client but isn't certain that he should try.

In many of the legal thrillers written before *The 13th Juror*, including John Grisham's *The Firm*, the reader wasn't treated to the kind of action that Lescroart introduced into the genre. Here, he puts Dismas Hardy in personal jeopardy in a number of places and puts him in conflict with Jennifer Witt's brother and father who display streaks of violence. Also, the author deftly weaves in Jennifer's history, describing how she grew up in an abusive family and showing its impact on her current behavior. Trying to identify other potential killers, the young attorney tracks down the victim's shady colleagues who may have had a motive to commit the crime. But in this quest, young Hardy becomes a target himself, or at least he believes he is.

Lescroart first chose the title, *One for the Money*. But his editor rejected that, and in a strange twist, another author, Janet Evanovich, used that title for the first book in a series that came out at the same time, launching her successful career. The final choice of a title for this book refers to a unique wrinkle in the law that allows a judge alone, acting as the 13th juror, to overturn a conviction. This fact coupled with the battered woman syndrome defense became the basis for this important novel.

By taking a sensitive social issue and weaving it into an action-packed legal story, Lescroart has created a special niche for his books and developed a devoted following. He specializes in compelling thrillers with a distinct mix of fast pace, controversial topics, and compelling characters. His close friend, Al Giannini who is a prosecutor of violent crimes in the San Francisco Bay area, puts it this way: "John uses the backdrop of the criminal justice system as a laboratory and crucible to get into the heads of the vivid people he creates."

Karna Small Bodman was on the air for fifteen years as a TV news anchor and reporter in San Francisco, Los Angeles, and Washington, D.C. She then served for six years in the Reagan White House, first as deputy press secretary and later as senior director of the National Security Council. When she left, she was the highest-ranking woman on the White House staff. Now she weaves many of her experiences into her political thrillers. Each focuses on a national security issue as well as a different area of the world while featuring many of the same characters. Her first novel, *Checkmate*, came out in 2007, *Gambit* in 2008 (featured on *The Today Show*), and *Final Finesse* in 2009. She is currently working on her fourth book, *Castle Bravo*.

95
Sandra Brown's
THE WITNESS (1995)

Deborah LeBlanc

Staggeringly prolific, Sandra Brown (1948–) arguably perfected a new genre by persistently pushing past the boundaries of formulaic romance novels. In 1979, after losing her job as a Dallas television personality, Brown decided to give writing a try. Arming herself with multiple romance novels and writing books, she set up a typewriter on a card table in a spare bedroom and, with two toddlers underfoot, wrote her first novel. With *Love's Encore* (1981), Brown began her long career, sometimes writing under different pseudonyms. Her first nom de plume was Rachel Ryan, a name created from the first names of her children. After beginning as a romance author, Brown, a former model, eventually focused on a new genre pioneered by one of her idols, Evelyn Anthony, a genre that combined romantic and thriller elements and came to be known as romantic suspense. Her numerous *New York Times* #1 bestsellers include *Unspeakable*, *The Alibi*, *The Switch*, *Chill Factor*, and *Ricochet*. Because of the expert way she combines elements, she was fittingly a recipient of the International Thriller Writers Thriller Master Award and the Romance Writers of America Lifetime Achievement Award.

As Sandra Brown's clout in the publishing industry grew, she fought against stereotypes, insisting that her publishers drop the heaving-bosom, bulging-biceps covers on her books. Those images were typical of the romance fiction she once wrote but were no longer appropriate to her work. She was now adding more intricate subplots, suspense, and even unhappy endings, and to her, the covers needed to reflect that change. The result—a near constant presence on the *New York Times* bestsellers list.

Brown's novel, *The Witness* (1995), is a landmark in the genre now known as romantic suspense. Although many loyal Brown romance fans acknowledge their initial reluctance in trying her suspense novels, most, if not all, agree that *The Witness* came as more than a pleasant surprise. Not only does the book contain everything one might expect from a Brown thriller—richly developed characters, sharp, on-point dialogue, and plenty of tasteful, evocative sex scenes—it also demonstrates her ability to twist and turn multiple subplots, while never losing sight of the main story, all the while driving the reader toward a masterfully constructed conclusion— one most readers never saw coming. Brown skillfully unfolds *The Witness* in a technique that weaves the past and present, and not only touches on topics often viewed as taboo, but actually thrusts them front and center, leaving ambiguity to writers more reluctant to take on controversy.

The story revolves around the relationship between Kendall Burn-wood, an idealistic public defender, and U.S. Marshal John McGrath. Mc-Grath is driving Kendall to Prosper, South Carolina, where she is scheduled to serve as a material witness against the Brotherhood, a paramilitary vigilante hate group who executed one of her clients. The ringleaders of this group are Kendall's husband, Matt, and her father-in-law, Gibb Burnwood, a well-respected, popular man in the community.

En route to Prosper, their car crashes into a ravine in Georgia, leaving Kendall to pull herself, her three-month-old baby, and McGrath from the wreckage. Once in the hospital, Kendall is careful not to disclose the true identity of the seriously injured McGrath, who is now hobbled by a leg injury and temporary amnesia. She hides his identity for good reason. If she testifies, Kendall knows she may face grievous retribution from Matt and Gibb, as well as the entire town of Prosper. The community is so entrenched in bigotry that it sees Kendall as a mortal enemy.

The push-pull generated by McGrath's memory loss and Kendall's terror sparks a sexual tension that is vividly and expertly consummated. Kendall's ultimate victory over seemingly impossible odds demonstrates Brown's ability to combine suspense, violence, intrigue, mystery, and sexual atmosphere. These elements come together so seamlessly that the reader forgets about genre and focuses on the characters and the story.

The literary history of this subject is complicated. In 1987, eight years prior to the publication of *The Witness*, Tess Gerritsen's first book, *Call after Midnight,* appeared. That novel is about a newlywed woman's search for her presumed-dead husband, and it too mixes elements of romance and suspense, although the former is emphasized over the latter. Gerritsen, a physician, eventually switched to writing medical thrillers (*Harvest*, 1996) and then began a criminal investigation series that frequently has a medical background (*The Surgeon*, 2001). Similarly, Tami Hoag began her career in the romance genre and subsequently switched to thrillers (*Still Waters*, 1992), but in her case, the strong action in her fiction is so dark and so dominant that the romantic element is difficult to find. Sandra Brown remains the author who is most identified with maintaining the balance in romantic suspense, and who has most explored its possibilities.

The Witness opened doors in the publishing industry that no one realized existed, creating new opportunities for other writers. Because of Brown's influence, many other novelists were attracted to this type of thriller and achieved careers, to the point that conferences of the Romance Writers of America frequently include sessions about thrillers while *Romantic Times* magazine also features articles and reviews about thrillers.

Deborah LeBlanc is an award-winning author and business owner from Lafayette, Louisiana. She is also a licensed death-scene investigator and an active member of two national paranormal investigation teams. She has been the president of the Horror Writers Association, the Writers' Guild of Acadiana, the Mystery Writers of America's Southwest Chapter, and an active member of Sisters in Crime, Novelists Inc., and International Thriller Writers. In 2004, she created the LeBlanc Literacy Challenge, an annual national campaign designed to encourage more people to read, and founded Literacy Inc., a nonprofit organization dedicated to fighting illiteracy in America's teens. Using a powerful ability to motivate, she also takes her passion for literacy to high schools around the country. Her novels include *Grave Intent*, *Morbid Curiosity*, and *Water Witch*.

96

David Baldacci's
ABSOLUTE POWER (1996)
Rhodi Hawk

David Baldacci (1960–) studied political science as an undergraduate at Virginia Commonwealth University and went on to earn his law degree from the University of Virginia. He wrote his first novel, *Absolute Power*, while still practicing law as a trial attorney. Since its publication in 1995, he authored numerous consecutive *New York Times* and worldwide best sellers, including *Total Control*, *The Camel Club*, *Divine Justice*, and *First Family*. He's also the cofounder, along with his wife, of the Wish You Well Foundation, a nonprofit organization dedicated to supporting literacy efforts across America. Still a resident of his native Virginia, he invites you to visit his foundation at www.wishyouwellfoundation.org.

I'm a Baldacci fan. I remember when *Absolute Power* came out in 1996, more than fourteen years ago. (Fourteen! It feels like it just hit the shelves.) At the time, the failed coup in the Soviet Union had long since wound down, and the media's political focus had turned inward to domestic affairs. Controversy. Aspersion. Mud. The presidential office was about to fall victim to that harbinger of the Information Age: the sex scandal. Remember watching President Clinton on CNN as he grappled with Paula Jones and Monica Lewinsky? When you think about it, coming up with the premise for *Absolute Power* seems like an obvious progression given the circumstances of the day. Until you count backward and realize that Baldacci had written it well before the Clinton scandals broke.

As for me, in 1996 I'd already ended my tour of duty for the U.S. Army and was living as a full-fledged civilian. But once you've been in the military, you tend to maintain a certain perspective, particularly when it comes to high-level government office, and for a soldier, the president of the United States is the commander in chief. (Ironic that you actually cast a vote for your top boss.) Also, my branch had been Military Intelligence, which is notorious for being long on secrets and short on tolerance when it comes to questioning authority. *Absolute Power*, from my perspective, still raises some fascinating questions.

The opening sequence is unforgettable. Luther is a high-tech burglar who's in the midst of robbing a mansion outside Washington, D.C., when one of the owners returns home unexpectedly. Luther hides in the master bedroom vault where, through a two-way mirror, he witnesses a sexual romp that goes wrong—and ends in homicide. The victim is the wealthy young lady of the house, and the assailant is none other than the president of the United States.

Baldacci describes what happens next in a straight-to-the-heart account from the perspective of each character, with Luther caught in the middle of it all. For me, the Secret Service agents hold particularly unique and compelling points of view. Baldacci shows how they're thinking of Timothy McCarthy, the true-life bodyguard who heroically threw himself into the line of fire to protect President Reagan; and of Clint Hill, who hadn't been close enough to save President Kennedy during that crucial moment, and how it haunted him for life. In *Absolute Power*, the Secret Service agents are suddenly torn between keeping the president safe and covering for his stupidity, and they don't have time to think. The decisions they make in the heat of the moment cannot be taken back.

It's a tricky thing to present the ensuing conspiracy and make it believable, and yet Baldacci's attention to character and technical detail accomplishes just that. It's believable, all right. And the possibilities still resonate to this day. The prose itself hadn't quite developed into the smoothness and mastery of Baldacci's later works, but that's a minor symptom of a first novel. He never lets up on the pace, and when you combine that intensity with the characters' heartbreaking relationships, not to mention the vividness of his world—law and politics from a point of view that feels incredibly authentic—the effect is mesmerizing.

When he was writing the book, Baldacci was already knee-deep into a career as a trial lawyer, during which he would finish work at about ten p.m. and then write into the wee hours, often until three in the morning. He's an advocate for hands-on field research, too, and for *Absolute Power* he spoke to Secret Service agents and firearms experts in the FBI. Even now, although the Internet has made it easier for writers to dig through information without ever having to change out of their bathrobes, he says he believes there's no substitute for going out and talking to the people who experience situations that build his stories.

Truth is, Baldacci himself is as interesting as his books, and not just because it's hard for me to take my eyes off his cover photo. (You'll have to cut me some slack here; the man *was* named one of the most beautiful people in the world by *People* magazine.) He and his wife Michelle are extremely active in numerous charities, including their own brainchild, the Wish You Well Foundation for literacy, and David is also the ambassador for the National Multiple Sclerosis Society. Oh, and did I mention he holds the key to the city for his ancestral home of Barga, Italy? And that his cousin is the governor of Maine? Seriously, this guy ain't faking it.

And yet he's as easygoing as they come. I had to ask him about a disconnect with *Absolute Power* that always bothered me: the great divide between the book and the film. For starters, the main character is absent from the movie. The main character! Jack Graham, the hot young lawyer who is defending Luther (and happens to be in love with Luther's daughter) doesn't exist in the film. Baldacci actually laughed about it when I asked him. He said the first drafts of William Goldman's screenplay were true to the book. "Then one day I got a call from Bill and he said, 'I have good news and bad news.'"

The good news, of course, was that the film was going straight to production with Clint Eastwood both directing and starring in the lead role. The bad news was that the story itself would be gutted.

Interestingly enough, after the film came out, Baldacci was confronted by a Secret Service agent, a big guy, and Baldacci was familiar enough with that world to recognize he was carrying a firearm beneath his jacket. He asked Baldacci where he got off portraying a movie where the SSA gets killed with a hypodermic needle to the neck.

"I didn't write it that way," Baldacci told him, and tried to explain that the book was very different from the movie.

But the (hulking, armed) SSA was having none of it: "Your book, your movie, pal."

Fortunately, there were enough people nearby to convince the SSA that Baldacci really did have little say in how the film unfolded.

Baldacci took it all in stride. He calls the book-movie process a great learning experience, and says he picked up a lot from Goldman. Also, having written several screenplays himself, Baldacci says it's just a completely different medium and you can't always expect the movie to turn out like the book.

Yeah, yeah, I know. Me, I can't help it; I missed Jack Graham in the movie. He's an everyday kind of guy who's accomplished a lot through a combination of fortitude, luck, and the relationships he's chosen. He has his flaws. We're never really sure he's going to succeed. His biggest driver both makes him heroic and gets him into trouble: the fact that he leads with his heart. But if I had to pick between the two, I would choose following Jack Graham in the book over watching him in the movie. You know what they always say about book vs. movie.

Rhodi Hawk has been fascinated by storytelling since her earliest memory, when her grandmother read to her from *Peter Pan* in Kensington Gardens. In her early career, she was a transcription linguist in U.S. Army intelligence, and later made a living as a technical writer during the Internet boom, working on her first novel in the early mornings and at night. Rhodi Hawk won the International Thriller Writers Scholarship for her first work of fiction, *A Twisted Ladder*. A compulsive traveler, she dabbles in the culinary arts.

97
Gayle Lynds's
MASQUERADE (1996)

Hank Phillippi Ryan

Gayle Lynds was born in Nebraska and grew up in Council Bluffs, Iowa, reading everything she could get her hands on. She earned her degree in journalism and began her career as an obituary writer for the *Arizona Republic*. Now, as she says, she "kills people—in her fiction—for a living." She is the award-winning author of eight international espionage novels, including *The Last Spymaster, The Coil, Mesmerized,* and *Mosaic* as well as the *New York Times* best seller, *Masquerade*. Her books are published in twenty countries. *The Last Spymaster* was chosen Novel of the Year by the Military Writers Society of America. With Robert Ludlum, she created the Covert-One series and wrote three of the novels: *The Paris Option, The Altman Code,* and *The Hades Factor,* which became a CBS miniseries. A member of the Association for Intelligence Officers, she is the cofounder (with David Morrell) of the International Thriller Writers organization. She lives in Southern California.

Women in the United States got the vote in 1920. It wasn't until 1996 that we got equality as espionage authors. And it almost didn't happen.

The true-life-behind-the-scenes story of *Masquerade* is as spellbinding as its fiction. It has suspense, charges of deception, high-echelon misjudgments, and back-channel controversy, not to mention a brave, beautiful, and tenacious heroine.

Gayle Lynds had a résumé to rival any author—she worked at a think tank, where she had top-secret clearances, inside information from the top levels of government, and a cadre of high-level pals. What she read for fun mirrored her real-life interests: the world of intelligence, intrigue, secret weapons, and politics on a global scale.

"On beaches and in airplanes, I saw everyone reading spy thrillers," Lynds said. "Men and women. But the authors were all men." In a world where the renowned Helen MacInnes (who died in 1985) held the sole female chair at the espionage writers' table, Lynds decided it was time to bring something new to territory that was long associated with Walther PPK-toting, tuxedo-sporting, code-breaking, martini-drinking alpha males. She wanted to crack the Berlin Wall of the male-dominated genre not only with a brilliant and resourceful female heroine, but also with a complex and innovative post-Cold War plot. It would be a contemporary and authoritative espionage thriller—written by a woman.

Masquerade—with its theme of stolen and multiple identities—stars Liz Sansborough, a woman who wakes from "an accident" to realize that she has no memories and no idea of her true identity. (Lynds insists she chose Sansborough from a British family tree, not because it could be translated as "without a city.") Her handler explains that Sansborough is a CIA agent who now has to be "retrained." Liz soon suspects the handsome handler—her husband?—is not who he seems. The problem is, if Liz has no past, how does she know who she really is? And how can she have a future?

Liz begins to realize there's one part of herself that's indelible—no accident can erase one's gut reactions. She trusts her instincts, but where did they come from? What's more, she can handle a weapon, knows judo, understands code breaking, can pick locks, and survive in the wild. If she's a spy, why doesn't she remember how she learned those skills? She's taken to a "training camp" where she stops taking her "medicine." After some disturbing discoveries, she goes on the run. Throwing in her lot with a dashing, mysterious, and out-of-favor operative, she begins an international quest not just to discover her identity— but to, well, save the world.

Meanwhile, the future of "The Carnivore," international assassin and arch-criminal, is also in play. The warring factions within the Agency battle for dominance—and for control over The Carnivore's fate. Will he surrender to Langley? Or remain at large?

Masquerade has mind control. Brainwashing. Psychological and physical manipulation. The struggle for world dominance. International intrigue. And blistering love scenes.

But at first, nobody wanted it.

Lynds's agent took it to a publisher in 1994. He waited for the call that he expected would bring a big-bucks offer for this groundbreaking thriller. Instead, the call was essentially the first salvo in the thriller suffrage movement.

As Lynds remembers it, the publisher told her agent, "I love this book, but no woman could have written it."

Lynds, shocked, had never considered that might be a reaction. "They literally thought someone else had written *Masquerade*. Apparently it was difficult for them to imagine that a woman could comprehend the field of espionage, that only a man could 'get it.'"

For an educated and experienced author, highly regarded in her field, the accusation was baffling. Demeaning. And ridiculous. "I would put a female killer up against a male any day of the week," Lynds says. "Women can be as resourceful and effective as any man. "

She never considered going undercover—changing her name to a man's or even to unisex initials, to get her cutting-edge espionage novel past the barriers of the old-boy network. "They wanted to make me a pseudo-male," she says. "Or to shelve my books in romance. I refused." Ironically, her first name is gender neutral. She was named after her Uncle Gale.

When *Masquerade* eventually found a publisher, Lynds's battle still wasn't over. The "stupid cover," as she calls it, of the first edition, features a voluptuous woman in a black bodysuit and high heels. "Just give me a cover like the boys get, I told them."

At first, critics saw the gender before the genre. Lynds was "aping her betters" and trying to "cut off" the private parts of male espionage authors, reviewers complained. "It was hard to be taken seriously with all the negativity," Lynds says. "I was pissed off."

Eventually, the public and the critics latched on to Lynds, and the book became a *New York Times* best seller in paperback. Ten years later, Peter Cannon of *Publishers Weekly* listed it in the top-ten spy novels ever written. It comes in at number eight—just after Ken Follett's *Eye of the Needle*, and ahead of *Above Suspicion* by Lynds's literary foremother, Helen MacInnes.

Lynds is an accidental icon. She insists her objective was telling a good story, not breaking barriers. But when she got push-back from the publishing world, she became as stubborn as one of her heroines. She felt that, if she failed, it would be harder for other female espionage authors. Persistence became a duty.

Finally, the barriers did come down. Now women espionage writers have the same opportunities as men. Lynds smiles when she's called "Queen of the Spy Thriller." In fact, she says, she hopes someone will come along and "knock me off."

Award-winning investigative reporter Hank Phillippi Ryan is currently on the air at Boston's NBC affiliate, where she has broken big stories for the past twenty-four years. Her features have resulted in new laws, people sent to prison, homes removed from foreclosure, and millions of dollars in refunds and restitution for consumers. Along with her twenty-six Emmy awards, Hank also received dozens of other journalism honors. She's been a legislative aide in the United States Senate (working on the Freedom of Information Act) and wrote for *Rolling Stone Magazine* (working with Hunter S. Thompson). Her first novel, *Prime Time*, won the prestigious Agatha Award for Best First Novel. It was a double RITA nominee for Best First Novel and Best Romantic Suspense Novel, and a Reviewers' Choice Award winner. Her Charlotte McNally thriller series includes *Face Time* (a Book Sense Notable Book), *Air Time*, and *Drive Time*. She is on the board of directors of New England Sisters in Crime and Mystery Writers of America.

98

Lee Child's
KILLING FLOOR (1997)

Marcus Sakey

Born in Coventry, England, Lee Child (1954–) is the best-selling author of the Jack Reacher series. He began his career in British television, where he worked for eighteen years before being laid off in 1995 due to corporate restructuring. Armed with six dollars in paper and pencils, he sat down to write what would become *Killing Floor*. Sales of the novel now number in the millions, and several sequels about his enormously popular character, including *Without Fail, One Shot, The Hard Way,* and *Nothing to Lose,* have been released. Reportedly, the name for Reacher came to him when he accompanied his wife to a grocery story, where she asked him to reach for something off the top shelf. "I'm a reacher," he thought, and was struck by the word. A devoted Yankees fan, the author lives in New York City.

Check this out:

> "I was arrested in Eno's Diner. At twelve o'clock. I was eating eggs and drinking coffee."

Seems simple, right? But with these few lines, Lee Child launched an internationally best-selling series and introduced a protagonist of iconic power, a hero built on classic mythic structure and yet inextricably a product of our time. Jack Reacher: former military policeman, wandering arbiter of morality, and caffeine addict.

At the time of this writing, there are more than thirteen books in the series. They run the gamut from mystery to thriller, from contemporary to flashback, from first to third person. They're published in forty-three countries and thirty languages and sell at an average of one per second. And the whole story begins here, with *Killing Floor* (1997), and Reacher sitting in a small-town diner, eating eggs and drinking coffee.

In this first novel, Reacher is six months out of what he had expected

to be a lifelong career in the military police, a victim of downsizing (as was
Child when he wrote the novel.) Since leaving the army, he's been wandering the country, living on his severance pay, and considering, in an idle
sort of way, what he'll do with the rest of his life. Today, though, all he
wants is to finish his breakfast and then see what he can find out about a
little-known bluesman who may have wandered through this small Georgia town called Margrave.

But this small town has secrets. A lot of them. Reacher is arrested on
suspicion of murder and locked in a holding cell. It doesn't take long to
prove his innocence, but by the time he does, he discovers that one of the
murder victims isn't a random stranger—it's Reacher's brother. To get payback, he'll tear Margrave apart.

The plot is complex and multilayered, schemes interweaving with
schemes, and a significant portion of the fun involves watching Reacher
navigate through them. While an intensely physical character—the only
description given of him is his huge size—his primary weapon is his mind.
He is a creature of logic who reasons his way to the solution. And unlike
many suspense novels, where the point is to distract readers with sleight of
hand, Child wants us along every step of the way. Reacher may be smarter
than we are, but his logic is sound and it's explained, and watching him
break the world down is a joy.

As he fights his way to the climax of *Killing Floor*, Reacher befriends
and falls for a female cop named Roscoe, one of the few people in town
with nothing to hide. In Roscoe, Child establishes what will become a tradition in his work. She's beautiful, yes, but more important, she's smart,
capable, and strong, without ever becoming some teenager's caricature of
feminine power.

This may explain, in part, the enormous female readership of what appear on the surface to be masculine action novels. But there are two other
factors that are more important to the popularity of the series. One is
Child's writing style; the other is the mythic structure of Reacher himself.

In discussions and reviews of popular fiction, the language tends to be
overlooked. Maybe this is academic snobbery; maybe it's because there is
often so much plot to relate. But any story, no matter the genre, is only as
good as its telling. Twists and surprises are one method to keep a reader
interested, and Child is terrific at them. But more crucial on a moment-
to-moment basis is the actual prose.

Writing is about rhythm and balance and enticement. It's a dance, a seduction. One good sentence eases a reader into the next one. At a glance, Child's basic structure and matter-of-fact description seem simplistic. But there is a subtle, calculated beat to it that pulls a reader through like a drum for a march. When someone says that they couldn't put a book down, that's only partly because they wanted to find out what happened; it's also because the rhythm of the prose never gave them the chance.

Child's other great triumph is in Reacher himself. The character is based on an archetype as old as storytelling; the knight-errant, the samurai without a master, the crack-shot cowboy who drifts into the company town. A wandering righter-of-wrongs, this character doesn't seek trouble, but when it finds him, he doesn't back down. Ever. In the real world, the ruthless and the selfish often succeed; in fiction, the knight-errant is there to stop them.

That's a universally appealing myth, and a terrific foundation. But it's Child's interpretation that makes Reacher so compelling. For one thing, there is the blue-collar Everyman basis of Reacher. He's not a tuxedoed James Bond playing high-stakes baccarat. He's a laid-off soldier who hangs out in diners. He doesn't drink martinis; he drinks coffee. And not from Starbucks. A man who travels lightly, he wears his ordinary clothes until they are dirty, and then instead of getting them washed, he throws them away. His only luggage is a tooth brush.

But Child's real twist on the myth goes beyond that. Typical knight-errant figures are bound by Judeo-Christian ideas of morality. They might kill, but generally as a last resort. They are willing to trust even when faithlessness has been demonstrated. They are, in a word, suckers, and the audience knows it.

But Reacher follows a different path. He has a code, but it's dictated by a rough common sense and a belief that evil must be punished. In *Killing Floor* alone, he shoots men in the back, makes promises of safety and immediately breaks them, fights viciously and sadistically and without mercy. He shatters noses and thumbs out eyeballs and cuts throats. He moves with moral certainty, leaving a trail of bodies, until the wrong in the world has been righted.

And we stay up way past bedtime, cheering him on.

According to Marcus Sakey, "ten years in advertising and marketing gave me the perfect experience to write about thieves and killers." His debut novel, *The Blade Itself*, was a *New York Times* Editor's Pick and named one of *Esquire Magazine's* five

Best Reads of 2007. His novels *At the City's Edge* and *Good People* have been called "Crime drama for the twenty-first century" (National Public Radio) and "Nothing short of brilliant" (*Chicago Tribune*). *The Amateurs* received similar praise. To research his books, he accompanied homicide detectives, toured a morgue, interviewed soldiers, rode with gang cops, and learned to pick a deadbolt in sixty seconds. Film rights for his work have sold to Ben Affleck and Tobey Maguire. A diehard Lee Child fan, he lives in Chicago.

99
Jeffery Deaver's
THE BONE COLLECTOR (1997)

Jeffrey J. Mariotte

Before he became a full-time fiction writer, Jeffery Deaver (1950–) was a folksinger, a journalist, and an attorney. In his ambitious thrillers, traces of all those crafts can be found—prose that sings, a keen eye for the decisive moment, and a deep knowledge of the law, of crime, and of police procedure. His novels have appeared on countless best-seller lists, his awards could fill cases, and the movies based on them have starred James Garner, Marlee Matlin, Denzel Washington, and Angelina Jolie. His numerous novels include the stand-alone thrillers *A Maiden's Grave*, *The Blue Nowhere*, *The Lesson of Her Death*, *Praying for Sleep*, and others, the Rune series, the John Pellam series (as William Jefferies), the Lincoln Rhyme series that began with *The Bone Collector*, the Kathryn Dance series, of which *The Sleeping Doll* was the first, and the Brynn McKenzie series, which debuted with *The Bodies Left Behind*.

Literary genres can be defined in terms of the intent of their works. Mysteries are meant to puzzle. Horror books are intended to frighten. Romance novels are designed to create sentimental emotion. If the purpose of thrillers is to thrill, then Jeffery Deaver is a consummate thriller writer.

I had been reading Jeffery Deaver for a while by the time *The Bone Collector* was published in 1997 (*Praying for Sleep*, *A Maiden's Grave*, and the Rune trilogy, in particular). Those books were entertaining, powerful thrillers. But *The Bone Collector* was a step above, the book that grabbed me and wouldn't let go until, gasping for breath, I managed to finish the last page and close the cover.

Deaver's earlier novels had been good, but now he had written a great one. In quadriplegic, former criminalist Lincoln Rhyme, he created a character destined to join the ranks of those to whom readers turn time and again. In addition, the book helped to establish a subgenre, one in which I've dipped my toes a time or two as the author of comic books and tie-in novels based on the TV shows *CSI: Crime Scene Investigation* and *CSI: Miami*.

It might not be entirely accurate to suggest that the megapopular *CSI* television franchise wouldn't exist without Lincoln Rhyme. Certainly, Patricia Cornwell had been writing books with strong forensic science themes since 1990. But the timing of the bestselling *The Bone Collector*, and the hit 1999 movie adaptation of the novel starring Denzel Washington and Angelina Jolie, certainly helped prepare audiences for the gruesome scenes that would confront them on *CSI: Crime Scene Investigation* and its spin-off shows.

It wasn't the novel's horrific parts that gripped me as much as it was the interaction between the crippled but brilliant Rhyme and third-year Patrol Officer and former model Amelia Sachs. They are two of the most cleverly matched characters in thriller history. Largely unfamiliar with forensic investigation techniques, Sachs becomes an appendage for the man who can't use his own, putting all her senses to work and reporting back to him. He leads her step-by-step, remotely, through what seemed to this reader to be the most accurately described crime scene investigation in all fiction at the time.

Their interaction is kicked off when Amelia finds a finger sticking up from the ground—bloody, stripped of skin, presumably the only visible part of a buried body—encircled by a woman's ring. Amelia wants to do things the right way, by the book, when she can remember what the book says. She's smart, ambitious, beautiful, healthy, and strong. A bit overzealous, maybe, but that rarely kills anyone. Her fast driving, however, just might.

Rhyme is bitter, impatient, rude, unhappily dependent on his aide, Thom, for the most basic bodily functions, suicidally depressed, and when we meet him, unshaven and ungroomed. And he stinks. He's also brilliant, intuitive, and almost preternaturally observant, the author of a couple of books on crime-scene investigation, and the former head of New York City's Central Investigation and Resource Department. His mind has an ironclad grasp on a vast array of topics, from the history, geology, sociology, and politics of New York to the various forensic sciences.

There doesn't seem to be any reason for the two to get along. We receive an early hint, though—the beautiful Sachs is so used to being viewed as an object of lust that coming into contact with a man who she believes will in no way react to her in a sexual way is a relief. It's an interesting psychological insight in a book full of them. Rhyme, for all his intellect, is almost entirely nonphysical, and Sachs, while smarter than the average street cop, is physical perfection. Put them together, as Deaver does, and you wind up with a single organism, the ideal crime-solving combination of brains, senses, guts, and functional limbs.

The character twists—carefully established and thoroughly believable, if unanticipated—surprise as much as the plot twists do. Deaver is determined to keep his readers wondering. All the necessary clues are provided, for those readers who can come close to matching Rhyme's erudition, but the twists are frequent and startling enough to cause mental whiplash. They demonstrate another characteristic of Deaver's work, the way in which the puzzle of a traditional mystery is supercharged by the extremes of the crimes that are committed until the novel's tone borders on horror. His experiment in mixing these genres makes his fiction noteworthy.

Compelling and intelligent characters combine with Deaver's narrative intensity and his fascinating well-researched background information to make his work—especially *The Bone Collector* and the rest of the Lincoln Rhyme series—an object lesson in how to write for maximum, satisfying thrills.

Jeffrey J. Mariotte is the award-winning author of the supernatural thrillers, *River Runs Red, Missing White Girl,* and *The Slab,* as well as, under the name Jeff Mariotte, tie-in novels and comic books, including some based on *CSI: Crime Scene Investigation* and *CSI: Miami.* He has also written dozens of original comic books, including the critically acclaimed horror-Western series, *Desperadoes,* and the graphic novel, *Zombie Cop.* A co-owner of San Diego independent genre bookstore Mysterious Galaxy, he lives on the Flying M Ranch in rural Arizona.

100
Dan Brown's
THE DA VINCI CODE (2003)

Steve Berry

A graduate of Phillips Exeter Academy and Amherst College, Dan Brown (1964–) worked as an English teacher before turning his efforts to writing full time. His interest in code breaking and covert government agencies led to his first book, *Digital Fortress* (1998). Focusing on the National Security Agency, the novel explored the tension between civilian privacy and national security. Brown's techno-thriller *Deception Point* (2001) centered on similar issues of morality in politics, national security, and classified technology. In 2000, Brown published *Angels & Demons*, a thriller that delved into the secret world of a religious group, the Illuminati, and featured Harvard professor of iconography and religious art, Robert Langdon. Brown brought him back in 2003's *The Da Vinci Code*, one of the best-selling novels of all time. The unparalleled success of that work landed all four of Brown's novels on the *New York Times* best-seller list during the same week in 2004.

Today, publishers, reviewers, bookstore owners, and even readers love to organize books into genres. But genres are just cubbyholes where writers and their stories are judiciously crammed, more out of convenience than for any artistic reason. It's easier to say "international suspense thriller" as opposed to "a story that involves unique colorful locales outside the United States, where the stakes are high and the intrigue paramount."

This habit may not be all bad. There is something to be said for brevity. Still, this particular genre—the international suspense thriller—possesses a history that is anything but short. Although others during the first half of the twentieth century wrote stories in a similar vein—Graham Greene being a notable example—Helen MacInnes, a Scottish novelist who started writing in the late 1930s, moved to the United States and became a citizen, and continued writing until her death in 1985, may well be the person who started the modern evolution of the international suspense thriller. At that time, the stories were called spy thrillers. But MacInnes transformed them into something altogether different.

Her locales were European; her heroes ordinary people; her villains either Nazis, Communists, or some other form of worldwide conspiracy. Her plots were strangely prophetic, since she wrote of organized world terrorism long before that evil became a clear reality. Her titles were alluring: *The Salzburg Connection*, *The Venetian Affair*, *North from Rome*, *Snare of the Hunter*.

We know a great deal about her because her personal papers are on file at Princeton University. Included within that cache are hundreds of fan letters that complemented her weaving of travel, history, and nostalgia into the convoluted plots. An exchange of letters between MacInnes and the director of the Swiss Tourist Bureau revealed the positive effect her novels had on European tourism. American reviews of her books (from the 1950s) described her suspense thrillers as "travelogues" and "Baedekers." Her United States publisher, Harcourt Brace and World, actively encouraged her to include European tourist destinations in her plots so as to promote sales. She obliged, and the technique worked. Nearly all of MacInnes's books were *New York Times* best sellers.

Through her, the international suspense thriller, as we know it today, began to form. But shaping that form fell to others. Robert Ludlum burst onto the scene in 1971 with *The Scarlatti Inheritance*. Frederick Forsyth came the same year with *The Day of the Jackal*. Clive Cussler emerged in 1973 with *The Mediterranean Caper*, and Ken Follett made his debut in 1978 with *Eye of the Needle*. These four writers were then not the megasellers they are today. Instead, they were fledgling craftsmen, anxious to see if a publisher or readers would care about their stories. Luckily for us, their vision proved correct. Combined, their works have spent countless weeks on every best-seller list that exists, and they have sold hundreds of millions of copies. Their careers have been long and varied. Each managed to survive an ever-changing political world, and make no mistake: the realm of the international suspense thriller is intricately linked to the real world. Any writer of the genre knows that the closer the fiction can be merged with reality, the better the story.

The decade from 1975 to 1985 was significant for the international suspense thriller. The Cold War provided enormous fodder, and the lingering remnants of Nazi Germany still held a fascination. Both subjects can be found in abundance within countless novels of that time. A cursory examination of *New York Times* best-seller lists from that decade reveals at least one international suspense thriller in the top ten for nearly every week.

Without question, it was a golden age for the genre. Then the Berlin Wall fell, the Iron Curtain dropped, the Soviet Union dissolved, and the Cold War ended. So fast in fact did these vast changes occur that international suspense novelists actually tried to keep that conflict alive a few more years within their fiction. But by the early 1990s, storylines had thinned. Writers tried to replace the genre's bread and butter with the Middle East, international assassins, and bio-threats. But the vital link between reality and fiction had disappeared. Reality took over, and international thrillers were no longer considered suspenseful.

The genre contracted a disease. Publishers quickly recognized its symptoms and pronounced the malady terminal. Unless you were one of the solidly established giants of the realm, which translated into a built-in readership, the chances of breaking in anew were slim. Editors crafted the death notice for the international suspense thriller by turning their attention to other genres.

The legal thriller rose to prominence. Scott Turow whetted the public's appetite in 1987 with *Presumed Innocent*. But a country lawyer from Oxford, Mississippi, became king with *The Firm* (1991). John Grisham went on, during the 1990s, to sell more books than any other writer.

The techno-thriller was born, thanks to the imagination of an insurance salesman who wrote a book in his spare time and managed to snag the attention of President Ronald Reagan. *The Hunt for Red October* (1984) launched not only Tom Clancy's career but the genre itself.

Dale Brown inaugurated the military thriller. The medical thriller matured through Robin Cook, Michael Palmer, and Tess Gerritsen. The financial thriller evolved through authors such as Stephen Frey and Christopher Reich.

Meanwhile, the international suspense thriller, the darling of the 1970s and 1980s, only languished. That is not to say new writers weren't able to launch careers during this time or continue successfully within the genre. Some in fact did. John Case, Robert Cullen, Jack DuBrul, Daniel Easterman, David Hagberg, Robert Harris, Joseph Kanon, John le Carré, Gayle Lynds, Glenn Meade, David Morrell, James Rollins, Justin Scott, and Daniel Silva, to name only a few. Still, for most of the unlucky souls who submitted international suspense thrillers for publication from 1992 to

2002, the standard response came in unison: sorry, at the moment, this does not fit our list. What should have been added was the proviso: and it's never going to fit until something dramatically changes.

That change came on March 18, 2003. The book that went on sale that day was from a relatively obscure thriller writer, Dan Brown, who'd managed to publish his first international suspense thriller in 1998. He did it again in 2000 and 2001. But those three earlier books barely garnered minimal reviews and sold only modestly. Few noticed them. His fourth manuscript was different. The story touched sensitive nerves and forced the reader to confront conclusions that, in their uniqueness and logic, were startling. Not that the novel was true or even purported to be actual history (remember it is fiction) or that it was even unique. (Katherine Neville blazed the trail for books that used history and puzzles long before with her ingenious *The Eight* in 1988 and then again in 1998 with *The Magic Circle*.) Instead, the story dared to challenge sacred religious beliefs in a fresh and entertaining manner.

Readers loved it. Even the title was intriguing. *The Da Vinci Code*. The book immediately climbed to #1 on every best-seller list. Its publishing run is unmatched. Approaching twenty million copies worldwide, no other hardcover fiction has performed as well. Also, those first three obscure thrillers, *Digital Fortress*, *Angels & Demons*, and *Deception Point*, have joined their sibling on the best-seller lists, selling in the millions.

Yet the effect of *The Da Vinci Code* started long before March 2003, and I'm an example of the good fortune that book brought. From 1997 until 2002, my agent, Pam Ahearn, submitted five of my international suspense thrillers to New York publishing houses. All were rejected a combined total of eighty-five times. On the eighty-sixth attempt, in April 2002, which was a resubmission of one of those manuscripts, the right editor, at the right moment, looking for that kind of story, found me. Why? He was Mark Tavani at Ballantine Books, which is part of Random House, and he knew that Doubleday, which is also part of Random House, had a book in production called *The Da Vinci Code* that seemed destined for great things.

The prepublication buzz had been phenomenal. Ten thousand advanced reader copies had been distributed (which by itself is astonishing). The excitement had risen to the point that those same editors, who only a few years before had sounded the death knell for the international suspense thriller, were now talking resurrection, looking for books that could ride the wind they firmly believed was about to start blowing their way. I was lucky enough to be offered a ticket in May 2002. Eventually three of the five manuscripts my agent submitted were bought by Ballantine. It wasn't that the stories had changed; they hadn't. But as in politics, in publishing timing is everything, too.

I wasn't alone. Other writers were given similar opportunities. Three who come directly to mind are Ted Bell (*Hawke*, 2003), Raelynn Hillhouse (*Rift Zone*, 2004), and Chris Kuzneski (*Sign of the Cross*, 2006). The genre suddenly sprang back to life. Even established giants are now hoisting their sails into that howling wind. John Grisham's *The Broker* (2009) was a radical departure from his usual legal thriller formula. Doubleday actively promoted the book as an international thriller.

So the genre has turned full circle. Life, then death, then life again. Such is the way of the world and publishing. Every few years a writer emerges who actually changes the way things are done. Jacqueline Susann did this in the 1960s with her innovative methods of self-promotion and marketing, many of which are standard practice today. Stephen King regenerated the horror genre in the 1970s with frightening tales about everyday things. The real contribution of Dan Brown and his marvelously inventive story is the effect that both he and his publisher had on the international suspense thriller. Together, they breathed life back into something that was all but dead. And, in the process, opened up opportunities for those of us who were out there searching for a chance.

Steve Berry lives on the Georgia coast. After twenty-nine years, he no longer practices law, but continues to serve as one of five members of the Camden County Board of Commissioners. He began writing in 1990, and though his undergraduate degree was in political science, it was Steve's interest in travel and history that led him to write international suspense thrillers. His many books include *The Amber Room*, *The Romanov Prophecy*, *The Third Secret*, *The Templar Legacy*, *The Alexandria Link*, *The Venetian Betrayal*, *The Charlemagne Pursuit*, and *The Paris Vendetta*. Steve's books have been translated into forty-three languages, for a total of nearly eight million copies in print worldwide. He also served as copresident of International Thriller Writers.

INDEX